'A brilliant mix of belly-laughs, profound insight and capti-
vating events delivered [with] Backman's pitch-perfect dialogue
and an unparalleled understanding of human nature.'
Shelf Awareness

'Insightful and touching, this is a sweet and inspiring story . . .
Fans of Backman's will find another winner in these pages.'
Publishers Weekly

'Impressive [and] heart-warming.'
Literary Review

'An author who specialises in the unforgettable outdoes
himself and in the process overshoots our rating system . . .
In the end 5*s are all I can offer but I feel that this is a novel
that deserves many, many more.'
Bookbag

'Britt-Marie's metamorphosis from cocoon to butterfly seems all
the more remarkable for the utterly discouraging environment in
which it takes place.'
Booklist

Fredrik Backman is a Swedish blogger, columnist and author. His debut novel *A Man Called Ove* was a number 1 bestseller across Scandinavia, has sold over one million copies worldwide, was a Richard & Judy summer read in the UK and an instant and enduring *New York Times* paperback bestseller, and has been made into an Oscar-nominated film. Fredrik's subsequent novels, *My Grandmother Sends Her Regards and Apologises* and *Britt-Marie Was Here*, also went straight to number 1 in Sweden on publication and have been read and loved around the world.

www.fredrikbackman.com

@Backmanland

FREDRIK BACKMAN

BRITT-MARIE WAS HERE

Translated from the Swedish
by Henning Koch

SCEPTRE

First published in Great Britain in 2016 by Sceptre
An imprint of Hodder & Stoughton
An Hachette UK company

First published in paperback in 2016

11

Copyright © Fredrik Backman 2016

Translation © by Henning Koch 2015

Paperback ISBN 9781473617230
eBook ISBN 9781473617223

Typeset in Sabon MT by Palimpsest Book Production Ltd, Falkirk, Stirlingshire

Printed and bound in Great Britain by Clays Ltd, Elcograf S.p.A

Hodder & Stoughton policy is to use papers that are natural, renewable and
recyclable products and made from wood grown in sustainable forests. The
logging and manufacturing processes are expected to conform to the
environmental regulations of the country of origin.

Hodder & Stoughton Ltd
Carmelite House
50 Victoria Embankment
London EC4Y 0DZ

www.sceptrebooks.co.uk

To my mother, who always made sure there was food in my stomach and books on my shelf.

'You love football because it's instinctive. If a ball comes rolling down the street you give it a punt. You love it for the same reason that you fall in love. Because you don't know how to avoid it.'

1

Forks. Knives. Spoons.

In that order.

Britt-Marie is certainly not the kind of person who judges other people. Far from it.

But surely no civilised person would even think of arranging a cutlery drawer in a different way from how cutlery drawers are supposed to be arranged?

We're not animals, are we?

It's a Monday in January. She's sitting at a desk in the unemployment office. Admittedly there's no cutlery in sight, but it's on her mind because it sums up everything that's gone wrong recently. Cutlery should be arranged as it always has been, because life should go on unchanged. Normal life is presentable. In normal life you clean up the kitchen and keep your balcony tidy and take care of your children. It's hard work – harder than one might think. In normal life you certainly don't find yourself sitting in the unemployment office.

The girl who works here has staggeringly short hair, Britt-Marie thinks, like a man's. Not that there's anything wrong with that, of course – it's modern, no doubt. The girl points at a piece of paper and smiles, evidently in a hurry.

'Just fill in your name, social security number, and address here, please.'

Britt-Marie has to be registered. As if she were a criminal. As if she has come to steal a job rather than find one.

'Milk and sugar?' the girl asks, pouring some coffee into a plastic mug.

Britt-Marie doesn't judge anyone. Far from it. But who would behave like that? A plastic mug! Are we at war? She'd like to say just that to the girl, but because Kent is always urging Britt-Marie to 'be more socially aware' she just smiles as diplomatically as she can and waits to be offered a coaster.

Kent is Britt-Marie's husband. He's an entrepreneur. Incredibly, incredibly successful. Has business dealings with Germany and is extremely, extremely socially aware.

The girl offers her two tiny disposable cartons of the sort of milk that doesn't have to be kept in the fridge. Then she holds out a plastic mug with plastic teaspoons protruding from it. Britt-Marie could not have looked more startled if she'd been offered roadkill.

She shakes her head and brushes her hand over the table as if it was covered in invisible crumbs. There are papers everywhere, in any old order. The girl clearly doesn't have time to tidy them up, Britt-Marie realises – she's probably far too busy with her career.

'OK,' says the girl pleasantly, turning back to the form, 'just write your address here.'

Britt-Marie fixes her gaze on her lap. She misses being at home with her cutlery drawer. She misses Kent, because Kent is the one who fills in all the forms.

When the girl looks like she's about to open her mouth again, Britt-Marie interrupts her.

'You forgot to give me a coaster,' says Britt-Marie, smiling, with all the social awareness she can muster. 'I don't want to make marks on your table. Could I trouble you to give me something to put my . . . coffee cup on?'

She uses that distinctive tone, which Britt-Marie relies on whenever she has to summon all her inner goodness, to refer to it as a 'cup' even though it is a plastic mug.

'Oh don't worry, just put it anywhere.'

As if life was as simple as that. As if using a coaster or

organising the cutlery drawer in the right order didn't matter. The girl – who clearly doesn't appreciate the value of coasters, or proper cups, or even mirrors, judging by her hairstyle – taps her pen against the paper, by the 'address' box.

'But surely we can't just put our cups on the table? That leaves marks on a table, surely you see that.'

The girl glances at the surface of the desk, which looks as if toddlers have been trying to eat potatoes off it. With pitchforks. In the dark.

'It really doesn't matter, it's so old and scratched up already!' she says with a smile.

Britt-Marie is screaming inside.

'I don't suppose you've considered that it's because you don't use coasters,' she mutters, not at all in a 'passive-aggressive' way, which is how Kent's children once described her when they thought she wasn't listening. Britt-Marie is not actually passive-aggressive. She's considerate. After she heard Kent's children saying she was passive-aggressive she was extra-considerate for several weeks.

The unemployment office girl looks a little strained. 'OK . . . what did you say your name was? Britt, right?'

'Britt-Marie. Only my sister calls me Britt.'

'OK, Britt-Marie, if you could just fill in the form. Please.'

Britt-Marie peers at the paper, which requires her to give assurances about where she lives and who she is. An unreasonable amount of paperwork is required these days just to be a human being. A preposterous amount of administration for society to let one take part. In the end she reluctantly fills in her name, social security number and her mobile telephone number. The address box is left empty.

'What's your educational background, Britt-Marie?'

Britt-Marie squeezes her handbag.

'I'll have you know that my education is excellent.'

'But no formal education?'

'For your information, I solve an enormous number of

crosswords. Which is not the sort of thing one can do without an education.'

She takes a very small gulp of the coffee. It doesn't taste like Kent's coffee at all. Kent makes very good coffee, everyone says so. Britt-Marie takes care of the coasters and Kent takes care of the coffee.

'OK . . . What sort of life experience do you have?'

'My latest employment was as a waitress. I had outstanding references.'

The girl looks hopeful. 'And when was that?'

'1978.'

'Ah . . . and you haven't worked since then?'

'I have worked *every day* since then. I've helped my husband with his company.'

Again the girl looks hopeful. 'And what sorts of tasks did you perform in the company?'

'I took care of the children and saw to it that our home was presentable.'

The girl smiles to hide her disappointment, as people do when they don't have the ability to distinguish between 'a place to live' and 'a home'. It's actually thoughtfulness that makes the difference. Because of thoughtfulness there are coasters and proper coffee cups and beds that are made so tightly in the mornings that Kent jokes with his acquaintances about how, if you stumble on the threshold on your way into the bedroom, there's 'a smaller risk of breaking your leg if you land on the floor than the bedspread.' Britt-Marie loathes it when he talks that way. Surely civilised people lift their feet when they walk across bedroom thresholds?

Whenever Britt-Marie and Kent go away, Britt-Marie sprinkles the mattress with bicarbonate of soda for twenty minutes before she makes the bed. The bicarbonate of soda absorbs dirt and humidity, leaving the mattress much fresher. Bicarbonate of soda helps almost everything, in Britt-Marie's experience. Kent usually complains about being late; Britt-Marie clasps her hands together over her stomach and says: 'I absolutely must be allowed to make the bed before we leave, Kent. Just imagine if we die!'

This is the actual reason why Britt-Marie hates travelling. Death. Not even bicarbonate of soda has any effect on death. Kent says she exaggerates, but people do actually drop dead all the time when they're away, and what would the landlord think if they had to break down the door only to find an unclean mattress? Surely they'd conclude that Kent and Britt-Marie lived in their own dirt?

The girl checks her watch.

'O . . . K,' she says.

Britt-Marie feels her tone has a note of criticism in it.

'The children are twins and we have a balcony. It's more work than you think, having a balcony.'

The girl nods tentatively.

'How old are your children?'

'Kent's children. They're thirty.'

'So they've left home?'

'Obviously.'

'And you're sixty-three years old?'

'Yes,' says Britt-Marie dismissively, as if this was highly irrelevant.

The girl clears her throat as if, actually, it's very relevant indeed.

'Well, Britt-Marie, quite honestly, because of the financial crisis and all that, I mean, there's a scarcity of jobs for people in your . . . situation.'

The girl sounds a bit as if 'situation' was not her first choice as a way of concluding the sentence. Britt-Marie smiles patiently.

'Kent says that the financial crisis is over. He's an entrepreneur, you must understand. So he understands these kind of things, which are possibly a little outside your field of competence.'

The girl blinks for an unnecessary amount of time. Checks her watch. She seems uncomfortable, which vexes Britt-Marie. She quickly decides to give the girl a compliment, just to show her goodwill. She looks around the room for something to compliment her about, and finally manages to say, with as generous a smile as she can muster:

5

'You have a very modern hairstyle.'

'What? Oh. Thanks,' she replies, her fingertips moving self-consciously towards her scalp.

'It's very courageous of you to wear your hair so short when you have such a large forehead.'

Why does the girl look offended, Britt-Marie wonders? Clearly that's what happens when you try to be sociable towards young people these days. The girl rises from her chair.

'Thanks for coming, Britt-Marie. You are registered on our database. We'll be in touch!'

She holds out her hand to say goodbye. Britt-Marie stands up and places the plastic mug of coffee in her hand.

'When?'

'Well, it's difficult to say.'

'I suppose I'm supposed to just sit and wait,' counters Britt-Marie with a diplomatic smile, 'As if I didn't have anything better to do?'

The girl swallows.

'Well, my colleague will be in touch with you about a jobseekers' training course, an—'

'I don't want a course. I want a job.'

'Absolutely, but it's difficult to say when something will turn up . . .'

Britt-Marie gets out a notebook from her pocket.

'Shall we say tomorrow, then?'

'What?'

'Could something turn up tomorrow?'

The girl clears her throat.

'Well, it could, or I'd rather s . . .'

Britt-Marie gets out a pencil from her bag, eyes the pencil with some disapproval and then looks at the girl.

'Might I trouble you for a pencil sharpener?' she asks.

'A pencil sharpener?' asks the girl, as if she had been asked for a thousand-year-old magical artefact.

'I need to put our meeting on the list.'

Some people don't understand the value of lists, but

Britt-Marie is not one of those people. She has so many lists that she has to keep a separate list to list all the lists. Otherwise anything could happen. She could die. Or forget to buy bicarbonate of soda.

The girl offers her a biro and says something to the effect of, 'Actually I don't have time tomorrow,' but Britt-Marie is too busy peering at the biro to hear what she's saying.

'Surely we can't write lists in *ink*?' she bursts out.

'That's all I've got.' The girl says this with some finality. 'Is there anything else I can help you with today, Britt-Marie?'

'Ha,' Britt-Marie responds after a moment.

Britt-Marie often says that. 'Ha.' Not as in 'ha-ha' but as in 'Aha,' spoken in a particularly disappointed tone. Like when you find a wet towel thrown on the bathroom floor.

'Ha.' Immediately after saying this, Britt-Marie always firmly closes her mouth, to emphasise this is the last thing she intends to say on the subject. Although it rarely is the last thing.

The girl hesitates. Britt-Marie grasps the biro as if it's sticky. Looks at the list marked 'Tuesday' in her notebook, and, at the top, above 'Cleaning' and 'Shopping,' she writes 'Unemployment office to contact me.'

She hands back the pen.

'It was very nice to meet you,' says the girl robotically. 'We'll be in touch!'

'Ha,' says Britt-Marie with a nod.

Britt-Marie leaves the unemployment office. The girl is obviously under the impression that this is the last time they'll meet, because she's unaware of how scrupulously Britt-Marie sticks to her lists. Clearly the girl has never seen Britt-Marie's balcony.

It's an astonishingly, astonishingly presentable balcony.

It's January outside, a winter chill in the air but no snow on the ground – below zero without any evidence of it being so. The very worst time of year for balcony plants.

After leaving the unemployment office, Britt-Marie goes to a supermarket that is not her usual supermarket, where she buys everything on her list. She doesn't like shopping on her own, because she doesn't like pushing the shopping trolley. Kent always pushes the shopping trolley, while Britt-Marie walks at his side and holds on to a corner of it. Not because she's trying to steer, only that she likes holding on to things while he is also holding on to them. For the sake of feeling that they are going somewhere at the same time.

She eats her dinner cold at exactly six o'clock. She's used to sitting up all night waiting for Kent, so she tries to put his portion in the fridge. But the only fridge here is full of very small bottles of alcohol. She lowers herself onto a bed that isn't hers, while rubbing her ring finger, a habit she falls into when she's nervous.

A few days ago she was sitting on her own bed, spinning her wedding ring, after cleaning the mattress extra-carefully with bicarbonate of soda. Now she's rubbing the white mark on her skin where the ring used to be.

The building has an address, but it's certainly neither a place to live nor a home. On the floor are two rectangular plastic boxes for balcony flowers, but the hostel room doesn't have a balcony. Britt-Marie has no one to sit up all night waiting for.

But she sits up anyway.

2

The unemployment office opens at 9.00. Britt-Marie waits until 9.02 before going in, because she doesn't want to seem pig-headed.

'You were supposed to contact me today,' she announces, not at all pig-headedly, when the girl opens her office door.

'What?' the girl exclaims, her face entirely liberated from any kind of positive emotion. She is surrounded by similarly dressed people clutching plastic mugs. 'Erm, look, we're just about to begin a meeting . . .'

'Oh, right. I suppose it's important?' says Britt-Marie, adjusting a crease in her skirt that only she can see.

'Well, yes . . .'

'And I'm not important, of course.'

The girl contorts herself as if her clothes have suddenly changed size.

'You know, I told you yesterday I'd be in touch if something turned up, I never said it would be tod—'

'But I've put it on the list,' says Britt-Marie, producing her notebook and pointing at it determinedly. 'I wouldn't have put it on the list if you hadn't said it, you must understand that. And you made me write it in ink!'

The girl takes a deep breath. 'Look, I'm very sorry if there's been a misunderstanding, but I have to go back to my meeting.'

'Maybe you'd have more time to find people jobs if you didn't spend your days in meetings?' observes Britt-Marie, as the girl shuts the door.

Britt-Marie is left on her own in the corridor. She notes there are two stickers on the girl's door, just under the handle. At a height where a child would put them. Both have footballs on them. This reminds her of Kent, because Kent loves football. He loves football in a way that nothing else in his life can live up to. He loves football even more than he loves telling everyone how much something costs after he's bought it.

During the big football championships, the crossword supplements are replaced by special football sections, and after that it's hardly possible to get a sensible word out of Kent. If Britt-Marie asks what he wants for dinner, he just mumbles that it doesn't matter, without even taking his eyes off the page.

Britt-Marie has never forgiven football for that. For taking Kent away from her, and for depriving her of her crossword supplement.

She rubs the white mark on her ring finger. She remembers the last time the morning newspaper replaced the crossword supplement with a football section, because she read the newspaper four times in the hope of finding a small, hidden crossword somewhere. She never found one, but she did find an article about a woman, of the same age as Britt-Marie, who had died. Britt-Marie can't get it out of her head. The article described how the woman had lain dead for several weeks before she was found, after the neighbours made a complaint about a bad smell from her flat. Britt-Marie can't stop thinking about that article, can't stop thinking about how vexatious it would be if the neighbours started complaining about bad smells. It said in the article that the cause of death had been 'natural'. A neighbour said that 'the woman's dinner was still on the table when the landlord walked into the flat.'

Britt-Marie had asked Kent what he thought the woman had eaten. She thought it must be awful to die in the middle of your dinner, as if the food was terrible. Kent mumbled that it hardly made any difference, and turned up the volume on the TV.

Britt-Marie fetched his shirt from the bedroom floor and put it in the washing machine, as usual. Then she washed it and reorganised his electric shaver in the bathroom. Kent often maintained that she had 'hidden' his shaver, when he stood there in the mornings yelling 'Briiitt-Mariiie' because he couldn't find it, but she wasn't hiding it at all. She was reorganising. There's a difference. Sometimes she reorganised because it was necessary, and sometimes she did it because she loved hearing him call out her name in the mornings.

After half an hour the door to the girl's office opens. People emerge; the girl says goodbye and smiles enthusiastically, until she notices Britt-Marie.

'Oh, you're still here. So, as I said, Britt-Marie, I'm really sorry but I don't have time for . . .'

Britt-Marie stands up and brushes some invisible crumbs from her skirt.

'You like football, I see,' Britt-Marie offers, nodding at the stickers on the door. 'That must be nice for you.'

The girl brightens. 'Yes. You too?'

'Certainly not.'

'Right . . .' The girl peers at her watch and then at another clock on the wall. She's quite clearly bent on trying to get Britt-Marie out of there, so Britt-Marie smiles patiently and decides to say something sociable.

'Your hairstyle is different today.'

'What?'

'Different from yesterday. It's modern, I suppose.'

'What, the hairstyle?'

'Never having to make up your mind.'

Then she adds at once: 'Not that there's anything wrong with that, of course. In fact it looks very practical.'

In actual fact it mainly looks short and spiky, like when someone has spilled orange juice on a shagpile rug. Kent always

11

used to spill his drink when he was having vodka and orange juice during his football matches, until one day Britt-Marie had enough and moved the rug to the guest room. That was thirteen years ago, but she still often thinks about it. Britt-Marie's rugs and Britt-Marie's memories have a lot in common in that sense: they are both very difficult to wash.

The girl clears her throat. 'Look, I'd love to talk further, but as I keep trying to tell you I just don't have time at the moment.'

'When do you have time?' Britt-Marie asks, getting out her notebook and methodically going through a list. 'Three o'clock?'

'I'm fully booked today—'

'I could also manage four or even five o'clock,' Britt-Marie offers, conferring with herself.

'We close at five today,' says the girl.

'Let's say five o'clock then.'

'What? No, we close at five—'

'We certainly can't have a meeting later than five,' Britt-Marie protests.

'What?' says the girl.

Britt-Marie smiles with enormous, enormous patience.

'I don't want to cause a scene here. Not at all. But my dear girl, civilised people have their dinner at six, so any later than five is surely a bit on the late side for a meeting, wouldn't you agree? Or are you saying we should have our meeting while we're eating?'

'No . . . I mean . . . What?'

'Ha. Well, in that case you have to make sure you're not late. So the potatoes don't get cold.'

Then she writes '18.00. Dinner' on her list.

The girl calls out something behind Britt-Marie but Britt-Marie has already gone, because she actually doesn't have time to stand here going on about this all day.

3

It's 16.55. Britt-Marie is waiting by herself in the street outside the unemployment office, because it would be impolite to go in too early for the meeting. The wind ruffles her hair gently. She misses her balcony so much, it pains her to even think about it — she has to squeeze her eyes shut, so tightly that her temples start hurting. She often busies herself on the balcony at nights while she's waiting for Kent. He always says she shouldn't wait up for him. She always does. She usually notices his car from the balcony, and by the time he steps inside, his food is already on the table. Once he's fallen asleep in their bed she picks up his shirt from the bedroom floor and puts it in the washing machine. If the collar is dirty she goes over it beforehand with vinegar and bicarbonate of soda. Early in the morning she wakes and fixes her hair and tidies up the kitchen, sprinkles bicarbonate of soda in the balcony flower boxes and polishes all the windows with Faxin.

Faxin is Britt-Marie's brand of window-cleaner. It's even better than bicarbonate of soda. She doesn't feel like a fully fledged human being unless she has a more or less full bottle at the ready. No Faxin? Anything could happen in such a situation. So she wrote 'Buy Faxin' on her shopping list this afternoon (she considered adding exclamation marks at the end, to really highlight the seriousness of it, but managed to contain herself). Then she went to the supermarket that isn't her usual, where nothing is arranged as usual. She asked a young person working there for Faxin. He didn't even know what it was. When Britt-Marie explained that it's her brand of window-cleaner, he just shrugged and suggested a different brand. At which point Britt-Marie got so angry that she got out her list and added an exclamation mark.

The shopping trolley was playing up and she even ran over her own foot with it. She closed her eyes and sucked in her cheeks and missed Kent. She found some salmon on sale and got some potatoes and vegetables. From a little shelf marked 'Stationery' she took a pencil and two pencil sharpeners and put them in her trolley.

'Are you a member?' asked the young man when she reached the till.

'Of what?' Britt-Marie asked suspiciously.

'The salmon is only on sale for members,' he said.

Britt-Marie smiled patiently.

'This is not my usual supermarket, you see. In my usual supermarket my husband is a member.'

The young man held out a brochure.

'You can apply here, it only takes a sec. All you do is fill in your name and address here an—'

'Certainly not,' said Britt-Marie immediately. Because surely there's some kind of limit? Do you really have to register and leave your name and address like some suspected terrorist just because you want to buy a bit of salmon?

'Well, in that case you have to pay full price for the salmon.'

'Ha.'

The young man looked unsure of himself.

'Look, if you don't have enough money on you I ca . . .'

Britt-Marie gave him a wide-eyed stare. She wanted so badly to raise her voice, but her vocal cords wouldn't cooperate.

'My dear little man, I have plenty of money. Absolutely plenty.' She tried to yell, and to slap down her wallet on the conveyor belt, but it was more like a whisper and a little pushing movement.

The young man shrugged and took her payment. Britt-Marie

wanted to tell him that her husband was actually an entrepreneur, and that she was actually well able to pay the full price for some salmon. But the young man had already started serving the next customer. As if she didn't make any difference.

At exactly 17.00 Britt-Marie knocks on the door of the girl's office. When the girl opens the door, she's wearing her coat.

'Where are you going?' asks Britt-Marie. The girl seems to pick up an incriminating note in her voice.

'I . . . well, we're closing now . . . as I told you, I have t—'

'Are you coming back, then? What time should I expect you?'

'What?'

'I have to know when I'm supposed to put on the potatoes.'

The girl rubs her eyelids with her knuckles.

'Yes, yes, OK. I'm sorry, Britt-Marie. But as I tried to tell you, I don't have the t—'

'These are for you,' says Britt-Marie, offering her the pencil. When the girl takes it, in some confusion, Britt-Marie also holds out a pair of pencil sharpeners, one of them blue and the other pink. She nods at these, and then she nods in a wholly unprejudicial way at the girl's boyish hairstyle.

'You know, there's no knowing what sort you people like nowadays. So I got both colours.'

The girl doesn't seem quite sure who Britt-Marie is referring to by 'you people'.

'Th . . . anks, I guess.'

'Now I'd like to be shown to the kitchen, if it's not too much bother to you, because otherwise I'll be late with the potatoes.'

The girl very briefly looks as if she's going to exclaim, 'Kitchen?' but at the last moment she holds back and, like small children next to bathtubs, seems to understand that protesting will only prolong the process and make it more tortuous. She simply gives up, points to the staff kitchen and takes the food bag from Britt-Marie, who follows her down the corridor.

15

Britt-Marie decides to acknowledge her civility with some sort of compliment of her own.

'That's a fine coat you have there,' she says at long last.

The girl's hand slides in surprise over the fabric of her coat.

'Thanks!' She smiles sincerely, opening the door to the kitchen.

'It's courageous of you to wear red at this time of year. Where are the cooking implements?'

With diminishing patience, the girl opens a drawer. One half is a jumble of cooking implements. The other holds a plastic compartment for cutlery.

A single compartment.

Forks, knives, spoons.

Together.

The girl's irritation turns to genuine concern.

'Are . . . you . . . Are you all right?' she asks Britt-Marie.

Britt-Marie has gone over to a chair to sit down, and looks on the verge of passing out.

'Barbarians,' she whispers, sucking in her cheeks.

The girl drops on to a chair opposite. Seems at a loss. Her gaze settles on Britt-Marie's left hand. Britt-Marie's fingertips are uncomfortably rubbing the white mark on her skin, like the scar of an amputated limb. When she notices the girl looking, she hides her hand under her handbag, looking as though she's caught someone spying on her in the shower.

Gently, the girl raises her eyebrows.

'Can I just ask . . . sorry, but . . . I mean, what are you really doing here, Britt-Marie?'

'I want a job,' Britt-Marie replies, digging in her bag for a handkerchief so she can give the table a rub-down.

The girl moves about, in a confused attempt to find a relaxed position.

'With all due respect, Britt-Marie, you haven't had a job in forty years. Why is it so important now?'

'I have had a job for forty years. I've taken care of a home. That's why it's important now,' says Britt-Marie, and brushes some imaginary crumbs off the table.

When the girl doesn't answer right away, she adds:

'I read in the newspaper about a woman who lay dead in her flat for several weeks, you see. They said the cause of death was "natural". Her dinner was still on the table. It's actually not very natural at all. No one knew she was dead until her neighbours reacted to the smell.'

The girl fiddles confusedly with her hair.

'So . . . you . . . sort of want a job, so that . . .' she says, fumblingly.

Britt-Marie exhales with great patience.

'She had no children and no husband and no job. No one knew she was there. If one has a job, people notice if one doesn't show up.'

The girl, still at work long after her day should be over, sits there looking for a long, long time at the woman who's kept her here. Britt-Marie sits with a straight back, like she sits on the chair on the balcony when she's waiting for Kent. She never wanted to go to bed when Kent wasn't home, because she didn't want to go to sleep unless someone knew she was there.

She sucks in her cheeks. Rubs the white mark.

'Ha. You believe it's preposterous, of course. I'm certainly aware that conversation isn't one of my strengths. My husband says I'm socially incompetent.'

The last words come out more quietly than the rest. The girl swallows and nods at the ring that is no longer on Britt-Marie's finger.

'What happened to your husband?'

'He had a heart attack.'

'I'm sorry. I didn't know he'd died.'

'He didn't die,' whispers Britt-Marie.

'Oh, I th—'

Britt-Marie interrupts her by getting up and starting to sort the cutlery as if it has committed some kind of crime.

'I don't use perfume, so I asked him to always put his shirt directly in the washing machine when he came home. He never

17

did. Then he used to yell at me because the washing machine was so loud at night.'

She stops abruptly, and gives the cooker a quick lecture about its buttons being the wrong way around. It looks ashamed of itself. Britt-Marie nods again and says:

'His other woman called me after he'd had his heart attack.'

The girl stands up to help, then sits down watchfully when Britt-Marie takes the filleting knife from the drawer.

'When Kent's children were small and stayed with us every other week, I made a habit of reading to them. My favourite was "The Master Tailor". It's a fairy tale, you understand. The children wanted me to make up my own stories, but I can't see the point of it when there are perfectly good ones already written by professionals. Kent said it was because I don't have any imagination, but actually my imagination is excellent.'

The girl doesn't answer. Britt-Marie sets the oven temperature. She puts the salmon in an oven dish. Then just stands there.

'It takes an excellent imagination to pretend one doesn't understand anything year in, year out, even though one washes all his shirts and one doesn't use perfume,' she whispers.

The girl stands up again. Puts her hand fumblingly on Britt-Marie's shoulder.

'I . . . sorry, I . . .' she starts to say.

She stops although she hasn't been interrupted. Britt-Marie clasps her hands together over her stomach and looks into the oven.

'I want a job because I actually don't think it's very edifying to disturb the neighbours with bad smells. I want someone to know I'm here.'

There's nothing to say to that.

When the salmon is ready they sit at the table and eat it without looking at each other.

'She's very beautiful. Young. I don't blame him, I actually don't,' says Britt-Marie at long last.

'She's probably a slag,' the girl offers.

18

'What does that mean?' asks Britt-Marie, looking uncomfortable.

'It's . . . I mean . . . it's something bad.'

Britt-Marie looks down at her plate again.

'Ha. That was nice of you.'

She feels as though she should say something nice back, so, with a certain amount of strain, she manages to say, 'You . . . I mean . . . your hair looks nice today.'

The girl smiles.

'Thanks!'

Britt-Marie nods.

'I'm not seeing as much of your forehead today, not like yesterday.'

The girl scratches her forehead, just under her fringe. Britt-Marie looks down at her plate and tries to resist the instinct to serve up a portion for Kent. The girl says something. Britt-Marie looks up and mumbles: 'Pardon me?'

'It was very nice, this,' says the girl.

Without Britt-Marie even asking.

4

And then Britt-Marie got herself a job. Which happened to be in a place called Borg. Two days after inviting the girl from the unemployment office to have some salmon, that's where Britt-Marie heads off to in her car. So we should now say a few words about Borg.

Borg is a community built along a road. That's really the kindest possible thing one can say about it. It's not a place that could be described as one in a million, rather as one of millions of others. It has a closed-down football pitch and a closed-down school and a closed-down chemist's and a closed-down off-licence and a closed-down healthcare centre and a closed-down supermarket and a closed-down shopping centre and a road that bears away in two directions.

There is a recreation centre that has admittedly not been closed down, but only because they haven't had time to do it yet. It takes time to close down an entire community, obviously, and the recreation centre has had to wait its turn. Apart from that the only two noticeable things in Borg are football and the pizzeria, because these tend to be the last things to abandon humanity.

Britt-Marie's first contact with the pizzeria and the recreation centre are on that day in January when she stops her white car between them. Her first contact with football is when one hits her, very hard, on the head.

This takes place just after her car has blown up.

You might sum it up by saying that Borg and Britt-Marie's first impressions of each other are not wholly positive.

If one wants to be pedantic about it, the actual explosion happens while Britt-Marie is turning into the parking area. On the passenger side. Britt-Marie is very clear about that, and if she had to describe the sound she'd say it was a bit like a 'ka-boom'. Understandably, she's in a panic, and she abandons both brake and clutch pedals, whereupon the car splutters pathetically. After a few unduly dramatic deviations across the frozen January puddles, it comes to an abrupt stop outside a building with a partially broken sign, the neon lights of which spell the name 'PizzRai'. Terrified, Britt-Marie jumps out of the car, expecting it (quite reasonably, under the circumstances) to be engulfed in flames at any moment. This does not happen. Instead, Britt-Marie is left standing on her own in the parking area, surrounded by the sort of silence that only exists in small, remote communities.

It's a touch on the annoying side. She adjusts her skirt and grips her handbag firmly.

A football rolls in a leisurely manner across the gravel, away from Britt-Marie's car and towards what Britt-Marie assumes must be the recreation centre. After a moment there's a disconcerting thumping noise. Determined not to be distracted from the tasks at hand, she gets out a list from her handbag. At the top it says, 'Drive to Borg.' She ticks that point. The next item on the list is, 'Pick up key from post office.'

She gets out the mobile phone that Kent gave her five years ago, and uses it for the first time. 'Hello?' says the girl at the unemployment office.

'Is that how people answer the phone nowadays?' says Britt-Marie. Helpfully, not critically.

'What?' says the girl, for a few moments still blissfully unaware that Britt-Marie has not necessarily walked out of the girl's life just because she's walked out of the unemployment office.

'I'm here now, in this place, Borg. But something is making

21

an awful racket and my car has blown up. How far is it to the post office?'

'Britt-Marie, is that you?'

'I can hardly hear you!'

'Did you say *blown up*? Are you OK?'

'Of course I am! But what about the car?'

'I don't know the first thing about cars,' tries the girl.

Britt-Marie releases an extremely patient exhalation of air.

'You said I should call you if I had any questions,' she reminds her. Britt-Marie feels it would be unreasonable for her to be expected to know everything about cars. She has only driven on a very few occasions since she and Kent were married – she never goes anywhere in a car unless Kent is there, and Kent is an absolutely excellent driver.

'I meant questions about the *job*.'

'Ha. That's the only important thing, of course. The career. If I'm killed in an explosion, that's not important of course,' states Britt-Marie. 'Maybe it's even good if I die. Then you'll have a job going spare.'

'Please Britt-Mar—'

'I can hardly hear you!!' bellows Britt-Marie, in a very helpful way, and hangs up. Then she stands there, on her own, sucking in her cheeks.

Something is still thumping on the other side of the recreation centre, which is still standing only because at the last councillors' meeting in December, there were so many other things already scheduled for closure. The local authority representatives were concerned it might cause a postponement of their annual Christmas dinner. In view of the importance of the Christmas dinner, the closure was pushed back to the end of January, after the holiday period of the local authority councillors. Obviously the communications officer of the local authority should have been responsible for communicating this to the personnel department, but unfortunately the communications officer went on holiday and forgot to communicate it. As a result, when the personnel department found that the local authority had a building without anyone to take care of it, a vacancy for a caretaker of the recreation centre was advertised with the unemployment office in early January. That was the long and the short of it.

Anyway, the job is not only exceptionally badly paid, but also temporary and subject to the decision regarding the closure of the recreation centre to be reached at the councillors' meeting in three weeks' time. And to top it all, the recreation centre is in Borg. The number of applicants for the position were, for these reasons, fairly limited.

But it just so happened that the girl at the unemployment office, who very much against her will ate salmon with Britt-Marie the day before yesterday, promised Britt-Marie that she would really try to find her a job. The next morning at 9.02, when Britt-Marie knocked on the girl's door to inform herself about how this was going, the girl tapped her computer for a while then eventually said: 'There is one job. But it's in the middle of nowhere and so badly paid that if you're receiving unemployment benefits you'll probably be out of pocket.'

'I don't get any *benefits*,' said Britt-Marie, as if they were a disease.

The girl sighed again and tried to say something about 'retraining courses' and 'measures' that Britt-Marie might be eligible for, but Britt-Marie made it clear that she certainly wouldn't welcome any of those measures.

'Please, Britt-Marie, this is just a job for three weeks, it's not really the kind of thing you want to be applying for at your . . . age . . . plus you'd have to move all the way to this place . . .'

Now Britt-Marie is in Borg and her car has blown up. It's hardly the best possible first day in her new job, one might say. She calls the girl back.

'Where can I expect to find the cleaning equipment?' asks Britt-Marie.

'What?' asks the girl.

'You said I should call if I had any questions about the job.'

The girl mutters something unintelligible, her voice sounding as if it's coming from inside a tin can.

'Now you have to listen to me, my dear. I fully intend to find the post office you have informed me about, and pick up the keys to the recreation centre, but I am not putting one foot inside the recreation centre until you inform me of the where-abouts of the cleaning equip—!' Once again she is interrupted by the ball rolling across the parking area. Britt-Marie dislikes this. It's nothing personal, she hasn't decided to pick on this football in particular. It's just that she just dislikes all footballs. Entirely without prejudice.

The football is being pursued by two children. They are exceedingly dirty, all three of them if you include the ball.

The children's jeans are all torn down their thighs. They catch up with the ball, kick it back in the opposite direction and once again disappear behind the recreation centre. One of them loses his balance and steadies himself by putting his hand against the window, where he leaves a black handprint.

'What's happening?' asks the girl.

'Shouldn't those children be at school?' Britt-Marie exclaims, reminding herself to put an extra exclamation mark after 'Buy Faxin!' on her list. If this place even has a supermarket.

'What?' says the girl.

'My dear girl, you have to stop saying "what?" all the time, it makes you sound so untalented.'

'What?'

'There are CHILDREN here!'

'OK, but please, Britt-Marie, I don't know anything about Borg! I've never been there! And I'm not hearing you – I think you . . . are you sure you're not holding the telephone upside down?'

Britt-Marie gives the telephone a scrutinising look. Turns it around.

'Ha,' she says into the microphone, as if the fault lay with the person at the other end of the line.

'OK, I can hear you at last,' says the girl encouragingly.

'I've never used this telephone. There are actually people who have other things to do than spending all day talking into their telephones, you understand.'

'Oh, don't worry. I'm just the same when I have a new telephone!'

'I'm certainly not worrying! And this is absolutely not a new telephone, it's five years old,' Britt-Marie corrects her. 'I've never needed one before. I've had things to get on with, you see. I don't call anyone except Kent, and I call him on the home telephone, like a civilised person.'

'But what if you're out, then?' asks the girl, instinctually unable to process what the world looked like before one could get hold of anyone, at any time of the day.

'My dear girl,' she explains patiently, 'If I'm out I'm with Kent.'

Britt-Marie was probably intending to say something else, but that's the point at which she sees the rat, more or less as big as a normal-sized flower pot, scampering across patches of ice in the parking area. Looking back, Britt-Marie is of the firm opinion that she wanted to scream very loudly. But unfortunately she did not have time for that, because everything abruptly went black and Britt-Marie's body lay unconscious on the ground.

Britt-Marie's first contact with football in Borg is when one hits her very hard on the head.

5

Britt-Marie wakes up on a floor. Somebody is leaning over her, saying something, but Britt-Marie's first thoughts are about the floor. She's worried that it may be dirty, and that people might think she's dead. These things happen all the time, people falling over and dying. It would be horrific, thinks Britt-Marie. To die on a dirty floor. What would people think?

'Hello, are you, what's-it-called? Deceased?' Somebody asks, but Britt-Marie keeps focusing on the floor.

'Hello, lady? Are you, you know, dead?' Somebody repeats and makes a little whistling sound.

Britt-Marie dislikes whistling, and she has a headache.

The floor smells of pizza. It would be awful to die with a headache while smelling of pizza.

She's not at all keen on pizza, because Kent smelled so much of pizza when he came home late from his meetings with Germany. Britt-Marie remembers all his smells. Most of all the smell of the hospital room. It was loaded with bouquets (it is common practice to receive flowers when you have a heart attack), but Britt-Marie can still remember that smell of perfume and pizza from the shirt by the side of his bed.

He was sleeping, snoring slightly. She held his hand a last time, without waking him. Then she folded up the shirt and put it in her handbag. When she came home she cleaned the collar with bicarbonate of soda and vinegar and washed it twice before she hung it up. Then she polished the windows with Faxin and freshened up the mattress and brought in the balcony boxes and packed her bag and turned on her mobile telephone for the first time in her life. For the first time in their life together. She thought the children might call and ask how things were with Kent. They didn't. They both sent a single text message.

There was a time just after their teenage years when they still promised to come to visit at Christmas. Then they started pretending to have reasons for cancelling. After a year or two they stopped pretending to have reasons for cancelling. In the end they stopped pretending that they were coming at all. That's how life went.

Britt-Marie has always liked the theatre, because she enjoys the way the actors get applauded at the end for their pretence. Kent's heart attack and the voice of the young, beautiful thing meant there'd be no applause for her. You can't keep pretending someone doesn't exist when she speaks to you on the telephone. So Britt-Marie left the hospital room with a shirt smelling of perfume and a broken heart.

You don't get any flowers for that.

'But, shit, are you . . . like . . . dead?' Somebody asks impatiently.

Britt-Marie finds it extremely impolite for Somebody to interrupt her in the midst of dying. Especially with such terrible language. There are certainly a good number of alternatives to 'shit', if you have a particular need to express such a feeling. She looks up at this Somebody standing over her, looking down.

'May I ask where I am?' asks Britt-Marie, in confusion.

'Hi there! At the health centre,' says Somebody cheerfully.

'It smells of pizza,' Britt-Marie manages to say.

'Yeah, you know, health centre is also pizzeria,' says Somebody, nodding.

'That hardly strikes me as hygienic,' Britt-Marie manages to utter.

Somebody shrugs his shoulders. 'First pizzeria. You know, they closed down that health centre. Financial crisis. What a shit. So now, you know, we do what we can. But no worry. Have first aid!'

27

Somebody, who actually seems to be a woman, points jovially at an open plastic case marked with a red cross on the lid, and 'First Aid' written on it. Then she waves a stinky bottle.

'And here, you know, second aid! You want?'

'Excuse me?' Britt-Marie squeaks, with her hand on a painful bump on her forehead.

Somebody, who on closer inspection is not standing over Britt-Marie but sitting over her, offers her a glass.

'They closed down the off-licence here, so now we do what we can. Here! Vodka from Estonia or some shit like that. Letters bloody weird, you know. Maybe not vodka, but same shit, burns your tongue but you get used to it. Good when you get those, what's-it-called? Flu blisters?'

Tormented, Britt-Marie shakes her head and catches sight of some red stains on her jacket.

'Am I bleeding?' she bursts out, sitting up in terror.

It would be terribly vexatious if she left bloodstains on Somebody's floor, whether it's been mopped or not.

'No! No! No shit like that. Maybe you get a bump on your head from the shot, huh, but that's just tomato sauce, you know!' yells Somebody and tries to mop Britt-Marie's jacket with a tissue.

Britt-Marie notices that Somebody is in a wheelchair. It's a difficult thing not to notice. Furthermore, Somebody seems intoxicated. Britt-Marie bases this observation on the fact that Somebody smells of vodka and can't quite manage to dab the tissue in the right place. But Britt-Marie doesn't have any prejudices about it.

'I was waiting here for you to stop looking deceased. Got hungry, you know, so I had a bit of lunch,' sniggers Somebody, pointing at a half-eaten pizza perched on a stool.

'Lunch? At this time of day?' mumbles Britt-Marie, because it isn't even eleven o'clock.

'If you hungry? Have pizza!' Somebody explains.

Only then does Britt-Marie register what was said.

'What do you mean, a bump from "the shot"? Have I been

shot?' she exclaims, fingering her scalp as if searching for a hole.

'Yeah, yeah, yeah. A football in the head, you know.' Somebody nods and spills vodka on the pizza.

Britt-Marie looks as if she may even have preferred a pistol to a pizza. She imagines that pistols are less dirty.

Somebody, who seems to be in her forties, helps her up, assisted by a girl in her early teens who has turned up at their side. Somebody has one of the worst hairstyles Britt-Marie has ever laid eyes on, as if she's combed her hair with a terrified animal. The girl's hair is more respectable, but her jeans are torn to shreds across her thighs. Probably modern.

Somebody sniggers, without a care in the world.

'Bloody brats, you know. Bloody football. But don't get angry, they weren't aiming at you!'

Britt-Marie touches the bump on her forehead.

'Is my face dirty?' she asks, simultaneously reproachful and anxious.

Somebody shakes her head and rolls back towards her pizza.

Britt-Marie's gaze falls self-consciously on two men with beards and caps, sitting at a table in a corner, with cups of coffee and morning newspapers. It seems abominable to her, lying there passed out in front of people who are trying to have their coffee. Yet neither of the men even glance at her.

'You only passed out a little,' says Somebody breezily, while shovelling the pizza into her mouth.

Britt-Marie gets out a small mirror from her handbag and starts rubbing her forehead. She found it very vexatious passing out, but nowhere near as vexatious as the thought of having passed out with a dirty face.

'How do you know if they were aiming at me?' she asks, with just a touch of criticism.

'They hit you!' laughs Somebody, throwing out her arms. 'If they aim, they don't hit. These kids bloody terrible at football, huh?'

'Ha,' says Britt-Marie.

'We're actually not that bad . . .' mutters the teenage girl standing next to them, looking offended.

Britt-Marie notices that she's holding the football in her hands. The way you hold a ball when that's what you have to do to stop yourself from repeatedly kicking it.

Somebody gestures encouragingly at the girl.

'My name's Vega. I work here!' the girl says.

'Shouldn't you be at school?' asks Britt-Marie, without taking her eyes off the football.

'Shouldn't you be at work?' answers Vega, holding the football as you do when you're holding on to someone you love.

Britt-Marie grips her handbag more firmly.

'Let me tell you something, I was on my way to work when I was hit on the head. I'm the caretaker of the recreation centre, I'll have you know. This is my first day.'

Vega's mouth opens in surprise. As if this, in some way, changes everything. But she remains silent.

'Caretaker?' asks Somebody. 'Why didn't you say so, lady! I've got one of them, what's-it-called? Registered letters! With the key!'

'I've been informed I'm to pick up the keys at the post office.'

'Are here! They closed down post office, you see!' shouts Somebody, rolling around behind the counter, still with the bottle of vodka in her hand.

There's a short silence. There's a tinkle from the door and a pair of dirty boots cross the unmopped floor. Somebody yells out:

'All right, Karl! I have packaging for you, wait!'

Britt-Marie turns around and is almost knocked to the ground by someone crashing into her shoulder. She looks up and sees a thick beard just below an unreasonably dirty cap, the whole appendage looking back at her.

There's a growl from somewhere between the beard and the cap: 'Look where you're going.'

Britt-Marie, who wasn't even moving, is deeply puzzled. Then she grips her handbag even more firmly and says:

'Ha.'

'*You* walked into *her*!' Vega hisses behind her.

Britt-Marie doesn't like it at all. She gets confused when anyone defends her – it doesn't happen very often.

Somebody comes back with Karl's 'packaging'; Karl looks with irritation at Vega and hostility at Britt-Marie. Then he nods grumpily to the two men at the corner table. They nod back even more grumpily. The door tinkles merrily behind Karl as he slopes out.

Somebody pats Britt-Marie encouragingly on the shoulder.

'Never bloody mind about him. Karl has . . . like . . . what do you say? A lemon up his arse, you know what I mean? Pissed off at life and the universe and everything. People around here don't like visitors from the city,' she says to Britt-Marie and nods at the men by the table when she says 'people'. They keep reading their newspapers and drinking their coffee as if neither of the women were there.

'How did he know I was from the city?'

Somebody rolls her eyes. 'Come on! I'll show you the recreation centre, huh!' she shouts and rolls off towards the door.

Britt-Marie looks at a section that leads off the pizzeria, healthcare centre, post office, or whatever it is. There are shelves of groceries in there. As if it were a minimarket.

'Could I ask, is this a grocer's?'

'They closed down the supermarket, you know, we do what we can!'

Britt-Marie remembers the dirty windows in the recreation centre.

'Might one ask if you have Faxin available here?' she asks.

Britt-Marie has never used any other brand than Faxin. She saw an advert for it in her father's morning newspaper when she was a child. A woman stood looking out of a clean window and underneath was written: 'Faxin Lets You See the World.' Britt-Marie loved that picture. As soon as she was old enough to have her own windows she polished them with Faxin, continued doing so daily for the rest of her life, and never had any problems seeing the world.

It was just that the world did not see her.

'I know, you know, but there's no Faxin now . . . you know?' says Somebody.

'What's that supposed to mean?' asks Britt-Marie, only a touch reproachfully.

'Faxin is not any more in manufacturer's . . . what's-it-called? Product range! Not profitable, you know.'

Britt-Marie's eyes open wide and she makes a little gasp.

'Is . . . but how . . . is that even legal?'

'Not profitable,' says Somebody with a shrug.

As if that's an answer.

'Surely people can't just behave like that?' Britt-Marie bursts out.

Somebody shrugs again. 'Never mind though, eh? I have another brand! You want Russian brand, good shit, over there—' she starts to say and gestures at Vega to run over and get it.

'Absolutely not!' Britt-Marie interrupts, walking towards the door as she hisses: 'I'll use bicarbonate of soda!'

Because you can't change Britt-Marie's way of seeing the world. Because once Britt-Marie has taken a position on the world there's no changing her.

6

Britt-Marie stumbles on the threshold. As if it's not just the people in Borg who are trying to push her away, but also the actual buildings. She stands on the wheelchair ramp leading up to the door of the pizzeria. Curls her toes, making her foot into a little fist in her shoe to dull the pain. A tractor goes past on the road in one direction, a truck in the other. And then the road lies desolate. Britt-Marie has never been in such a small community, only driven through places like this sitting next to Kent in the car. Kent was always very sneering about them.

Britt-Marie regains her composure and grips her handbag more firmly as she steps off the wheelchair ramp and crosses the large gravelled parking area. She walks fast, as if she's being chased by someone. Somebody rolls behind her. Vega takes the football and runs towards a group of other children, who are all wearing jeans that are torn across their thighs. After a couple of steps, Vega stops, peers at Britt-Marie and mumbles:

'Sorry the ball hit your head. We weren't aiming at you.'

Then she says quite curtly to Somebody:

'But we could have hit it if we'd been aiming!'

She turns around and shoots the ball past the boys into a wooden fence between the recreation centre and the pizzeria. One of the boys is at the receiving end, and he fires it into the fence again. Only then does Britt-Marie realise where the thumping sounds in Borg come from. One of the boys takes aim at the fence but instead manages to shoot the ball right back to Britt-Marie, which, if you consider the angle, is quite an impressive feat as far as underachievements go.

The ball rolls back slowly to Britt-Marie. The children seem to be waiting for her to kick it back. Britt-Marie moves out of the way as if the ball was trying to spit at her. The ball rolls past. Vega comes running.

'Why didn't you kick it?' she asks, perplexed.

'Why on earth would I want to kick it?'

They glare at each other, filled with mutual conviction that the opposing party is utterly deranged. Vega kicks the ball back to the boys and runs off. Britt-Marie brushes some dust from her skirt. Somebody takes a gulp of vodka.

'Bloody brats, you know. Crap at football. They couldn't hit the water from, you know? A boat! But they don't have nowhere to play, right? Bloody crap. The council closed down the football ground. Sold the land and now they're building flats there. Then the financial crisis and all that shit and now: no flats like they said, and no football pitch either.'

'Kent says the financial crisis is over,' Britt-Marie informs her amicably.

Somebody snorts.

'Maybe that Kent bloke has, what's-it-called? His head up his arse, huh?'

Britt-Marie doesn't know if she's more offended because she doesn't know what this means, or because she has an idea of what it means.

'Kent probably knows more about this than you do. He's an entrepreneur, you have to understand. Incredibly successful. Does business with Germany,' she says, putting Somebody to rights.

Somebody looks unimpressed. Points at the children with her vodka bottle and says:

'They closed down the football team when they closed down the pitch. Good players moved to crap team in town.'

She nods down the road towards what Britt-Marie has to assume is 'town', then back at the children.

'Town. Twenty kilometres that way, huh? These are, you know, the kids left behind. Like your what's-it-called? Faxin! Discontinued product line. You have to be profitable. So this Kent, huh, he may have his arse full of head, huh? Maybe financial crisis cleared out of the city, you know, but it likes Borg. It's living here now, the bastard!'

Britt-Marie notes the clear distinction between how she speaks of the 'town' twenty kilometres away and the city Britt-Marie comes from. There are two different levels of contempt. Somebody takes such a big hit on her bottle that her eyes tear up as she goes on:

'In Borg, everyone drove trucks, you know. There was, what's-it-called, a trucking company here! Then you know, the bastard financial crisis. More people in Borg now than trucks, and more trucks than jobs.'

Britt-Marie keeps a firm grasp on her handbag and feels a need, for reasons that are not entirely apparent, to defend herself.

'There are rats here,' she therefore informs Somebody, not at all unpleasantly.

'Rats have to live somewhere, don't they?'

'Rats are filthy. They live in their own dirt.'

Somebody digs in her ear. Looks at her finger with interest. Drinks some more vodka. Britt-Marie nods and adds in a tone that, in every possible way, is extremely helpful:

'If you got involved in keeping things a bit cleaner here in Borg, then maybe you wouldn't have so much of a financial crisis.'

Somebody doesn't give the impression that she's been listening very carefully.

'It's one of those, what's-it-called? Myths? Dirty rats. It's a myth, huh. They're, what's-it-called? Clean! Wash themselves like cats, you know, with tongue. Mice are crappy, crap everywhere, but rats have toilets. Always crap in same place, huh.' She points at Britt-Marie's car with her bottle.

'You should move the car. They'll shoot football at it, huh.'

Britt-Marie shakes her head patiently.

'It certainly cannot be moved, it exploded as I was parking it.'

Somebody laughs. She pushes her wheelchair around the car, and looks at the football-shaped dent in the passenger door.

'Ah. Flying stone.' She chuckles.

'What's that?' asks Britt-Marie, reluctantly following behind and glaring at the football-shaped dent.

'Flying stone. When the car workshop call insurance company, huh. Then the workshop say, "flying stone",' chuckles Somebody.

Britt-Marie fumbles after her list in her handbag.

'Ha. Might I ask where I'll find the nearest mechanic?'

'Here,' says Somebody.

Britt-Marie peers sceptically. At Somebody, obviously, not at the wheelchair. Britt-Marie is not one of those types who judges people.

'You repair cars, do you?'

Somebody shrugs.

'They shut down the car workshop, huh. We do what we can. But never bloody mind that now! I show you the recreation centre, yeah?'

She holds up the envelope with the keys. Britt-Marie takes it, looks at Somebody's bottle of vodka and keeps a firm grip on her handbag.

Then she shakes her head.

'That's perfectly all right, thank you. I don't want to create any bother.'

'No bother for me,' says Somebody and nonchalantly rolls her wheelchair back and forth.

Britt-Marie smiles superbly.

'I wasn't alluding to your bother.'

Then she briskly turns around and marches off across the gravelled courtyard, in case Somebody gets the idea of trying to follow her. She lifts out her bags and flower boxes from the car and drags them over to the recreation centre. Unlocks the door and steps inside, and locks it behind her. Not that she dislikes this Somebody person, not at all.

It's just that the smell of vodka reminds her of Kent.

She looks around. The wall is thumping from the outside,

and there are rat tracks in the dust on the floor. So Britt-Marie does what she always does when facing emergencies in life: she cleans. She polishes the windows with a rag dipped in bicarbonate of soda, and wipes them with newspaper dampened with vinegar. It's almost as effective as Faxin, but doesn't quite feel as good. She wipes the kitchen sink with bicarbonate of soda and water and then mops all the floors, then mixes bicarbonate of soda and lemon juice to clean the tiles and taps in the bathroom, and then mixes bicarbonate of soda and toothpaste to polish the washbasin. Then she sprinkles bicarbonate of soda over her balcony boxes, as otherwise there'll be snails.

The balcony boxes may look as if they only contain soil, but underneath there are flowers waiting for spring. The winter requires whoever is doing the watering to have a bit of faith, in order to believe that what looks empty has every potential. Britt-Marie no longer knows whether she has faith or just hope. Maybe neither.

The wallpaper of the recreation centre looks indifferently at her. It's covered in photos of people and footballs.

Everywhere, footballs. Every time Britt-Marie glimpses another one in the corner of her eye, she rubs things even more aggressively with her sponge. She keeps cleaning until the thumping against the wall stops and the children and the football have gone home. Only once the sun has gone down does Britt-Marie realise that the lights inside only work in the kitchen. So she stays in there, stranded on a little island of artificial, fluorescent light, in a soon-to-be-closed-down recreation centre.

The kitchen is almost completely taken up by a draining board, a refrigerator and two wooden stools. She opens the refrigerator to find it empty apart from a packet of coffee. She curses herself for not bringing any vanilla essence. If you mix vanilla essence with bicarbonate of soda, the refrigerator smells fresh.

She stands hesitantly in front of the coffee percolator. It looks modern. She hasn't made coffee in many years, because Kent makes very good coffee, and Britt-Marie always finds it's best to wait for him. But this percolator has an illuminated button, which strikes Britt-Marie as one of the most marvellous things she has seen in years, so she tries to open the lid where she assumes the coffee should be spooned in. It's stuck. The button starts blinking angrily.

Britt-Marie feels deeply mortified by this. She tugs at the lid in frustration. The blinking intensifies, upon which Britt-Marie tugs at it with such insistence that the whole machine is knocked over. The lid snaps open and a mess of coffee grounds and water sprays all over Britt-Marie's jacket.

They say people change when they go away, which is why Britt-Marie has always loathed travelling. She doesn't want change.

So it must be on account of the travelling, she decides afterwards, that she now loses her self-possession as never before. Unless you count the time Kent walked across the parquet floor in his golf shoes soon after they were married.

She picks up the mop and starts beating the coffee machine with the handle as hard as she can. It blinks. Something smashes. It stops blinking. Britt-Marie keeps hitting it until her arms are trembling and her eyes can no longer make out the contours of the draining board. Finally, out of breath, she fetches a towel from her handbag. Turns off the ceiling light in the kitchen. Sits down on one of the wooden stools in the darkness, and weeps into the towel.

She doesn't want her tears to drip on to the floor. They could leave marks.

7

Britt-Marie stays awake all night. She's used to that, as people are when they have lived their entire lives for someone else.

She sits in the dark, of course, otherwise what would people think if they walked by and saw the light left on as if there was some criminal inside?

But she doesn't sleep, because she remembers the thick layer of dust on the floor of the recreation centre before she started cleaning, and if she dies in her sleep she's certainly not going to risk lying here until she starts smelling and gets all covered in dust. Sleeping on one of the sofas in the corner of the recreation centre is not even worth thinking about, because they were so filthy that Britt-Marie had to wear double latex gloves when she covered them with bicarbonate of soda. Maybe she could have slept in the car? Maybe, if she were an animal.

The girl at the unemployment office kept insisting that there was a hotel in the town twenty kilometres away, but Britt-Marie can't even think of staying another night in a place where other people have made her bed. She knows that there are some people who do nothing else but dream of going away and experiencing something different, but Britt-Marie dreams of staying at home where everything is always the same. She wants to make her own bed.

Any time she and Kent are staying at a hotel she always puts up the 'Do Not Disturb' sign, and then makes the bed and cleans the room herself. It's not because she judges people, not at all;

it's because she knows that the cleaning staff could very well be the sort of people who judge people, and Britt-Marie certainly doesn't want to run the risk of the cleaning staff sitting in a meeting in the evening, discussing the horrible state of Room 423.

Once, Kent made a mistake about the check-in time for the flight when they were going home after a hotel visit, although Kent still maintains that 'those sods can't even write the correct time on the sodding ticket', and they had to run off in the middle of the night without even having time to take a shower. So, just before Britt-Marie rushed out of the door, she ran into the bathroom to turn on the shower for a few seconds, so there would be water on the floor when the cleaning staff came, and they would therefore not come to the conclusion that the guests in Room 423 had set off wearing their own dirt.

Kent snorted at her and said she was always too bloody concerned about what people thought of her. Britt-Marie was screaming inside all the way to the airport. She had actually mainly been concerned about what people would think of Kent.

She doesn't know when he stopped caring about what people thought of her.

She knows that once upon a time he did care. That was back in the days when he still looked at her as if he knew she was there. It's difficult to know when love blooms; suddenly one day you wake up and it's in full flower. It works the same way when it wilts − one day it is just too late. Love has a great deal in common with balcony plants in that way. Sometimes not even bicarbonate of soda makes a difference.

Britt-Marie doesn't know when their marriage slipped out of her hands, when it became worn and scratched up no matter how many coasters she used. Once he used to hold her hand when they slept, and she dreamed his dreams. Not that Britt-Marie didn't have any dreams of her own, it was just that his were bigger, and the one with the biggest dreams always wins in this world. She had learned that. So she stayed home to take care of his children, without even dreaming of having any of her own. She stayed home another few years to make a

40

presentable home and support him in his career, without dreaming of her own. She found she had neighbours who called her a 'nag-bag' when she worried about what the Germans would think if there was rubbish in the foyer or the stairwell smelled of pizza. She made no friends of her own, just the odd acquaintance, usually the wife of one of Kent's business associates.

One of them once offered to help Britt-Marie with the washing-up after a dinner party, and then she set about sorting Britt-Marie's cutlery drawer with knives on the left, then spoons and forks. When Britt-Marie asked, in a state of shock what she was doing, the acquaintance laughed as if it was a joke, and said 'Does it really matter?' They were no longer acquainted. Kent said that Britt-Marie was socially incompetent, so she stayed home for another few years so he could be social on behalf of the both of them. A few years turned into more years, and more years turned into all years. Years have a habit of behaving like that. It's not that Britt-Marie chose not to have any expectations, she just woke up one morning and realised they were past their sell-by date.

Kent's children liked her, she thinks, but children become adults and adults refer to women of Britt-Marie's type as 'nag-bags'. From time to time there were other children living in their block; occasionally Britt-Marie got to cook them dinner if they were home alone. But the children always had mothers or grandmothers who came home at some point, and then they grew up, and Britt-Marie became a 'nag-bag'. Kent kept saying she was socially incompetent and she assumed this had to be right. In the end all she dreamed of was a balcony and a husband who did not walk on the parquet in his golf shoes, who occasionally put his shirt in the laundry basket without her having to ask him to do it, and who now and then said he liked the food without her having to ask. A home. Children who, although they weren't her own, came for Christmas in spite of everything. Or at least tried to pretend they had a decent reason not to. A correctly organised cutlery drawer. An evening at the theatre every now and again.

Windows you could see the world through. Someone who noticed that Britt-Marie had taken special care with her hair. Or at least pretended to notice. Or at least let Britt-Marie go on pretending.

Someone who came home to a newly mopped floor and a hot dinner on the table and, on the odd occasion, noticed that she had made an effort. It may be that a heart only finally breaks after leaving a hospital room in which a shirt smells of pizza and perfume, but it will break more readily if it has burst a few times before.

Britt-Marie turns on the light at six o'clock the following morning. Not because she's really missing the light, but because people may have noticed the light was on last night, and if they've realised Britt-Marie has spent the night at the recreation centre she doesn't want them thinking she's still asleep at this time of the morning.

There's an old television by the sofas, which she could turn on to feel less lonely, but she avoids it because there will most likely be football on it. There's always football nowadays, and faced with that option Britt-Marie would actually prefer to be lonely. The recreation centre encloses her in a guarded silence. The coffee percolator lies on its side and no longer blinks at her. She sits on the stool in front of it, remembering how Kent's children said Britt-Marie was 'passive-aggressive'. Kent laughed in that way that he did after drinking vodka and orange in front of a football match, his stomach bouncing up and down and the laughter gushing forth in little snorting bursts through his nostrils, and then he replied: 'She ain't bloody passive-aggressive, she's aggressive-passive!' And then he laughed until he spilled vodka on the shagpile rug.

That was the night Britt-Marie decided she had had enough and moved the rug to the guest room, without a word. Not because she's passive-aggressive, obviously. But because there are limits.

She wasn't upset about what Kent had said, because most likely he didn't even understand it himself. On the other hand she was offended that he hadn't even checked to see if she was standing close enough to hear.

She looks at the coffee percolator. For a fleeting, carefree moment the thought occurs to her that she might try to mend it, but she comes to her senses and moves away from it. She hasn't mended anything since she was married. It was always best to wait until Kent came home, she felt. Kent always said 'women can't even put together IKEA furniture' when they watched women in television programmes about house building or renovation. 'Quota-filling,' he used to call it. Britt-Marie liked sitting next to him on the sofa solving the crossword. Always so close to the remote control that she could feel the tips of his fingers against her knee when he fumbled with it to flip the channel to a football match.

Then she fetches more bicarbonate of soda and cleans the entire recreation centre one more time. She has just sprinkled another batch of bicarbonate of soda over the sofas when there's a knock at the door. It takes Britt-Marie a fair amount of time to open it, because running into the bathroom and doing her hair in front of the mirror without functioning lights is a somewhat complicated process.

Somebody is sitting outside the door with a box of wine in her hands.

'Ha,' says Britt-Marie to the box.

'Good wine, you know. Cheap. Fell off the back of a lorry, huh!' says Somebody quite smugly.

Britt-Marie doesn't know what that means.

'But, you know, I have to pour into bottle with label and all that crap, in case tax authority asks about it,' says Somebody. 'It's called "house red" in my pizzeria, if tax authority asking, OK?' Somebody partly gives Britt-Marie the box and partly throws it at her before she forces her way inside, the wheelchair slamming across the threshold, to have a look around.

Britt-Marie looks at the goo of melted snow and gravel left behind by the wheels, with marginally less horror than if it had been excrement.

'Might I ask how the repair of my car is progressing?' asks Britt-Marie.

Somebody nods exultantly.

'Bloody good! Bloody good! Hey, let me ask you something, Britt-Marie: do you mind about colour?'

'I beg your pardon?'

'You know, the door I got, huh. Bloody lovely door, huh. But maybe not same colour as car. Maybe . . . more like yellow.'

'What's happened to my door?' Britt-Marie asks, horrified.

'Nothing! Nothing! Just a question, huh! Yellow door? Not good? It's, what's-it-called? Oxidised! Old door. Almost not yellow any more. Almost white now.'

'I will certainly not tolerate a yellow door on my white car!'

Somebody waves the palms of her hands in circles.

'OK, OK, OK, you know. Calm, calm, calm. Fix white door. No problem. Don't get lemon in arse now. But white door will have, what's-it-called? Delivery time!'

She nods at the wine in a carefree manner.

'You like wine, Britt?'

'No,' answers Britt-Marie, not because she dislikes wine, but because if you say you like wine, people may come to the conclusion that you're an alcoholic.

'Everyone likes wine, Britt!'

'My name is Britt-Marie. Only my sister calls me Britt.'

'Sister, huh? There's, what's-it-called? Another one of you? Nice for the world!'

Somebody grins, as if this is a joke. At Britt-Marie's expense, Britt-Marie assumes.

'My sister died when we were small,' she informs Somebody, without taking her eyes off the wine box.

'Ah . . . what the hell . . . I . . . what's-it-called? Condole,' says Somebody sadly.

Britt-Marie curls up her toes tightly in her shoes.

'Ha. That's nice of you,' she says quietly.

'The wine is good but a bit, what's-it-called? Muddy! You have to strain it a few times with a coffee filter, huh, everything

OK then!' she explains expertly, before looking at Britt-Marie's bag and Britt-Marie's balcony boxes on the floor. Her smile grows.

'I wanted to give to you, you know, as your congratulations-for-new-job present. But now I can see it's more like a, what's-it-called? Moving-in present!'

Offended, Britt-Marie holds the box of wine in front of her as if it's making a ticking sound.

'I'd like to point out to you that I don't live here.'

'Where did you sleep last night, then?'

'I didn't sleep,' says Britt-Marie, looking as if she'd like to toss the wine box out of the door and cover her ears.

'There's one of them hotels, you know,' says Somebody.

'Ha, I suppose you also have a hotel on your premises. I could imagine you do. Pizzeria and car workshop and post office and grocer's shop and a hotel? Must be nice for you, never having to make up your mind.'

Somebody's face collapses with undisguised surprise.

'Hotel? Why would I have one of those? No, no, no, Britt-Marie. I keep to my, what's-it-called? Core activity!'

Britt-Marie shifts her weight from left foot to right, and finally goes to the refrigerator and puts the wine box inside.

'I don't like hotels,' she announces and closes the door firmly.

'No, damn it! Don't put wine in fridge, you get lumps in it!' yells Somebody.

Britt-Marie glares at her.

'Is it really necessary to swear all the time, as if we were a horde of barbarians?'

Somebody propels her chair forward and tugs at the kitchen drawers until she finds the coffee filters.

'Shit, Britt-Marie! I show. You must filter. It's OK. Or, you know, mix with Fanta. I have cheap Fanta, if you want. From China!'

She stops herself when she notices the coffee percolator. The remains of it, at least. Britt-Marie, filled with discomfort, clasps her hands together over her stomach and looks as if she'd like to brush some invisible specks of dust from the opening of a black hole, and then sink into it herself.

'What . . . happened?' asks Somebody, eyeing first the mop and then the mop-sized dents in the coffee percolator. Britt-Marie stands in silence, with flaming cheeks. She may quite possibly be thinking about Kent. Finally she clears her throat, straightens her back and looks Somebody right in the eye as she answers:

'Hit by a flying stone.'

Somebody looks at her. Looks at the coffee machine. Looks at the mop.

Then she starts laughing. Loudly. Then coughing. Then laughing even louder. Britt-Marie is deeply offended. It wasn't meant to be funny. At least she doesn't think it was; she hasn't said anything that was supposed to be funny in years, as far as she can remember. So she's offended by the laughter, because she assumes it's at her expense and not because of the actual joke. It's the sort of thing you assume if you've spent a sufficient amount of time with a husband who is constantly trying to be funny. There was not space in their relationship for more hilarity than his. Kent was funny and Britt-Marie went into the kitchen and took care of the washing-up. That was how they divided up their responsibilities.

But now Somebody sits here laughing so much that her wheelchair almost topples over. This makes Britt-Marie insecure, and her natural reaction to insecurity is irritation. She goes to the vacuum cleaner in a very demonstrative way to attack the sofa covers, which are covered in bicarbonate of soda.

Somebody's laughter slowly turns into a titter, and then into general mumbling about flying stones. 'That's bloody funny, you know. Hey, you know there's a bloody big package in your car, huh?'

As if this would in any way be a surprise to Britt-Marie. Britt-Marie can still hear a trace of tittering in her voice.

'I'm well aware of that,' she says tersely. She can hear Somebody rolling her wheelchair towards the front door.

'You want, you know, some help carrying it inside?'

Britt-Marie turns on the vacuum cleaner by way of an answer. Somebody yells to make herself heard:

'It's no trouble, Britt-Marie!'

Britt-Marie rubs the nozzle as hard as she can over the sofa cushions.

Repeatedly, until Somebody gives up and yells: 'Well, you know, have Fanta like I said if you want some for wine! And pizza!' Then the door closes. Britt-Marie turns off the vacuum cleaner. She doesn't want to be unfriendly, but she really doesn't want any help with the package. Nothing is more important to Britt-Marie right now than her reluctance to be helped with the package.

Because there's a piece of furniture from IKEA inside.

And Britt-Marie is going to assemble it herself.

8

From time to time a truck drives through Borg and, whenever this happens, the recreation centre shakes violently – as if, Britt-Marie thinks, it was built on the fault line between two continental shelves. Continental shelves are common in crossword puzzles, so it's the sort of thing she knows about. She also knows that Borg is the kind of place Britt-Marie's mother used to describe as 'the back of beyond', because that was how Britt-Marie's mother used to describe the countryside.

Yet another truck thunders past. A green one. The walls shake.

Borg used to be the sort of community trucks came home to, but nowadays they only drive past. The truck makes her think of Ingrid. She remembers that she had time to see it through the back window when she was a child, on the very last day that she can recall thinking of herself as such. It was also green.

Britt-Marie has wondered the same thing an infinite number of times over the years: whether she had time to scream. And whether it would have made a difference. Their mother had told Ingrid to put on her belt, because Ingrid never put her belt on, and for that exact reason Ingrid had not put it on. They were arguing. That's why they didn't see it. Britt-Marie saw it because she always put her belt on, because she wanted her mother to notice. Which she obviously never did, because Britt-Marie never had to be noticed, for the simple reason that she always did everything without having to be told.

It came from the right-hand side. Green. That's one of the

few things Britt-Marie remembers. It came from the right and there was glass and blood all over the back seat of their parents' car. The last thing Britt-Marie remembered before she passed out was that she wanted to clean it up. Make it nice. And when she woke up at the hospital that is precisely what she did. Clean. Make things nice. When they buried her sister and there were strangers in black clothes drinking coffee in her parents' home, Britt-Marie put coasters under all the cups and washed up all the dishes and cleaned all the windows. When her father began to stay at work for longer and longer, and her mother stopped talking altogether, Britt-Marie cleaned. Cleaned, cleaned, and cleaned.

She hoped that sooner or later her mother would get out of bed and say, 'How nice you've made everything,' but it never happened. They never spoke about the accident, and, because they didn't, they also couldn't talk about anything else. Some people had pulled Britt-Marie out of the car; she doesn't know who, but she knows that her mother, silently furious, never forgave them for saving the wrong daughter. Maybe Britt-Marie didn't forgive them either. Because they saved the life of a person who from that day devoted herself to just walking around being afraid of dying and lying there stinking. One day she read her father's morning newspaper, and saw an advertisement for a brand of window-cleaner. And in this way a life went by.

Now she's sixty-three and she's standing at the back of beyond, looking out at Borg through the kitchen window of the recreation centre, missing Faxin and her view of the world.

Obviously, she stands far enough from the window for no one outside to be able to see her looking out. What sort of impression would that make! As if she just stood there all day staring out, like some criminal. But her car is still parked in the gravelled courtyard. She has accidentally left her keys inside and the IKEA package is still in the back seat. She doesn't know exactly how she's supposed to get it inside the recreation centre, because it's so very heavy. She can't really say why it's so heavy because she doesn't know exactly what's inside. The idea was to buy a stool, not unlike the two stools in the kitchen at the recreation centre, but after she had made her way to the IKEA self-service warehouse and found the appropriate shelf she found that all the stools had been sold.

Britt-Marie had taken all morning to make the decision that she was going to buy and assemble a stool, so this anticlimax left her standing there, frozen to the spot, for such a length of time that she began to worry that someone in the warehouse would see her there looking mysterious. What would people think? Most likely, that she was planning to steal something. Once this thought was firmly established, Britt-Marie panicked and with superhuman powers managed to drag over the next available package to her cart, in almost every conceivable way managing to convey the impression that this was the package she had been after all along. She hardly remembers how she got it into the car. She supposes that she was overcome with that syndrome they often talk about on the TV, when mothers pick up huge boulders under which their children are lying trapped. Britt-Marie is invested with that sort of power when she starts entertaining suspicions of strangers looking at her and wondering whether she's a criminal.

She moves further away from the window, just to be on the safe side. At exactly twelve o'clock she prepares the table by the sofas for lunch. Not that there's much of either a table or a lunch, just a tin of peanuts and a glass of water, but the fact is that civilised people have lunch at twelve, and if Britt-Marie is anything in this world she's certainly civilised. She spreads a towel on the sofa before she sits down, then empties the tin of peanuts on to a plate. She has to force herself not to try to eat them with a knife and fork. Then she washes up and cleans the whole recreation centre again so carefully that she almost uses up her whole supply of bicarbonate of soda.

There's a little laundry room with a washing machine and a tumble drier. Britt-Marie cleans the machines with her last bit of bicarbonate of soda, like a starving person putting out her last bait on her fishing line.

Not that she was thinking of doing any washing, but she can't bear the thought of them all dirty. In a corner behind the tumble-drier she finds a whole sack of white shirts with numbers on them. Football jerseys, she understands. The entire recreation centre is hung with pictures of various people wearing those shirts. Very likely they're covered in grass stains, of course. Britt-Marie can't for the life of her understand why anyone would choose to practise an outdoor sport while wearing white jerseys. It's barbaric. She wonders whether the cornershop/pizzeria/car workshop/post office would even be likely to sell bicarbonate of soda.

She fetches her coat. Just inside the front door, next to several photos of footballs and people who don't know any better than to kick them, hangs a yellow jersey with the word 'Bank' printed above the number '10'. Just beneath is a photo of an old man holding up the same jersey with a proud smile.

Britt-Marie puts on her coat. Outside the front door is a person, who is clearly just about to knock on it. The person has a face and the face is full of snuff. This, in every possible way, is an awful way of establishing the very short-lived acquaintance between Britt-Marie and the face, because Britt-Marie loathes snuff. The whole thing is over in twenty seconds, when the snuff-face moves off while mumbling something that sounds distinctly like 'nag-bag'.

At which point Britt-Marie picks up her telephone and dials the number of the only person her telephone has ever called. The girl at the unemployment office doesn't answer. Britt-Marie calls again, because actually a telephone is not a thing you decide whether or not to answer.

'Yes?' says the girl at long last, with food in her mouth. 'Sorry. I'm having my lunch.'

'Now?' Britt-Marie exclaims, as if the girl was joking. 'My dear girl, we're not at war. Surely it's not necessary to be having your lunch at half past one?'

The girl chews her lunch quite hard. Bravely tries to change the topic of conversation:

'Did the pest control man come? I had to spend hours calling around but in the end I found someone who promised to make an emergency visit, and—'

'She was a pest control woman. Who took snuff,' Britt-Marie goes on, as if this explains everything.

'Right,' says the girl again. 'So did she deal with the rat?'

'No, she most certainly did not,' Britt-Marie affirms. 'She came in here wearing dirty shoes and I'd just mopped the floor. Taking snuff as well, she was. Said she was putting out poison, that's how she put it, and you can't just do that, do you really think one can just do that? Put out poison just like that?'

'N . . . o?' guesses the girl.

'No, you actually can't. Someone could die! And that's what I said. And then she stood there rolling her eyes with her dirty shoes and her snuff, and she said she'd put out a trap instead, and bait it with Snickers! Chocolate! On my newly mopped floor!' Britt-Marie says all this in the voice of someone screaming inside.

'OK,' says the girl and immediately wishes she hadn't, because she realises it is not OK at all.

'So I said it will have to be poison, then, and do you know what she told me? Listen to this! She said if the rat eats the poison you can't know for certain where it will go to die. It could die in a cavity in the wall and lie there stinking! Have you ever heard of such a thing? Do you know that you called in a woman who takes snuff and thinks it's absolutely in order to let dead animals die in the walls and stink the place out?'

'I was only trying to help,' says the girl.

'Ha. A fine lot of help that was. Some of us actually have other things to do than hanging about dealing with pest control women all day long,' says Britt-Marie well-meaningly.

'I couldn't agree more,' says the girl.

There's a queue in the cornershop. Or the pizzeria. Or the post office. Or the car workshop. Or whatever it is. Either way, there's a queue. In the middle of the afternoon. As if people here don't have anything better to do at this time.

The men with beards and caps are drinking coffee and reading the newspapers at one of the tables. Karl is standing at the front of the queue. He's picking up a parcel. How very nice for him, thinks Britt-Marie, having all this leisure time on his hands. A cuboid woman in her thirties stands in front of Britt-Marie, wearing her sunglasses. Indoors. Very modern, muses Britt-Marie.

She has a white dog with her. Britt-Marie can't think it's very hygienic. The woman buys a pack of butter and six beers with foreign lettering on the cans, which Somebody produces from behind the counter. Also four packs of bacon and more chocolate biscuits than Britt-Marie believes any civilised person could possibly need. Somebody asks if she'd like to have it on credit. The woman nods grumpily and throws it all in a bag. Britt-Marie would obviously never consider the woman to be 'fat', because Britt-Marie is absolutely not the kind of person who pigeon-holes people like that, but it does strike her how wonderful it must be for the woman to go through life so untroubled by her cholesterol levels.

'Are you blind, or what?' the woman roars as she turns around and charges directly into Britt-Marie.

Britt-Marie opens her eyes wide in surprise. Adjusts her hair.

'I most certainly am not. I have quite perfect vision. I've spoken to my optician about it. "You have quite perfect vision," he said!'

'In that case could you possibly get out of the way?' grunts the woman and waves a stick at her.

Britt-Marie looks at the stick. Looks at the dog and the sunglasses.

She mumbles 'Ha . . . ha . . . ha . . .' and nods apologetically before she realises that nodding won't make any difference. The blind woman and the dog walk through her more than they walk past her. The door tinkles cheerfully behind them. It doesn't have the sense to do anything else.

Somebody rolls past Britt-Marie and waves encouragingly at her.

'Don't worry about her. She's like Karl. Lemon up her arse, you know.'

She makes a gesture with her arm, which Britt-Marie feels is supposed to indicate how far up the latter the former is stuck, and then piles up a stack of empty pizza boxes on the counter.

Britt-Marie adjusts her hair and adjusts her skirt and instinctively adjusts the topmost pizza box, which isn't quite straight, and then tries to adjust her dignity as well and say in a tone that is absolutely considerate:

'I should like to know how the repair of my car is progressing.'

Somebody scratches her hair.

'Sure, sure, sure, that car, yeah. You know, I have something to ask you, Britt-Marie: is a door important to Britt-Marie?'

'Door? Why . . . what in the world do you mean?'

'You know, only asking. Colour: important for Britt-Marie, I understand. Yellow door: not OK. So I ask you, Britt-Marie: is a door important to Britt-Marie? If not important then Britt-Marie's car is, what's-it-called? Finish repaired! If a door is important . . . you know. Maybe, what's-it-called? Longer delivery time!'

She looks pleased. Britt-Marie does not look pleased.

'For goodness sake, I must have a door on the car!' she fumes.

Somebody waves the palms of her hands defensively.

'Sure, sure, sure, no get angry. Just ask. Door: a little longer!' She measures out a few centimetres in the air between her thumb and index finger to illustrate how short a period of time 'a little longer' really is.

Britt-Marie realises that the woman has the upper hand in these negotiations.

Kent should have been here; he loves negotiating. He always says you have to compliment the person you're negotiating with. So Britt-Marie collects herself and says:

'Here in Borg people seem to have all the time in the world to go shopping in the afternoon. It must be nice for you to have so much leisure.'

Somebody raises her eyebrows.

'And you? You're very busy?'

With a deep patience, Britt-Marie puts one hand in the other.

'I am *extremely* busy. Very, very busy indeed. But as it happens

I am out of bicarbonate of soda. Do you sell bicarbonate of soda in this . . . shop?'

She says the word 'shop' with divine indulgence.

'Vega!' Somebody roars at once so that Britt-Marie jumps into the air and almost knocks over the pile of pizza boxes.

The child from yesterday turns up behind the counter, still holding the football. Beside her stands a boy who looks almost exactly the same as her, but with longer hair.

'Bicarbonate of soda for the lady!' says Somebody with an exaggerated theatrical bow at Britt-Marie, which is not at all appreciated.

'It's her,' whispers Vega to the boy.

The boy immediately looks as if Britt-Marie is a lost key. He runs into the stockroom and stumbles back out with two bottles in his arms. Faxin. All the air goes out of Britt-Marie.

She assumes that she has what is sometimes in crossword clues known as an 'out-of-body experience'. For a few moments she forgets all about the grocery shop and the pizzeria and the men with beards and cups of coffee and newspapers. Her heart beats as if it's just been released from prison.

The boy places the bottles on the counter like a cat that's caught a squirrel. Britt-Marie's fingers brush over them before her sense of dignity orders them to leave off. It's like coming home.

'I . . . I was under the impression that they'd been discontinued,' she whispers.

The boy points eagerly at himself: 'Chill! Omar fixes everything!'

He points even more eagerly at the bottles of Faxin.

'All the foreign trucks stop at the petrol station in town! I know them all there! I fix whatever you like!'

Somebody nods wisely.

'They shut down petrol station in Borg. Not, you know, profitable.'

'But I fix petrol in can, if you like, free home delivery! And I can get you more Faxin if you want!' the boy hollers.

Vega rolls her eyes.

'I'm the one who told you she needed Faxin,' she hisses at the boy and puts the jar of bicarbonate of soda on the counter.

'I'm the one who fixed it!' the boy maintains, without taking his eyes off Britt-Marie.

'This is my younger brother Omar,' sighs Vega to Britt-Marie.

'We're born the same year!' protests Omar.

'In January and December, yeah,' snorts Vega. If anything, Britt-Marie notices, the brother looks slightly older than her. Still a child, but approaching that age when they can become quite pungent.

'I'm the best fixer in Borg. The king of the castle, you know. Whatever you need, come to me!' says Omar to Britt-Marie, winking confidently without paying any attention to his sister, who's kicking him on the shin.

'Twit,' says Vega with a sigh.

'Cow!' answers Omar.

Britt-Marie doesn't know if she should be concerned, or proud that she actually knows that this means something bad, but she doesn't have much time to reflect on this before Omar is lying on the floor, holding his lip. Vega goes out of the door with the football in one hand and the other hand still formed into a fist.

Somebody titters at Omar.

'You have, what's-it-called? Marshmallows for brains! Never learn, do you?'

Omar wipes his lip and then looks as if he's letting go of the whole business. Like a small child forgetting to cry over a dropped ice cream when he catches sight of a glittering power ball.

'If you want new hubcaps for your car I can fix it. Or anything. Shampoo or handbags or anything. I'll fix it!'

'Maybe some plasters?' hollers Somebody mischievously and points at his lip.

Britt-Marie keeps a firm grip on her handbag and adjusts her hair, as if the boy has offended the both of them.

'I certainly don't need either shampoo or a handbag.'

Omar points at the bottles of Faxin.

'Those are thirty kronor each but you can have them on credit.'

'On *credit*?'

'Everyone shops on credit in Borg.'

'I certainly don't shop on credit! I can see maybe you don't understand such a thing in Borg, but there are some of us that can pay our way!' hisses Britt-Marie.

That last bit just slips out of her. It wasn't quite how she meant to put it.

Somebody is not grinning any more. Both the boy and Britt-Marie have red faces, caused by different kinds of shame. Britt-Marie briskly lays down the money on the counter and the boy picks it up and runs out of the door. Soon the thumping can be heard again. Britt-Marie stays where she is and tries to avoid Somebody's eyes.

'I didn't get a receipt,' Britt-Marie states in a low voice, which is not at all incriminating.

Somebody shakes her head and smacks her tongue.

'What does he look like, IKEA or something? He doesn't have, what's-it-called? Limited company, you know. Just a kid with a bicycle.'

'Ha,' says Britt-Marie.

'What else you want?' asks Somebody, her tone noticeably less hospitable as she puts the jar of bicarbonate of soda and the bottles of Faxin in a bag.

Britt-Marie smiles as helpfully as she can.

'You have to understand that one has to get a receipt. Otherwise one actually can't prove that one isn't a criminal,' she explains.

Somebody rolls her eyes, which Britt-Marie feels is unnecessary.

Somebody presses a few keys on her till. The money tray opens, revealing not very much money at all inside, and then the till spits out a pale yellow receipt.

'That'll be six hundred and seventy-three kronor and fifty öre,' says Somebody.

Britt-Marie stares back as if she's got something stuck in her throat.

'For bicarbonate of soda?'

Somebody points out of the door.

'For dent in car. I have done one of those, what's-it-called? Bodywork inspection! I don't want to, what's-it-called? Insult you, Britt-Marie! So you can't have credit. Six hundred and seventy-three kronor and fifty öre.'

Britt-Marie almost drops her handbag. That's how grave the situation is.

'I have . . . who . . . for goodness' sake. No civilised person walks around with that much cash in her handbag.'

She says that in an extra-loud voice. So that everyone in there can hear, in case one of them is a criminal. On the other hand, only the bearded coffee-drinking men are there, and neither of them even look up, but still. Criminal types do sometimes have beards. Britt-Marie actually has no prejudices about that.

'Do you take cards?' she says, registering a certain amount of rising heat along her cheekbones.

Somebody shakes her head hard.

'Poker players do cards, huh, Britt-Marie. Here we do cash.'

'Ha. In that case I'll have to ask for directions to the nearest cash machine,' says Britt-Marie.

'In town,' says Somebody coldly, crossing her arms.

'Ha,' says Britt-Marie.

'They closed down the cash machine in Borg. Not profitable,' says Somebody with raised eyebrows, nodding at the receipt.

Britt-Marie's gaze flickers desperately across the walls, in an attempt to deflect attention from her blood-red cheeks. There's a yellow jersey hanging on the wall, identical to the one in the recreation centre. With the word 'Bank' written above the number '10' on its back.

Somebody notices her looking at it, so she closes the till, knots the bag of bicarbonate of soda and Faxin, and pushes it across the counter.

'You know, no shame here with credit, huh, Britt-Marie. Maybe shame where you come from, but no shame in Borg.'

Britt-Marie takes the bag without knowing what to do with her eyes.

Somebody takes a slug of vodka and nods at the yellow jersey on the wall.

'Best player in Borg. Called "Bank", you know, because when Bank play for Borg it was like, what's-it-called? Like money in the bank! Long time ago. Before financial crisis. Then, you know: Bank got ill, huh. Like another sort of crisis. Bank moved away. Gone now, huh.'

She nods out of the door. A ball thumps against the fence.

'Bank's old man trained all the brats, huh. Kept them going. Kept all of Borg going, huh? Everyone's friend! But God, you know, God got a shit head for numbers, huh. The sod gives both profitable and unprofitable person heart attack. Bank's dad died a month ago.'

The wooden walls creak and groan around them, as old houses do, and old people. One of the men with papers and cups of coffee fetches more coffee from the counter. Britt-Marie notes that you get a free top-up here.

'They found him on the, what's-it-called? Kitchen floor!'

'Pardon me?'

Somebody points at the yellow jersey. Shrugs.

'Bank's old man. On the kitchen floor. One morning. Just dead.'

She snaps her fingers. Britt-Marie jumps. She thinks of Kent's heart attack. He had always been very profitable. She takes an even firmer grip on her bag of Faxin and bicarbonate of soda. Stands in silence for so long that Somebody starts to look concerned.

'Hey, you need something else? I have that, what's-it-called? Baileys! Chocolate spirit! You know, it's a copy, but you can put O'boy and vodka in it, and then, it's OK to drink, if you drink it, you know . . . fast!'

Britt-Marie shakes her head briskly. She walks towards the door, but something about that kitchen floor may possibly cause her some hesitation. So she cautiously turns around, before she changes her mind, and then turns around again.

Britt-Marie is not a very spontaneous person, one certainly

needs to be clear about that. 'Spontaneous' is a synonym for 'irrational' — that's Britt-Marie's firm view, and if there's one thing Britt-Marie isn't, it's irrational. This is not so very easy for her, in other words. But at last she turns around, then changes her mind and turns around another time, so that by the end she's facing the door when she lowers her voice and asks, with all the spontaneity that she can muster:

'Do you possibly stock Snickers chocolate bars?'

Darkness falls early in Borg in January. Britt-Marie goes back to the recreation centre and sits by herself on one of the kitchen stools, with the front door open. The chill doesn't concern her. Not the waiting either. She is used to it. You do get used to it. She has plenty of time to think about whether what she is going through now is a sort of life crisis. She has read about them. People have life crises all the time.

The rat comes in through the open door at twenty past six. It settles on the threshold and focuses a very watchful gaze on the Snickers bar, which is on a plate on top of a little towel. Britt-Marie gives the rat a stern look and cups one hand firmly in the other.

'From now on we have dinner at six o'clock. Like civilised people.'

After thinking this over for a certain amount of time, she adds:

'Or rats.'

The rat looks at the Snickers. Britt-Marie has removed the wrapper and placed the chocolate in the middle of the plate, with a neatly folded napkin next to it. She looks at the rat. Clears her throat.

'Ha. I'm not especially good at starting these types of conversations. I'm socially incompetent, you see, that's what my husband says. He's very socially gifted, everyone says that. An entrepreneur, you see.'

When the rat doesn't answer, she adds:

'Very successful. Very, very successful.'

She briefly considers telling the rat about her life crisis. She imagines she'd like to explain that it's difficult knowing who you are, once you are alone, when you have always been there for the sake of someone else. But she doesn't want to trouble the rat with it. So she adjusts a crease in her skirt and says, very formally:

'I would like to propose a working arrangement. For your part, it would mean that a dinner would be arranged for you every evening at six o'clock.'

She makes an explanatory gesture at the chocolate.

'The arrangement, if we find it mutually beneficial, would mean that, if you die, I won't let you lie and smell bad in the wall. And you will do the same for me. In case people don't know we are here.'

The rat takes a tentative step towards the chocolate. Stretches its neck and sniffs it. Britt-Marie brushes invisible crumbs from her knee.

'It's the sodium bicarbonate that disappears when one dies, you have to understand. That's why people smell. I read that after Ingrid had died.'

The rat's whiskers vibrate with scepticism. Britt-Marie clears her throat apologetically.

'Ingrid was my sister, you have to understand. She died. I was worried she'd smell bad. That's how I found out about sodium bicarbonate. The body produces sodium bicarbonate to neutralise the acidic substances in the stomach. When one dies, the body stops producing the sodium bicarbonate, so the acidic substances eat their way through the skin and end up on the floor. That's when it smells, you have to understand.'

She thinks about adding that she has always found it reasonable to assume that the human soul is found in the sodium bicarbonate. When it leaves the body, there's nothing left. Only complaining neighbours. But she doesn't say anything. Doesn't want to cause bother.

The rat eats its dinner but doesn't comment on whether or not it enjoyed it.

Britt-Marie doesn't ask.

9

Everything begins in earnest this evening. The weather is mild, the snow turns to rain as it falls from sky to earth. The children play football in the dark, but neither the dark nor the rain seems to concern them in the least. The parking area is only blessed with light here and there, where it's cast by the neon sign of the pizzeria, or from the kitchen window where Britt-Marie stands hidden behind the curtain watching them, but, to be quite honest, most of them are so bad at football that more light would only have a marginal effect on their ability to hit the ball.

The rat has gone home. Britt-Marie has locked the door and washed up and cleaned the whole recreation centre one more time. She is standing by the window looking out at the world. From time to time the ball bounces through the puddles on to the road, and then the children play Rock, Paper, Scissors to decide who has to go and fetch it.

Kent used to tell David and Pernilla when they were small that Britt-Marie couldn't play with them because she 'didn't know how', but that isn't true. Britt-Marie knows perfectly well how to play Rock, Paper, Scissors. She just doesn't think it sounds very hygienic to keep stones in paper bags. As for the scissors, it's not even worth thinking about. Who knows where they've been?

Of course Kent is always saying Britt-Marie is 'so darned negative'. It's a part of her social incompetence. 'Darn it! Just be happy instead!' Kent fetches the cigars and takes care of the guests and Britt-Marie does the washing-up and takes care of the home, and that's how they have divided up their lives. Kent is a bit happy, darn it, and Britt-Marie is darned negative. Maybe that's how it goes. It's easier to stay optimistic if you never have to clear up the mess afterwards.

The two siblings, Vega and Omar, play on opposing sides. She is calm and calculating, gently moving the ball with the insides of her feet, as you might twiddle your toes against someone you love while sleeping. Her brother, on the other hand, is angry and frustrated, hunting the ball down as if it owes him money. Britt-Marie doesn't know the first thing about football, but anyone can see that Vega is the best player in the parking area. Or at least the least bad one.

Omar is constantly in his sister's shadow. They are all in her shadow. She reminds Britt-Marie of Ingrid.

Ingrid was never negative. As always with people like this, it's difficult to know whether everyone loved Ingrid because she was so positive, or if she was so positive because everyone loved her. She was one year older than Britt-Marie, and five centimetres taller – it doesn't take much to put someone in your shadow. It never mattered to Britt-Marie that she was the one who receded into the background. She never wanted much.

Sometimes she actually yearned to want something, so much that she could hardly bear it. It seemed so vital, wanting things. But usually the feeling passed.

Ingrid, of course, was always falling to bits with wanting things – her singing career, for instance, and the celebrity status she was predestined to achieve, and the boys out there in the world who were so much more than the usual ones on offer in their apartment block. The usual boys who, Britt-Marie realised, were infinitely too unusual to even look at Britt-Marie, and yet were far too usual in every way to deserve her sister.

They were brothers, the boys on their floor. Alf and Kent. They fought about everything. Britt-Marie couldn't understand it. She followed her sister everywhere. It never bothered Ingrid. Quite the opposite. 'It's you and me, Britt,' she used to whisper at nights when she told her the stories of how they were going to live in Paris in a palace filled with servants. That was why she called her little sister 'Britt' – because it sounded American.

Admittedly it seemed a bit obscure why you would have an American name in Paris, but Britt-Marie had certainly never been the sort of person who opposed things needlessly.

Vega is grim, but when her team scores in the dark yard, in the rain, in a goal made of two soft-drink cans, her laugh sounds just like Ingrid's. Ingrid also loved to play. As with all people like that, it's difficult to know if she was the best because she loved the games, or if she loved them because she was the best.

A little boy with ginger hair gets hit hard in the face with the ball. He falls headlong into a muddy puddle. Britt-Marie shudders. It's the same football they shot at Britt-Marie's head, and when she sees the mud on it she wants to give herself a tetanus shot. Yet she has difficulties taking her eyes off the game, because Ingrid would have liked it.

Of course, if Kent had been here he would have said the children were playing like big girls' blouses. Kent is able to describe almost anything bad by adding, before or after, that it's a bit of a 'big girl's blouse', Britt-Marie is actually not especially fond of irony, but she notes a certain amount of that very thing, in the fact that the only player out there not playing like a girl's blouse is the girl.

Britt-Marie finally comes to her senses and leaves the window before anyone out there starts getting any ideas. It's gone eight, so the recreation centre is steeped in darkness. Britt-Marie waters her balcony boxes in the dark. Sprinkles bicarbonate of soda over the soil. She misses her balcony more than anything. You're never quite alone when you can stand on a balcony – you have all the cars and houses and the people in the streets. You're among them, but also not. That's the best thing about balconies. The second best is standing out there early in the morning before Kent has woken up, closing your eyes and feeling the wind in your hair. Britt-Marie used to do that, and it felt like Paris. Of course she has never been to Paris, because Kent doesn't do any business there, but she has solved an awful lot of crossword clues about Paris. It's the world's most crossword-referenced city, full of rich and famous celebrities with their very own cleaners. Ingrid used to go on about how they'd have their own servants, which was the only bit of the dream Britt-Marie wasn't sure about – she didn't want them to think that Britt-Marie's sister was so bad at cleaning that she had to employ someone to do it. Britt-Marie had heard their mother talking about those sorts of mothers with contempt, and Britt-Marie didn't want anyone talking about Ingrid like that.

So while Ingrid would excel at everything out there in the world, Britt-Marie imagined herself being really good at things inside of it. Cleaning. Making things nice. Her sister noticed this. Noticed her. Britt-Marie did her hair every morning, and her sister never forgot to say, 'Thanks, you did that really well, Britt!' while she turned her head in front of the mirror to a tune from one of her vinyl records. Britt-Marie never had records. You don't need any when you have an older sister who truly sees you.

When there's a bang on the door Britt-Marie jumps as if someone just drove an axe through it. Vega is standing outside, but without an axe. Worse still, she's dripping mud and rain on the floor. Britt-Marie screams on the inside.

'Why don't you turn on the lights?' asks Vega, squinting into the darkness.

'They don't work, dear.'

'Have you tried changing the bulbs?' asks Vega with a frown, as if she has to totally control herself not to add 'dear' at the end of her question.

Omar pops up next to her. He has mud in his nostrils. Inside his nostrils. Britt-Marie cannot get her head around how something like that could happen. Surely there's such a thing as gravity.

'You need to buy light bulbs. I have the baddest low-energy bulbs! Special price!' he says eagerly, producing a rucksack from somewhere.

Vega kicks him on the shin and looks at Britt-Marie with the strained diplomacy of the teenager.

'Can we watch the match here?' she asks.

'What . . . match?' asks Britt-Marie.

'*The* match!' Vega replies, not entirely unlike how you'd say '*the* Pope' if someone asked, 'what Pope?'

Britt-Marie switches her hands around on her stomach, and then re-clasps them together.

'The match in what?'

'Football!' Vega and Omar burst out.

'Ha,' mutters Britt-Marie and looks with revulsion at their muddy clothes. Not at the children, obviously. At their clothes. Britt-Marie is obviously not revolted by children.

'He always let us watch it here,' says Vega and points at the photo on the wall inside the door of the elderly man with the 'Bank' jersey in his hands.

In another photo just next to it stands the same man in front of a truck, and he's wearing a white jacket on which 'Borg FC' is written on one of his breast pockets and 'Coach' on the other. It could have done with a wash, Britt-Marie notes.

'I have not been informed about this. You'll have to contact the man, in that case.'

The silence depletes the air between them of oxygen.

'He's dead,' says Vega at long last, looking down at her shoes.

Britt-Marie looks at the man in the photo. Then at her hands.

'That's . . . ha. Very sad to hear it. But I actually can't be held responsible for it,' she says.

Vega peers at her with hate. Then shoves Omar in the side and hisses:

'Come on, Omar, let's get out of here. Never bloody mind about her.'

She has already turned around and started walking away when Britt-Marie notices the other children, three of them, waiting a few metres away. All in their early teens. One with ginger hair, one with black and another with high cholesterol. She senses the accusation in their eyes.

'Can I ask why you don't watch the football in the pizzeria

or the car workshop or whatever it is, if it's so important?' asks Britt-Marie in a polite and not at all confrontational manner.

Omar kicks his ball across the parking area and says in a quiet voice:

'They drink in there. If they lose.'

'Ha. And if they win?'

'Then they drink even more. So he always let us watch in here.'

'And I suppose in these parts you wouldn't have homes of your own to go to, with televisions in them? Would you?'

'There isn't space for the whole team at anyone's house,' snaps Vega suddenly, 'and besides, we watch the matches together. Like a team.'

Britt-Marie brushes some dust off her skirt.

'I was under the impression that you didn't have a team any more.'

'We have a team!' roars Vega and stamps back towards Britt-Marie.

'We're here, aren't we? We're here! So we are a team! Even if they take our bloody pitch and our bloody club and our trainer has a bloody heart attack and goes and bloody dies on us we're a team!'

Britt-Marie is practically shaking as the child's furious eyes focus on her. This is certainly no suitable way for a human being to express herself. But tears are now running down the child's cheeks, and Britt-Marie can't properly determine whether the child is going to give her a hug or a wallop.

Britt-Marie looks as if she would find either alternative similarly threatening.

'I have to ask you to wait here,' she says in a panic, and closes the door.

That's how it all happens before everything begins in earnest.

Britt-Marie stands inside the door, breathing in the smell of wet potting soil and bicarbonate of soda. She remembers the smell of alcohol and the sound of Kent's football matches. He never went on to the balcony. So the balcony belonged to

Britt-Marie and no one else, which was something quite unique. She always lied and said she had bought the plants, because she knew he'd say something horrible if she told him she'd found them in the garbage room and sometimes in the street. Left behind by some neighbours when they moved away. Plants reminded her of Ingrid, because Ingrid loved things that were alive. And for this reason Britt-Marie repeatedly saved homeless plants, to give her the strength to remember a sister whose life she was not even able to save once. You couldn't explain things like this to Kent.

Kent doesn't believe in death, he believes in evolution. 'That's evolution,' he said, nodding approvingly, on one occasion when he was watching a nature programme in which a lion killed an injured zebra: 'It's sorting out the one that's weak, right? It's about the survival of the species, you have to get that. If you're not the best from the start, you have to accept the consequences and leave space for someone stronger, right?'

You can't discuss balcony plants with a person like that.

Or the feeling of missing someone.

Britt-Marie's fingertips are trembling slightly when she picks up the mobile.

The girl from the unemployment office answers on the third attempt.

'Hello?' says the girl in a panting voice.

'Is that how you answer the phone? Out of breath?'

'Britt-Marie? I'm at the gym!'

'That must be very nice for you.'

'Has something happened?'

'There are some children here. They say they want to see some sort of match here.'

'Oh yeah, the match! I'm going to watch it as well!'

'I wasn't notified that my range of duties included taking care of children . . .'

The girl at the other end of the line groans in what is, to be honest, quite an uncalled-for way.

'Britt-Marie, sorry, but I'm not supposed to talk on the phone in the gym.'

68

Then she exclaims, without a thought:

'But . . . you know . . . it's a good thing, isn't it? If the children are there watching the football and you drop dead, they'll know all about it!'

Britt-Marie laughs curtly. Then there's a silence for a very, very long time.

The girl inhales grimly, and there's a sound of a jogging machine stopping.

'OK, sorry Britt-Marie, I was joking. It was a silly thing for me to say. I didn't mean it that way . . . hello?'

Britt-Marie has already hung up. She opens the door half a minute later with the newly washed football jerseys neatly folded into a pile in her arms.

'But you're not coming in with those muddy clothes, I have just mopped the floors!' she says to the children before she stops herself.

There's a policeman standing among them. He's small and chubby and has a head of hair like a lawn the day after an impromptu barbecue.

'What have you done now?' Britt-Marie hisses at Vega.

The policeman looks ambivalent. The woman who stands in front of him is very different to the one the children described. Fussy, yes, and bossy, clearly, but something else as well. Determined, immaculately neat, and somehow . . . unique. He stares dumbly for a moment while he tries to think of something to say to her, but in the end decides the most civic thing he can do is to hold out a big glass jar towards Britt-Marie.

'My name is Sven. I just wanted to welcome you to Borg. This is jam.'

Britt-Marie looks at the jam jar. Vega looks at Sven. At a loss, Sven scratches himself on various parts of his police uniform.

'Blueberry jam. I made it myself. I did a course. In town.'

Britt-Marie gives him a careful once-over from top to bottom and back again. She stops in both directions when she comes to the uniform shirt, which is tight over his stomach.

'I don't have a jersey in your size,' she informs him.

Sven blushes.

'No, no, no, of course, that's not what I meant. I want . . . just welcome to Borg, just that. That's all I wanted to say.'

He presses the jam jar into Vega's hands and totters away from the threshold into the parking area, heading towards the pizzeria. Vega looks at the jam jar. Omar looks at Britt-Marie's bare ring finger and grins.

'Are you married?' he asks.

Britt-Marie is shocked at herself when she notices how quickly she blurts out:

'I'm divorced.'

It's the first time she's said it out loud. Omar's grin widens as he nods at Sven.

'Sven is free, just so you know!'

Britt-Marie hears the other children tittering. She presses the jerseys into Omar's arms, snatches the jam jar from Vega and disappears into the gloom of the recreation centre. About half a dozen children remain on the threshold, rolling their eyes.

That's how it all begins.

10

Football is a curious game, because it doesn't ask to be loved.
It demands it.

Britt-Marie wanders about inside the recreation centre like a
confounded spirit whose grave someone has opened in order to
start a discotheque.

The children sit on the sofa, wearing the white jerseys and
drinking soft drinks. Britt-Marie has obviously ensured that they
are sitting on towels, because she doesn't have enough bicarbonate of soda to clean all the children. It goes without saying
that they have coasters under their soft drinks. Admittedly there
weren't any proper coasters, so Britt-Marie has used two pieces
of toilet paper folded over. Necessity has no rule, but even necessity has to understand that you can't just put a soft-drink can
on the table.

She also puts glasses in front of the children. One of them,
the one that Britt-Marie would obviously never refer to as 'over-
weight' but who looks as if he's had quite a few soft drinks
belonging to other children, tells her cheerfully that he'd 'rather
just drink straight from the can.'

'You certainly won't, here we drink from glasses,' Britt-Marie
interjects with uncompromising articulation.

'Why?'

'Because we're not animals.'

The boy looks at his lemonade can, thinks about it, and then
asks:

'What animal apart from human beings can drink from a can?'

Britt-Marie doesn't answer. Instead she picks up the remote controls from the floor and puts them on the table. As soon as she's done it she bounces back in terror when the until-now timid boys on the sofa all roar 'Nooo!' as if she's flung the remote controls in their faces.

'No remotes on the table!' hisses the lemonade boy fearfully.

'That's the worst jinx! We'll lose if you do that!' yells Omar and runs up to throw them back on the floor.

'What do you mean, "we'll lose"?' asks Britt-Marie, as if he's taken leave of his senses.

Omar points at the grown men on the TV, who quite clearly do not even know he exists.

'We will!' he repeats with conviction, as if this somehow explains anything.

Britt-Marie notes that he's wearing his football jersey back to front.

'I don't appreciate yelling indoors. I also don't appreciate the wearing of clothes back to front like gangsters,' she points out, picking up the remotes from the floor.

'We'll lose if we wear our shirts the right way around!'

Britt-Marie doesn't even know how to respond to such nonsense, so she takes the remote controls and the children's muddy clothes into the laundry. When she turns around after starting the washing machine, the ginger-haired boy is standing in front of her. He looks embarrassed. Britt-Marie cups one hand into the other and doesn't look ready for more conversation.

'They're superstitious, everything has to be the same as the last time we won,' says the boy, at the same time explanatory and defensive. He suddenly looks slightly nervous. 'I'm the one who shot the football at your head yesterday. I didn't do it on purpose. I'm pants at aiming. I hope it didn't ruin your hair,' he says. 'Your hair is . . . nice,' he adds with a smile, then turns to go back to the sofa.

Britt-Marie keeps her eyes on him and by and large doesn't entirely dislike him. He sits on the far side against the wall behind the boy with black hair and the boy who's had the most soft drink, so that he's out of sight.

'We call him Pirate,' says Vega.

She has popped up next to Britt-Marie. Apparently it's what she does: pops up, all the time. Her jersey is slightly too big. Or her body too small, possibly.

'Pirate,' echoes Britt-Marie, in the way that Britt-Marie echoes when she has to drum up all the well-meaning feelings she's capable of, in order not to have to explain that 'Pirate' is not much of a name for anyone except an actual pirate.

Vega points to the other two children on the sofa.

'And that's Toad. And that's Dino.'

And there goes the limit of Britt-Marie's well-meaningness.

'For goodness' sake, those aren't even proper names!'

Vega doesn't look as if she understands what this is supposed to mean.

'It's because he's a Somalian,' she says, pointing at one of the boys, as if this explains everything.

When Britt-Marie doesn't look as if it does explain everything, Vega sighs in a very bored sort of way and explains:

'When Dino moved to Borg and Omar heard that he was a "Somalian" he thought it sounded like a "sommelier", you know one of those people who drink wine on the TV. So we called him "Wino". And it rhymes with "Dino". So now we just call him "Dino".'

Britt-Marie stares at Vega as if Vega had just fallen asleep drunk in Britt-Marie's bed.

'So your real names weren't good enough, I suppose, were they?'

Vega doesn't seem to comprehend the difference.

'He can't have the same name as us, can he? Or we wouldn't know who to pass to when we're playing.'

Britt-Marie snorts hard through her nose, because that's how Britt-Marie's irritation comes steaming out when it grows too large inside her head.

'Surely the boy has a proper name,' she fumes.

Vega shrugs.

'He didn't do much talking when he moved here, so we didn't know what his name was, but he laughed when we called him Dino and we liked it when he laughed. So he kept the name.

'Toad we called Toad because he can burp so loud that it's just sick. And Pirate we call Pirate because we . . . I don't know, we just do.'

She nods towards the ginger-haired boy, who still can't be seen. Britt-Marie smiles graciously and says:

'And I don't suppose there are any girls' teams for you to play in? No, of course not.'

Vega shakes her head.

'All the girls play for the team in town.'

Britt-Marie nods with absolute, absolute helpfulness.

'I suppose that team wasn't good enough for you, was it?'

Vega looks annoyed.

'This is my team!' she says.

A player on the TV lies rolling about on the pitch. Omar uses the stoppage time to climb up on one of the kitchen stools and start changing the light bulbs on credit. Britt-Marie circles nervously.

Vega starts looking around as if there's a person missing.

'Where's the ball?' she calls out into the room.

'Shit! Outside!' Omar cries, looking out at the rain outside the window.

'You can't possibly be thinking about bringing that ball in here!' gasps Britt-Marie in terror.

'It can't just stay out there in the rain!' says Vega, with a similar level of terror in her voice, as if this was a question of a human life.

Before Britt-Marie has time to realise what's going on, a chain of Stones and Scissors being put in Paper Bags is initiated across the room, until ginger-haired Pirate in some way loses and is on his way up from the sofa towards the door in a fluid movement.

'Mother of God! Not in your newly washed jersey! No!' She catches hold of his collar but he's already wearing his shoes and has already gone over the threshold. Britt-Marie, in absolute agitation, gets into her own shoes and runs after him.

The boy is standing two metres away, with the muddy football in his arms.

'Sorry,' he mumbles, staring down at the leather.

Britt-Marie doesn't know if he is apologising to her or to the football. She holds her hands over her hair so the rain doesn't ruin her coiffure. The boy peers at her, smiling sincerely, and then, embarrassed, looks down at the ground.

'Can I ask you something?' he says.

'Excuse me?' says Britt-Marie, the rain running down her face.

'Would you help me fix my hair?' he mumbles, avoiding eye contact.

'I'm sorry, what was that?' asks Britt-Marie, while she keeps her gaze focused on a patch of mud left by the football on the boy's newly washed jersey.

'I have a date tomorrow. I was going to, I was thinking, I wanted to ask if you could help me fix my hair,' he manages to say.

Britt-Marie nods as if this was quite typical.

'I don't suppose you have any hairdressers in Borg, oh no. I suppose that will also be my responsibility now, is that what you mean? Is it?'

The boy shakes his head at the ball.

'Your hair's really nice. I was thinking you're good at doing hair, because your hair is nice. There isn't a hairdresser in Borg because it closed down.'

The rain tails off somewhat. Britt-Marie is still holding the palms of her hands like a pitched roof over the top of her head, and the rain is running down into her sleeves.

'Is that what it's known as these days? A "date"?' she says, a touch thoughtfully.

'What did you call it before?' asks the boy, peering up from the ball.

'In my days it was known as a "meeting",' says Britt-Marie firmly.

Possibly she's not an expert at this, she'd be willing to admit. She has only ever been for two meetings with boys. One of them she ended up marrying. The rain stops completely while they are standing there, she and the boy with the ginger hair and the muddy football.

'We say date, or at least I do,' mumbles the boy.

Britt-Marie takes a deep breath and avoids his avoidance of eye contact.

'You really must understand that I can't give you an answer now, because I have my list in my handbag,' she says in a low voice.

The boy immediately starts nodding with altogether worrying enthusiasm.

'It doesn't matter! I can make it any time tomorrow!'

'Ha. I imagine school isn't of much concern here in Borg.'

'It's still Christmas holiday.'

And then their silence is so abruptly broken by the children's howls of euphoria from within that Britt-Marie is startled and makes a grab for the boy's jersey, and the boy in turn is so surprised that he tosses the ball into her arms. She gets mud on her jacket. Half a second later the men in the pizzeria burst into fits of braying, until the neon sign above the door rattles.

'What's going on?' Britt-Marie wants to know, with panic in her eyes, as she throws the ball on the ground.

'We scored a goal!' howls the Pirate boy ecstatically.

'What do you mean, "we"?' asks Britt-Marie.

'Our team!'

'I thought you didn't have a team!'

'But I mean: our team, the one we're supporting! On the TV!' the boy tries to explain.

'But how is it your team if you don't *play* in it?'

The boy thinks this over for a moment. Then he seems to take a firmer grip on the ball.

'We've supported this team for longer than most of the players in it. So it's more our team than theirs.'

'Preposterous,' snorts Britt-Marie.

In the next second the sound of a front door being slammed cuts through the January night. Britt-Marie spins around in pure dismay and starts running towards it. The boy runs after. The door is locked from the inside.

'Like, they've locked it so we can't come in! Because we were out here when we scored!' puffs Pirate, jubilant and out of breath.

'What on earth are you trying to say?' Britt-Marie demands and tugs frantically at the door handle.

'I mean it's important that we stay out here, because while we were out here we scored! We're bringing good luck out here!' hollers the boy as if that's reasonable. Britt-Marie stares at him as if it certainly isn't. But then they stand in the parking area, despite the rain that's falling again, and Britt-Marie doesn't say anything else.

Because it's the first time in an absolute age that anyone has told Britt-Marie it's important for her to be somewhere.

Football is a curious game in that way. Because it doesn't ask to be loved.

11

The children open the door at half-time to let Britt-Marie and Pirate back in. Britt-Marie spends the second half in front of the mirror in the bathroom. Firstly because she doesn't want to come out and risk having to talk to any of the children, and secondly because their team scores again so they forbid her from coming out until the match is over. So Britt-Marie stays in there and dries her hair and brings them luck and has a life crisis. It's possible to do all of these things at the same time. Her mirror image belongs to someone else, someone whose face has been touched by many winters. The winters have always been the worst, both for the balcony plants and for Britt-Marie. It's the silence that Britt-Marie struggles most of all to live with, because while immersed in silence you don't know if anyone knows you are there, and winter is also the quiet season because the cold insulates people. Makes the world soundless.

It was the silence that paralysed Britt-Marie when Ingrid died.

Her father started coming home later and later from his work, and at a certain point he started to come home so late that Britt-Marie would already be asleep by the time he walked in. Then she woke up one morning and he was only just coming home. And in the end she woke up one morning and he hadn't come home at all. Her mother said less and less about it. Stayed in bed for longer and longer in the mornings. Britt-Marie meandered around the flat as children do when they have to live in silent worlds. Once she knocked over a vase just so her mother would yell at her from the bedroom. Her mother didn't yell. Britt-Marie swept up the glass herself. And never knocked over a vase again. The next day her mother stayed in bed until Britt-Marie had made dinner. The day after that she got up even later. And in the end she didn't get up at all. Of course several of her mother's girlfriends sent beautiful flowers, and condolences, but they were too busy with their lives to pay their respects to someone who was anyway already dead. Britt-Marie cut little notches in the flower stalks and put them in newly washed vases. She cleaned the flat and polished all the windows and the day after when she took out the rubbish she met Kent on the stairs. They stared at one another as children who have turned into adults tend to do. He had been married with two children, but he had recently been divorced and had now come back to the house to visit his mother. He smiled when he saw Britt-Marie. Because in those days he used to see her.

Britt-Marie rubs her ring finger in front of the mirror. The white line there is like a tattoo. Taunting her. There's a knock on the bathroom door.

Pirate is standing outside.

'Ha . . . Did you win?'

'2–0!' nods Pirate blissfully.

'Because actually I have only stayed in here all this time because you told me so. I have no intestinal problems,' says Britt-Marie very seriously.

Pirate nods, in some confusion, mumbles 'Ooo . . . K' and points at the front door, which is open.

'Sven is here again.'

The policeman stands on the threshold and lifts his hand in a fumbling wave. Britt-Marie draws back, deeply affronted but not sure why, and closes the bathroom door behind her. Once she has fixed her hair properly she takes a deep breath and re-emerges.

'Yes?' she says to the policeman.

The policeman smiles and holds out a piece of paper, which he drops just as he's giving it to Britt-Marie.

'Whoops, whoops, sorry, sorry, I just thought I'd give you this. Well, I thought, or we, we thought . . .'

He makes a gesture towards the pizzeria. Britt-Marie assumes he means he has spoken to Somebody. He smiles again. Clasps his hands together on top of his stomach, then changes his mind and crosses his arms just below his chin.

'We were thinking you need somewhere to live, of course, of course, and I understood you didn't want to stay at the hotel in town . . . Not that you can't live anywhere you want to. Of course! We just thought this might be a good alternative for you. Perhaps?'

Britt-Marie looks at the paper. It's a handwritten, misspelled advertisement for a room that's available for rent. At the bottom is an image of a little man wearing a hat, who appears to be dancing. The relationship between the man and the advertisement is extremely unclear.

'I'm the one who helped her make the ad,' says the policeman enthusiastically. 'I did a course in it, in town. She's a very nice lady, the one who's letting the room, I mean, she's just moved back to Borg. Or, I mean, it's just temporary, of course, she's selling the house. But it's here in Borg, not far at all . . . it's walkable but I can give you a lift, if you like?'

Britt-Marie's eyebrows inch closer together. There's a police car parked outside.

'In that?'

'Yes, I heard your car's at the workshop. But I can drive you, it's no trouble at all!'

'It's obviously not a problem for you. Whereas I'm supposed to be driven around this community in a police car, am I, so everyone thinks I'm a criminal, is that what you are telling me?'

The policeman looks ashamed of himself.

'No, no, no. Of course, you wouldn't want that.'

'I certainly would not,' says Britt-Marie 'Was there anything else?'

He shakes his head despondently and turns to leave. Britt-Marie closes the door.

The children stay in the recreation centre until she has tumble-dried their clothes.

Clothes that cannot be tumble-dried she hangs up to dry, so the children can pick them up the day after. Most of them go home in their football jerseys. In a certain sense this is how Britt-Marie turns into their team coach. It's just that no one has told her about it yet.

None of the children thank her for doing their laundry. The door closes behind them and the recreation centre is steeped in the sort of silence that only children and footballs can fill. Britt-Marie puts away plates and soft-drink cans from the sofa table. Omar and Vega have left their plates on the draining board. They haven't washed them up or put them in the dishwasher, haven't even rinsed them off. All they've done is put them there.

Kent also used to do that sometimes as if expecting to be thanked for it. As if he wanted Britt-Marie to know that when the plate was back in its place, washed and dried, in the cupboard tomorrow, he had certainly done his allotted share of the task.

There's a knock at the front door of the recreation centre. It's not a civilised hour, so Britt-Marie assumes that it's one of the children who's forgotten something. She opens with a:

'Ha?'

Then she sees that it's the policeman standing outside again. He smiles awkwardly. Britt-Marie immediately changes the tone to a:

'Ha!'

Which is something quite different. At least the way Britt-Marie says it. The policeman swallows and seems to be drumming up some courage. A little too abruptly he whips out a bamboo curtain, almost smacking it into Britt-Marie's forehead.

'Sorry, yes, well, I just wanted to . . . this is a bamboo screen!' he says and almost drops it into the mud.

'Ha . . .' says Britt-Marie, more guarded now.

He nods enthusiastically.

'I made it! I did a course in town. "Far Eastern Home Design".'

He nods again. As if Britt-Marie is supposed to say something. She doesn't. He holds the bamboo screen in front of his face.

'You can hold it against the window. So no one sees it's you.'

He points cheerfully at the police car. Then at the bamboo screen.

Then at the rain that has started falling again. As rain does in Borg. Which must obviously be quite pleasant for the rain, not having anything better to do with its time.

'And you can keep it over your head when we go out to the car, like an umbrella, so you don't ruin your hair.' He swallows again and fingers the bamboo.

'You don't have to, of course, of course. I was just thinking that you have to live somewhere while you're in Borg. I was thinking, so to speak, well, hmm, you understand. That it's hardly suitable for a lady to live in a recreation centre, so to speak.'

They stand in silence for a long time after that. Britt-Marie switches her hands the other way, and then at long last exhales deeply with immeasurable patience. Not at all a sigh. Then she says:

'I need to get my things.'

He nods eagerly. She closes the door and leaves him out there in the rain.

That is how it goes on – the thing that has started.

12

Britt-Marie opens the door. He gives her the bamboo screen and she gives him the balcony boxes.

'I was told there was a large flat-pack from IKEA in the back seat of your car, should I load it into my car?' he asks helpfully.

'You certainly shall not!' answers Britt-Marie, as if he had suggested setting fire to it.

'Of course not, of course not,' he says apologetically.

Britt-Marie sees the men with the beards and caps leave the pizzeria. They nod at the policeman, he waves back. They seem not to see Britt-Marie at all.

The policeman hurries off towards his patrol car with the balcony boxes, then he hurries back to walk alongside Britt-Marie. He doesn't hold her arm, but he does position his arm a few centimetres under hers without actually touching her. So he can catch her in case she slips.

She holds the bamboo screen like an umbrella over her hair (because in fact bamboo screens work quite brilliantly as umbrellas), and keeps it in a firm grip over her head throughout the journey, so the policeman doesn't notice that her hairstyle has been ruined.

'I should like to stop by a cash machine on the way, so I can pay for the room,' she says. 'If it's no bother to you. I obviously don't want to cause you any bother,' she adds in a bothered tone of voice.

'It's no bother at all!' says the policeman, who seems free of any kind of bothered tendencies. He doesn't mention the fact that the nearest cash machine is actually a twenty-kilometre detour.

He talks all the way, just as Kent used to do when they were in the car. But it was different, because Kent always told her things, whereas the policeman asks her questions. It irritates Britt-Marie. You do get irritated by someone taking an interest in you, when you're not used to it.

'What did you think of the match, then?' he asks.

'I was in the toilet,' says Britt-Marie.

She gets incredibly irritated when she hears herself saying this. Because anyone making hasty conclusions might believe she has serious intestinal problems. The policeman doesn't answer straight away, so she comes to the conclusion that he is indeed sitting there making hasty conclusions, and she doesn't at all appreciate that he is doing so. So she adds sharply:

'I actually don't have serious intestinal problems, but it was important for me to be in the toilet, otherwise apparently something would have gone wrong in the match.'

He laughs. She doesn't know if it's at her expense. He stops when he notices that she doesn't much appreciate it.

'How did you end up here in Borg?'

'I was offered employment here.'

She has her feet semi-buried among empty pizza boxes and paper bags from the hamburger place. In the back seat is a painter's easel and a jumble of brushes and canvases.

'Do you like paintings?' the policeman asks her, in an upbeat mood, when he sees her looking at them.

'No.'

He fidgets with embarrassment at the steering wheel.

'I mean, I don't mean my own paintings, of course. I'm just a bit of a happy amateur. I'm doing a course in watercolour painting in town. No, I mean paintings in general. Real paintings. Beautiful paintings.'

There's something inside Britt-Marie that wants to say, 'Your paintings are also beautiful,' but another more down-to-earth part of her answers in its place:

'We don't have any paintings at home. Kent doesn't like art.'

The policeman gives her a silent nod. They drive into town, which is actually also more like a large village than a proper town. Similar to Borg, just a bit more of it. Heading in the same direction, but not as quickly. Britt-Marie stops at a cash machine next to a tanning salon, which Britt-Marie doesn't find so very hygienic because she's read that solariums cause cancer, and you can hardly say cancer is hygienic.

It takes a bit of time to get her money out, because she's so careful about hiding her code that she ends up pressing the wrong buttons. She is also hardly helped along by the fact that she still has a bamboo screen on top of her head.

But the policeman doesn't tell her to hurry up. She realises to her own surprise that she likes this. Kent always told her to hurry up, however quickly she was doing something. She gets back into the police car, and starts feeling she ought to say something sociable. So she takes a deep breath and points at the empty takeaway boxes and bags on the floor, and says:

'I don't suppose they were offering a cookery course in town, oh no.'

The policeman lights up.

'Yes, as a matter of fact, I did a sushi-making course – Have you ever made sushi?'

'Certainly not. Kent doesn't like foreign food.'

'True, true, well, there isn't much cooking when you make sushi. Mainly just . . . cutting. And I haven't done it so many times, actually, to be honest with you. I mean since I did the course. It's not much fun cooking for yourself, if you understand what I mean?'

He smiles with embarrassment. She doesn't smile at all.

'No,' she says.

They drive back into Borg. Finally the policeman seems to build up enough courage to bring up another subject:

'Well, anyway, it's nice of you to take on the youngsters like you have. Borg is not an easy place to grow up in these days. The young people need someone, as you know, to see them.'

'I have not taken anyone on, they are certainly not my responsibility!' protests Britt-Marie.

'I don't mean it like that, of course, I just mean they *like* you. The young people. I haven't seen them liking anyone since their last coach died.'

'What do you mean, their "last coach"?'

'I, well, yes, I suppose I just mean they are very glad you moved here,' says the policeman, opting for 'they' when really he would have preferred to say 'we', and then he asks:

'What did you do before you came here?'

Britt-Marie doesn't answer. Instead she glares out of the window at the houses they are passing. Outside almost every one of them, a 'For Sale' sign has been hammered into the lawn, so she states drily:

'There don't seem to be many people living in Borg who want to stay in Borg.'

The corners of the policeman's mouth do what the corners of mouths do when trying to overcome wistfulness.

'The financial crisis hit hard here, after the trucking company laid off all the drivers. Those who have signs up are the ones who still have hopes of selling. The others have given up, young people escape to the cities, and only the oldies like us stay on, because we're the only ones who still have jobs.'

'The financial crisis is over. My husband told me that, he's an entrepreneur,' Britt-Marie informs him, keeping both her hair and the white mark on her ring finger well hidden under the bamboo screen. He looks away, awkwardly, while she firmly stares out of her window at a community in which even those who live there would rather not.

'And you're also keen on football, I understand,' she says at last.

'I was once told that "You love football because it's instinctive. If a ball comes rolling down the street you give it a punt. You love it for the same reason that you fall in love. Because

86

you don't know how to avoid it".' The policeman smiles, slightly embarrassed.

'Who made this suggestion?'

'The children's old coach said it once. Lovely, isn't it?'

'Ludicrous,' says Britt-Marie, although part of her wants to say 'poetic'.

He grips the steering wheel even harder.

'Probably so, probably so, I just mean that . . . I mean everyone loves football, don't they? So to speak?'

She doesn't say a word.

They pass the cornershop, carry on for a few moments, then stop outside a small, grey, squat house built on two floors. In a garden on the other side of the road stand two women who are so old that they look as if they lived in this community before it became a community. Leaning on their Zimmer frames, they cast suspicious glances at the police car. Sven waves at them as he and Britt-Marie get out of the car; they do not wave back. It has stopped raining, but Britt-Marie is still holding the bamboo screen over her hair. Sven rings the doorbell of the house. A blind woman, no less cube-shaped than the house itself — although Britt-Marie would never dream of referring to her as 'fat' — opens the door.

'Hi Bank,' says Sven cheerfully.

'Hello Sven. So you've brought her along?' says Bank indifferently, waving her stick towards Britt-Marie. 'The rent for the room is two hundred and fifty kronor a week, no credit. You can only rent it until I get the house sold,' Bank goes on, grunting, and stomps back into the house without inviting them in.

Britt-Marie enters behind her, slightly on her tiptoes because the floor is so dirty that she doesn't even want to walk on it in her shoes. The white dog lies in the hall, surrounded by carelessly packed removal crates in utter disarray. Britt-Marie assumes this is all because of carelessness, not the fact that this 'Bank' person is blind. Although Britt-Marie doesn't have preconceived opinions, she's quite convinced that even blind people can be careless.

All over the house are photos of a girl in a yellow football jersey, and in a few of them she is standing next to the old man who is also in the photos at the recreation centre. In these pictures he is younger. He must have been about Britt-Marie's age when they found him on the kitchen floor in that house, Britt-Marie realises. She doesn't know if that makes her old. She hasn't had so many people to compare herself to in recent years.

Sven stands by the door with the balcony boxes and her bag in his arms.

He's about the same age as her, and this feels rather old when she looks at him.

'We miss your dad very much, Bank. All of Borg misses him,' he says wistfully into the hall.

Bank doesn't answer. Britt-Marie doesn't know what to do, so she snatches the balcony boxes from Sven. He takes off his police cap, but remains on the threshold as men of that kind always do because as far as they are concerned it is not appropriate to go inside a lady's home without an invitation.

Britt-Marie doesn't invite him in, although it irks her to see him standing there on her threshold, in uniform. She sees the ancient women on the other side of the road, still standing in the garden glaring at them.

What will the neighbours think?

'Was there anything else?' she says, although what she really means is, 'Thanks.'

'No, no, nothing at all . . .'

'Thank you,' says Britt-Marie so that it sounds more like 'Goodbye' than 'Thanks'.

He nods awkwardly and turns around. When he has got halfway to the car, Britt-Marie takes a deep breath and clears her throat and only raises her voice a little:

'For the lift. I should like to . . . well, what I'm saying is: I should like to thank you for the lift.'

He turns around and his whole face lights up. She quickly shuts the door before he gets any ideas.

Bank goes up the stairs. Seems to use the stick more as a

sort of walking cane than for orienting herself. Britt-Marie comes stumbling after with the balcony boxes and the bag in her arms.

'Toilet. Washbasin. You'll have to eat somewhere else, because I don't want the smell of frying in the house. Make yourself scarce in the daytime, because that's when the estate agent brings buyers over,' she snorts and starts moving off towards the staircase.

Britt-Marie goes after her and says diplomatically:

'Ha. I should like to apologise for my behaviour earlier. I was unaware of your being blind.'

Bank grunts something and tries to go downstairs, but Britt-Marie hasn't finished.

'But I'd like to point out that you actually can't expect people to know you're blind when they have only seen you from behind,' she says helpfully.

'God damn it, woman, I'm not blind!' roars Bank.

'Ha?'

'I have impaired vision. Close up I can see just fine.'

'How close?'

'I can see where the dog is. The dog sees the rest,' says Bank, pointing at the dog, about a metre away on the stairs.

'Well, then you're practically blind.'

'That's what I said. Goodnight.'

'I'm certainly not the sort of person who gets hung up on semantics, I really am not, but I did certainly hear you say "blind" . . .'

Bank looks like someone weighing up the possibility of causing damage to the wall with the front of her head.

'If I say I'm blind, people are too ashamed to ask any more questions, and they leave me in peace. If I say I have impaired vision they want to prattle on endlessly about the difference between that and being properly blind. Goodnight now!' she concludes, and moves on down the stairs.

'Might I ask why you have a stick and a dog and sunglasses if you're not even blind?'

'My eyes are sensitive to light, and I had the dog before my eyes started playing up. It's a normal bloody dog. Goodnight!'

The dog looks as if it has taken offence at this.

'And the stick?' Britt-Marie asks.

'It's not a blind stick, it's a walking cane. I have a bad knee. And it's also quite convenient when people don't get out of the way.'

'Ha,' says Britt-Marie. Bank shoves the dog out of the way with the cane.

'Payment in advance. No credit. And I don't want to see you here in the daytime. Goodnight!'

'Could I ask when you expect to sell this house?'

'As soon as I find anyone barmy enough to want to live in Borg.'

Britt-Marie stands at the top of the stairs, which seem desolate and very steep as soon as Bank and the dog are out of sight. A moment later the front door slams and the house drowns in the silence that follows.

Britt-Marie looks around. It's raining again. The police car has gone. A lone truck goes by. Then more silence. Britt-Marie feels cold on the inside.

She takes the bedclothes off the bed and covers the mattress in bicarbonate of soda.

She gets her list out of her bag. There's nothing on it. No items to tick. Darkness comes sweeping in through the window, enveloping Britt-Marie. She doesn't turn on any lights. She finds a towel in her bag and weeps into it, while standing up. She doesn't want to sit on the mattress until it has been properly cleaned.

It's past midnight by the time she notices the door. It's next to one of the windows, facing out on to nothing. Britt-Marie has difficulties at first believing what she is seeing. She has to go and fetch a bottle of Faxin, then clean all the window glass in the door, before she can even bring herself to touch the door handle. It's stuck. She pulls at it for all she's worth, wedges herself against the door frame and uses her body weight, which admittedly isn't much. For a fleeting moment she sees the world through the glass and thinks about Kent and all the things he always said she couldn't do, and in that moment something makes her gather all her strength in a furious show of defiance that finally overpowers the door. She flies backwards through the room when the door opens wide. Rain falls in over the floor.

Britt-Marie sits leaning against the bed, breathing heavily and staring out.

It's a balcony.

13

A balcony can change everything.

It's six in the morning and Britt-Marie is enthusiastic. It's a new experience for her. Somebody's state of mind would rather have to be described as the hungover, irascible kind. Britt-Marie has woken her, by knocking on the door of the pizzeria at six o'clock to ask her, excitedly, for a drill.

Somebody grudgingly opens up, and informs Britt-Marie that the pizzeria and all its other financial activities are closed at this time of day. Britt-Marie then questions why Somebody is there at all, because, as far as Britt-Marie can see, it can't possibly be hygienic to live in a pizzeria. Somebody explains as well as she can in her condition – eyes half-closed, with various scraps of food on her jersey that never quite made it to her mouth or for one reason or another came back out again – that she was 'too much drunk' after the football match last night to make it home. Britt-Marie nods appreciatively at this, and says she thought this was a wise decision, because one really shouldn't drink and drive. She doesn't look at the wheelchair at all when she says it.

Somebody mutters and tries to close the door. But, as we already said, Britt-Marie is enthusiastic, and will not be deterred. For Britt-Marie now has somewhere to put her balcony boxes.

Everything changes when you have somewhere to put your balcony boxes. Britt-Marie feels ready to take on the world. Or, at least, Borg.

Somebody doesn't seem to respond so very well to enthusiasm at six in the morning, so Britt-Marie asks if Somebody happens to own an electric drill. And in fact Somebody does own one. She fetches it. Britt-Marie takes it with both hands and accidentally turns it on and, as a result of this, happens to drill Somebody's hand just a little. Somebody then takes back the drill and demands to know what Britt-Marie was intending to do with the drill. Britt-Marie announces that she plans to put up a picture.

So now Somebody is in the recreation centre, hungover and a little irascible, with a drill in her hand. Britt-Marie stands in the middle of the room, looking enthusiastically at the picture. She found it in the recreation centre storage room early this morning, because Bank, as we know, had ordered her to make herself scarce in the house in the daytime, and in any case Britt-Marie was having trouble sleeping, what with all the emotions surfacing after the discovery of the balcony. The picture had been leaning up against the wall behind an unmentionable pile of rubbish, covered in a layer of dust so thick that it looked like volcanic ash. Britt-Marie took it inside the recreation centre and cleaned it with a damp rag and bicarbonate of soda. It looks very stylish now.

'I've never put up a picture before, you have to understand,' explains Britt-Marie very considerately when she notices that Somebody is looking exhausted.

Somebody finishes her drilling and then hangs up the picture. It's not actually a painting, just a very, very old information chart with a black-and-white map of Borg. 'Welcome to Borg' it says at the top. For someone who loathes travelling, Britt-Marie has always had a great love of maps. There's something reassuring about them, she's always found, ever since Ingrid used to speak to her at night about Paris, while they were children. You can look at a map and point at Paris. Things are understandable when you can point at them. She nods soberly at Somebody.

'We don't have any pictures at home, me and Kent, you have to understand. Kent doesn't like art.'

Somebody raises her eyebrows at the information chart when Britt-Marie mentions 'art'.

'Could we possibly hang it a little higher?'

'Higher?'

'It's very low,' Britt-Marie observes, obviously not in a critical way.

Somebody looks at Britt-Marie. Looks at her wheelchair. Britt-Marie looks at the wheelchair too. 'But obviously it's fine where it is, also. Obviously.'

Somebody mutters something best not heard by anyone and rolls off towards the door, back to the pizzeria across the car park. Britt-Marie follows her because she needs Snickers and bicarbonate of soda.

Inside there's an overwhelming smell of cigarette smoke and beer. The tables are covered in dirty glasses and crockery. Somebody roots around behind the counter, grunting something to the effect of, 'Headache tablets, where does Vega keep that shit?' She disappears into the kitchen.

Britt-Marie is tentatively reaching for two dirty plates when Somebody, as if she can sense what she is up to, yells:

'Don't touch washing-up!'

Britt-Marie opens the cutlery drawer and starts arranging the cutlery in the right order. Somebody rolls forward and closes the cutlery drawer. Britt-Marie inhales patiently.

'I'm just trying to make things look nice around here.'

'Stop changing! I won't find a crap!' Somebody exclaims when Britt-Marie turns her attention to the cupboard where drinking glasses are kept, not as if she's choosing to do it but rather as if she has no choice.

'It's quite extraordinary how you manage to find anything here at all,' Britt-Marie informs her.

'You're putting in wrong place!' Somebody objects.

'Ha, ha, whatever I do is wrong, of course, isn't that always the case?'

Somebody mumbles something incoherent, throws her arms up at the ceiling as if it's the fault of the ceiling, and rolls out of the kitchen. Britt-Marie stays where she is and tries to stop herself from opening the cutlery drawer again. It works fairly well for about fifteen seconds. When she goes out of the kitchen she finds Somebody sitting in the shop eating fist-sized piles of cornflakes straight from the pack.

'You could at least use a plate,' says Britt-Marie and fetches a plate.

Somebody, extremely displeased, eats fist-sized piles of cornflakes straight from the plate.

'I don't suppose you're having any natural yoghurt with that, are you?'

'I am, what's-it-called? Lactose intolerant.'

'Ha,' says Britt-Marie tolerantly, and rearranges a few cans on a shelf.

'Please Britt-Marie, don't move shit,' whispers Somebody, like you do when you have a severe headache.

'You mean my cleaning is wrong as well, is that what you mean?' asks Britt-Marie and goes over to the till, where she starts sorting cartons of cigarettes into colour-coded piles.

'Stop!' Somebody yells and tries to snatch them out of Britt-Marie's hands.

'I'm only trying to make it a bit nice in here!'

'Not together!' whines Somebody and points at one brand of cigarettes with foreign letters on the cartons, and another that doesn't have foreign letters. 'Because of tax authority!' says Somebody, looking very serious as she points at the cartons with the foreign letters: 'Flying stones!'

Britt-Marie looks like she needs something to grab hold of, so she doesn't lose her balance.

'You mean they're contraband?'

'Nah, you know, Britt-Marie. These, huh, they fall off a lorry,' says Somebody apologetically.

'That's *illegal*!'

Somebody rolls back into the kitchen. She opens the cutlery drawer and swears very loudly, then a long harangue follows in which Britt-Marie can only make out, 'Comes here for to borrow drill and hang picture, I want to sleep but oh no, I'm criminal, Mary Poppins out there is starting recreation centre and moving crap around.'

Britt-Marie stays in the demarcation area between the groceries and the pizzeria, rearranging cans and cigarette cartons. In actual fact she only meant to buy some bicarbonate of soda and Snickers and then leave, but as it doesn't seem responsible to purchase bicarbonate of soda from someone who is clearly drunk, she has decided to wait until Somebody sobers up.

Somebody seems to have decamped to the kitchen, so in the meantime Britt-Marie does what she always does in these types of situations: she cleans. It looks quite decent when she's finished, it really does. Unfortunately there are no flowers, but there is a vase on the counter next to the till with a white piece of tape stuck to it, where someone has written, 'Tips'. It's empty. Britt-Marie washes it out and puts it back next to the till. Then she gets all the coins out of her handbag and drops them in. She tries to make them look fluffy, as if they were potting soil. By the time she has finished, the vase looks a good deal more decorative.

'Maybe you wouldn't develop so many allergies if you kept things a little more hygienic in here,' she explains considerately to Somebody when Somebody comes out of the kitchen.

Somebody massages her temples, spins the wheelchair around and disappears back into the kitchen. Britt-Marie keeps working on the coins in the vase to make them look even more decorative.

The front door tinkles and the two men with beards and caps step inside. They also look hungover.

'I have to ask you to wipe your feet outside,' Britt-Marie informs them at once. 'I've just mopped the floor, you see.' They look bemused, but comply.

'Ha. How can we help you?' asks Britt-Marie when they come back in.

'Coff . . . ee?' the men manage to say and look around as if

96

they have stepped into a parallel dimension where there's a pizzeria just the same as the one where they usually drink their coffee, except this one is clean.

Britt-Marie nods and goes into the kitchen. Somebody is sleeping with a can of beer in her hand, and her head resting in the cutlery drawer. Britt-Marie cannot find any tea-towels, so she takes two kitchen rolls, carefully lifts Somebody's head and pushes the kitchen rolls into the cutlery drawer as cushions, on to which she gently lowers Somebody's head. She makes coffee in an entirely normal coffee percolator unaffected by flying stones, and serves this to the men with caps and beards. Stands there by their table for a while, in the vague hope that one of them might say that the coffee's decent. Neither of them do.

'Ha. Are you intending to solve the crossword?'

The men stare at her as if she has just addressed them without using vowels, then go back to their newspapers. Britt-Marie nods helpfully.

'If you don't have the intention of solving it, may I?'

The men look a little as if she has asked whether they're planning on using their kidneys in the foreseeable future or if she can take them.

'Who are you, anyway?' asks one of the men.

'I'm Britt-Marie.'

'Are you from the city?'

'Yes.' She smiles.

The men nod, as if this explains everything.

'Buy your own bloody newspaper, then,' says one of them. The other grunts in agreement.

'Ha,' says Britt-Marie and decides not to offer them a top-up.

Somebody keeps sleeping in the kitchen; possibly it is Britt-Marie's fault because she's made her too comfortable, but nonetheless Britt-Marie feels obliged to take care of the customers until Vega comes in. Not that there's a particularly large number of customers. Or any at all, you might say, if you were being pedantic about it. The only one who comes in is the ginger-haired boy whose name is Pirate, even though that's not a name. He diffidently asks if Britt-Marie has time to do his hair. She informs him that she is terribly busy right now. He nods, excited, and waits in a corner.

'If you're just going to stand there you may as well help out,' says Britt-Marie eventually.

He nods so eagerly it's a wonder he doesn't bite his tongue.

Vega shows up. She stops in the doorway and looks as if she's come to the wrong place.

'What's . . . happened here?' she pants, as if the pizzeria has been burgled in the night by a group of pedants, who have cleaned it up as a way of making a political statement.

'What are you trying to say?' says Britt-Marie, a bit offended.

'It's so . . . clean!' She heads for the kitchen, but Britt-Marie stops her.

'She's sleeping in there.'

Vega shrugs.

'She's hungover. She always is when the football's been on.'

Karl, who always seems to have some parcel to pick up, walks in.

'Can we be of assistance?' asks Britt-Marie, in every way mindful of providing good service, without any hint of incrimination.

'I'm picking up a parcel,' says Karl, not at all mindful of anyone's good service.

His sideburns reach all the way to his chin, Britt-Marie notes. They look like snowdrops – one of Britt-Marie's favourite flowers – except in his case the snowdrops are upside down.

'We haven't had any parcels today,' says Vega.

'I'll wait, then,' says Karl, and goes over to the cap-wearing men.

'And obviously you are not ordering yourself anything. You're just going to sit here,' says Britt-Marie in a thoroughly, thoroughly friendly way.

Karl stops. The men at the table look at him as if to clarify that, as far as they are concerned, he should not be negotiating with terrorists.

'Coffee,' Karl rumbles at last.

Pirate is already on his way with the jug.

The next person who steps inside is Sven. A smile lights up his round little face when he catches sight of Britt-Marie.

'Hello Britt-Marie!'

'Wipe your shoes.'

He nods eagerly. Goes outside and then comes back inside again.

'Nice to see you here,' he says.

'Ha. Are you working today?' asks Britt-Marie.

'Yes, yes, of course, of course.' He nods.

'It's not so easy knowing, you seem to keep your uniform on whether you're working or not,' says Britt-Marie, not at all critically.

Sven doesn't entirely look as if he's sure what she's talking about. Instead, his gaze alights on what is clearly a foreign carton of cigarettes, left on the counter next to the till after Somebody and Britt-Marie's argument about smuggling.

'Interesting letters, those . . .' he says enquiringly.

Britt-Marie and Vega's eyes meet, and the girl's sense of panic transmits back.

'Those are mine!' Britt-Marie exclaims and snatches up the cigarettes.

'Oh,' says Sven, surprised.

'It's certainly no crime to smoke!' says Britt-Marie, although she certainly thinks it ought to be.

Then she makes herself exceedingly, exceedingly busy with rearranging a shelf in the grocery section.

'Has everything worked out with the room at Bank's?' asks Sven behind her, but to Britt-Marie's relief he's interrupted by Vega groaning:

'Nooo, not him . . .'

Britt-Marie looks out of the window. A BMW has stopped in the parking area. Britt-Marie knows that because Kent has a BMW. The door makes a tinkling sound and a man more or less the same age as Somebody and a boy more or less the same age as Vega come walking in.

It is unclear which one of them Vega doesn't want to see. The man is wearing a very expensive jacket, Britt-Marie knows this because Kent has one just the same. The boy is wearing a beaten-up tracksuit top, on which the name of the town twenty kilometres away is written, followed by the word 'Hockey'. He looks at Vega with interest and she looks at him with contempt. The man smiles jeeringly at the men in the corner, and they look back at him as if hoping that by doing so they'll eventually set him on fire. He looks away and starts jeering at Vega instead.

'Frantic business activity here, as usual?'

'Why? Are you here to give someone the sack?' Vega answers acidly, then, pretending to have suddenly realised something, slaps her forehead dramatically: 'Oh no! That's right, you can't because you don't work here! And where you work there's no one left to sack, because you already sacked them all!'

The man's eyes go black. The boy looks spectacularly uncomfortable.

The man thumps two soft-drink cans on the counter.

'Twenty-four kronor,' says Vega indifferently.

'We're having pizzas as well,' says the man, trying to regain the upper hand.

'The pizzeria is closed,' says Vega.

'What do you mean?'

'The pizza baker is temporarily out of order.'

The man snivels disdainfully and slaps a five-hundred krona note on the counter.

'A pizzeria without pizzas, seems a pretty effective business venture you have here.'

'A bit like a trucking company with one manager and no drivers,' Vega responds sarcastically.

The man clenches his fist on the counter, but from the corner of his eye he sees Karl getting out of his chair, though the other two men are doing their best to make him sit back down.

'I'm six kronor short here,' he says grimly at Vega, after examining the change she's flung back.

'We don't have any coins left,' Vega says through her teeth.

Sven is standing beside them now. He looks unsure of himself. 'It might be best if you leave now, Fredrik,' he says.

The man's gaze moves from Vega to the policeman. It stops on the vase, where the tips are kept.

'No problem,' he says, his face cracking open in a scornful smile as he stuffs his hand into the vase and fishes out six kronor.

He grins at Sven, then at the boy with the ice hockey tracksuit top. The boy looks down at the floor and walks back to the door. Sven stays where he is, beaten. The man with the expensive jacket makes eye contact with Britt-Marie.

'Who are you?' asks the man.

'I work at the recreation centre,' says Britt-Marie, glaring at the fingerprints on the newly polished vase for the tips.

'I thought the council had closed it down? Bloody waste of taxpayers' money if you ask me. Invest them in juvenile detention centres, that's where the kids end up anyway!'

Britt-Marie looks helpful.

'My husband has a jacket like that,' she says.

'Your husband has good taste,' says the man with a grin.

'Except his is the right size,' says Britt-Marie. There's a long, long silence. Then Vega first, and Sven after, burst into peals of laughter. Britt-Marie can't think what they're laughing about. The boy runs out, the man marches behind him and slams the door so hard that the fluorescent tube up on the ceiling flickers. The BMW does a wheelspin as it leaves the parking area.

Britt-Marie doesn't know where to look. Sven and Vega are still laughing loudly, which makes her uncomfortable. She assumes it must be at her expense. So she also hurries towards the door.

'I have time for your hair now,' she whispers to Pirate and then flees across the parking area.

The door closes with a merry tinkling.

14

All marriages have their bad sides, because all people have weaknesses. If you live with another human being you learn to handle these weaknesses in a variety of ways. For instance, you might take the view that weaknesses are a bit like heavy pieces of furniture, and based on this you must learn to clean around them. To maintain the illusion.

Of course the dust is building up unseen, but you learn to repress this for as long as it goes unnoticed by guests. And then one day someone moves a piece of furniture without your say-so, and everything comes into plain view. Dirt and scratch marks. Permanent damage to the parquet floor. By then it's too late.

Britt-Marie stands in the bathroom at the recreation centre, looking at all of her worst sides in the mirror. She's afraid – she's fairly certain this is her worst side. More than anything she'd like to go home. Iron Kent's shirts and sit on her own balcony. More than anything she'd like everything to go back to normal.

'Do you want me to leave?' asks Pirate anxiously from the doorway.

'I'm not going to tolerate your laughing at me,' says Britt-Marie with all the strictness she can summon.

'Why would I laugh at you?' asks Pirate.

She sucks in her cheeks without answering. Hesitant, he holds out a carton of cigarettes with foreign lettering.

'Sven said you forgot this.'

Britt-Marie takes it, dismayed. Contraband. Which she has now either stolen or bought on credit, depending on how positively you want to look at it. This is all highly vexatious, because Britt-Marie is not even sure now what sort of criminal she is. But there's no doubt that she's a criminal. Although Kent would certainly agree with Somebody that there's nothing criminal about withholding cigarettes from the tax authorities and the police. 'Get over it, darling! It's not cheating if you don't get caught!' he always used to say when she was signing off her tax return, and she asked what all those other pieces of paper were that Kent's accountant had slipped into the envelope. 'Don't worry, they're completely legal tax deductions! Get on with it!' he'd say reassuringly. Kent loved deductions and loathed tax bills. Britt-Marie never dared admit to him that she did not understand the rights and wrongs of it.

Pirate gently touches her shoulder.

'They weren't laughing at you. In the pizzeria, I mean. They were laughing at Fredrik. He was the boss at the trucking company when they all got fired, so they don't like him.'

Britt-Marie nods and tries to look as if, in fact, she hadn't been especially worried about it in the first place. Pirate seems encouraged by this response, because he goes on:

'Fredrik trains the hockey team in town, they're wicked! The tall one who was with him in the pizzeria is his son, he's as old as me but he's almost got a beard already! You get that? Sick, isn't it? He's wicked at football as well but Fredrik wants him to play hockey because he thinks hockey's better!'

'Why on earth does he think that?' asks Britt-Marie, because on the basis of her slight knowledge of hockey it seems to her one of the few things in the universe that is more ludicrous than football.

'Probably because it's expensive. Fredrik likes things that most people can't afford,' says Pirate.

'Why are you so dreadfully amused by football, then?' asks Britt-Marie.

Pirate seems to find the question mystifying.

'What do you mean? People like football just because they like football, that's all.'

Ludicrous, thinks Britt-Marie, but she buttons up. Instead, she points to a bag in the boy's hand.

'What's that?'

'Scissors and a comb and products and stuff!' says the boy blissfully.

Britt-Marie doesn't ask what he means by 'products' but she notes that he has a heck of a lot of jars, anyway. She fetches a stool from the kitchen, puts down towels on the floor and gestures for him to take a seat. Then she washes his hair and cuts the uneven bits. She used to do that for Ingrid.

Suddenly words come tumbling out of her; she can't understand why on earth she had to open her mouth, but:

'From time to time I feel unsure whether people are laughing at me or something else, you must understand. My husband says I don't have a sense of humour.'

She is quickly silenced by her common sense. Embarrassed, she clamps her lips together.

The boy stares at her in the mirror with consternation.

'That's a horrific thing to say to someone!'

Britt-Marie doesn't answer. But she agrees. It is a horrific thing to say to someone.

'Do you love him? Your husband?' asks the boy so suddenly that Britt-Marie almost snips him in the ear.

She brushes down his shoulder with the back of her hand. Buries her gaze in his scalp.

'Yes.'

'Why isn't he here, then?'

'Because sometimes love isn't enough.'

Then they remain silent until Britt-Marie has finished cutting, and Pirate's unruly washing-up brush has been tenderly coaxed into a hairstyle as neat as biological circumstances will allow. He stays where he is, admiring himself in the mirror. Britt-Marie cleans up and looks out into the parking area. Two young men are standing there, neither of them even twenty years old, smoking and leaning against a big black car. They're wearing the same kind of jeans, ripped across the thighs, as the children in the football team. But these two are no children. They look like the sort of young men who would make Britt-Marie take a firmer grip on her handbag while passing. Not that she judges people, not at all, but one of these men actually has tattoos on his hands.

'That's Sami and Psycho,' says Pirate behind her.

He sounds scared.

'Those are not names,' Britt-Marie informs him.

'Sami is a name, I think. But Psycho is called Psycho because he's a psycho,' says Pirate quietly, as if he doesn't dare utter their names too loudly.

'I don't suppose they have jobs to go to?'

Pirate shrugs.

'No one here has a job. Apart from some really old people.'

Britt-Marie puts one hand in the other. Then the other in the one. While trying not to be offended.

'The one on the right has tattoos on his hands,' she notes.

'That's Psycho. He's mad. Sami's all right, but Psycho's . . . you know, he's dangerous. You have to avoid any trouble with him. My mother says I'm not allowed in Vega and Omar's house when Psycho's there.'

'Why on earth would he be in Vega and Omar's home?'

'Sami is their older brother.'

The door of the pizzeria opens. Vega emerges with two pizzas and hands them to Sami. He kisses her on the cheek. Psycho grins insolently at her. She looks at him as if she just bought a new bag and he vomited in it. Then he slams the door. The black car pulls out of the parking area.

'They don't eat in the pizzeria when Sven's there, Vega said they're not allowed to,' explains Pirate.

'Ha. Quite understandable. Because she knows they're worried about the police, of course.'

'No, because she knows the police are afraid of them.'

Societies are like people in that way. If you don't ask too

many questions and don't shift any heavy furniture around, there's no need to notice their worst sides. Britt-Marie brushes down her skirt. Then she brushes Pirate's sleeve. She'd like to change the subject, and without further ado he helps her out:

'Has Vega asked you yet?'

'About what?' asks Britt-Marie.

'If you want to be our coach?'

'Absolutely not!'

Extremely offended, she cups one hand into the other and asks:

'Anyway, what does that mean?'

'I mean a trainer. We have to have one. There's a challenge cup in town; you can only enter if you have a team with a coach.'

'A cup? Like a competition?'

'Like a cup.'

'In this weather? Outdoors? That's ludicrous!'

'No, I mean it's an indoor competition. In a sports centre, in town,' says Pirate. Britt-Marie is about to say a few choice words about the sort of people who like to kick balls around indoors when there's a knock on the door. A boy is standing outside, of about the same age as Pirate. Long-haired, one might also add.

'Ha?' says Britt-Marie.

'Is Ben, like, here?' asks the boy.

It seems fairly unclear what the meaning of 'like' is in the construction of the sentence. As if the boy just asked, 'Is Ben almost here?'

'Who?' says Britt-Marie.

'Ben? Or, like, what they call him in his team. Pirate?'

'Ha. Ha. Ha. He is here, but he's occupied,' says Britt-Marie firmly and is about to close the door.

'With what, sort of thing?' asks the boy.

'He's meeting someone. Or he has a date. Or whatever it's called.'

'I know. With me!' says the boy with a frustrated groan.

Britt-Marie, who is not encumbered with any prejudice, puts one hand in the other and says:

'Ha.'

The boy is chewing gum. She dislikes that. It's actually quite all right to dislike chewing gum, even if you are a person without any prejudices.

'It's, like, epically lame saying "date",' says the boy.

'It was Pir . . . it was Ben who said it. In my time we said "meeting",' says Britt-Marie, defending herself.

'Also epically lame,' snorts the boy.

'What do you say, then?' asks Britt-Marie, just a touch critically.

'Nothing. Just "out", sort of thing,' says the boy.

'I have to ask you to wait here,' says Britt-Marie and firmly closes the door.

Pirate stands in the bathroom, fixing his hair. He starts jumping up and down on the spot when he sees her in the mirror.

'Is he here? Isn't he fantastic?'

'He's strikingly rude,' says Britt-Marie, but Pirate obviously can't hear anything, because the sound of his jumping echoes quite a lot in the bathroom.

Britt-Marie takes a piece of toilet paper, carefully picks a hair off Pirate's jumper and folds it into the toilet paper, then flushes it down the toilet.

'I was under the impression that you went on dates with girls.'

'I do go on dates with girls sometimes,' says Pirate.

'But this is a boy,' says Britt-Marie.

'This is a boy,' confirms Pirate with a nod, as if they are playing some sort of parlour game, the rules of which have not been explained to him.

'Ha,' says Britt-Marie.

'Do you have to decide on one or the other?'

'I know nothing about that. I don't have any prejudices about it,' Britt-Marie assures him.

Pirate adjusts his hair, smiles and asks:

'Do you think he'll like my hair?'

Britt-Marie doesn't seem to have heard his question, and instead she says:

'Your friends in the football team obviously don't know that you go on dates with boys. Obviously I won't mention it.'

Pirate looks surprised.

'Why wouldn't they know?'

'Have you told them?'

'Why wouldn't I have told them?'

'What did they say?'

'They said "OK".' Then he looks unsure. 'What else should they have said?'

'Ha, ha, obviously nothing, obviously,' says Britt-Marie in a way you could describe as not at all defensive, and then adds: 'I have no prejudices about this!'

'I know,' says Pirate.

Then he smiles nervously.

'Is my hair looking nice?'

Britt-Marie can't quite bring herself to answer, so she just nods. She picks off one last hair from his jumper, and awkwardly holds it in her hand. He hugs her. She can't think why on earth he would get it into his head to do such a thing.

'You shouldn't be alone, it's a waste when someone whose hair looks as nice as yours is alone,' he whispers.

He's almost at the door when Britt-Marie, still holding his hair in her hand, collects herself, clears her throat and whispers back:

'If he doesn't say your hair is looking lovely, then he doesn't deserve you!'

Pirate turns around, runs back through the room and hugs her again. She pushes him away, friendly but firm, because one mustn't forget one's boundaries He asks her if he can borrow her mobile phone. She looks doubtful, and warns him not to run up a large bill. He takes it, dials his own number, lets it ring once then hangs up. Then he tries to embrace her again, laughs when she squirms, and runs off. The door closes.

Fifteen minutes later Britt-Marie gets a text message: 'He said it! :)'

The recreation centre goes quiet around her. She vacuums up

all the hair from the floor just to make some noise. Washes and tumble-dries the towels.

Then she dusts all the pictures, taking extra care with the information chart and map, which Somebody hung a metre lower than all the other frames.

She removes the wrapper from a Snickers bar, puts it on a plate, puts the plate on a towel and leaves it on the threshold. Opens the front door. Sits for a long time on her stool trying to feel the wind in her hair. At long last she picks up the telephone.

'Hello?' says the girl at the unemployment office.

Britt-Marie inhales deeply.

'It was impolite of me to say that you had a boy's hairstyle.'

'Britt-Marie?'

Britt-Marie swallows, with concentration.

'Obviously I shouldn't have got involved in that, I mean the sort of hairstyle you have. Or if you go out on dates with boys or girls. Not at all.'

'You didn't mention anything about . . . that.'

'Ha. Ha. Ha. It's not beyond the realm of possibility that I just thought it, maybe so. In either case it was impolite of me,' says Britt-Marie irritably.

'What . . . but I mean, what do you mean by . . . what's wrong with my hairstyle?'

'Nothing at all. That's what I'm saying,' insists Britt-Marie.

'I'm not . . . I mean, I'm . . . I don't like . . .' says the girl defensively in a slightly overbearing voice.

'That's not for me to stick my nose into.'

'I mean, not that . . . you know . . . there's anything wrong with being that way! Or not,' the girl persists.

'I certainly haven't said anything of the kind!'

'Nor me!' protests the girl.

'Well, then,' says Britt-Marie.

'Absolutely!' says the girl.

There's such a long silence between them that at long last the girl says 'Hello?' because she thinks Britt-Marie has hung up. And that's when Britt-Marie hangs up.

The rat is one hour and six minutes late for dinner. It rushes in and lunges at the biggest possible piece of Snickers that it could carry, stops for a second and stares at Britt-Marie, then runs back outside into the darkness. Britt-Marie wraps the rest of the chocolate in plastic cling film and puts it in the fridge. Washes up the plate. Washes and tumble-dries the towel and hangs it in its place. Through the window she sees Sven emerging from the pizzeria. He stops by the police car and looks over at the recreation centre. Britt-Marie hides behind the curtain. He gets in the car and drives off. For a short moment she was afraid he was going to come over and knock on the door. Then she got disappointed when he didn't.

She turns off all the lights except in the bathroom. The sheen of the lone light bulb finds its way out from under the door and lights up the exact area of the wall where Somebody hung up the information chart, slightly too low but obviously not too low. 'Welcome to Borg', Britt-Marie reads, while she sits on a stool in the darkness and looks at the red dot that first made her fall in love with the picture. The reason for her love of maps. It's half worn away, the dot, and the red colour is bleached. Yet it's there, flung down there on the map halfway between the lower left corner and its centre, and next to it is written, 'You are here'.

Sometimes it's easier to go on living, not even knowing who you are, when at least you know precisely where you are while you go on not knowing.

15

People sometimes refer to darkness as something that falls, but in places like Borg it doesn't just fall, it collapses. It engulfs the streets in an instant. In cities there are so many people who don't want to sit at home all night that you can open dedicated premises and run entertainment industries that are open only at these times. But, in Borg, life is encapsulated once darkness falls.

Britt-Marie locks the door of the recreation centre and stands on her own in the parking area.

Her pockets are full of neatly folded toilet paper, because she did not find an envelope. The sign above the pizzeria is turned off, but she can make out the shadow of Somebody moving around inside. Something in Britt-Marie wants to go and talk to her, possibly to buy something. Another considerably more rational something orders her to do no such thing. It's dark outside. It's not civilised to walk into shops when it's dark outside.

She stands by the door, listening to the radio inside, which is playing some sort of pop music. Britt-Marie knows this because she's not at all unfamiliar with pop music. There are many crossword questions about it, and Britt-Marie likes to keep herself informed. But this particular song is new to her; a young man is singing in a cracked voice about how you can either be 'someone' or 'no one at all'.

Britt-Marie is still holding on to the carton of cigarettes covered in foreign letters. She doesn't know how much foreign cigarettes cost, but she gets out a considerably larger than reasonable amount of money from her handbag and folds it in the toilet paper until it looks like a small envelope with a phenomenal capacity for water absorption. Then she carefully tucks it under the door.

The young man keeps singing on the radio. As hard as he can. About nothing much.

'Love has no mercy,' he sings. Again and again. Love has no mercy. Kent wells up in Britt-Marie's chest until she can't breathe.

Then she walks by herself along a road that heads out of a community in two directions. As darkness collapses. Towards a bed and a balcony that are not her own.

The truck comes up on her right, from behind. Too close. Too fast.

That's why she throws herself across to the other side of the road. The human brain has a monstrous ability to recreate memories of such clarity that the rest of the body loses all sense of time. An approaching truck can make the ears believe they are hearing a mother screaming, can make the hands believe they are cutting themselves on glass, can make the lips taste blood. Deep inside, Britt-Marie has time to yell Ingrid's name a thousand times.

The truck thunders by, so close that her heart can't tell whether it's been run over or not, in a rain of hard lumps of mud gouged out of the road surface. Britt-Marie takes a few tottering steps; her coat is wet and dirty, there's a howling in her ears. Maybe a single second passes and maybe a hundred. She blinks at the headlights with a growing awareness that the howling is not coming from inside. There's actually a car sounding its horn. She hears someone yelling. She holds up her hand to shield her eyes from the headlights of the BMW. Fredrik, the man who came to the café earlier, is standing in front of her, shouting furiously.

'Are you bloody senile or what, you old bat!? What are you doing walking in the middle of the fucking road! I almost killed you!'

The way he puts it, it's as if her death would have been an inconvenience to him more than anyone else. She doesn't know what to say. Her heart is racing so frantically that it's giving her a stitch. Fredrik throws out his arms.

'Can you hear what I'm saying or are you a retard?'

He takes two steps towards her. She doesn't know why. Looking back on it, she's unsure whether he was intending to hit her, but neither of them ever find out, because he's interrupted by another voice. A different kind of voice. Cold.

'Problem?'

Fredrik turns around first, so that Britt-Marie has time to see his eyes register the danger before she has time to see what he's worried about. He swallows.

'No . . . she was wal . . .'

Sami is standing a few metres away, with his hands in his pockets. He is twenty years old at most but, judging by the suffocating grip of his presence in the darkness, you might describe him as a 'spirit of violence'. Britt-Marie wonders whether in a crossword this might be rendered as 'God of aggression'. Vertical, fifteen letters. People have time to think of all sorts of things while they face up to what they imagine is their imminent violent death, and this happens to be the first thing that comes to Britt-Marie's mind. Fredrik stutters indecipherably. Sami says nothing. Another young man is moving up behind him. He's taller. It's not at all difficult to guess why he's known as Psycho. His mouth is grinning, but it's not so much a grin as a display of teeth.

Britt-Marie has heard tell of this sort of thing on the natural history programmes Kent used to watch when there was no football on the TV. Human beings are the only animals that smile as a gesture of peace, whereas other animals show their teeth as a threat. This is perfectly understandable now; she can see the animal inside the human being.

Psycho's smile grows wider. Sami doesn't take his hands out of his pockets. Doesn't even raise his voice.

'Don't you touch her,' he says, nodding towards Britt-Marie, while keeping his gaze fixed on Fredrik.

Fredrik totters back to his BMW. His self-confidence seems

to grow with every step he takes towards it, as if the car is giving him superpowers. But he waits until he's standing right by the door before he hisses:

'Retard! This whole bloody place is completely retarded!'

Psycho takes half a step forward. The BMW does a wheelspin in the mud and gravel and makes its escape in the rain. Britt-Marie has time to see the boy in the passenger seat, the one who's the same age as Ben and Vega and Omar, but taller and more grown up. Wearing the tracksuit top on which it says 'Hockey'. He looks scared.

Psycho looks at Britt-Marie. Displays his teeth. Britt-Marie turns around and does her absolute best to walk briskly without breaking into a run, because in the natural history programmes they always say you shouldn't try to run away from wild animals. She hears Sami calling out behind her, without anger or menace, in fact almost softly:

'See you around, Coach!'

She's a hundred and fifty metres away when she finally has the courage to stop and catch her breath. When she turns around the two men have gone back to a group of other young men on a patch of asphalt between some apartment blocks and a cluster of trees. The black car is there, with its engine running and the headlights on. The young men are moving about in the beams of light. Sami yells something and surges forward, kicking his right leg into the air. Then he punches his fists up and cheers loudly at the sky.

It takes Britt-Marie a minute to understand what they are doing.

They're playing football.

Playing.

The temperature drops below zero in the night. Rain turns to snow.

Britt-Marie stands on the balcony watching all this happening. She finds herself spending an inordinate amount of time thinking about sushi and how you make it.

114

She cleans the mattress. Hangs up her coat. When she hears Bank coming back and closing the door downstairs, she paces around the room three times and thumps her feet as hard against the floor as she can. Just to clarify that she's there. Then she sleeps the dreamless sleep of exhaustion, because she couldn't even begin to say whose dreams she might have.

The sun is already up when she wakes. She almost falls out of bed when she realises. Waking up long after the late-rising January sun! What will people think? Still half asleep, she's making her way to her clothes when she realises why she's woken up. Someone is knocking on the door. The whole thing is terribly vexatious, actually, waking up at an hour when people are actually quite entitled to knock on your door.

She fixes her hair as quickly as she can, then stumbles down almost the entire length of the stairs, very nearly breaking her neck. It's the sort of thing that happens every few minutes – people falling down stairs and killing themselves. She just about manages to land on her two feet at the bottom, in the hall, and then sets about gathering her wits. After a certain amount of hesitation she rushes into the kitchen, which is obviously as dirty as you can possibly imagine, and then looks in all the drawers until she finds an apron.

She puts this on.

'Ha?' she says with raised eyebrows when she opens the door.

She adjusts her apron, as you do when you are interrupted by someone knocking at your door while you are busy with the washing-up. Vega and Omar are standing there.

'What are you doing?' asks Vega.

'I'm busy,' Britt-Marie answers.

'Were you asleep?' asks Omar.

'Certainly not!' Britt-Marie protests, while adjusting both her hair and her apron.

'We heard you coming down the stairs,' says Vega.

'That's not a crime, is it?'

'Cool it, will you, we only asked if you were asleep!'

Britt-Marie clasps her hands together.

'It's possible that I may have overslept, it's not something that happens often.'

'Did you have something you had to get up for?' asks Omar.

Britt-Marie doesn't have a convincing answer to that one. There's a silence for a few moments, until Vega's patience runs out and she gets to the point with a frustrated groan:

'We were wondering if you wanted to eat with us tonight.'

Omar nods energetically.

'And then we're wondering if you want to be our new coach, for our team!'

Then Omar shrieks, 'Ouch!' and Vega hisses, 'Idiot!' and tries to kick him again on the shin, but this time he gets out of the way.

'We wanted to invite you for dinner so we could ask you to be our coach. Sort of like when they offer a contract in *proper* football teams,' says Vega sourly.

'I'm not particularly taken with football,' says Britt-Marie as politely as she can, which quite possibly is not very politely at all.

'You don't need to do anything, all you have to do is sign a bloody form and come to our bloody training sessions!' protests Vega.

'There's this wicked knock-out competition in town. The council is organising it, and any team can take part, but you have to have a coach.'

'There has to be someone else in Borg you could give this assignment to,' says Britt-Marie and starts backing away into the hall.

'No one else has time,' says Vega.

'But we were thinking you don't have anything to do, sort of thing!' says Omar with a cheerful nod.

Britt-Marie pauses and looks thoroughly offended.

Adjusts her apron.

'I'll have you know I have a great deal to do.'

'Like what?'

'I have a list!'

'But I mean, God, this will hardly take any time at all, you only have to be there when we're training in case one of the competition organisers comes by! So they can see we have a sodding coach!' Vega groans.

'We're training at six this evening, in the parking area by the recreation centre,' says Omar with a nod.

'But I don't know anything about football!'

'Nor does Omar, but we still let him play with us,' says Vega.

'You bloody what!?' Omar exclaims.

Vega, apparently losing her patience, shakes her head at Britt-Marie.

'Never bloody mind, then! We thought you had it in you to be decent about it. This is Borg, so it's not like there are so many other bloody adults to choose from. You're the only one.'

Britt-Marie has nothing to say to that. Vega starts going down the steps and makes an irritated gesture at Omar to come with her. Britt-Marie stays in the doorway, keeping her hands clasped together while opening and closing her mouth repeatedly, until at long last she calls out:

'I can't at six o'clock!'

Vega turns around. Britt-Marie stares at her apron.

'Civilised people have their dinner at six. You actually can't play football in the middle of your dinner.'

Vega shrugs. As if it doesn't make any difference.

'OK. Come over to ours and have dinner at six, then, and we'll train afterwards.'

'We're having tacos!' says Omar, nodding, with great satisfaction.

'What's tacos?'

The children stare at her.

'Tacos,' says Omar, as if the problem could only have been that she didn't hear him properly.

'I don't eat foreign food,' says Britt-Marie, even though what she really means is, 'Kent doesn't eat foreign food.'

Vega shrugs her shoulders again.

'If you don't eat the tortillas it's like having salad.'

'We live in one of the high-rises, block two, second floor,' says Omar and points down the road.

Of course it's not there and then that Britt-Marie becomes the coach of a football team. It's just the point at which someone tells her that's what she's become.

She closes the door. Removes her apron. Puts it back in the drawer. Then cleans the kitchen, because she doesn't know how not to. Then she goes upstairs and fetches her mobile. The girl at the unemployment office picks up after a single ring.

'Do you know anything about football?'

'Is that Britt-Marie?' asks the girl, although she should have learned by now.

'I need to know how one trains a football team,' Britt-Marie informs her. 'Do you need a permit from the local authority for that type of thing?'

'No . . . or what I mean is . . . what do you mean?' says the girl.

Britt-Marie exhales. But does not sigh.

'My dear, if for example you want to have your balcony glazed you need a permit. I'm assuming the same thing applies to football teams. Surely they're not beyond the rule of law just because the players run about kicking things all over the place?'

'No . . . I've . . . or, I mean I assume their parents have to sign some letter to say they're allowed to play in the team,' says the girl dubiously.

Britt-Marie makes a note of that on her list. Nods soberly to herself and asks:

'Ha. So can I ask, what's the first thing you have to do at football practice?'

'I'd say . . . but I don't know . . . the first thing you do at training . . . I mean, is to take the register?'

'I beg your pardon?'

'You have a register. You tick off the people who are there,' says the girl.

'A list?'

'Yes . . .?'

Britt-Marie has already hung up.

She may not know a lot about football, but even the gods know that no one is more skilled at lists than Britt-Marie.

16

Dino opens the door. He laughs when he sees Britt-Marie, who assumes she has pressed the wrong doorbell, but in fact it turns out Dino always has his dinner with Vega and Omar, and Dino isn't necessarily laughing at her. Apparently, in spite of her first impressions, that is how things are done in Borg. People seem to have their dinners at other people's homes just like that, and then go around laughing as if they hadn't a care in the world. Omar comes running into the hall and points at Britt-Marie.

'Take off your shoes, Sami gets really pissed off otherwise because he just mopped the floor!'

'I do not get pissed off!' comes a voice from the kitchen, sounding fairly pissed off.

'He's always in a foul one when it's our cleaning day,' explains Omar to Britt-Marie.

'Maybe I wouldn't be in a foul one if WE had a fucking cleaning day, but it's always ME who has a fucking cleaning day in this place. EVERY DAY!' yells Sami from the kitchen.

Omar nods meaningfully at Britt-Marie.

'You see. Pissed off.'

Vega turns up in the doorway with a slumped upper-body posture, waving an invisible bottle of spirits, in imitation of Somebody.

'You know, Britt-Marie, Sami he has, what's-it-called? Citrus fruit up the anus, huh?'

Dino and Omar laugh until they are hyperventilating.

Britt-Marie responds with a brisk series of polite nods, because this is as close as she gets to laughing out loud. She removes her shoes, goes into the kitchen and nods cautiously at Sami. He points at a chair.

'The food is ready,' he says and removes his apron, before immediately roaring towards the hall:

'GRUB'S UP!'

Britt-Marie checks her watch. It's exactly six o'clock.

'Are we waiting for your parents?' she asks considerately.

'They're not here,' says Sami and starts putting coasters on the table.

'I suppose they're delayed, coming home from work,' Britt-Marie says pleasantly.

'Mum drives a truck. Abroad. She's not home much,' says Sami curtly, putting glasses and bowls on the coasters.

'And your father?'

'He cleared off.'

'Cleared off?'

'That's right. When I was small. Omar and Vega were just born. I guess he couldn't take it. So we don't talk about him in this home. Mum took care of us. THE FOOD'S READY NOW SO COME HERE BEFORE I FUCKING BEAT THE HELL OUT OF YOU!'

Vega, Omar and Dino saunter into the kitchen and start devouring their food, hardly stopping to chew it; it might as well have been liquidised and served up with straws.

'But who takes care of you now, then, when your mother's not here?' asks Britt-Marie.

'We take care of us,' says Sami, offended.

She doesn't know exactly what common conversational practice is after that, so she gets out the carton of cigarettes with the foreign letters on it.

'Of course I usually bring flowers when I'm invited for dinner, but there's no florist in Borg. I've noticed you like cigarettes. I suppose cigarettes must be like flowers for someone who likes cigarettes,' she explains, as if to defend herself.

121

Sami takes the carton of cigarettes. He looks almost emotional. Britt-Marie sits in a spare seat and clears her throat.

'You're not afraid of cancer, I suppose?'

'There are worse things to be afraid of,' says Sami with a smile.

'Ha,' says Britt-Marie, and picks up something from her plate that she has to assume is a taco.

Omar and Vega start talking at the same time. Mostly about football, as far as Britt-Marie can make out. Dino says almost nothing, but he laughs the whole time. Britt-Marie doesn't understand what he's laughing at. He and Omar don't even need to say anything before they burst out laughing, all they have to do is look at one another. Children are unfathomable that way.

Sami points at Omar with his fork.

'How many times do I have to tell you, Omar? Take your fucking elbows off the fucking table!'

Omar rolls his eyes. Removes his elbows.

'I don't get why you can't have your elbows on the table. What difference does it make?'

Britt-Marie observes him intensely.

'It makes a difference, Omar, because we're not animals,' she explains.

Sami looks at Britt-Marie appreciatively. Omar looks at them both with puzzlement.

'Animals don't have elbows,' he objects.

'Eat your fucking food,' says Sami.

When Omar and Dino are done, they stand up and run into another room, still laughing. Vega puts her plate on the draining board and looks as if she's expecting a diploma for effort. After that she also runs off.

'You could say thanks for the food,' Sami calls out after them, pissed off.

'THANKS FOR THE FOOD!' the children roar from an indefinable part of the flat.

Sami stands up and clatters demonstratively with the plates in the sink. Then he looks at Britt-Marie.

'Right. So you didn't like the food, then?'

'Excuse me?' says Britt-Marie.

Sami shakes his head, says something to himself punctuated by several 'fucking' references, then snatches up the carton of cigarettes and disappears on to the balcony.

Britt-Marie stays in the kitchen on her own. Eats what she is almost sure must be tacos. They taste less odd than she expected. She stands up, puts what's left of the food into the fridge, washes up and dries the plates and cutlery and opens the cutlery drawer. Leans over it, catches her breath. Forks-knives-spoons. In the right order.

Sami is standing on the balcony, smoking, when she comes out.

'Very nice dinner, Sami. Thanks for that,' she says, one hand firmly clasped in the other.

He nods.

'Sometimes it's nice if someone says it tastes good without your having to ask every time, you get what I mean?'

'Yes' she says. Because she does get it.

Then she feels that it would be in order to say something polite, so she says:

'You have a very nice cutlery drawer.'

He looks at her for a long time, and then grins.

'You're OK, Coach.'

'Ha. Ha. You're also . . . OK. Sami.'

He drives them all to their practice session in his black car. Vega argues loudly with him all the way – which, in Borg, is not very far. Britt-Marie doesn't understand what the argument is about, but it seems to have something to do with that Psycho fellow. Something about money. When they stop, Britt-Marie has a sense that something ought to be done to change the subject, because this Psycho makes her nervous in much the same way as too much talk about poisonous spiders. So she says:

'Do you also have a team, Sami? You and those boys you were playing with the other night?'

'No, we don't have a . . . team,' says Sami, and looks as if it was a bit of a strange question.

'So why do you play football, then?' asks Britt-Marie, puzzled.

'What do you mean, "why"?' asks Sami, just as puzzled.

Neither of them are able to come up with a good answer.

The car stops. Vega, Omar and Dino jump out. Britt-Marie checks the contents of her bag to make sure she hasn't forgotten anything.

'Are you ready, Britt-Marie?' asks Vega, as if she's already bored.

Britt-Marie nods with a good deal of concentration and points at her bag.

'Yes, yes, obviously I'm ready. I should like to tell you that I have made a list!'

Sami parks the car with the engine running, so that the head-lights illuminate the parking area. The children put out four fizzy-drink cans as goalposts. Fizzy-drink cans are magical in this way – they can transform parking areas into football pitches by their mere existence.

Britt-Marie holds up her list.

'Vega?' she asks, loud and clear, while the children run about kicking the ball with varying degrees of success.

'What?' says Vega, who's standing right in front of her.

'Is that a "yes"?'

'What are you talking about?'

Britt-Marie taps her pen against the list with extreme patience.

'My dear, I am reading the register. What one does is, one reads out the names and then each respective person says "yes". It's common practice.'

Vega squints disapprovingly.

'You can see I'm standing here!'

Britt-Marie nods considerately.

'My dear, if we could just tick people off in any old way there wouldn't be any point doing the register, you have to understand.'

'Never mind about your bloody register! Let's just play!' Vega says and kicks the ball.

124

'Vega?'

'YEEES!? Jesus . . .'

Britt-Marie nods intently and ticks Vega's name off on the list. Once she's done the same with the other children, she distributes handwritten notes to them with a short, very formal message followed by two neat lines at the bottom, where it is written 'Parental signature'. Britt-Marie is very proud of the notes. She has written them in ink. Anyone who knows Britt-Marie understands what an outstanding achievement it is for Britt-Marie to control her compulsion never to write anything in ink. People really do change when they travel.

'Do both parents have to sign?' asks Pirate, who has arranged his hair so neatly that it really pains Britt-Marie when, in the next second, a ball strikes his head.

'Sorry! I was aiming at Vega!' yells Omar.

Vega and Omar end up having a fight. The other children fling themselves into the chaos. Britt-Marie walks around in circles, trying to figure out how to give Vega and Omar their notes among all the flying fists, but in the end she gives up and walks determinedly across the parking area and hands their slips to Sami instead. He is sitting on the bonnet of the black car, drinking one of the goalposts.

Britt-Marie brushes dust off every part of herself. Football is certainly not very hygienic.

'You need help?' asks Sami.

'I'm not familiar with what a football coach is supposed to do when the players fight like wild dogs,' Britt-Marie admits.

'You let them run – you know, idiot!' grins Sami.

'I'm certainly not an idiot!' protests Britt-Marie.

'No, it's an exercise. It's called "Idiot". I'll show you.'

He slides off the bonnet and walks around the car. Britt-Marie follows him. Clasps one hand in the other and asks, not at all accusingly:

'Might I trouble you for an answer as to why you don't train these children yourself, if you know so much about this football thing?'

Sami gets half a dozen soft-drink cans out of the boot. Hands one of them to Britt-Marie.

'I don't have time,' he says.

'Maybe you would if you didn't spend such an inordinate amount of time buying soft drinks,' Britt-Marie notes.

Sami laughs again.

'Come on, Coach, you do get that the council wouldn't let someone with my criminal record coach a youth team,' he says. As if it's hardly worth mentioning. Britt-Marie keeps an extra-firm grip on her handbag after that. Not because she judges people, obviously, but because there's a pretty strong wind in Borg tonight. No other reason.

'Idiot', the way it's done in Borg, is an exercise based on half a dozen soft-drink cans being positioned at intervals of a couple of metres. The children stand by the fence between the recreation centre and the pizzeria, then they run as fast as they can to the first soft-drink can, and as fast as they can back to the fence, then as fast as they can to the second soft-drink can a little further away, and then back as fast as they can. And then to the third soft-drink can, and so on.

'For how long are they supposed to do that?' asks Britt-Marie.

'As long as you like,' says Sami.

'For goodness' sake, I can't make them do that!' Britt-Marie objects.

'You're the coach now. If they don't do what you tell them they can't play in the competition.'

It sounds quite deranged, in Britt-Marie's opinion, but Sami doesn't go into more detailed explanations because his telephone starts ringing.

'What did you say the exercise was called?' asks Britt-Marie.

'Idiot!' says Sami and then answers 'Yeah' into his telephone, as people do who have no use for either exclamation marks or question marks.

Britt-Marie mulls this over at length until at long last she manages to say:

'That's a good name for both the exercise and the person who came up with it.'

By now, Sami has started walking back to his car with the telephone pressed to his ear, so he can't hear her. No one can. But this doesn't actually concern Britt-Marie so much. The children run between the soft-drink cans and Britt-Marie stands there beside them with a sort of happy fizziness in her whole body, repeating 'A good name for the exercise and the person who came up with it' very, very quietly to herself. Over and over again.

It's the first time for as long as she can remember that she has intentionally made a joke.

17

In the children's defence, they didn't do it on purpose. Or rather, it was obviously done on purpose but none of them believed Toad would actually hit the mark, so to speak. They never hit anything they aim at. Especially not Toad, who's the youngest and worst player in an already dismal team.

It so happens that Bank, in an even blacker mood than usual, comes walking across the parking area with her white dog in the middle of a training session.

Omar sees her go into the pizzeria or the cornershop or car workshop or whatever it is, and after a while come out again with one bag that seems to contain chocolate and another that seems to contain beer. Omar elbows Toad in the side and says:

'You think she has superpowers?'

Toad answers with a sound made by children whose mouths are full of goalpost. Omar gestures in an explanatory way to Britt-Marie, as if Britt-Marie might be more receptive to his line of reasoning, which must be reckoned as fairly exaggerated optimism.

'You know, what the hell, in films blind types get superpowers! Like Daredevil!'

'I'm not familiar with Daredevil,' explains Britt-Marie with as much amicability as she can drum up, considering how enormously stupid this conversation is.

Bank moves across the parking area with her stick in her

hand, next to and slightly behind the white dog. Omar points at her exultantly:

'Daredevil! Is a superhero! Except blind! So he has super-senses instead. You think she does? Could she sort of sense it if you shot a football at her head even though she couldn't see it?'

'She is not blind. She merely has impaired vision,' says Britt-Marie. Omar, who has long since stopped listening to Britt-Marie, turns around and says:

'Do it, Toad!'

Toad, who happens to have the ball at that moment, doesn't seem to think it's a very good idea. But then Omar utters those golden words that have the magical power to obliterate every child's self-restraint anywhere in the world:

'You don't have the guts to do it!'

In fairness to Toad, he obviously never thought he'd hit her. They're all quite surprised that he does.

Most surprised of all, obviously, is Bank.

'WHATTHEBLOODY . . .!' she roars.

The children stand still at first, their mouths agape. Like you do. Then Omar starts tittering. Then Vega follows suit. Bank storms towards them, incandescent, her stick cleaving the air.

'WAS THAT FUNNY? BRATS!'

Britt-Marie clears her throat and almost holds out her arms.

'Please . . . Bank, he didn't mean to, he obviously wasn't aiming at you, he obviously wasn't. It was obviously an accident.'

'ACCIDENT! ACCIDENT, YEAH!' howls Bank, and it's a little unclear what she means by this.

'What do you mean not on purpose? He was aiming, wasn't he?' yells Omar confidently, while at the same time moving out of cleaving range behind Britt-Marie.

'Did you really?' Britt-Marie asks Toad in astonishment.

'WHO DID THIS!?' yells Bank, her entire face throbbing like a single thick vein emerging from her throat.

Toad, paralysed, nods and backs away. Britt-Marie enthusiastically clasps one hand in the other, and doesn't quite know what to do with herself.

'But . . . it's absolutely marvellous!' she manages to blurt out.

'WHAT *ARE* YOU SAYING, YOU OLD BAT?' howls Bank.

At this stage, everything that's reasonable inside Britt-Marie insistently tries to curb her enthusiasm, but clearly it doesn't have much success, because Britt-Marie leans in and whispers chirpily:

'They never hit anything they aim at, you see. This is really an excellent sign of progress!'

Bank stares at Britt-Marie. At least she seems to be staring. It's difficult to know for sure, with those sunglasses. Britt-Marie gulps hesitantly.

'It's obviously not marvellous that he hit . . . you. That is obviously not what I mean. But it is excellent that he hit . . . anything at all.'

Bank leaves the parking area in a hailstorm of the ugliest and most colourful words Britt-Marie has ever heard. Britt-Marie actually didn't even know it was possible to combine words for genitalia with words describing other parts of the body in that way. You don't even come across that level of verbal innovation in crosswords.

A thoughtful silence envelops the parking area. Obviously, it's the voice of Somebody that breaks it.

'Like I said about that one. Lemon. Up the. Arse.'

She's sitting in the pizzeria doorway, grinning in the direction of Bank.

Britt-Marie brushes her skirt down.

'I wouldn't want to suggest that you're wrong, I certainly wouldn't. But I do really think that on this occasion Bank's problem was not a lemon in the arse, but a football in the head.'

They all laugh. Britt-Marie doesn't get angry about it. It's a new feeling for her.

The boy with the tracksuit jacket with 'Hockey' written on it walks out of the pizzeria with a pizza box in his hands. He fails to hide his interest in the football training, realises his mistake, and tries to quickly get moving, but Vega has already seen him.

'What are you doing here?' she calls out.

'Buying pizza,' says the boy in the tracksuit repentantly.

'Don't you have pizza in town, or what?'

The boy looks down at his pizza box.

'I like the pizza here.'

Vega clenches her fists but doesn't say anything else. The boy squeezes past Somebody in the doorway and runs out towards the road. The BMW is parked a hundred metres down the road, with its engine running.

Somebody turns to Vega with a grimace.

'He's not his dad. Dad can be pig, kid could be good. You should know if anyone.'

Vega looks as if the words have wounded her. She turns around and kicks the ball so hard that it flies over the fence into the darkness.

Somebody rolls a few metres towards Britt-Marie, nods at the pizzeria.

'Come! Have something for you!'

By this stage, Toad has drunk all the goalposts and Vega kicks off a noisy dispute with Sami, of which Britt-Marie can only distinguish something about 'Psycho' and 'owes money', by which she comes to the conclusion that the training session is over. She's unsure whether she should be doing anything in particular, such as blowing a whistle or similar, but she chooses not to. Mainly because she doesn't have a whistle.

Inside the pizzeria, Somebody slides a fistful of money and a piece of paper across the counter.

'Here. This change, and this receipt, huh.'

She gestures towards the bottom of the door, where Britt-Marie pushed the money through last night.

'Next time, you can, what's-it-called? Come in!' She grins.

When Britt-Marie doesn't seem to know what to say, she adds:

'You left too much money for cigarettes, Britt-Marie. You are, what's-it-called? Either your maths is crap or you're very generous, huh? I think: Britt-Marie is generous, huh? Not like that Fredrik, for example, he's so mean he yells every time he takes a shit!'

She nods cheerfully. Britt-Marie mumbles 'Ha' repeatedly. Neatly folds the receipt and puts it in her handbag. Takes the change and puts it in the vase for tips. Somebody rolls half a turn forward, then half a turn back.

'It looked nice, you know. Looked nice when you . . . cleaned, huh. Thanks!' she says.

'It was not my intention to hide your belongings so you could not find them,' says Britt-Marie, directing her voice into her handbag.

Somebody scratches her chin.

'The cutlery, huh. Fork, knife, spoon. That order. I can, what's-it-called? Get used to it!'

Britt-Marie sucks in her cheeks. Goes to the door. She has reached the threshold when she stops and summons her strength and says:

'I should just like to inform you that there's no urgency, at the moment, to have my car repaired.'

Somebody looks out of the door at the children and their football pitch. She nods. Britt-Marie also nods. It's the first time for as long as Britt-Marie can remember that she has had a friend. The children take off their dirty jerseys and drop them off in the recreation centre, without Britt-Marie even having offered to wash them. There's no one left in the parking area by the time she's washed and tumble-dried the jerseys and put them in a neat pile, ready for tomorrow's training. Borg is empty except for a lone silhouette by the bus stop on the road. Britt-Marie didn't even know there was a bus stop there until she saw someone waiting by the streetlight.

She doesn't recognise Pirate until she's just a few metres away. His red hair is tangled and muddy and he stands motionless as if trying to ignore that she's there. Her common sense tries to make her walk away. But instead she says:

'I was under the impression that you lived in Borg.'

He keeps a firm grip on the note that Britt-Marie handed out at the start of the training session.

'It says here you have to have both your parents' signatures. So I have to go and ask my father to sign it.'

Britt-Marie nods.

'Ha. Have a good evening, then,' she says and starts walking towards the darkness.

'You want to come with me?' he calls out after her.

She turns around as if he's out of his mind. The paper in his hands is stained with sweat.

'I . . . it . . . I think it would feel better for me if you were there,' he manages to say.

It's obviously wholly ludicrous. Britt-Marie is scrupulous about telling him that throughout the whole bus journey.

Which takes almost an hour. And ends abruptly in front of an enormous white building. Britt-Marie is holding on to her handbag so tightly that she gets cramp in her fingers. She is, in spite of everything, a civilised person with a normal life to get on with.

Civilised people with normal lives are actually not in the habit of visiting prisons.

18

'Bloody gangsters', Kent always used to call them, the people who were responsible for things such as street violence, extortionate taxes, pickpocketing, graffiti in public toilets, and hotels where all the deckchairs were occupied when Kent came down to the pool. All things of this kind were caused by 'gangsters'. It was an effective system, always having people there to blame for everything without ever having to define who they really were.

Britt-Marie never found out what he really wanted. What would have satisfied him? Would a lot of money have been enough, or was every last penny required? One time when David and Pernilla were teenagers they gave him a coffee mug with a message on it: 'He Who Dies with the Most Toys Wins'. They said it was 'ironic' but Kent seemed to take it as a challenge. He always had a plan, there was always a 'bloody big deal' just around the corner. His company was just about to strike bigger and bigger deals in Germany, the flat they inherited from Britt-Marie's parents could finally be converted to a freehold so they could sell it for more money. Just a few more months. Just a few years. They got married because Kent's accountant said it made sense from a 'tax-planning perspective'. Britt-Marie never had a plan, she hoped it would be enough if you were faithful and in love. Until the day came when it wasn't enough.

'Bloody gangsters,' Kent would have said if he'd been sitting with Britt-Marie this evening, in the little waiting room in the prison. 'Put the criminals on a deserted island with a pistol each, and they'll clean up the sorry mess themselves.' Britt-Marie never liked him talking like that, but she never said anything. Now when she thinks about it she has difficulties remembering the last time she said anything at all, until one day she left him without a word. Because of this it always feels as if the whole thing was her fault.

She wonders what he's doing now. If he feels well and wears clean shirts. If he takes his medicine. If he looks for things in kitchen drawers and yells out her name before he remembers that she's no longer there. She wonders if he is with her, the young and beautiful woman, and if she likes pizza. Britt-Marie wonders what he would say if he knew she was sitting in a waiting room in a prison full of gangsters.

If he'd be worried. If he'd tell a joke at her expense. If he'd touch her and whisper that everything would be all right, like he used to do in the days after she had buried her mother.

They were very different people in those days. Britt-Marie doesn't know if it was Kent or herself who changed first. Or how much of it was her fault. She was ready to say 'everything' if she could only have her life back.

Pirate sits next to her, holding her hand, and Britt-Marie clutches his very hard in return.

'You mustn't tell my mum we were here,' he whispers.

'Where is she?'

'At the hospital.'

'Was she in an accident?'

'No, no, she works there,' says Pirate, before adding as if explaining a law of nature: 'All the mums in Borg work at the hospital.'

Britt-Marie doesn't know what to say to that.

'Why do they call you Pirate?' she asks instead.

'Because my father hid the treasure.'

As soon as she hears this, she decides she'll never call him 'Pirate' again.

A thick metal door opens and Sven stands in the doorway, sweaty and red-nosed, with his police cap in his hands.

'Is Mum livid again?' says Ben at once, with a sigh.

Sven slowly shakes his head. Puts his hand on the boy's shoulder.

Meets Britt-Marie's eyes.

'Ben's mother is on the night shift. She called me as soon as they called from here. I came as quick as I could.'

Britt-Marie would like to hug him, but she's a sensible person. The guards won't let Ben see his father because it isn't visiting hours, but after much persuasion Sven manages to get them to agree to take the paper into the prison. They come back with a signature. Next to the signature his father has written: 'LOVE YOU!'

Ben holds the paper so hard on their way back that it's illegible by the time they get to Borg. Neither he, Britt-Marie nor Sven utter a single word. There's not much you can say to a teenager who has to ask strangers in uniform for permission to see his father. But when they drop Ben off outside his house and his mother comes out, Britt-Marie feels it's appropriate to say something encouraging, so she makes an attempt with:

'It was very clean, Ben, I have to say. I have always imagined prisons to be dirty places, but this one certainly seemed very hygienic. That is something to be pleased about at least.'

Ben folds the paper with his father's signature without meeting her eyes, and then hands it to her. Sven quickly says:

'You should keep that, Ben.'

Ben nods and smiles and holds the paper even more tightly.

'Is there training tomorrow?' he murmurs.

Britt-Marie fumbles for her list in her bag, but Sven calmly assures him:

'Of course there's training tomorrow, Ben. Usual time.'

Ben peers at Britt-Marie. She tries to nod affirmatively. Ben starts up the path, then turns, smiles faintly and waves. They wait until he's buried his face in his mother's arms. Sven waves, but she doesn't see, just presses her face into her boy's hair and whispers something.

Sven drives slowly through Borg. Clears his throat uncomfortably as you do when you have a bad conscience.

'They haven't had such an easy time, Ben and her. She's working triple shifts so they can keep the house. He's a good boy, and his dad wasn't a bad man. Well, sure, I know what he did was wrong, tax evasion is a crime. But he was desperate. Financial crises can make people desperate, and desperation makes people foolish . . .'

He goes silent. Britt-Marie doesn't say anything about the financial crisis being over. For various reasons it doesn't strike her as appropriate on this particular occasion.

Sven has cleaned up the police car. All the pizza boxes have been removed from the floor, she notes. They drive past the patch of asphalt, where Sami and Psycho are playing football again this evening with their friends.

'Ben's father is not like them. I just want you to understand that he isn't a criminal. Not in the same way as those boys,' explains Sven.

'Sami is not like those boys either!' protests Britt-Marie, and the words slip out of her quickly: 'He's no gangster, he has a spectacularly well-organised cutlery drawer!'

Sven's laughter comes abruptly, deep and rolling, like a lit fire to warm your hands.

'No, no, there's nothing wrong with Sami. He just keeps bad company . . .'

'Vega seems to be of the opinion that he owes people money.'

'Not Sami, but Psycho does. Psycho always owes people money,' says Sven, and his laughter fades, spills on to the floor and disappears.

The police car slows down. The boys playing football see it, but they hardly react. There's a certain swagger about their disregard for the police. Sven narrows his eyes.

'Sami didn't have an easy time growing up either. More disasters have hit that family than you'd consider fair by anyone's reckoning, if you ask me. He's both mother and father as well as older brother to Vega and Omar, and that's not a responsibility anyone should put on the shoulders of a kid who hasn't even turned twenty.'

Possibly Britt-Marie wants to ask what this means, the bit about 'both mother and father', but she manages not to, so he continues:

'Psycho is his best friend, and has been since they were big enough to kick that ball around. Sami could have been a really good player, everyone saw his talent, but he was too busy surviving, perhaps.'

'What does that mean?' asks Britt-Marie, slightly wounded by the way Sven says it, as if she should understand, without an explanation.

Sven holds up his palm apologetically.

'Sorry, I . . . was thinking out loud. He, they, how should I explain it? Sami, Vega and Omar's mother did all she could but their father, he . . . he was not a good man, Britt-Marie. When he came home and had his anger attacks, people heard him all over Borg. And Sami was hardly old enough to go to school back then, but he took his younger siblings' hands and ran for it. Psycho met them outside their door, every time. Psycho carried Omar on his back and Sami carried Vega, and then they ran into the forest. Until their dad fell into a drunken stupor. Night after night, until their dad just cleared out one day. And then that thing happened with their mother . . . it . . .'

He falls silent, as you do when you realise once again that you're thinking out loud. He doesn't try to hide that he's hiding something, but Britt-Marie doesn't stick her nose in. Sven smooths the back of his hand over his eyebrows.

'Psycho grew into a properly dangerous lunatic, Sami knows that, but Sami's not the sort of person to turn his back on someone who once carried his younger siblings on his back. Maybe in a place like Borg you don't have the luxury of being able to choose your best friend.'

The police car once again starts rolling slowly down the road. The boys' football match continues. Psycho scores, roars something into the night and runs around the pitch with his arms extended as if he was an aircraft. Sami laughs so much that he keels over, hands on his knees. They look happy.

Britt-Marie doesn't know what to say, or what to believe.

She has never met a gangster with a correctly organised cutlery drawer.

Sven's gaze loses itself in some place where the headlights end and darkness begins.

'We do what we can in Borg. We always have done. But there's a fire burning in those boys, and sooner or later it will consume everyone around them, or themselves.'

'That was nicely put,' says Britt-Marie.

He smiles bashfully.

She looks down into her handbag. Then she dismays herself by going further:

'Do you have any children yourself?'

He shakes his head. Looks out of the window as you do if you don't have any children, yet in spite of all have a whole village full of children.

'I was married, but . . . ah. She never liked Borg. She said it was a place where you came to die, not live.'

He tries to smile. Britt-Marie wishes she had brought the bamboo screen along.

He bites his lip. When they should turn off by Bank's house, he seems to hesitate, then summons his courage and says:

'If it isn't, I mean, if it's not inconvenient to you I'd like to show you something.'

She doesn't protest. He smiles in a way you'd hardly notice. She smiles in a way no one could ever notice.

He drives the police car through Borg and out the other side. Turns off down a gravel track. It apparently goes on for ever, but when they finally stop it suddenly seems inconceivable that they were just in a built-up area. The car is surrounded by trees, and the silence is of a sort that only exists where there are no people.

'It's . . . well . . . ah. It's probably ridiculous, of course, but this is my . . . well, my favourite place on earth . . .' mumbles Sven.

He blushes. Looks like he wants to turn the car around and drive away fast and never mention it again. But Britt-Marie opens her door and gets out.

They are standing on a rock over a lake held tight by trees on all sides.

Britt-Marie peers down over the edge until she feels a queasiness in her stomach. The sky is clear and bright with stars. Sven opens his door and comes up behind her and clears his throat.

'I . . . ah. It's silly, but I wanted you to see that Borg can be beautiful as well,' he whispers.

Britt-Marie closes her eyes. She feels the wind in her hair.

'Thank you,' she whispers back.

They don't speak on the way back. He gets out of the car outside Bank's house, runs around and opens Britt-Marie's door. Then he opens the door of the back seat and fumbles with something, coming back with a well-thumbed plastic folder.

'It's . . . ah, it's just . . . something,' he manages to say.

It's a drawing. Of the recreation centre and the pizzeria, and in between the children playing football. Britt-Marie in the middle of the picture. Everything done in pencil. Britt-Marie holds on to it a little too hard, and Sven removes his police cap a little too suddenly.

'Well, it's probably silly, of course, of course it is, but I was thinking . . . there's a restaurant in town . . .'

When Britt-Marie doesn't answer at once he adds briskly:

'A proper restaurant, I mean! Not like the pizzeria here in Borg, but a nice one. With white tablecloths. And cutlery.'

It will be quite a long time before Britt-Marie realises that he tries to hide his insecurity with jokes, rather than the other way around. But when she does not immediately seem to understand, he holds up his palm and apologises:

'Not that there's anything wrong with the pizzeria, of course not, of course not, but . . .'

He's holding his police cap in both hands now, and looking

like considerably younger men do when they want to ask considerably younger women something specific. There is so much inside Britt-Marie that yearns to know what it is. But the sensible part inside her has already gone into the hall and closed the door.

19

'The other woman' is what it's called, but Britt-Marie always had difficulties viewing Kent's other woman as that. Maybe because she herself knew how it felt to be that woman. Admittedly Kent had already divorced when he came back to the house that day, a lifetime earlier, after Britt-Marie had buried her mother, but his children never saw it that way. Children never see it that way. As far as David and Pernilla were concerned, Britt-Marie was the other woman regardless of how many fairy tales she read them and how many dinners she cooked – and maybe Kent also regarded her as such. And despite the number of shirts she had washed, maybe Britt-Marie never quite felt like the primary woman herself.

She sits on the balcony watching the morning dawdling over Borg, as mornings in Borg have a habit of doing in January. Daylight comes apparently without any need for the sun to rise. She is still holding Sven's drawing.

He is not an especially good drawer, far from it, and if she'd been more critical by nature she might have had reservations about what the blurred contours and irregular silhouettes were saying about the way he saw her. But at least he saw her. It's difficult to steel oneself against that.

She fetches her mobile and calls the girl at the unemployment office.

The girl's voice answers very gaily, so Britt-Marie understands it has to be the telephone answering machine. Obviously she intends to hang up, because she doesn't find it appropriate leaving messages on answering machines unless you're calling from a hospital or selling narcotics. But for some reason or other she doesn't hang up; instead she sits in silence after the peep and declares at last:

'This is Britt-Marie. One of the children in the football team hit something he was aiming for today. I felt you might be interested to hear that.'

She feels silly when she hangs up. Obviously the girl won't be interested in that. Kent would have laughed at her if he was here.

Bank is sitting in the kitchen having soup when Britt-Marie comes down the stairs. The dog is sitting next to the table, waiting. Britt-Marie stops in the hall and looks at the soup plate. She wonders how the soup was cooked, because she sees no saucepan and the kitchen doesn't have a microwave. Bank is slurping.

'Did you have something to say, or is it just that you never saw a blind person having soup before?' she asks without lifting her head.

'I was under the impression you had *impaired vision*.'

Bank slurps loudly by way of an answer. Britt-Marie presses the palms of her hands against her skirt.

'You like football, I understand,' she says, nodding at the photographs on the walls.

'No,' says Bank.

Britt-Marie clasps her hands together over her stomach and looks at the rows of photographs on the wall, each one of them of Bank and her father and at least one football.

'I've become a sort of coach for a team.'

'I heard.' She starts slurping again. Doesn't raise her head. Britt-Marie brushes some specks of dust from various objects in the hall.

'Ha. At any rate I noticed all the photographs, so I felt it was appropriate under the circumstances, bearing in mind your obvious experience of football, that I asked you for a piece of advice.'

'A piece of advice about what?'

'About football.' She doesn't know if Bank rolls her eyes, but it certainly feels as if she does. The dog goes into the living room. Bank walks behind, running her stick along the walls.

'Where are these photos you're talking about?' she asks.

'Higher up.'

Bank's stick taps the glass of one of the framed photos, in which a younger version of herself is standing, wearing a jersey so badly stained that not even bicarbonate of soda would have helped. Bank leans towards the photo until her nose is almost touching the glass. Then she moves around the room and taps systematically at all the photos, as if memorising where they are.

Britt-Marie stands in the hall and waits for what she considers to be an appropriate length of time, until the whole thing stops being merely uncomfortable and starts getting downright odd. Then she puts on her coat and opens the door. Just before it closes, Bank grunts behind her:

'You want some good advice? That team can't play. Nothing you do will make any difference.'

Britt-Marie whispers, 'Ha,' and walks out.

She locks herself into the laundry at the recreation centre. Sits on one of the stools while her skirt, still muddy from the truck incident, spins around in the washing machine. Once she has got dressed and fixed her hair, she stands for a long time in the kitchen observing the coffee percolator that was destroyed by flying stones.

Britt-Marie decides to assemble an entire piece of IKEA furniture that day and for some reason ends up doing so at the pizzeria. It takes the best part of ten hours, because there are actually three items of furniture – one table and two chairs. Intended for balconies. Britt-Marie pushes them as far as they'll go into a corner, puts out kitchen roll as a tablecloth, and then sits there on her own eating pizza that Somebody has baked for her. It is a remarkable day in Britt-Marie's life, unique even among the consistently remarkable days she's had since arriving in Borg.

Sven has his dinner at another table in the pizzeria, but they have their coffee together. Without saying anything to one another. Just trying to get used to the presence of the other person. As you do when it's been a long time since anyone's presence had a physical effect on you. A long time since a person could be sensed without physically touching at all.

Karl comes in to pick up a parcel. Sits down at a table in the corner and has a cup of coffee beside the men with caps and beards. They continue to intentionally ignore Britt-Marie, as if this might make her disappear. Vega comes in with the football under her arm, as dirty as only a child can get in the short distance between her older brother's car and a pizzeria. Omar comes in behind her and, when he sees Britt-Marie's newly assembled balcony furniture, immediately tries to flog her some furniture polish.

When Britt-Marie walks out to go to the training session, Sven stands up with his police cap in his hands, but he doesn't say anything and she speeds up to make sure he doesn't have the opportunity.

Ben's mother is standing outside the door. She is wearing her hospital clothes and holding something in her hands.

'Hello Britt-Marie. We haven't met, but I'm Ben's mo—'

'I'm aware of who you are,' says Britt-Marie guardedly, as if preparing to be spattered with mud again by a passing truck.

'I just wanted to say thank you for, well . . . for seeing Ben. Not many grown-ups do,' says Ben's mother, and holds out what she has in her hands.

It's a bottle of Faxin. Britt-Marie is dumbstruck. Ben's mother clears her throat awkwardly.

'I hope it doesn't seem silly. Ben asked Omar what you liked and Omar said you liked this. He gave us a special deal, so we . . . well, Ben and I, we wanted to say thanks. For everything.'

Britt-Marie holds the bottle as if she's afraid of dropping it. Ben's mother takes a step back, then stops and adds:

'We want you to know there's another Borg than the one

145

with a couple of old blokes sitting in a pizzeria boozing all day. There are the rest of us as well. Those of us who haven't given up.'

With that she turns around before Britt-Marie has a chance to respond, gets into a little car and drives off. The training begins and Britt-Marie calls the register and makes a note on her list, and the children do 'the Idiot', because that's the next item on Britt-Marie's list after 'Take register'.

The children hardly complain at all, the one exception being when Vega asks if they've practised enough, and Britt-Marie says they have, and Vega immediately gets stirred up and yells something about how this team will never improve if their coach goes easy on them!

Children are beyond understanding, this much is abundantly clear. So Britt-Marie writes in her list how they have to 'do the Idiot' more and that's precisely what they do. After that they gather in a ring around Britt-Marie and look like they expect her to say something, and Britt-Marie goes to Sami, who's sitting on the bonnet of his black car, and asks him what sort of thing this might be.

'Ah, you know. They've been running and now they want to play. Give them a pep talk and just toss the ball to them.'

'A pep talk?'

'Something encouraging,' he clarifies.

Britt-Marie thinks about it for a while, then turns to the children and says with all the encouragement she can muster:

'Try not to get too dirty.'

Sami laughs. The children look utterly perplexed, and start a practice match. Toad, who's the goalkeeper at one end, lets in more goals than anyone else. Seven or eight, one after the other. Every time it happens his face turns completely scarlet and he roars: 'Come on now! Let's TURN THIS THING AROUND!'

Sami laughs about that every time. This makes Britt-Marie nervous, so she asks:

'Why is he behaving like that?'

'He has a dad who supports Liverpool,' Sami answers without elaboration.

He grabs two cans from the back of the car, and gives one of them to Britt-Marie. 'If you have a dad who supports Liverpool you always fucking think you can turn anything around. You know! Ever since that Champions League final.'

Britt-Marie sips her soft drink from the can and thinks that, by doing this, she is finally beyond all limits of honour and decency. So she decides she might as well say what she feels:

'I don't want to be unpleasant in any way, Sami, because you have a quite impeccable cutlery drawer. But by and large I find everything you say utterly mystifying!'

Sami guffaws.

'You too, Britt-Marie. You too.'

Then he tells her about a football game, almost a decade ago, at a time when Vega and Omar were hardly out of their nappies, yet nonetheless sat there with him and Psycho in the pizzeria. Liverpool were up against Milan in the Champions League final. Britt-Marie asks whether this is a competition, and Sami answers that it's a cup, and Britt-Marie asks what a cup is, and Sami says it's a sort of competition, whereupon Britt-Marie points out that he could just have said that from the start instead of giving himself airs and graces.

Sami gives a deep breath, which is not at all a sigh.

Then he explains that Milan were in the lead by 3–0 at half-time, and no team in any final of any football competition for as long as Sami can remember had ever been so exposed and outplayed as Liverpool in this match. But in the changing rooms, one of the players from the Liverpool team stood yelling like a madman at the others, because he would not go along with a world where there were certain things that could not be turned around. In the second half he headed in a goal to make it 3–1, then waved his arms like crazy and ran back down the pitch. When his team scored again to make it 3–2 he was on his way to heaven, because he and all the others saw it now, saw that there was an avalanche in motion and no one could stop them from turning it around. Not with walls, moats and ten thousand wild horses would it be possible to hold them back.

They equalised to make it 3–3, survived extra time, then won on penalties.

You can't tell someone with a father who supports Liverpool that everything can't be turned around after that.

He looks at Vega and Omar and smiles.

'Or an older brother, I suppose. It could be an older brother too.'

Britt-Marie sips her goalpost. 'It sounds almost poetic, the way you describe it.'

Sami grins.

'Football is poetry for me, you know. I was born in the summer of 1994, right in the middle of the World Cup.'

Britt-Marie doesn't have a clue what that's supposed to mean, but she doesn't ask because she thinks there has to be some limit to the anecdotes, even if they happen to be poetic.

'Does Toad's dad come here to watch him play?' she asks.

'He's standing right there,' says Sami, pointing at the pizzeria.

Karl stands in the doorway drinking coffee. He has a red cap on his head. Looks almost happy. It's a very remarkable day for Britt-Marie. A remarkable game.

Sven is waiting for her in the pizzeria at the end of the session. He offers her a lift home, but she insists that there's no need. Then he asks her if he can drive her balcony furniture back instead, and at long last she agrees to that. He's carried it out and loaded it and almost got into the driver's seat when she closes her eyes and summons all the energy she has in order to blurt out:

'I have dinner at six.'

'Sorry?' says Sven after his head has popped up on the other side of the police car.

She digs her heels into the mud.

'It's not as if I have to have a white tablecloth on the table. But I want cutlery and I want us to eat at six.'

'Tomorrow?' he says effervescently.

She nods grimly and gets her list out.

When the police car has disappeared down the road, Vega, Omar and Sami call out to her from the other side of the parking area. Sami is grinning. Vega shoots the ball all the way across the gravel and mud, and it comes to a stop a metre away from her. Britt-Marie puts her list in her handbag and holds on to the latter so hard that her knuckles turn white, as you do when you have waited a whole life for something to begin.

Then she takes a few very small steps forward and kicks the football as hard as she can.

Because she no longer knows how not to.

20

Today is the day after, and it's one of the absolutely worst days of Britt-Marie's life. She has a bump on her head and apparently she has broken two fingers. At least that is what Ben's mother tells her, and Ben's mother is a nurse, after all, so Britt-Marie has to assume she is qualified to comment on such matters. They are sitting on a little bench behind a curtain at a hospital in town. Britt-Marie has a plaster on her forehead and her hand in a bandage, and she's doing her absolute utmost not to cry. Ben's mother keeps her hand on her sore wrist, but she doesn't ask how all this happened. Britt-Marie is grateful for that, because she'd rather no one ever found out.

Having said that, this is how it all did happen:

To begin with, Britt-Marie slept all night through, which was the first time since she had come to Borg. She slept the unreflective sleep of a child, and she woke up in great spirits. Another day. This alone should immediately have made her suspicious, because little good can come of waking up all enthusiastic like that. She leapt out of bed and immediately started cleaning Bank's kitchen. Not because she needed to but rather because Bank wasn't at home and the kitchen was just there when Britt-Marie came down the stairs. Simply put, she had never met a kitchen she did not want to clean. After this was done, she took a walk through Borg to the recreation centre. Then cleaned it from top to bottom. Made sure all the pictures were hanging straight, even the ones with footballs in them. She stood absolutely still in front of them and looked at her reflection in the glass of the frames.

Then rubbed the white mark on her ring finger. People who have not worn a wedding ring for almost their entire lives are unaware of how a mark like that looks. Some people take theirs off from time to time – while doing the washing-up, for instance – but Britt-Marie had never once taken off her ring until the day she took it off once and for all. So the white mark is permanent, as if her skin had another colour when she was married. As if this is what is left of her, underneath, if you scrape off everything she turned into.

With this thought in mind Britt-Marie set off for the pizzeria, to wake up Somebody. They drank coffee and Britt-Marie enquired in a friendly way about postcards and whether Somebody happened to stock them. Somebody did indeed. They were extremely old and had the caption 'Welcome to Borg' written across them. That was how you knew they were old, said Somebody; it was a long time since anyone uttered those words.

Britt-Marie wrote a postcard to Kent. Her message was very short. 'Hello. This is from Britt-Marie. Sorry for all the pain I have caused you. I hope you are feeling well. I hope you have clean shirts. Your electric shaver is in the third drawer in the bathroom. If you need to get on to the balcony to polish the windows you have to wiggle the door handle a bit, pull it towards you and give the door a little shove. There is Faxin in the broom cupboard.' She wanted to describe how much she missed him. But didn't. Didn't want to cause any bother.

'Might I ask for directions to the nearest postbox?' she asked Somebody.

'Here,' Somebody replied and pointed to the palm of her hand.

Britt-Marie immediately looked sceptical, but Somebody promised that her postal service was 'the fastest in town!'

Then the two women had a short discussion about the yellow jersey hanging on the wall in the pizzeria, with the word 'Bank' emblazoned on its back, because Britt-Marie couldn't quite manage to stop looking at it.

As if it was a clue to some mystery. Somebody explained helpfully that Bank did not know it had been hung up there, and if she found out she would probably be so angry that Somebody thought she might behave like a person 'with something shoved up her arse, like a whole bloody what's-it-called? Lemon tree orchard!'

'Why?'

'You know, Bank hate football, huh! What's-it-called? No one like memories of good time when times are bad, huh?'

'I was under the impression that you and Bank were good friends.'

'We are! We were! Best mates before, you know. The whole thing with eyes. Before Bank moved, huh.'

'But you never talk about football?'

Somebody laughed drily.

'In the old days – Bank loved football, huh. Loved more than life. Then this thing with eyes, huh. Eyes took football from her, so now she hates football. You understand? That's how life is, huh? Love, hate, one or the other. So she went away. Long, long time, huh. Bank's old man not like Bank at all, huh, without football they had nothing to, what's-it-called? Converse about! Then the old man died. Bank came here to bury and sell the house, huh. She and me now, we are more like, what's-it-called? Drinking buddies! You could say, we talk less now. Drink more.'

'Ha. Might one ask where she went when she left Borg?'

'You know, here and there, when you have lemon in your arse you don't want to sit still, do you?' laughed Somebody.

Britt-Marie didn't laugh. Somebody cleared her throat.

'She was in London, Lisbon, Paris, I got one of them postcards! Have it somewhere, huh. Bank and dog, around the world. You know, sometimes I think she left because she was angry. But sometimes I think she went because this thing with eyes gets worse and worse, you know? Maybe Bank want to see the world before completely blind, you see?'

She found the postcard from Paris. Britt-Marie wanted so badly to hold it in her hand, but she stopped herself. Instead, she tried to distract both Somebody and herself by pointing at the wall and asking:

'Why is the jersey yellow? I was under the impression that football jerseys in Borg are white.'

'National team.'

'Ha. Is that something special?'

'It's . . . national team,' said Somebody, as if she found the question odd.

'Is it hard to get into that?'

'It's . . . national team,' answered Somebody, looking bemused.

Britt-Marie was annoyed by this, so she didn't ask anything else. Instead she suddenly blurted out, to her own consternation:

'How did it happen? How did Bank lose her sight?'

Not that Britt-Marie is the sort who sticks her nose into other people's business, obviously, but still. She did wake up feeling enthusiastic today, and obviously anything can happen when you do. Her common sense was yelling at her inside, but by then it was already too late.

'Disease. Bloody crap. Came, what's-it-called? Sneaking along! Many years. Like financial crisis . . .'

Somebody's eyebrows sank towards her jumper. 'You know, Britt-Marie, people say Bank good IN SPITE this thing with the eyes, huh. I say Bank good BECAUSE this thing with her eyes. You understand? Had to fight harder than everyone else. Therefore – she became the best. What's-it-called? Incentive! You understand?'

Britt-Marie wasn't entirely sure that she did. She wanted to take the chance of asking Somebody how it had come to pass that she was in a wheelchair, but at this point the sensible part of Britt-Marie put a stop to things, and in this she was backed up by common practice, because it certainly wasn't seemly to ask questions of this nature. So the conversation tailed off. Whereupon Somebody rolled back one full turn of the wheels, and then forward one turn.

'I fell off one of them boats. When I was small, huh. If you wondering.'

'I certainly wasn't wondering!' insisted Britt-Marie.

'I know, Britt, I know,' said Somebody, grinning. 'You don't have prejudice. You get that I am human, huh. Happen to have the wheelchair. I not wheelchair that happens to have human in it, huh.' She patted Britt-Marie on the arm and added: 'That is why I like you, Britt. You are also human.'

Britt-Marie wanted to say she also liked Somebody, but she was sensible about it.

So they didn't say anything else. Britt-Marie bought a Snickers for the rat and asked if Somebody happened to know of anywhere that sold flowers.

'Flower? For who?'

'For Bank. It strikes me as impolite when I am renting a room from her for all this time that I have never offered her so much as a flower, it's common practice to give flowers.'

'But Bank likes beer! Take her beer instead, huh?'

Britt-Marie didn't find this very civilised, but she accepted that beer might be a little like flowers to someone who liked beer. She insisted on Somebody finding a bit of cellophane, which Somebody failed to do, but after a few minutes Omar showed up in the doorway and cried: 'You need cellophane? I have some! Special price for a friend!'

Because that is clearly how things happen in Borg.

With this cellophane, which came at a price that Britt-Marie was certainly not prepared to categorise as very friendly at all, Britt-Marie wrapped up a can of beer to make it look decorative, with a little bow at the top and everything. Then she went to the recreation centre, left the front door ajar and put a plate with the Snickers on the threshold. Next to the plate she put a note, written neatly in ink: 'Out on a date. Or a meeting. Or whatever it's called nowadays. No need to put away your plate when you have finished, it's no trouble at all for me.' She wanted to write something about how she hoped the rat would find someone else to share its dinner with, because she did not feel the rat deserved to eat alone. Loneliness is a waste of both rats and people. But her common sense ordered her not to get involved in the rat's personal choices about social relationships, so she left it at that.

She turned off the lights and waited for dusk, because, conveniently enough, at this time of year the sun set well in advance of dinnertime. Once she had made sure that no one could see her, she briskly set off for the bus stop on the road leading out of Borg in two directions, and left in one of those two available directions, on a bus. It felt like an adventure. Like freedom. Not to the extent that she was unconcerned about the state of the seat, obviously, so she tidily spread four white napkins over it before sitting down. You had to have some limits, after all, even when you were out adventuring.

But in spite of all: it felt like something new, travelling on a bus on her own.

All the way, she rubbed the white mark on her ring finger.

The tanning salon next to the cash machine in the town was deserted. Britt-Marie followed the instructions on a machine that told her to put coins in it. Its display started flashing, and then half a dozen large fluorescent tubes in the hard plastic bed turned themselves on.

Britt-Marie is no connoisseur when it comes to solariums, and as a result she was possibly not very familiar with the basic functions of the machine. Her idea had been to sit on a stool next to the lit-up bed, sticking her hand into the light and gently closing the lid on top of it. How long she would have to sit there bronzing her hand into one without a white mark on it she did not know, but she imagined that the process could not be more elaborate than cooking salmon in the oven. Her plan was to simply remove her hand now and then and see how it was all going.

It must have been something to do with the soporific humming of the machine, perhaps, as well as the heat of it, especially as she had gone around all day being enthusiastic – that was how it happened. Her head slumped, as one's head has a way of doing when one goes to sleep on a stool, and then her forehead struck the lid of the tanning machine very hard, and her hand got horribly twisted under the lid. She rolled on to the floor and passed out, and now she's in hospital. With a bump on her head and broken fingers.

Ben's mother is sitting next to her, patting her on the arm.

The cleaning staff found her, and this makes Britt-Marie even more indignant, because everyone knows how cleaning staff gossip at their meetings.

'Don't be upset, things like this happen to the best of us,' whispers Ben's mother encouragingly.

'No, they don't,' says Britt-Marie, so that her voice cracks. She slips off the bench. Ben's mother holds out her hand but Britt-Marie glides away. 'Enough people in Borg are giving up, Britt-Marie. Don't become one of them, please.'

Britt-Marie may want to retort something, but humiliation and common sense compel her to leave the room. The children from the football team are sitting in the waiting room. Quite decimated, Britt-Marie avoids their eyes. This is something new to her – the feeling of having yearned for something, only to collapse on the ground. Britt-Marie is not used to hoping.

So she walks past the children and wishes with all her heart that they were not here.

Sven is waiting with his cap in his hands. He has brought a little basket with baguettes in it.

'Well, ah, I thought that . . . well, I thought you wouldn't want to go to the restaurant now . . . after all this, so I made a picnic. I thought . . . but, yeah, maybe you'd rather just go home. Of course.' Britt-Marie shuts her eyes hard and holds her bandaged hand behind her back. He looks down into his basket.

'I bought the baguettes but I wove the basket myself.'

Britt-Marie sucks her cheeks in and bites them. There's no way Sven and the children knew what she was doing in the salon, but this makes her feel all the more ridiculous. So she whispers:

'Please, Sven, I just want to go home.'

So Sven drives her to Bank's house, even though she wishes he wouldn't. And wishes he'd never seen her like this. She hides her hand under the bamboo screen and more than anything she'd like to be taken back to her proper home. Her real life. And be dropped off there. She's not ready for enthusiasm.

He tries to say something when they stop, but she gets out before he has time. He's still standing outside his police car with his cap in his hands when she closes the front door. She stands motionless on the other side, holding her breath until he leaves.

She cleans Bank's house from top to bottom. Has soup for dinner, alone. Then slowly walks up the stairs, fetches a towel and sits on the side of the bed.

21

Bank comes home spectacularly drunk somewhere between midnight and dawn. She is carrying a pizza box from Somebody's pizzeria, and is singing songs so uncivilised that they'd make a sailor blush. Britt-Marie sits on the balcony and the dog seems to look up at her, establishing eye contact as Bank stands there swearing and fidgeting with the key in the lock. The dog almost appears to shrug its shoulders in weary resignation. Britt-Marie can empathise.

The first thump from downstairs is the sound of a picture frame being knocked off the wall by Bank's stick. The second thump is followed by a splintering sound, when the frame hits the floor and the sheet of glass on a photograph of a football-playing girl and her father is broken and scatters all over the floor. This continues methodically for almost an hour. Bank wanders about on the ground floor, here and there, then here again, smashing all her memories, not furiously and violently but with the simple, systematic approach of grief. One by one the pictures are broken, until only empty walls and abandoned nails remain. Britt-Marie sits motionless on the balcony and wishes she could call the police. But she doesn't have Sven's telephone number.

And then finally the noise stops. Britt-Marie stays on the balcony until she realises Bank must have given up and gone to sleep. Shortly afterwards she hears soft steps on the stairs, a creak of her door, and then feels something touching the tips of her fingers. The dog's nose. It lies beside her, sufficiently far away not to be intrusive, but close enough for each to sense the other's presence in case of movement. After that everything is quiet until morning comes to Borg, to the extent that morning comes at all to Borg.

When Britt-Marie and the dog finally dare to come downstairs, Bank is sitting on the floor in the hall, leaning against the wall. She smells of alcohol. Britt-Marie doesn't know if she's sleeping, but she's certainly not about to lift her sunglasses to check, so instead she just fetches a brush and starts sweeping up the glass. Collects all the photographs and puts them in a neat pile. Stacks the frames one against the other in a corner. Gives the dog breakfast.

Bank is still not moving by the time Britt-Marie puts on her coat and makes sure she has her list in her handbag, but Britt-Marie nonetheless collects herself and puts the beer next to her and says:

'This is a present. I should like to insist that you don't drink it today, because it seems to me that you had quite enough yesterday, and if you're ever to smell like a civilised person again you'll need a bath in bicarbonate of soda and vanilla essence, but don't think I'm trying to stick my nose into your business.'

Bank is sitting so still that Britt-Marie has to lean forward to assure herself that she is breathing. The fact that Bank's breath seems to be burning off the surface of Britt-Marie's retinas indicates that she's doing exactly that. Britt-Marie blinks and straightens up and suddenly hears herself saying the following:

'I suppose I have to assume you're not the sort of person whose father was a supporter of Liverpool. You see, I've been informed that anyone whose father supported Liverpool never gives up . . . Or an older brother. As I understand it, in some cases the same thing also goes for an older brother who supports Liverpool.'

She stands on the front porch and has all but closed the front

159

door behind her when she hears Bank mumbling from inside the gloom:

'Dad was a Tottenham supporter.'

Somebody is sitting in the kitchen of the pizzeria and smelling just like Bank, though her mood is a good deal better. If she notices Britt-Marie's bandaged hand she certainly says nothing about it. She hands Britt-Marie a letter that 'some bloke from town' apparently brought in.

'Something about that football coach. "For the attention of the coach".'

'Ha,' says Britt-Marie. She reads the paper without properly understanding what it means – something about 'the need for registration' and 'a licence'.

She is far too busy to concern herself with some silly letter, so she stuffs it in her bag and sets about serving coffee to the men with caps and beards, who have their heads buried in their newspapers. She doesn't ask for the crossword supplements and they don't offer her any either. Karl picks up a parcel and has some coffee. When he's done, he takes his cup to the counter, nods at Britt-Marie without looking at her and mumbles, 'Thanks, that was nice.'

Britt-Marie's common sense prevents her from asking what he could possibly be getting in the post all the time, which is probably just as well. Those parcels could have anything in them. Maybe he's building a bomb. That's the sort of thing you read about. Admittedly Karl seems a taciturn sort of man who mostly keeps himself to himself and doesn't bother other people, but in fact this is precisely the sort of person neighbours describe whenever a bit of bomb-making has been going on.

Crossword puzzle writers like bombs, so Britt-Marie knows all about it.

Sami and Psycho come in after lunch. Psycho lingers by the door, with something doleful in his eyes as he scans the premises, apparently looking for something he's lost. Britt-Marie must be

160

visibly unsettled by this, because Sami gives her a calming look and then turns to Psycho and says:

'Can you go and check if I left my phone in the car?'

'Why?' asks Psycho.

'Because I'm fucking asking you to!'

Psycho does something with his lips as if he's spitting without any saliva in his mouth. The door tinkles cheerfully behind him. Sami turns to Britt-Marie.

'Did you win?'

Britt-Marie stares at him, nonplussed. His face cracks open in a purposeful grin as he points at her bandaged fingers:

'Looks like you've been in a fight. What kind of state did you leave the other lady in?'

'I'll have you know it was an accident,' protests Britt-Marie, praying she'll be able to avoid going into the details.

'OK, Coach, OK,' laughs Sami, with a flurry of play punches in the air. He produces a bag, gets out three football jerseys from it and puts them on the counter. 'This is Vega, Omar and Dino's kit. I've washed them over and over, but some of the stains won't bloody go away whatever I do.'

'Have you tried bicarbonate of soda?'

'Would that help?'

Britt-Marie has to grab hold of the till to contain her enthusiasm.

'I . . . it's . . . I can try to get rid of the stains for you. It's no trouble at all!'

Sami nods gratefully.

'Thanks, Coach. I could do with a few pointers. I mean the stains on these kids' clothes, anyone would think they live in the fucking trees.'

Britt-Marie waits until he has left with Psycho before she goes to the recreation centre. The stains do go away with bicarbonate of soda. She also washes towels and aprons for Somebody, even though Somebody insists there's no need. Not that Somebody has a problem with Britt-Marie doing the washing for her, it's more because she really doesn't think the laundry needs doing.

They have a brief dispute about this. Somebody calls Britt-Marie 'Mary Poppins' again and Britt-Marie retorts that she's a 'filthy little piglet'. Somebody bursts out laughing about this, at which point the argument runs out of steam.

Britt-Marie puts out some Snickers for the rat. She doesn't wait until it appears, because she doesn't want to explain how things went with her date. Not that she's sure the rat will be keen to know about it, but either way she's not ready to talk about it yet. Afterwards, she goes back to the pizzeria to have her dinner with Somebody, because Somebody seems to care either too little or too much about Britt-Marie to ask.

Sven doesn't pass by the pizzeria that evening, but Britt-Marie catches herself leaping out of her chair, her heart racing, every time there's a tinkle from the door. It wouldn't have annoyed her even if he showed up in the middle of their meal. But it's never Sven. Just one or other of the children, until they're all assembled, with crisp, clean football jerseys, because the children seem to have someone at home taking care of that.

This fills Britt-Marie with a sort of hope for Borg. That there are still people here who understand the value of a freshly washed football jersey.

The children are on their way out to start their training when the boy turns up in the doorway. He is wearing his tracksuit top with 'Hockey' written on it, but there's no sign of his dad.

'What the hell are you doing here?' Vega wants to know.

The boy pushes his hands deep into his pockets and nods at the football in her hands.

'I was hoping to play with you – can I?'

'You can clear off to town and play there!' hisses Vega.

The boy's chin is resting against his collarbone, but he doesn't back off.

'The football team in town trains at six o'clock. That's when I have my hockey training. But I noticed that you train later . . .'

Britt-Marie has a clear perception of needing to defend that decision, so she says:

'You actually can't train in the middle of dinner!'

'Not in the middle of hockey either,' says the boy.

'You don't belong here, bloody rich kid,' sneers Vega as she elbows past him. 'We're not as good as the team in town, anyway, so why don't you clear off and play with them if you want to play football!'

Still he doesn't back off. She stops. He raises his chin.

'I couldn't give a shit if you're good. I just want to play. That's how a team is made.'

Vega pushes her way outside with a choice of words that, as far as Britt-Marie is concerned, is far from civilised, but Omar gives the boy a soft shove in the back and says:

'If you can get the ball off her you're in. I don't think you've got the guts to do it, though.'

The boy has rushed across the parking area before the sentence comes to an end. Vega elbows him in the face. He stumbles on to his knees with blood in his nostrils, but at the same time he sticks out his foot and scoops out the ball, in a long hook. Vega falls and scrapes her entire body through the gravel, a warlike expression in her eyes. Omar nudges Britt-Marie, standing in the pizzeria doorway, and points at them with excitement: 'Check it out now, when Vega gives him, like, the worst sliding tackle!'

'What does that mean?' asks Britt-Marie, but she soon finds out when Vega darts across the pitch and, a few metres behind the boy, catapults herself through the air with both legs stretched out, sliding across the gravel until she collides with the boy's feet and sends his body into a wild half-somersault through the gloom.

That is how Britt-Marie comes to realise why all the children in Borg have jeans that are ripped across their thighs. Vega stands up and puts her foot on the ball in a gesture not so much of ownership but of domination. The boy brushes himself off a bit, displaying an alarming need for bicarbonate of soda, and digs sharp pebbles out of the skin of his face. Vega looks at Britt-Marie, shrugs her shoulders and snorts:

'He's OK.'

Britt-Marie gets out the list from her handbag.

'Would you be good enough to state your name?' she asks.

'Max,' says the boy.

Omar, with great seriousness, points first at Vega and then at Max.

'You CANNOT play in the same team when we're playing two-goals!'

Then they do the Idiot. Play two-goals. And they are a team. Sami couldn't come tonight to light up the pitch with his headlights, but there's another vehicle in the same place with its headlights turned on. It's Karl's truck, with such an impressive amount of rust down its sides it seems unlikely that such a length of time could have passed since the invention of trucks.

22

When the woman and the man in the red car stop at the far end of the parking area, neither Britt-Marie nor the children react at first, because they're starting to get used to new players and spectators turning up at Borg football team's training sessions as if it was the most natural thing in the world. Only when Max points at them and says, 'They're from town, aren't they? She's the head of the district football association, my dad knows her', does play stop and the players and coach wait suspiciously for the strangers to present themselves.

'Are you Britt-Marie?' asks the woman as she comes closer.

She is neatly dressed, as is the man. The red car is extremely clean, notes Britt-Marie with an initial sense of approval from her old life, which is quickly replaced by an instinctual scepticism that she has picked up in Borg for all things that seem neat and clean. 'I am,' answers Britt-Marie.

'I dropped off a document for you earlier today, have you had time to look through it?' asks the woman, with a gesture at the pizzeria.

'Ha. Ha. No, no, I haven't. I have been otherwise engaged.'

The woman looks at the children. Then at Britt-Marie.

'It's about the rules of the competition, the January Cup, for which this . . . *team* . . . has been entered.'

She says the word 'team' in much the same way as Britt-Marie says 'cup' when she's got a plastic mug in her hand.

'Ha,' says Britt-Marie, picking up her notebook and pen, as if arming herself.

'You are named as the football coach in the application. Do you have a licence for that?'

'I beg your pardon?' says Britt-Marie, while at the same time writing 'licence' in her notebook.

'L-i-c-e-n-c-e,' the woman repeats, pointing at the man beside her as if he was someone Britt-Marie ought to recognise: 'The District Football Association and the County Council only allow teams to participate in the January Cup if they have a coach with a local authority coaching licence.'

Britt-Marie writes, 'Acquire local authority coaching licence' in her notebook.

'Ha. Might I trouble you to tell me how I can get my hands on such a licence? I will immediately see to it that my contact at the unemployment office ensures th—'

'But good Lord, it's not something you just PICK UP! You have to do an entire COURSE in it!' the man next to the woman in front of the red car bursts out a touch hysterically.

Angrily he waves his hand over the parking area. 'You're not a proper team! You don't even have a pitch to train on!'

At this stage Vega gets fed up, because Vega's patience is quite clearly of the very shortest kind, and she hisses back at him:

'Hey, you miserable old sod, are we playing football here or not?'

'What?' says the old sod.

'Are you deaf? I said: are we playing bloody football here or are we bloody not?' roars Vega.

'Well?' says the old sod with a mocking smile, throwing out his arms.

'If we're playing football here then it *is* a bloody football pitch,' Vega establishes.

The old sod looks at Britt-Marie in shock, as if he feels she ought to say something. Britt-Marie actually feels this would not be so appropriate, because just for once, apart from her use of language, she feels that Vega is absolutely right. So she stays silent. The woman next to the old sod clears her throat.

'There's an absolutely excellent football club in town, I'm quite sure that—'

'We have an absolutely excellent football club here!' Vega interrupts.

The woman is breathing spasmodically through her nostrils.

'We have to have rules and regulations for the January Cup. Otherwise more or less anyone could turn up and play. That would be chaotic, you have to understand that. If you don't have an accredited trainer we can't let you participate, unfortunately; in that case you'll have to reapply next year and then we'll process the—'

The voice that interrupts her, somewhere in the dark between the red car and Karl's truck, is hungover and in no mood to be talked back to, this much is amply clear.

'I have a licence. Write my name on the paper if it's so damned important.'

The woman stares at Bank. All the others do the same. Where Bank is staring, without being at all prejudicial about it, is unclear. But the dog is at least looking at Britt-Marie. Britt-Marie peers back at it shiftily, as a conspiring criminal type might do.

'Good God, is SHE back in Borg?' hisses the old codger to the woman as soon as he catches sight of Bank.

'Shush!' shushes the woman.

Bank steps out of the shadows and waves her stick in the direction of the woman and the old codger, so that she accidentally strikes the old codger quite hard on his thigh. Twice.

'Oh dear,' Bank says apologetically, then points the stick at the woman.

'Put my name down. I suppose you haven't forgotten it,' she says, and happens to strike the old codger fairly hard across one of his arms three or possibly four times.

'I didn't even know you were back in Borg,' the woman says with a cold smile.

'Now you do.'

'We . . . I mean . . . the regulations of the competition stipulate that . . .' the woman tries to say.

Bank groans, loud and hungover.

'Shut your mouth will you, Annika, just shut your mouth. The kids just want to play. There used to be a time when we also just wanted to play, and old blokes like this one tried to stop us.'

Bank thrusts her stick in the direction of the old sod when she says that last bit, but this time he manages to jump out of the way. The woman stands there for a good while, and seems to be pondering a variety of answers. She looks younger and younger for every moment that passes. She opens her mouth, then closes it again. Finally, in a resigned sort of way, she writes down Bank's name in her papers. The old sod is still spitting and hissing when they get into the red car and leave Borg behind as they head back to town.

Bank doesn't waste any time on superficialities. In her hungover condition her patience seems comparable to Vega's. She waves her stick menacingly at the children and mutters:

'If you're not blind you must have noticed by now that I am, pretty well. But I have no need to watch you play to get the fact that you're useless. We have a few days until their idiotic cup, so we have to use that time as well as we can to make you as un-useless as possible.'

She thinks about this for a moment and then adds:

'You should probably keep your expectations low.'

It's not an excellent pep talk, far from it. Possibly, Britt-Marie has a sense that she liked Bank better when she hardly did any talking. But of course Omar is the first of them to drum up enough courage to disagree with her, partly because he dares say what the whole team is thinking, and partly because he's dumb enough to do it.

'Shit! Fat chance we've got with a blind coach!'

Britt-Marie clasps her hands together.

'You're not supposed to say things like that, Omar. It's incredibly uncivilised.'

'She's blind! What can she know about football?'

'It's actually more a case of impaired vision,' Britt-Marie points out, adding with a slight note of outrage: 'It has nothing to do with corpulence.'

Omar swears. Bank just nods calmly. She points her stick at the football with a precision that makes even Omar feel slightly caught out.

'Give the ball here,' she says, and at the same time whistles to her dog. The dog shuffles off at once and positions itself immediately behind Omar.

Omar's eyes flick nervously between the dog behind him and Bank in front of him.

'Right . . . what I . . . hold on, I didn't mean . . .'

Bank runs forward with a surprising turn of speed to claim the ball. At the same time the dog, behind Omar, places itself with its legs wide apart and starts peeing. The dog pee forms itself into a neat round puddle in the gravel. Bank's foot caresses the leather football and makes a sudden movement as if about to kick it hard at Omar's head. He ducks and throws himself back, startled, stumbling over the dog and stepping neatly into the puddle.

Bank stops abruptly with her foot on the ball. Points with her stick at Omar and mutters:

'At least I know what a dummy shot is. And even if I'm almost blind I'd bet quite a lot of money you're standing in dog pee right now. So maybe we could agree that at least I know more about football than you do?'

Vega stands at the edge of the wee-pool, fascinated by all this.

'How did you teach the dog to do that?'

Bank whistles for the dog. Scratches its nose. Opens her jacket pocket and lets it have what's inside.

'The dog knows lots of tricks. I had it before I went blind. I know how to train things.'

Britt-Marie is already on her way to the recreation centre to fetch bicarbonate of soda.

When she comes back to the parking area, the children are playing football so you can hear it. It has to be experienced before you can understand it, the difference between silent and non-silent football. Britt-Marie stops in the darkness and listens. Every time one of the children gets the ball, their teammates are shouting: 'Here! I'm here!'

'If you can be heard then you exist,' mutters hungover Bank, massaging her temples.

The children play. Call out. Explain where they are. Britt-Marie squeezes her container of bicarbonate of soda until it has dents in it.

'I'm here,' she whispers, wishing that Sven was here so she could tell him.

It's a remarkable club. A remarkable game.

They part ways at the end of the training session. Toad goes back with his dad in the truck, Sami picks up Vega, Omar and Dino. Max wanders home on his own, along the road. Ben is met by his mother. She waves at Britt-Marie and Britt-Marie waves back. Bank doesn't say a word on the way home and Britt-Marie feels it's inappropriate to challenge destiny. Above all she does not believe it is appropriate to challenge a stick that has been both in the mud and inside at least one person's mouth this evening. So she makes do with silence.

Back at the house, Bank opens the cellophane around the beer and drinks it straight from the bottle. Britt-Marie goes and fetches a glass and a coaster.

'Enough's enough, actually,' she says firmly to Bank.

'You're a bloody nag-bag, did anyone ever tell you that?'

'Many times,' says Britt-Marie and, depending on what sort of system you are using, you could say that Britt-Marie finds her second real girlfriend tonight.

On her way to the stairs, she changes her mind, turns around and asks:

'You said your father supports Tottenham. If it's not too much trouble, what does that mean?'

Bank drinks her beer from the glass. Slumps in her chair. The dog lays its head in her lap.

'If you support Tottenham you always give more love than you get back,' she says.

Britt-Marie cups her uninjured hand over the bandage on the other. There's certainly an awful lot of unnecessary complication about liking football.

'I assume what you mean by that is that it's a bad team.'

The corners of Bank's mouth bounce up.

'Tottenham is the worst kind of bad team, because they're almost good. They always promise that they're going to be fantastic. They make you hope. So you go on loving them and they carry on finding more and more innovative ways of disappointing you.'

Britt-Marie nods as if this sounded reasonable. Bank stands up and states:

'In that sense his daughter was always like his favourite team.'

She puts the empty bottle on the kitchen counter and, without relying on the stick, walks past Britt-Marie into the living room.

'The beer was nice. Thanks.'

Britt-Marie sits on the edge of her bed for hours that evening. She stands on the balcony, waiting for a police car. Then back to the bed. She doesn't cry, isn't despondent; in fact it's almost the other way around. She's almost eager. Just doesn't know what to do with herself. Like a sort of restlessness. The windows are polished, the floors have been scoured, and the balcony furniture wiped down. She's poured bicarbonate of soda into the flower pots and onto the mattress. She rubs the fingers of her uninjured hand across the bandages that cover the white mark that used to be covered by the wedding ring. So in a way she did achieve the desired result of her visit to the tanning salon, even if not in the exact way she had thought. Nothing has gone as she thought it would since she came to Borg.

For the first time since she got here, she accepts this may not be something altogether bad.

When she hears the knock at the front door she has been

hoping for it for so long that at first she thinks it must be a figment of her imagination. But then there's another knock, and Britt-Marie jumps out of bed and stumbles down the stairs like a complete lunatic. It's obviously not at all like her, highly uncivilised in every possible way. She has not run down the stairs like this since she was a teenager, when your heart reaches the front door before your feet. For a moment she stops and summons all the common sense at her disposal, in order to fix her hair and adjust all the invisible creases in her skirt.

'Sven! I . . .' she has time to say, holding on to the door handle.

Then she just stands there. Trying, but failing, to breathe. She feels her legs giving way beneath her.

'Hello my darling,' says Kent.

23

'Sweet boys don't get to kiss pretty girls,' Britt-Marie's mother sometimes used to say. Even though what she really meant was that pretty girls should not kiss sweet boys, because when dealing with sweet boys there's absolutely no certainty of being able to look forward to a reliable income.

'We have to pray that Britt-Marie finds a man who can support her, otherwise she'll have to live in the gutter, because she has absolutely no talents of her own,' Britt-Marie used to hear her say into the telephone. 'I got her for my sins,' she also used to say, into the telephone if she was drunk, or pointedly at Britt-Marie after tippling sherry.

It's impossible to be good enough for a parent after losing a sister who in all important respects was a better version of yourself. Britt-Marie did try, nonetheless. But with a father who came home later and later and, in the end, not at all, she did not have very many options. Instead, Britt-Marie learned not to have any expectations of her own, and to put up with her mother's scepticism about her prospects.

Alf and Kent lived on the same floor, and they fought, as brothers tend to do. Sooner or later they both wanted the same girl. Whether they wanted Britt-Marie because they really did want her, or because brothers always want what their brothers want, she was never quite sure. If Ingrid had been there they would have courted her instead, Britt-Marie had no illusions about that. You tend not to if you're used to living in someone's shadow. But the boys were persistent, competed, fought for her attention in very different ways.

One of the brothers was too insensitive to her, always going on about how much money he was going to make; the other was too kind. Britt-Marie didn't want to disappoint her mother, so she chose Alf and ruled out Kent.

Kent stood in the stairwell with flowers in his hands and his eyes closed when she walked off with his brother. By the time she came back he had gone.

She was only with Alf for a short length of time. He was weary, she remembers. Already bored. Like a victor after the adrenalin has worn off. One morning he left her to go and do his military service and was gone for months.

The morning that he was due back, Britt-Marie spent hours in front of the mirror for the first time in her life and tried on a new dress. Her mother gave her a look, and said:

'I see you're trying to make yourself look cheap. Well, mission accomplished.' Britt-Marie tried to explain that this was modern. Her mother told her not to raise her voice, it made her sound very ordinary. Britt-Marie tried gently to explain that she wanted to surprise Alf at the train station, and her mother snorted: 'Oh, he'll be surprised all right.' She was right.

Britt-Marie turned up in an old dress and with sweaty hands and her heart clattering like horse's hooves on cobblestones. Obviously she had heard the stories of how soldiers have a girl in every town, she had just never thought this would be true of Alf. At least she'd never thought he'd have two girls in the same town.

She'd been sitting all night in the kitchen weeping into a towel when her mother finally got out of bed and scolded her for making too much noise. Britt-Marie told her about the other girl she'd seen Alf with. 'Ha, what did you expect when you picked a man like that?' hissed her mother before going back to bed. She got up later than usual the following day. In the end she didn't get up at all. Britt-Marie found a job as a waitress instead of getting herself an education, so she could take care of things at home. Brought dinner into the bedroom for her mother, who had stopped talking, yet was capable now and then of sitting up in the bed and saying, 'Ha, working as a waitress – it must be nice for you not to feel you owe more to your parents after all the advantages we've given you. I don't suppose any education was good enough for you, you obviously prefer to stay here at home and live off my savings instead.'

The flat grew increasingly quiet. And finally absolutely silent. Britt-Marie polished the windows and waited for something new to begin.

One day, Kent was just standing there on the landing. The day after her mother's funeral. He spoke of his divorce and his children.

Britt-Marie had been hoping for so long that she thought this must be a figment of her imagination, and when he smiled at her it felt like sunlight on her skin. She made his dreams her own. His life became her life. She was good at this, and people want to do the things they're good at. People want someone to know they are there.

Now Kent stands in her doorway in Borg, holding flowers. He smiles. Sunlight on her skin. It's hard not to want to go back to your normal life once you know how difficult it is to start again.

'Were you waiting for someone?' asks Kent insecurely, and once again he is like that boy on the landing.

Britt-Marie shakes her head in shock. He smiles.

'I got your postcard. And I . . . well . . . the accountant checked your cash withdrawals,' he says almost with embarrassment and gestures at the road towards town.

When Britt-Marie doesn't know what to say he goes on:

'I asked for you in the pizzeria. That woman in the wheelchair didn't want to say where you were, but a couple of old blokes drinking coffee there were pretty keen to tell me. Do you know them?'

'No,' whispers Britt-Marie, unsure whether he's making that up. Kent holds out the flowers.

'Darling . . . I . . . damn it, I'm sorry! Me, her, that woman, it never meant a thing. It's over. You're the one I love. Damn it. Darling!'

Britt-Marie looks with concern at the stick he's using to prop himself up.

'What on earth's happened to you?'

He waves dismissively at her.

'Ah, don't make a fuss about that, the doctors just wanted me to have it for a while after the heart attack, that's all. The chassis has rusted up a bit, after it's been parked up in the garage for half the winter!' He grins, with a nod at his legs.

She wants to hold his hand.

It doesn't feel natural to have to invite him in. It never did, not even when they were teenagers. At her mother's she wasn't allowed to bring boys into the bedroom, so the first time Britt-Marie brought a boy in there, it was Kent. After her mother's death. That boy stayed. Made her home his own and his life hers. So now it seems very natural to them both to be driving around Borg in their BMW, because in many ways they were always at their best when they were in the car. He in the driver's seat, she the passenger. At this moment they can pretend they have only been passing through, and leave Borg, as you do with places you send postcards from.

They drive into town and back. Kent keeps his hand on the gearstick, so that Britt-Marie can carefully reach out with the tips of her fingers of the hand that is not injured, and put them on top of his. Just to feel that they are both heading in the same direction. His shirt is creased and has coffee stains over his stomach. Britt-Marie remembers Sami talking about how some children look as if they live in the trees, and Kent does look as if he fell out of a tree in his sleep, hitting every branch on his way down. He smiles apologetically.

'I couldn't find that blasted iron, darling. There's no order to anything when you're not at home. You know that.'

Britt-Marie doesn't answer. She's worrying about what people will think. Will they say he had a wife who left him while he was walking about with a stick and everything? Her ring finger feels cold, and she's infinitely grateful for the bandage, which stops Kent seeing it. She knows he let her down, but she can't get away from the feeling that she also let him down. What is love worth if you leave someone when he needs you the most?

Kent coughs and takes his foot off the accelerator, although the road lies empty ahead of them.

Britt-Marie has never seen him slow down for no particular reason.

'The doctors say I haven't been so well. For a long time, I mean. I haven't been myself. I've been given some darned tablets, antidepressants or whatever they're called.'

The way he says it is the same as when he's talking about his plans, as if they are all a foregone conclusion.

As if what made him come home late smelling of pizza was nothing but a production fault, perfectly easy to mend. Now everything is fine.

She wants to ask why he never called her, after all she had a mobile telephone with her. But she realises he would have assumed she couldn't switch it on. So she stays quiet about it. He peers out of the window as they drive back into Borg.

'Darned strange place for you to end up in, isn't it? What was it your mum used to call the countryside? "Sheer mediocrity"? She was darned funny, your mum. And it is a bit ironic that you should end up in the sticks out here, isn't it? You, who hardly put your foot outside our flat in forty years!'

He says it as a joke. She can't quite accept it in that spirit. But when they stop outside Bank's house he's breathing so heavily that she can hear the pain he's in. His tears are the first she's ever seen in his eyes. There were no tears there even when he buried his own mother, while clutching Britt-Marie's hand.

'It's over. With her. That woman. She never meant a thing. Not like you, Britt-Marie.'

He holds the fingers of her unscathed hand, caresses them gently and says in a low voice:

'I need you at home, darling. I need you there. Don't throw away a whole life we've lived together just because I made one stupid mistake!'

Britt-Marie brushes invisible crumbs from his shirt. Breathes in the fragrance of the flowers in her arms.

'Boys are not allowed in my bedroom. Not then and not now either,' she whispers.

He laughs out loud. Her skin is burning.

'Tomorrow?' he calls out behind her as she's getting out of the car.

She nods.

Because life is more than the shoes your feet are in. More than the person you are. It's the togetherness. The parts of yourself in another. Memories and walls and cupboards and drawers with compartments for cutlery, so you know where everything is.

A life of adaptation towards a perfect organisation, a stream-lined existence based on two personalities. A shared life of everything that's normal. Cement and stone, remote controls and crosswords, shirts and bicarbonate of soda, bathroom cabinets and electric shavers in the third drawer. He needs her for all that. If she's not there, nothing is as it should be.

She goes up to her room. Opens drawers. Folds towels.

The mobile rings, the display showing the number of the girl from the unemployment office, but Britt-Marie declines the call. Sits on her own on the balcony all night. With her packed bags next to her.

24

'You look at me as if you're judging me. I should like to inform you that I don't appreciate it at all,' Britt-Marie affirms. When she doesn't get an answer, she continues more diplomatically:

'It may not be your intention to look at me as if you're judging me, but that is how it feels.'

When she still gets no answer, she sits down on a stool with her hands clasped together in her lap, and points out:

'I should like to point out that the towel has been left where it is so you can wipe your paws on it. Not as a decoration.'

The rat eats some Snickers. Doesn't say anything. But Britt-Marie senses she is being judged. She snorts defensively.

'Love doesn't necessarily have to be fireworks and symphony orchestras for every human being, I do believe you can look at it like that. For some of us love can be other things. Sensible things!'

The rat eats Snickers. Makes a foray over the towel. Goes back to the Snickers.

'Kent is my husband. I am his wife. I'm certainly not going to sit here and be lectured by a rat,' Britt-Marie clarifies. Then she collects her thoughts a bit, switches her hands around and adds:

'Not that there's anything wrong with that, of course. Being a rat. I'm sure it's quite excellent.'

The rat makes no attempt to be anything but a rat. Britt-Marie's next words come out in a long exhalation.

'It's just that I've been a melancholic for a long time, you have to understand.'

The rat eats Snickers. The children play football in the parking area outside the recreation centre. Britt-Marie sees Kent's BMW through the doorway. He's playing with the children. They like him; everyone likes Kent when they first meet him. It takes years to see his bad side. With Britt-Marie it's the other way around.

In fact she doesn't know if 'melancholic' is the right word. She looks for a better expression, as in a crossword. Vertical: 'Dejected individual'. 'As felt by a non-happy person'. Or possibly: 'Greek for black, followed by stomach ache'.

'Maybe "heavy-hearted" would be a better word,' she tells the rat.

She has been feeling heavy-hearted for a long time now.

'It may seem ludicrous to you, but in some ways I've had less time to be heavy-hearted in Borg than I did at home . . . It's not as if I've been forced into the life I've lived. I could have made changes. I could have found myself some employment,' says Britt-Marie, and she can hear that she's actually defending Kent rather than herself.

But on the other hand it's quite true. She could have found herself a job. It was just that Kent thought it would be good if she waited a while. Just a year or so. Who else would take care of everything at home, he asked, and by his way of asking it was clear to her that he wasn't volunteering to do it himself.

So after waiting at home with her mother for a few years, Britt-Marie waited at home with Kent's children for a few years, and then Kent's mother became ill and Britt-Marie waited at home with her quite a bit for another few years. Kent felt it was best that way, obviously just during a transitional period until all of Kent's plans had fallen into place, and, of course, it was best for the whole family if Britt-Marie was at home in the afternoons in case the Germans wanted to have dinner. When he said 'the whole family' he was obviously referring to everyone in the family except Britt-Marie. 'Corporate entertainment is tax-deductible,' Kent always explained, but he never explained who would benefit by it.

A year turned into several years, and several years turned into all the years. One morning you wake up with more life behind you than in front of you, not being able to understand how it's happened.

'I could have found myself employment. It was my choice to stay at home. I'm not a victim,' Britt-Marie points out.

She doesn't say anything about how close she got. She went to job interviews. Several of them. She didn't tell Kent about them, obviously, because he would only have asked what salary she'd get, and if she had told him he would have laughed and said: 'Isn't it bloody better then if I pay you to stay at home?' He would have meant that as a joke but she would not have been able to take it in that spirit, and so, as a result, she never said anything. She was always there in good time for the interviews, and there was always someone else waiting there in the visitors' room. Almost exclusively young women. One of them started talking to Britt-Marie, because she couldn't imagine that someone so old was there for the same job as herself. She had three children and had been left by her husband. One of the children had an illness. When she was called in for her interview, Britt-Marie stood up and went home. You could say a lot of things about Britt-Marie, but she was certainly not someone who'd steal a job from someone more in need of it.

Obviously she doesn't tell the rat about this, she doesn't want to make herself out to be some sort of martyr. And then, of course, you never know what sort of life experiences the rat has had.

Maybe it lost its whole family in a terrorist attack, for instance; it's the sort of thing you read about.

'There's a lot of pressure on Kent, you have to understand,' she explains.

Because there is. Providing for a whole family takes time, and has to be respected.

'It takes a long time to get to know a person,' says Britt-Marie

181

to the rat, her voice growing progressively quieter with every word.

Kent digs his heels in when he walks. Not everyone notices these kinds of things, but that's how it is. He curls up when sleeping, as if he's cold, irrespective of how many blankets she gently spreads over him. He's afraid of heights.

'And his general knowledge is outstanding, especially when it comes to geography!' she points out.

Geography is a very good skill to share the sofa with when solving crossword puzzles. Not so very easy to acquire, actually. Love doesn't have to be fireworks for everyone. It could be a question of capital cities with five letters or knowing exactly when it's time to reheel your shoes.

'He could change.' Britt-Marie wants to say it in a loud, clear voice, but instead it comes out in a whisper.

But he might, certainly. He doesn't even need to become an entirely new person, it's enough if he can become who he used to be before he was unfaithful.

He is taking medicine, after all, and they can do really amazing things with medicine nowadays.

'A few years ago they cloned a sheep, can you imagine?' says Britt-Marie to the rat.

At this point the rat decides to leave.

She puts away the plate. Washes up. Cleans. Polishes the window and looks out at Kent playing football with Omar and Dino. She can also change, she's sure about that. She doesn't have to be so boring. Life may not turn out differently if she goes home with Kent, but at least it will go back to normal.

'I'm not ready for an unusual life,' says Britt-Marie to the rat before she remembers that it has gone.

It takes time to get to know a person. She is not ready to get to know a new one. She has decided she has to learn to live with herself as she is.

She stands in the doorway watching Kent score a goal. He props himself up against the stick and leaps into the air, making a pirouette. It could not possibly be the sort of behaviour the doctors would recommend after a heart attack, but Britt-Marie stops herself from criticising him, because he looks so happy. She assumes there could also be advantages, health-wise, in being happy after a heart attack.

Omar nags about having a ride in the BMW, justifying this by the argument that it's 'wicked as hell', and Britt-Marie realises this must be something good, so she manages to stop herself from criticising this as well. Kent manages to tell the boys how much it cost, which seems to impress them terrifically. The third time around he lets Omar drive, and Omar looks as if he's just been given permission to ride a dragon.

Sven isn't wearing his uniform when he steps out of the pizzeria, so she hardly notices him until they're just a few metres apart. He looks at the BMW, looks at Britt-Marie, and clears his throat.

'Hello, Britt-Marie,' he says.

'Hello,' she says, surprised.

She holds on to her handbag very hard. He digs his hands deep into his pockets like a teenager. He's wearing a shirt and his hair is water-combed. He doesn't say it was for her sake, and before she has time to say anything irrational her common sense blurts out:

'That's my husband!'

She points at the BMW. Sven's hands sink even deeper into his jacket pockets.

Kent stops the car when he sees them, gets outside with his stick swinging self-confidently in one hand. He reaches out to Sven and his handshake is a little longer and harder than it needs to be.

'Kent!' Kent crows.

'Sven,' Sven mumbles.

'My husband,' Britt-Marie reminds him.

Sven's hand goes back to his jacket pocket. His clothes seem to be rubbing uncomfortably.

Britt-Marie's grip on her handbag gets harder and harder,

until her fingers hurt, and maybe also some other parts of her. Kent grins jauntily.

'Nice kids! That curly-haired one wants to be an entrepreneur, did he tell you?'

He laughs in the direction of Omar. Britt-Marie looks down at the ground. Sven is grim when he looks up at Kent.

'You can't park there,' he notes, moving his elbow towards the BMW without taking his hand out of his pocket.

'Oh right,' Kent says dismissively, tiredly waving his hand at him.

'I'm telling you you can't park there and we don't let teenagers drive cars around here. It's irresponsible!' Sven says insistently, with a ferocity Britt-Marie has never seen in him before.

'Relax, will you,' Kent grins, with a superior air.

Sven is vibrating. He points through the lining of his jacket with both index fingers.

'Either bloody way you can't park there, and it's illegal to let minors drive your car. You just have to accept that, wherever you come from . . .'

The last words are spoken at a much lower volume. As if they have already started regretting themselves. Kent supports himself against his stick and coughs, slightly at a loss.

He looks at Britt-Marie, but she doesn't look back at him, so he peers at Sven instead.

'What's the matter with you – what are you, a cop?'

'Yes!' says Sven.

'Well I'll be damned,' laughs Kent, immediately sobering up his face and straightening his back and making a scornful salute.

Sven blushes and fixes his gaze on the zipper of his jacket. Britt-Marie's breathing speeds up and she steps forward as if she's about to move between them physically. In the end she just puts her feet down hard in the gravel and says:

'Please Kent, why don't you just move the car. It is actually in the middle of the football pitch.'

Kent sighs, then nods mischievously at her, and holds up both hands as if someone is threatening him.

'Sure, sure, sure, if the sheriff insists. No problem. Just don't shoot!'

He takes a few demonstrative steps forward and leans over Britt-Marie. She can't remember the last time he kissed her on the cheek.

'I checked into the hotel in town. Bloody rat-hole, you know how it is in places like this, but I noticed there was a restaurant opposite. It looked OK, under the circumstances,' he says so Sven will hear. When he says 'circumstances' he makes a superior sort of gesture at the pizzeria and the recreation centre and the road. He revs the engine more than he needs to when he moves the car. When he's done, he gives his business card to Omar, because Kent likes giving people his business card almost as much as he likes telling people what his belongings cost. The boy is deeply impressed. Britt-Marie realises that she doesn't know at what exact point Sven turned around and left, only that he's gone now.

She stands alone outside the pizzeria. If something within her has been knocked down and shattered, she tries to tell herself, it is all her own fault, because these feelings she has inside should never have been set free in the first place. It is far too late to start a new life.

She has dinner with Kent at the restaurant in town. It has white tablecloths and a menu without photographs and seems to have a serious attitude about the cutlery. Or at least it does not treat it like a joke. Kent says he feels alone without her. 'Lost' is the word he uses. He seems to be taking her seriously, or at least he isn't treating her as a joke. He's wearing his old, broken belt, she notices, and she realises this is because he did not find his usual one that she mended just before she left. She wants to tell him it's lying neatly rolled up in the second drawer of the wardrobe in the bedroom. Their bedroom. She wants him to shout out her name.

But all he does is scratch his beard stubble and try to sound unconcerned when he asks:

'But this coppper, then . . . is he . . . how did you become . . . friends?'

Britt-Marie does her utmost to sound similarly unconcerned when she answers:

'He's just a policeman, Kent.'

Kent nods and blinks with emphasis.

'You have to trust me when I say I know I made a mistake, darling. It's over now. I'll never ever have contact with her again. You can't punish me for the rest of my life because of just one false move, right?' he says, and softly grabs her bandaged hand across the table.

He's wearing his wedding ring. She can feel the white mark on her finger, it's burning and denouncing her. He pats the bandage, as if not even reflecting on why it's there.

'Come on now, darling, you've made your point. Loud and clear! I understand!'

She nods. Because it's true. Because she never wanted him to suffer, only that he should know that he was wrong.

'You obviously think this thing with the football team is ludicrous,' she whispers.

'Are you joking? I think it's absolutely fantastic!'

He lets go of her hand as soon as the food comes, and she immediately misses it. Feels like you do when you come out of the hairdresser after having more hair taken off than you wanted.

She places her napkin neatly in her lap, pats it tenderly as if it was sleeping, and whispers:

'Me too. I also think it's fantastic.'

Kent lights up. Leans forward. Looks deep into her eyes.

'Hey darling, let's put it like this: you stay here until the kids have played in this cup that the curly-haired one was going on about today. And then we go home. To our life. OK?'

Britt-Marie inhales so deeply that her breath starts faltering halfway through.

'I would appreciate that,' she whispers.

'Anything for you, darling,' says Kent with a nod, and then

stops the waitress to ask for the pepper mill even though he hasn't tried the food yet.

It's normal food, of course, but before common sense puts the brakes on, Britt-Marie briefly considers telling Kent about how she has tried tacos. She wants him to know that there have been a lot of things going on in her life lately. But she stops herself, because it probably doesn't really matter now, and anyway Kent wants to tell her things about his business affairs with the Germans.

Britt-Marie orders French fries with her food. She doesn't eat French fries because she doesn't like them, but she always orders them anyway whenever she goes with Kent to restaurants; she always worries that he won't have enough food to satisfy him.

While he's reaching across the table for her fries, Britt-Marie peers out of the window and for a moment she has a feeling that there was a police car in the street. But this could merely have been a figment of her imagination. Ashamed of herself, she looks down at her napkin. Here she is, a grown woman, with fantasies of emergency vehicles. What would people think?

Kent drives her to football practice, and waits in his BMW until it's over. Bank is also there, so Britt-Marie lets her take care of the training while Britt-Marie mainly just stands there holding on to the list. When it's over, Britt-Marie can hardly remember what they did, or if she even spoke to the children, or said goodbye to them.

Kent drives her and Bank and the dog back to Bank's house. Bank and the dog hop out without asking how much the car cost, which seems to upset Kent terribly. Bank accidentally taps her stick against the paintwork and it's almost certainly not deliberate the first two times. Kent fiddles with his telephone and Britt-Marie sits waiting next to him, because she's very good at doing that. Finally he says:

'I have to go and see the accountant tomorrow. There are big things in motion with the Germans, you know, big plans!'

He nods persistently, to show just how big the plans are.

Britt-Marie smiles encouragingly. She opens the door at the same time as the thought strikes her, and as a result she asks without really thinking it through:

'What football team do you support?'

'Manchester United,' he answers, surprised, looking up from his telephone.

She nods and gets out.

'That was a very nice dinner, Kent. Thank you.'

He leans across the seat and looks up at her.

'When we're home we'll go to the theatre, just the two of us. OK, darling? I promise!'

She stays in the hall with the door open until he's driven off. Then she sees the ancient women in the garden opposite, staring at her while leaning against their Zimmer frames. She hurries inside.

Bank is in the kitchen having some bacon.

'My husband supports Manchester United,' Britt-Marie informs her.

'Might have bloody known,' says Bank.

Britt-Marie doesn't have a clue what that's supposed to mean.

25

Britt-Marie devotes the next morning to cleaning the balcony furniture. She'll miss it. The women with the Zimmer frames on the other side of the road emerge to pick up their newspapers from the postbox. In a sudden fit of wanting to seem sociable, Britt-Marie waves at them, but they only glare back at her and slam the door.

Bank is frying bacon when she comes downstairs, but obviously she hasn't turned on the extractor fan. It must be nice for Bank, thinks Britt-Marie, not to be bothered about the smell of burnt pork or concerned about what the neighbours might think.

Hesitantly she places herself in the doorway between the hall and the kitchen. As Bank seems unaware of her presence, she clears her throat twice, because she has a feeling that she may, after all, owe her landlady an explanation.

'I suppose you feel you're owed an explanation about this whole business of my husband,' she says.

'No,' says Bank firmly.

'Oh,' says Britt-Marie, disappointed.

'Bacon?' grunts Bank, and pours a lick of beer into the pot.

'No thanks,' says Britt-Marie, not at all disgusted by this, and goes on:

'He is my husband. We never actually divorced. I just haven't been at home for a while. Almost like a holiday. But now I'm going home, you have to understand. I understand very well that perhaps you don't understand this sort of thing, but he is my husband. It's certainly not an appropriate thing, to leave one's husband at my age.'

Bank looks as one does when one doesn't want to discuss Britt-Marie and Kent's relationship.

'Sure you don't want any bacon?' she mutters.

Britt-Marie shakes her head.

'No thank you. But I want you to understand that he's not a bad man. He made a mistake, but anyone can make a mistake. I'm sure he had masses of opportunities to make a mistake before, without ever doing it. You can't write off a human being for ever, just for the sake of a single mistake.'

'It's good bacon,' says Bank.

'There are obligations. Marital obligations. One doesn't just give up,' Britt-Marie explains.

'I would have offered you eggs if there were any eggs. But the dog had them. So you'll have to make do with bacon.'

'You can't just leave each other after a whole life.'

'So you'll have some bacon, then?' Bank establishes, and turns on the extractor fan.

You might infer from this that she's more bothered about the sound of Britt-Maries's voice than the smell of fried bacon. So Britt-Marie stamps her foot on the floor.

'I don't eat bacon! It's not good for the cholesterol. Kent has also cut down, I can tell you, he was at the doctor in the autumn. We have an exceedingly capable doctor. He's an immigrant, you know. From Germany!'

Bank turns up the extractor fan to its maximum level, so that Britt-Marie has to raise her voice to make herself heard over all the noise, and as a result she's almost shouting when she points out:

'It's actually not very appropriate leaving your husband when he's just had a heart attack! I'm not that sort of a woman!'

The plate is slammed down on the table in front of her, so the fat splashes over the rim.

'Eat your bacon,' says Bank.

Britt-Marie gives it to the dog. But she doesn't say anything else about Kent. Or at least she tries not to. Instead she asks:

'What does it mean when someone supports Manchester United or whatever it's called?'

Bank answers with her mouth full of bacon.

'They always win. So they've started believing they deserve to.'

'Ha.'

Bank doesn't say anything else. Britt-Marie stands up and washes up her plate. Dries it. Stands there in case Bank has something else to add, but when Bank starts behaving as if she's forgotten that Britt-Marie is even there, Britt-Marie clears her throat and says with irrepressible emphasis:

'Kent is not a bad man. He has not always won.'

The dog looks at Bank as if it feels Bank ought to have a bad conscience. Bank seems to pick up on this, because she continues eating, in an even surlier silence than usual. Britt-Marie has already left the kitchen and put on her coat and neatly stashed her list away in her handbag when the dog growls from the kitchen and Bank groans loudly by way of an answer, and then at long last calls out into the hall:

'You want a lift?'

'Excuse me?' says Britt-Marie.

'Shall I drive you to the recreation centre?' asks Bank.

Britt-Marie goes to the kitchen doorway and stares at her and almost drops her handbag.

'Drive? How . . . I . . . no, that's fine . . . thank you. I don't want to . . . I don't know . . . I'm certainly not judging, but how . . .'

She stops when she sees the satisfied grin on Bank's face.

'I'm almost blind. I don't drive. I was joking, Britt-Marie.'

The dog signals its encouragement. Britt-Marie adjusts her hair.

'Ha. That was . . . nice of you.'

'Don't worry so much, Britt-Marie!' Bank calls out after her,

191

and Britt-Marie has absolutely no idea what to say to that sort of absurd notion.

She walks to the recreation centre. Cleans. Polishes the windows and looks out of them. She sees other things now than when she first came to Borg. Faxin can do that for a person.

She serves up the Snickers by the door. Walks across the football pitch that she used to think was just a parking area. Sven's car is parked outside the pizzeria. Britt-Marie takes a deep breath before she walks inside.

'Hello,' she says.

'Britt! All right there!' yells Somebody and rolls out of the kitchen gripping a pot of coffee.

Sven is standing by the till, wearing his uniform. Quickly he removes his police cap and holds it in his hands.

'Hello, Britt-Marie,' he says. He smiles, and seems to grow a few centimetres taller.

Then comes another voice from the window:

'Good morning, darling!'

Kent is sitting at a table, drinking coffee. He has taken off his shoes and has one of his feet propped up on a chair. It's one of his main talents. He can sit anywhere drinking coffee and looking as comfortable as if he was in his own living room. No one is quite his equal when it comes to making himself at home anywhere, without being invited to do so.

Sven shrinks again. As if he's leaking air. Britt-Marie tries not to look as if her heart has jumped twice inside of her.

'I thought you were going to your accountant,' she manages to say.

'I'm going in a minute, that kid Omar just wanted to show me a couple of things first,' says Kent, smiling as if he has all the time in the world, and then he winks playfully at Sven and points out loudly:

'Don't worry, Sheriff, I haven't parked illegally today. I'm on the other side of the road.'

Sven wipes the palms of his hands on his trouser legs and looks down at the floor as he answers:

'You can't park there either.'

Kent nods with feigned seriousness.

'Does the sheriff want to issue a fine? Will the sheriff accept cash?'

He takes out his wallet, which is so thick that he has to have a rubber band around it to get it into his trouser back pocket, and puts it on the table. Then he laughs as if all this is just a joke. He's good at that, Kent – good at looking as if everything is just a joke. Because if it is, then no one can take offence, and then Kent can always say: 'Ah, come on, don't you have a sense of humour?' The person with less of a sense of humour always loses in this world.

Sven looks down at the floor.

'I don't issue parking fines. I'm not a traffic warden.'

'OK, Sheriff! OK! But the sheriff himself obviously parks wherever the sheriff feels like parking.' Kent grins and nods at the police car, which can be seen through the window.

Before Sven has time to answer, Kent hollers at Somebody:

'Don't worry about the sheriff's coffee, I'll pay for it! I mean it's us taxpayers who pay the sheriff's salary anyway, so just put it on our bill!'

Sven doesn't answer. He just puts some cash on the counter and says in a low voice to Somebody:

'I can pay for my own coffee.'

Then he glances at Britt-Marie and mumbles:

'I'll have it to take away, if that's all right.'

She wants to say something. Doesn't have time.

'Check this out, darling! I had these printed for Omar!' yells Kent and waves a fistful of business cards.

When every available person in the pizzeria does not immediately run to his table, Kent stands up very elaborately and sighs as if none of them have a sense of humour. Then he walks up to the counter in his socks, which makes Britt-Marie scream inside, and hands Sven a business card.

'Here, Sheriff! Take a business card!'

Then he grins at Britt-Marie and shows her one of them, on which it is written: '*Omar – Entrepreneur*'.

'There's a printing place in that town place. They printed these on the bloody double this morning, over the moon they were, poor things don't get any customers!' Kent tells them jovially and makes emphatic quotation marks in the air when he says 'town'.

Sven stands there swallowing hard. As soon as Somebody has poured his coffee into a paper mug, Sven takes it and walks directly towards the door.

When he passes Britt-Marie he slows down and meets her eyes very briefly.

'Have a . . . have a good day, won't you,' he mumbles.

'You . . . well, I mean . . . you too,' says Britt-Marie, sucking in her cheeks.

'Be careful out there, Sheriff!' Kent yells in an American accent.

Sven stands still, with his gaze focused on the floor. Britt-Marie has time to see his fist, clenched until his knuckles turn white, before he forces it into his trouser pocket like an animal into a sack. The door tinkles cheerfully behind him.

Britt-Marie stands in front of the till, feeling at a loss. One curious thing Kent can do is that he can feel so at ease in a place that Britt-Marie immediately feels like a stranger. He thumps her back and waves the business cards around.

'Please, Kent. Could you not at least put on your shoes?' she whispers.

Kent looks at his socks in surprise. Waves his big toe through a hole in one of them.

'Sure, sure, darling. Of course. I have to get going now anyway. Give these to the kid when he comes in!'

He shakes his wrist in a dramatic way, so that his watch makes a rattling sound. It's a very expensive one, Britt-Marie knows that and everyone knows it who's ever run into Kent while queuing up to pay at the petrol station. Then he presses the business cards into her hand and kisses her cheek.

'I'll be back this evening!' he cries on his way out of the door, and the next second he's gone.

Britt-Marie stands there, more at a loss than ever. When she doesn't know what to do with herself she deals with it in her usual way. She cleans.

Somebody lets her get on with it. Either because she doesn't care or precisely because she does care.

Omar turns up at lunchtime. He immediately starts chasing Britt-Marie around the pizzeria as if they were the last two people on the planet and she was holding the last bag of crisps.

'Is Kent here? Is he coming? Is he here?' he hollers, tugging at her arm.

'Kent is with his accountant. He'll be back this evening.'

'I've fixed him the coolest rims for his BMW! Wicked! You want to check them? He's getting a special price for them . . . you know!'

Britt-Marie doesn't ask what this means, because she assumes that some truck or other, despite never being scheduled to stop in Borg, has left the community slightly lighter than when it pulled in.

When Britt-Marie gives the boy the business cards he goes abruptly silent. Holds them as if they were made of priceless silk. The door tinkles and Vega comes in. She doesn't even look at Britt-Marie.

'Hello Vega,' says Britt-Marie.

Vega ignores her.

'Hello Vega!' Britt-Marie repeats.

'Check these ULTIMATE business cards, they're wicked. I got them off Kent!' Omar yells, his eyes glittering.

Vega takes in this information with indifference and storms into the kitchen. Soon you can hear that she's washing up. It sounds like something is crawling about in the sink while she attempts to beat it to death. Somebody rolls out of the kitchen and shrugs apologetically at Britt-Marie.

'Vega very angry, you know.'

'How do you know?' asks Britt-Marie.

'Teenager. Washing up without being told. Bloody angry when that happening, huh?'

Britt-Marie has to admit there's a good logic to that.

'Why is she so angry?'

Omar answers eagerly:

'Because she knows Kent's been here, so she's twigged you'll be clearing out!'

He doesn't sound too upset about it himself, because the opportunity of exchanging a football coach for an investor in tyre rims seems like an acceptable deal to him.

'I'm staying in Borg until after the competition' says Britt-Marie, directing this as much to herself as to anyone else.

The boy doesn't look as if he's been listening. He doesn't even bother correcting her by saying it's called a 'cup'. Britt-Marie almost wishes he would. The men with beards and caps come in, drink coffee and read newspapers without any acknowledgement of Britt-Marie, but there's a certain ease about them today, as if they know that soon they won't have to pretend not to notice her.

Evidently Vega has run out of things to slam about, so she comes storming out of the kitchen towards the front door.

'Ha. I suppose you're leaving?' says Britt-Marie in a well-meaning way.

'As if you're bothered,' hisses Vega.

'Will you be back in time for training?'

'Bloody difference does it make?'

'At least put a jacket on? It's cold out ther—'

'Go to hell, you old bat! Go back to your crappy life with your shitty bloke!'

The girl slams the door, which tinkles cheerfully. Omar gathers up his business cards and runs after her. Britt-Marie calls out to him but he either doesn't hear, or doesn't care.

After that, Britt-Marie cleans the entire pizzeria in grim silence. No one tries to stop her.

When she's done she sinks on to a stool in the kitchen. Somebody sits next to her, drinking a beer and watching her thoughtfully.

'Beer, Britt-Marie. You want?'

Britt-Marie blinks at her.

'Yes, you know what? Absolutely. I think I'd absolutely like to have a beer.'

So they drink beer without saying anything else. Britt-Marie must have had two or three sips of hers when the door tinkles again.

She just about has time to see the young man coming inside, and she's certainly not used to having alcohol levels of this magnitude in her blood at this time of the afternoon, which may be the reason why she does not immediately notice that the man is wearing a black hood over his head.

But Somebody does notice. She puts down her beer. Rolls up behind Britt-Marie and tugs at the arm of her jacket.

'Britt-Marie. Down on the floor. Now!'

And that's when Britt-Marie sees the pistol.

26

It's a very strange thing staring into the barrel of a gun. It embraces you. You fall into it.

A few hours later some police from town come to the pizzeria to ask Britt-Marie if she can describe the young man, what he was wearing and whether he was short or tall and spoke with a dialect or accent. The only description she's able to give them is, 'He was holding a pistol.' One of the police explains she 'mustn't take it personally' because a robbery is only about the money.

This may be easy for the police to say, but it is actually extremely difficult to have a pistol pointed at one and NOT take it personally – at least that is Britt-Marie's considered opinion.

'Open the fucking till then, for Christ's sake!' hisses the robber at her.

She will come to remember this afterwards, being addressed as if she's an instrument, not a person. Somebody tries to roll up to the till but Britt-Marie is in the way and seems frozen to the spot.

'OPEN IT!' bellows the robber so that both Somebody and the men with caps instinctively cover their faces with their hands, as if this might help.

But Britt-Marie does not move. Her terror paralyses her so she's not even capable of feeling afraid. Why she reacts the way she does is something she's incapable of understanding, but there are an awful lot of things you are not equipped to know about yourself until you have a pistol pointing at your face. And so, to Britt-Marie's own surprise and the consternation of Somebody and the men with caps, she hears some words coming out of her mouth:

'First you have to buy something.'

'OOOPEN IT!' howls the robber.

But Britt-Marie doesn't move. She puts her bandaged hand into the other. Both hands are trembling, and Britt-Marie thinks briefly that surely there are limits, but in the final analysis it's been the sort of day that Britt-Marie feels has gone beyond the limit. So she replies in a wholly considerate way:

'You have to put in an amount before you can open the till, you see. Otherwise the receipt is wrong.'

The pistol judders up and down in the robber's hand. Equal amounts of fury and surprise.

'JUST BLOODY PUT IN ANYTHING THEN!'

Britt-Marie changes her hands around. Her fingers are slippery with sweat. But something within her decides, against her most reasonably protesting common sense, that this is a good point in Britt-Marie's life to stand her ground a bit.

'You have to understand you can't just put anything in. Then the receipts aren't right.'

'I COULDN'T GIVE A FUCK ABOUT YOUR FUCKING RECEIPTS, YOU OLD BAG . . .!' screams the robber.

'There's no need to raise your voice,' Britt-Marie interrupts firmly, and then goes on patiently to tell him:

'And there's certainly no cause to use that sort of language!'

Somebody's wheelchair comes careering across the floor and tackles Britt-Marie at thigh-height, sending Somebody, the wheelchair and Britt-Marie to the floor. The sound of the gunshot into the ceiling leaves a piercing ringing sound in Britt-Marie's ears that makes her lose all sense of direction. Fragments of glass from the fluorescent tube come snowing down and she doesn't know if she is lying on her back or her stomach, where the walls are, or where the floors. She can feel Somebody's heavy breathing in her ear and far away something seems to be making a tinkling sound.

Then she hears Vega and Omar's voices.

'What the he . . .' Vega manages to say, and Britt-Marie instinctively gets to her feet at that point, even though her ears are still ringing and her common sense is telling her to sharpen up and stay there on the floor like a civilised person.

There's a lot you can't know about a person until you become one with her. What her capabilities are. The courage she has. The robber turns to Vega and Omar with his sense of shock radiating heatedly through the holes in his balaclava.

'What are you doing here?'

'Psycho?' whispers Omar.

'THE HELL YOU DOING HERE? I WAITED UNTIL YOU'D GONE! WHAT YOU BLOODY DOING HERE, FUCKING KIDS?'

'I forgot my jacket,' Vega manages to say.

Psycho furiously waves his pistol at her, but Britt-Marie is already standing between the pistol barrel and the children. She stretches her arms out behind her to make sure she's covering the girl and the boy with her body, but she doesn't move an inch. She's frozen to the spot, held in place by a whole lifetime of thwarted ambitions.

'That's just about enough now!' she hisses menacingly.

She actually can't remember ever having done anything menacing in her entire life.

There's a slightly ambivalent atmosphere in the pizzeria after that; that is probably how you'd have to describe it. Psycho clearly doesn't quite know what to do with his pistol and, until he makes his decision, no one else in the pizzeria knows what to do about it either. Britt-Marie looks at his shoes with annoyance.

'I just mopped the floor.'

'SHUT YOUR FUCKING MOUTH, MOTHERFUCKER!'

'I certainly will not!'

Psycho has broken into a sweat, which drips from the holes

in his balaclava. He spins his pistol two turns around the pizzeria at eye-level, sending the men with caps down on the floor again. Then he stares hatefully at Britt-Marie one last time, and runs.

The bell on the door tinkles obediently and Britt-Marie's body starts melting on to the floor, although Vega and Omar are doing their best to hold her up with their trembling arms. Her coat is wet with tears, but she can't tell if they are hers or the children's, or exactly at what point she stops being in their arms and instead they are in hers. When she realises that they are about to fall, she summons the strength to stand on her own two feet. Because that is what women like Britt-Marie do. They find the strength when they have to do something for others.

'Sorry sorry sorry sorry sorry,' pants Vega.

'Shhhh,' whispers Britt-Marie and rocks both her and Omar in her arms.

'Sorry for calling you an old bat,' sobs Vega.

'It's certainly nothing I haven't heard before,' Britt-Marie says to calm her.

Gently she sits the children down on two chairs. Wraps them in blankets and makes hot chocolate with real cocoa, because that was what Kent's children used to want when they woke in the night after having horrible nightmares. Admittedly the quality of the cocoa is a little dubious, because Somebody boasts that it's 'almost cocoa, huh! From Asia!' – but in any case the children are too shaken up to be concerned about it.

Omar keeps stammering about how they have to find Sami, and Vega repeatedly calls her older brother's mobile. Britt-Marie tries to calm them by saying that she's quite certain Sami had nothing to do with the robbery, upon which the two children stare open-mouthed at her and Omar whispers:

'You don't get it. When Sami finds out that Psycho pointed a gun at us he'll find him and kill him. We have to get hold of Sami!'

But Sami isn't picking up. The children get more and more frightened. Britt-Marie wraps them up even tighter in blankets and makes more hot chocolate. Then she does what she can.

What she knows. She fetches a broom and a mop and bicarbonate of soda and sweeps up the glass and swabs the floor.

When she's done with that she stands behind the till, holding on for all she's worth so that she doesn't pass out. Somebody gets her a headache tablet and another beer. The men with caps and beards get up from their table, bring their coffee cups to the counter and silently put them down in front of Britt-Marie. Then they take off their caps, look down at their newspapers and start rifling through them until they find what they are looking for and duly hand these over to Britt-Marie.

Crossword supplements.

27

Britt-Marie doesn't know if it's Kent or Sven's voice she hears first.

Sven comes because Vega has called him, Kent comes because Omar has called him.

The police car and the BMW both come ploughing into the parking area. The two men come stumbling in, white-faced, standing crestfallen inside the door and looking at the shot-to-pieces fluorescent tube on the ceiling. Then they stare at Britt-Marie. She sees their fear. Sees how they are plagued by bad conscience because they weren't here to protect her. She sees how much this pains them, this missed opportunity to be her hero. They gulp, they don't seem to know which foot to stand on. Then they instinctively do what almost all men in that situation would do.

They start arguing with each other about whose fault this is.

'Is everyone OK?' Sven asks first of all, but he's interrupted by Kent, who points across the premises with his whole arm and orders everyone:

'Now let's take it easy until the police get here!'

Sven spins around like an offended mannequin.

'What do you think I'm wearing, you damned yuppie! A carnival outfit?'

'I mean the real police, the kind that can STOP robberies!' splutters Kent.

Sven takes two small, angry steps forward and lifts his chin:

'Of course, of course, you would have stopped it with your WALLET if you'd been here!'

Their white faces turn red in an instant. Britt-Marie has never seen Sven angry in this way before, and judging by the facial expressions of Vega, Omar and Somebody, none of them have either. Kent, who immediately senses his leadership position in the room is under threat, tries to raise his voice even more to take command of the situation.

'Are you OK, kids?' he asks Omar and Vega.

'Don't you ask them if they're OK! You don't even KNOW these children!' Sven says, cutting him off and furiously pushing Kent's pointing hand away, then turns to the children and points with his own whole arm. 'Are you OK, kids?'

Vega and Omar nod, confused. Somebody tries to say something but she doesn't have a chance. Kent pushes in front of Sven and waves the palms of his hands about.

'Everyone calm down now so we can call the police.'

'I'm STANDING RIGHT HERE!'

Britt-Marie's ears are still ringing. She clears her throat and says:

'Please Kent. Please Sven. Can I just ask you to calm yourselves dow—'

But the men are not listening to her, they continue rowing and gesticulating as if she were something you could just switch off with a remote control.

Kent snorts something about how Sven couldn't 'protect a hand with a glove' and Sven snorts back that he's sure Kent is 'very brave inside his BMW with the doors locked'. Kent yells that Sven shouldn't get ideas about himself because he's nothing but 'a copper in a little crappy village' and Sven yells back that Kent shouldn't think he can just come here and 'buy people's admiration with business cards and shit like that!' Upon which Kent yells that 'the kid wants to be a bloody entrepreneur, doesn't he!' upon which Sven yells that 'being an entrepreneur is not a job' upon which Kent rails at him, 'What, so you want him to be a cop instead, do you? Huh? What sort of pay does a policeman take home?' Upon which Sven flies into a rage: 'We get a two and a half per cent raise every year and I have very good yields on my pension funds! I've done a course in it!'

Britt-Marie tries to step between them, but they don't notice her.

'I've done a *cooouuurse*,' Kent imitates disdainfully.

'Hey! It's an offence to pull at a policeman's uniform, damn it!' roars Sven and grabs hold of Kent's shirt.

'Watch the shirt! Do you have any idea how much this cost!?'

'You vain ponce, no wonder Britt-Marie left you!'

'Left me!? You think she'll be staying here with y-o-u, you glorified security guard!?'

Britt-Marie waves her arms as hard as she can in front of them, trying to make them see her.

'Please Kent! Please Sven! Stop at once! I just mopped this floor!'

But it's useless, as each of the men has just employed their respective right arms to put the other in a headlock, and they have started tottering about doubled over in a swearing, panting dance, and seconds later, with a mighty crash, the front door of the pizzeria shatters into splintered wood when the two men tumble through it like drunken bears. They land in an indecorous pile in the gravel and, in so doing, seem to draw even more attention to their physical imperfections.

Britt-Marie runs forward and stares at them. They stare up at her, suddenly silent and well aware of the trouble they have caused.

Kent tries to get on his feet first.

'Darling, you can see for yourself, can't you? The bloke is a complete idiot!'

'He started it!' Sven protests at once, crawling to his feet next to Kent.

And that's the point when Britt-Marie has had enough. Enough of the whole thing. She's been shouted at and pushed and threatened with pistols and now she has to mop the floor one more time because of splinters of wood all over the pizzeria. Enough is enough.

They don't hear her the first, second or third time. But then she fills her lungs with air and says as emphatically as she can:

'I should like to ask you to leave.'

When they still don't listen to her she does something she hasn't done in twenty years, not since one of her flowers was blown off the balcony. She yells.

'GET OUT OF HERE! THE PAIR OF YOU!'

The pizzeria grows more silent than it could possibly have been even if a new pistol-wielding robber had stepped inside. Kent and Sven are left standing with their mouths wide open, making noises that would probably have been words if they had closed their mouths between the syllables. Britt-Marie digs her heels even deeper into the floor and points at the broken door.

'Get out. At once.'

'But for God's sake, darl—' Kent begins to say, but Britt-Marie chops her bandaged hand through the air in what could probably have qualified as a new form of martial arts and abruptly silences him.

'You might have asked how I hurt my hand, Kent. You might have asked, because then I might have believed that you actually cared.'

'I thought, oh come on now, darling, I thought you'd got your hand caught in the dishwasher or some shit like that . . . you know how it is. I didn't think it was anything seri—'

'Because you didn't ask!'

'But . . . darling . . . don't get all piss—' stammers Kent.

Sven sticks out his chest towards him.

'Exactly! Exactly! Get out of here, you bloody yuppie, Britt-Marie doesn't want you here! Don't you underst—' he starts saying, brimming with self-confidence.

But Britt-Marie's hand cleaves the air in front of him so that he staggers back at the draught.

'And you, Sven! Don't tell me what I feel! You don't know

me! Not even I know myself, quite clearly, because this is certainly not normal behaviour for me!'

Somewhere on the premises Somebody is trying not to laugh. Vega and Omar look as if they'd like to keep notes so they never forget any of the details. Britt-Marie collects herself and adjusts her hair and brushes some wooden splinters from her skirt and then places her bandaged hand neatly in the other, and clarifies in an altogether well-meaning, considerate way:

'Now I'm going to clean in here. Good afternoon to you both.'

The bell above the door tinkles dolefully and half-heartedly behind Kent and Sven. They stay outside for a good while yelling 'See what you've done?' at each other. Then everything goes silent.

Britt-Marie starts cleaning.

Somebody and the children hide in the kitchen until she has finished. They daren't even laugh.

28

Admittedly it is not the two policemen's fault, it really isn't.

They've come to Borg from town and are just trying to do their jobs as best they can.

But Britt-Marie is possibly just slightly irascible. That is how you get when people shoot at you.

'We can appreciate that you're in shock, but we need our questions answered,' one of the policemen tries to explain.

'I see you're not at all concerned about stomping in with muddy shoes on a newly mopped floor, I see that, it must be very nice for you.'

'We've already said we're sorry about that. Really sorry. But as we've already explained now several times we have to question all the witnesses on the scene,' the other policeman tries to say.

'My list has been destroyed.'

'What do you mean?'

'You asked for my testimony. My list is destroyed. None of all this was on my list when I left home this morning, so now my entire list is in disarray.'

'That's not quite what we meant,' says the first policeman.

'Aha. So now my testimony is wrong as well, is it?'

'We need to know if you got a good look at the perpetrator,' the other policeman attempts to say.

'I should like to inform you that I have perfectly good vision. I've spoken to my optician about it. He's an excellent optician, you should understand. Very well brought up. He doesn't walk around indoors with muddy shoes.'

The police emit synchronised sighs. Britt-Marie exhales very pointedly back.

'It would be a great help to us if you could describe the perpetrator,' one of the policemen asks.

'Of course I can do that,' hisses Britt-Marie.

'And how would you describe him?'

'He had a pistol!'

'But you really don't remember anything else? Any distinguishing characteristics?'

'Isn't a pistol a distinguishing characteristic?' wonders Britt-Marie.

This is the moment when the police decide to go back into town.

Britt-Marie mops the floor again. So hard that in the end Somebody has to stop her.

'Careful with mop, Britt-Marie, expensive mop for God's sake!' she grins.

Britt-Marie does not think this is the best of days to roll about in your wheelchair, grinning at people, she certainly doesn't. But Somebody makes sure she drinks her beer and eats a bit of pizza, and then she hands over her car keys.

'I was under the distinct impression that the car had not been repaired yet!' Britt-Marie bursts out.

Somebody shrugs, ashamed of herself.

'Ah, you know. Been ready many days, huh, but . . . you know.'

'No. I absolutely don't know at all.'

Somebody guiltily rubs her hands in her lap.

'The car is ready many days. But if Britt has no car: can't drive off and leave Borg, huh?'

'So you pulled the wool over my eyes? You lied to my face?' Britt-Marie says in an injured tone of voice.

'Yes,' Somebody admits.

'Might I ask why you did that?'

Somebody shrugs. 'I like you. You're, what's-it-called? A breath of fresh air! Borg is boring without Britt, huh?'

Britt-Marie doesn't have a particularly good answer to hand for this, it has to be said. So Somebody fetches another beer and calls out, as if in passing:

'But Britt, you know, let me put question to you: how do you feel about blue car?'

'What do you mean by that?' pants Britt-Marie.

Then they spend a fairly lengthy amount of time on the football pitch, arguing about this, because Somebody is quite persistent about explaining that she could without any trouble respray Britt-Marie's car the same colour as the new blue door. It wouldn't be any trouble at all. In fact, Somebody is almost a hundred per cent sure that at some point she registered a paint-shop business with the local authority.

In the end Britt-Marie gets so worked up about this that she takes her notebook and tears out her list for the whole day, and starts one completely fresh. She has never done this in her whole life, but desperate times call for desperate measures.

She walks back through Borg with Vega and Omar, because Britt-Marie has by this point consumed half a can of beer, meaning it's quite out of the question for her to get behind the wheel. Especially not in a car with a blue door. What would people think? Omar stays absolutely silent until they get home, which is more minutes of silence than Britt-Marie has ever heard from him since they first got to know each other.

Vega keeps calling Sami without getting an answer. Britt-Marie tries to convince her that Sami may not have heard news of the robbery, but Vega tells her that this is Borg. Everyone knows everything about everyone in Borg. So Sami knows and Sami isn't answering because he's busy tracking Psycho down and killing him.

Under these circumstances, Britt-Marie can't bring herself to leave the children on their own, so she goes up to the flat with them and starts making dinner. They have it at exactly six o'clock. The children eat staring down at their plates, as children do who have learned to expect the worst. When Britt-Marie's telephone rings the first time they bounce up, but it's only Kent so Britt-Marie doesn't answer. When Sven calls a minute later she doesn't answer either, and when the girl from the unemployment office calls three times in a row she switches off the telephone.

Vega calls Sami again. Gets no answer. That's when she starts washing up, without anyone having asked her, and then Britt-Marie realises the situation is really serious.

'I'm sure nothing serious has happened,' says Britt-Marie.

'The hell you know about it?' Vega says.

Omar mumbles from the table:

'Sami is never late for dinner. He's a dinner-Nazi.'

Then he picks up his plate and puts it in the dishwasher. Voluntarily. Which is the point at which Britt-Marie understands something extremely drastic has to be done, so she concentrates on breathing in and out half a dozen times, and then she hugs the children hard. When they burst into tears she does the same.

When the doorbell finally rings they're stumbling over one another to get there. None of them gives a second thought to the fact that if this was Sami coming back he would just have opened the door with his key, so when they tug at the door handle only to find the white dog sitting outside, Omar feels disappointed, Vega is angry and Britt-Marie anxious. Because these seem to be their most basic emotions in life.

'You can't come in with dirty paws,' Britt-Marie informs the dog.

The dog glances at its paws, and seems overwhelmed by a lack of self-confidence.

Next to it stands Bank, and next to her stand Max, Ben, Dino and Toad.

Bank points her stick, gently poking Britt-Marie in the stomach.

'Hi there, Rambo!'

'How dare you!' protests Britt-Marie instinctively.

'You scared off the robber,' explains Toad. 'Like Rambo. That means you're an ice-cool motherfucker!'

Britt-Marie patiently puts her bandaged hand in the other and turns her eyes to Ben. He smiles and nods encouragingly.

'And that's, like, good.'

Britt-Marie absorbs this information and then her eyes wander all the way back to Bank.

'Ha. Very nice of you to say so.'

'Don't mention it,' mutters Bank impatiently and makes a gesture at her wrist, as if she was wearing a watch:

'What about training?'

'What training?' asks Britt-Marie.

'The training!' answers Max, who's wearing his national hockey team jersey and dancing up and down as if he needs the loo.

Britt-Marie uncomfortably rocks back and forth from her heels to her toes.

'I assumed it was self-evident that it had been cancelled. In view of the circumstances.'

'What circumstances?'

'The robbery, my dear.'

Max looks as if he's working his brain hard to bring clarity to what these two separate things could feasibly have to do with each other. Then he comes to the only possible logical conclusion: 'Did the robber nick the ball?'

'I'm sorry?'

'If he didn't nick the ball we can still play, can't we?'

The group gathered on the landing takes this conclusion into consideration, and when none of them seems able to come up with any rational line of argument to oppose it, there's not much else to do.

So they play. In the yard outside the apartment block, between the refuse room and the bicycle stand, using three gloves and a dog as the goalposts.

Max tackles Vega just as she's about to score, and she takes two swings at him with both fists. He backs off. She roars: 'Don't touch me, rich kid!' They all shuffle away. Omar avoids the ball as if it's frightening to him.

The black car stops on the road just as Toad has hit one of the goalposts on the nose for the third time, and it's refusing to take part any more. Omar rushes into Sami's arms, and Vega turns around and marches into the house without a word.

The goalpost is having some sweets from Bank's pocket and getting scratched behind its ears as Sami draws closer.

'Hey there, Bank,' he says.

'Did you find him?' asks Bank.

'No,' says Sami.

'Lucky for Psycho!' yells Toad excitedly, waving his thumb and index finger like a pistol, then cutting this activity short when Britt-Marie gives him a look as if he just refused to use a coaster.

Bank pokes Sami's stomach with her stick.

'Lucky for Psycho. But mainly lucky for you, Sami.'

She heads for home with Max, Dino, Toad and Ben in tow. Before they go around the corner Ben stops and calls out to Britt-Marie:

'You're still coming tomorrow, aren't you?'

'Coming to what?' Britt-Marie wants to know, and is met by a collective stare from the group as if she's lost her reason.

'To the cup! Tomorrow's the cup!' thunders Max.

Britt-Marie brushes her skirt so they don't see she's got her eyes closed and is sucking her cheeks in.

'Ha. Ha. Obviously I will. Obviously.'

She doesn't say anything about how it will be her last day in Borg. They don't say anything either.

She sits in the kitchen until Sami comes out of Vega and Omar's bedroom.

'They're sleeping,' he says with a somewhat forced smile.

Britt-Marie stands up, collects herself and informs him coolly:

'I don't want to stick my nose in, because I'm certainly not the sort of person who does that, but if it's true that you were intending to do away with this Psycho tonight for the sake of

Vega and Omar, I should like to clarify to you that it's not suitable for a gentleman to run around doing away with people.'

He raises his eyebrows. She closes her fingers around her handbag.

'I'm not a gentleman,' he says with a smile.

'No, but you could become one!'

He laughs. She doesn't laugh. So he stops laughing.

'Ah, drop it, I wouldn't have killed him. He's my best friend. He's just so fucking sick in the head, you get what I mean? He owes people money. The wrong kind of people. So he's desperate. He didn't think Vega and Omar would be there.'

'Right,' says Britt-Marie.

'That's not to say you're not important as well!' Sami corrects himself.

'Sorry. I need a cig,' says Sami with a sigh, and only then does Britt-Marie realise his hands are trembling.

She goes with him on to the balcony, coughing dubiously and not at all demonstratively. He blows the smoke away from her and apologises.

'Sorry, is this bothering you?'

'I should like to ask if you have any more cigarettes,' says Britt-Marie without blinking an eye.

He starts laughing.

'I didn't think you were a smoker.'

'I'm certainly not,' she says defensively. 'I've just had a long day.'

'OK, OK,' he smirks, handing her one and lighting it for her.

She takes slight, shallow puffs. Closes her eyes.

'I'd like you to know that you're certainly not the only one with tendencies to live a wild, irresponsible existence. I smoked any number of cigarettes in my youth.'

He laughs out loud, and she feels it's more at her than with her, so she goes on to clarify her statement:

'For a period in my youth I was actually employed as a waitress!'

She nods with emphasis, just to underline that she's by no

means just making this up off the top of her head. Sami looks impressed and gestures at her to take a seat on an upside-down drinks crate.

'You want a whisky, Britt-Marie?'

Britt-Marie's common sense has obviously locked itself in its room, because suddenly Britt-Marie hears herself saying:

'Yes, absolutely, you know what, Sami? I would like one very much!'

And so they drink whisky and smoke. Britt-Marie tries to blow some smoke rings, because she knows she wished she could do this at the time when she was working as a waitress. The chefs knew how to do it. It looked so very relaxing.

'Dad didn't leave, we chased him away, me and Magnus,' Sami tells her without any preamble.

'Who's Magnus?'

'He likes "Psycho" better, people don't get as scared of a "Magnus",' says Sami with a grin.

'Ha,' says Britt-Marie, but it's actually more of a 'huh?' than a 'ha'.

'Dad hit Mum whenever he'd been drinking. No one knew about it, you know, but once Magnus was picking me up to go to football training when we were small, and he'd never seen anything like it. He comes from a right nuclear family, his dad worked for an insurance company and drove an Opel, sort of thing. But he . . . I don't bloody know. He saw me step in between Mum and Dad, and I got a hiding from Dad as usual, and then out of fucking nowhere Magnus was standing there yelling, with a knife at Dad's throat. And I don't think I got it until then, that not all kids lived like we did. Not all kids were afraid every time they came home. Omar cried. Vega cried. So, you know . . . it felt like that was enough right there. See what I mean?'

Britt-Marie coughs smoke through her nose. Sami pats her helpfully on the back and fetches water for her. Then stands by the balcony railing, peering over the edge as if he's measuring the distance to the ground.

'Magnus helped chase Dad away. You don't find friends like that just anywhere.'

'Where's your mother, Sami?'

'Just away for a while, she'll be back soon,' Sami attempts.

Britt-Marie collects herself and points her cigarette at him menacingly.

'I may be many things, Sami, but I'm no idiot.'

Sami empties his glass. Scratches his head.

'She's dead,' he admits at last.

Exactly how long it takes Britt-Marie to get absolutely clear about the whole story, she can't say. Night has fallen over Borg, and she thinks it may be snowing. When Sami, Vega and Omar's father left, their mother took on more driving work with the trucking company. Year after year. When the trucking company fired all its drivers she started working for foreign companies, whenever she could find them, to the best of her ability. Year after year, as mothers do. One evening she got caught up in a traffic jam, got delayed, and her bonus hung in the balance. So she drove through the night in bad weather, in a truck that was too old. At dawn she met an oncoming car, the driver of which was reaching for his mobile, so that he'd veered on to the wrong side of the road. She swerved, the tyres of the truck lost their purchase on the road in the rain and the whole thing overturned. There was a deluge of blood and glass, and three children sat waiting three thousand kilometres away for the sound of a key in the front door.

'She was a bloody good mum. She was a warrior,' whispers Sami.

Britt-Marie has to refill her glass before she manages to say: 'I am so very, very sorry, Sami.'

It may sound paltry and less than you might expect. But it's all she's got.

Sami pats her on the arm understandingly, as if he's the one to console her and not the other way around.

'Vega's afraid, even though she mainly seems angry. Omar is angry, though you'd probably think he was afraid.'

'And you?'

'I don't have time to feel things, I have to take care of them.'

'But . . . how . . . I mean . . . the authorities,' Britt-Marie starts, in a welter of disconnected thoughts.

Sami lights her another cigarette, then one for himself.

'We never informed anyone that Dad cleared off. He must be abroad somewhere, but he's still registered at this address. We had his old driving licence, so Omar bribed a truck driver at the petrol station to go to the police in town pretending to be him and signing some papers. We got a couple of thousand on Mum's insurance. No one else ever asked anything about it.'

'But you can't just . . . Good God, Sami, this is not *Pippi Longstocking*, is it! Who will take care of the children—'

'I will. I will take care of them,' he says simply, cutting her short.

'For . . . how long?'

'As long as I can. I get the fact they'll catch us out pretty soon, I'm not an idiot. But I only need a bit of time, Britt-Marie. Just a bit. I have plans. I just have to show that I can support them financially, you understand? Otherwise they'll take Vega and Omar and put them in some fucking children's home. I can't let them do that. I'm not the type that just walks out.'

'They might let you take care of the children. If you explain it exactly as it is, they might—'

'Look at me, Britt-Marie. Criminal record, unemployed and mates with people like Psycho. Would you let me take care of two children?'

'We can show them your cutlery drawer! We can explain that you have the potential to become a gentleman!'

'Thanks,' he says and puts his hand on her shoulder.

She leans against him.

'And Sven knows everything?'

Sami runs his hands over her hair to calm her.

'He's the one who took the international call from the police who found the truck. He came here to give us the news. Cried as much as we did. It's like having a parent in the army, you know, when your mum drives a truck. If someone in uniform comes to your door you know what it's about.'

'So . . . Sven . . .'

'He knows everything.'

Britt-Marie's eyes blink very hard as they stare at his shirt. It's a curious thing to do. A grown woman on a young man's balcony in the middle of the night, just like that. What on earth would people think about that?

'I was under the impression that one became a policeman because one believed in rules and regulations.'

'I think Sven became a policeman because he believes in justice.'

Britt-Marie straightens up. Wipes her face down.

'We're going to need more whisky. And if it's not too trouble-some, I should like to ask for a bottle of window-cleaner as well.'

After a considerable amount of reflection she adds:

'Under present circumstances I could see myself making do with any old brand.'

29

Britt-Marie wakes up with a headache of the most spectacular kind. She's lying in her bed in Bank's house. A neighbour seems to be drilling into the wall. The whole room sways when she gets up. She's sweating, her body aching and her mouth laced with a sort of sharp bitterness. Britt-Marie is obviously a woman with a certain amount of life experience, so she understands her condition immediately. The day after she has drunk more alcohol in Sami's home than her total intake in the last forty years there can only be one reasonable conclusion:

'I've got flu!' she explains to Bank in a knowing sort of way, when she comes down to the kitchen.

Bank is making bacon and eggs. The dog sniffs the air and moves a little further away from Britt-Marie.

'You smell of spirits,' Bank states, without quite managing to stop herself looking amused.

'That's right. Which is obviously why I feel the way I do today,' says Britt-Marie with a nod.

'I thought you said you'd come down with flu,' says Bank.

Britt-Marie nods helpfully.

'But my dear, that's precisely what I'm saying! It's the only reasonable explanation. When you drink alcohol your immune system is knocked out, you have to understand. And that's why I've got the flu.'

'Flu, right then,' mumbles Bank and puts the eggs on the table for Britt-Marie.

Britt-Marie closes her eyes, holding back her nausea, and gives the eggs to the dog. Bank puts a glass of cold water in front of her instead. Britt-Marie drinks. Flu makes people dehydrated. She's read all about it.

'Mine and Kent's children were ill all the time; if it wasn't one thing it was another – but as for myself I am never ill. "Britt-Marie, you're as healthy as a nut kernel!" That's what my doctor always says, he really does!'

When neither Bank nor the dog answer, Britt-Marie breathes deeply and her eyes blink forlornly. Her words seem drained of oxygen when she corrects herself:

'I mean Kent's children.'

She drinks her water in silence. The dog and Bank have their eggs. They go with her to meet the football team, because Britt-Marie is not the sort of woman who bunks off work just because she has flu. The dog makes a demonstrative loop around the flower bed outside the house because it stinks as if someone has vomited there in the course of the night.

Somebody is sitting inside the broken front door of the pizzeria, drinking coffee, when they get there. She grimaces when Britt-Marie comes too close, and Britt-Marie pulls an even uglier face back.

'It stinks in here. Have you been smoking inside?' she asks, almost with a note of accusation.

Somebody wrinkles her nose.

'And you, Britt? Have you been, what's-it-called? On fire and trying to put it out with whisky?'

'I'll have you know that I've got the flu,' snorts Britt-Marie.

Bank pokes Somebody's wheelchair with her stick.

'Stop going on now and give her a Bloody Mary.'

'What's that?' asks Britt-Marie as brightly as she's able.

'It helps against . . . flu,' mutters Bank.

Somebody disappears into the kitchen and comes back with a glass filled with what looks like tomato juice. Britt-Marie sips it sceptically, before spitting it out at the dog. It does not look at all pleased about it.

'This tastes of p-e-p-p-e-r!' splutters Britt-Marie.

The dog goes to sit in the gravel, carefully placing itself upwind. Bank holds out her stick with her arm straightened to make sure she's out of spitting range. Somebody frowns and fetches a cloth to wipe down the table between them, while muttering:

'Don't know what flu you have, Britt, but do me a favour, huh, what's-it-called? Don't light a match near your breath before you brush your teeth, huh? Pizzeria has no fire insurance, you know.'

Britt-Marie certainly has no idea what that's supposed to mean. But she makes her polite apologies to Somebody and Bank and explains she has a few things to do in the recreation centre and actually can't stay here all morning making a fuss about things. Then she briskly walks across the parking area, continues in a controlled manner into the recreation centre toilet and locks the door behind her.

When she comes out Sven is squatting by the pizzeria door, putting the hinges back in. He stumbles to his feet and removes his police cap when he catches sight of her. There's a toolbox at his feet. He tries to smile.

'I just thought that I, well, that I would mend the door. I thought . . .'

'Ha,' says Britt-Marie and looks at the wood splinters around his feet.

'Yes, I mean, I'll sweep up here. It was . . . I'm, I mean, I'm sorry!'

He looks as if that last bit is about more important things than wood splinters. He moves out of the way, and she slinks past. Holding her breath even though she has brushed her teeth.

'I'm, I mean, I'm very sorry about yesterday,' he says wretchedly to her back.

She stops without turning around. He clears his throat.

'I mean, I never meant to make you feel . . . the way you felt. I would never want to be the one to make you feel . . . like that.'

She closes her eyes and nods. Waits until her common sense has silenced the part of her that wishes he'd touch her.

'I'll get the vacuum cleaner,' she whispers after that. She knows he's looking at her as she walks away. Her steps become awkward, as if she's forgotten how to walk without putting one foot on top of the other. All her words to him are like staying in a hotel, new and curious and tentatively fumbling for switches on the wall, repeatedly turning on different lights than those she wanted to turn on.

Somebody comes rolling after her into the kitchen, where she's opening the broom cupboard to get out the pizzeria's vacuum cleaner.

'Here. Came for you.'

Britt-Marie stares at the bouquet in her hands. Tulips. Purple. Britt-Marie loves purple tulips, to the extent that Britt-Marie can love anything without viewing it as an unseemly burst of emotion. Tenderly she holds it in her hands and does her utmost not to get the shivers. 'I love you', it says on the card. From Kent.

It takes years to get to know a human being. An entire life. It's what makes a home a home.

At a hotel you're only a visitor. Hotels don't know your favourite flowers.

She fills her lungs with tulips; during one long inhalation she is there again, at her own draining board and in her own broom cupboard and rugs that she knows the whereabouts of because she put them there herself. White shirts and black shoes and a damp towel on the bathroom floor. All Kent's things. All Kent-things. You just can't rebuild things like that. You wake up one morning and realise that you're too old to check in to a hotel.

She doesn't meet Sven's eyes when she comes back out of the kitchen. Is grateful that the noise of the vacuum cleaner is drowning out all the things that should not be said.

Then come Vega, Omar, Ben, Toad and Dino, exactly on time, and Britt-Marie busies herself with fitting them out in their newly washed football kits. Vega looks searchingly at Britt-Marie and asks if she's hungover, because actually she looks hungover, says the girl. Britt-Marie makes it clear in every possible way that she's certainly no such thing, that she's merely come down with the flu.

'Ah. That sort of flu. Sami had that this morning as well,' laughs Omar.

The first little tinkle from the friendly bell above the door, after Sven has mended it, rings out when the men with beards and caps come in to drink their coffee and read their newspapers. But one of them asks when the first match is starting and when Omar tells them, the men check their wristwatches. As if for the first time in ages they have a schedule to keep to.

The second tinkle from the bell above the door comes when the two ancient women with Zimmer frames come dragging themselves over the threshold.

One of them rivets her eyes into Britt-Marie and points at her.

'Err yow thoon she oa treena de boos?'

Britt-Marie can't tell if these are words or sounds. Vega leans forward and whispers:

'She's asking if you're our coach.'

Britt-Marie nods without taking her eyes off the tip of the ancient woman's finger, as if it's about to open fire. At this confirmation, the ancient woman produces a bag from a little shelf under the handle of the Zimmer frame, and presses it into Britt-Marie's arms.

'Frout aia de boos!'

'She says it's fruit for the boys in the team,' Vega interprets helpfully.

'Ha. I should like to inform you there's also a girl in the team,' informs Britt-Marie.

The ancient woman glares at her. Then she glares at Vega and the football jersey she's wearing. The other ancient woman pushes her way forward and grunts something you can't hear to the first ancient woman, whereupon the first ancient woman points at Vega and glares at Britt-Marie:

'Shera havan esstrofrout!'

'They're saying I should have extra fruit,' says Vega, pleased to hear this and taking the bag from Britt-Marie to peer inside.

'Ha,' says Britt-Marie, frenetically adjusting her skirt in every possible way she can think of.

When she looks up again the two ancient women are standing so close to her that you couldn't get an A4 sheet of paper between them. The women point at her and Bank.

'Yer yunguns shall teek th' chouldrin un goo ter de blousted folk in toon un tall erm Borg ainnit derd! We ainitt derd hire! Tell doose bastourds dait, hire wha' I see?'

'She's saying you and Bank have to take us to town and tell those bastards Borg isn't dead,' says Vega with her mouth full of apple.

Bank stands on the other side of Britt-Marie with a grin on her face.

'And she called you a "young one", Britt-Marie.'

Britt-Marie, who wasn't even referred to as a 'young one' when she was young, can't quite think what to say to that. So she just pats one of the women's Zimmer frames, slightly at a loss, and says:

'Ha. Thank you, then. Thank you kindly.'

The women grunt and drag themselves out again. Somebody fetches the keys to the white car with the blue door and, in between chewing, Vega informs Britt-Marie that they have to pick up Max on the way.

'Ha. I was under the impression that you didn't like him,' says Britt-Marie with surprise.

'ARE YOU GOING TO START NOW AS WELL!?' roars Vega at once, so that the apple sprays out of her mouth and ricochets between them.

Omar laughs loudly and mockingly, Vega chases him out into the parking area with apples and mangos whizzing past the back of his head.

Britt-Marie closes her eyes and squeezes her eyelids tightly until her headache retreats. Then she nervously fidgets with the car keys, coughs quietly and holds them out to Sven without making eye contact.

'It's not appropriate driving a car when you have . . . the flu.'

Sven removes his cap when they get into the car. He doesn't even need to say he's doing it out of empathy. He doesn't want Britt-Marie to start worrying about what people might think if she's driven to the football competition by a policeman. Especially not in a white car with a blue door.

Nor does he say anything about how there are considerably more passengers and dogs in the car than what is suitable from both a legal and a hygienic point of view, especially as the dog and Toad have to sit in the boot because there isn't any other space available. In the end he does timidly point out that the car needs filling up. And asks her if she'd like him to do it. She answers that there's certainly no need for that, because she can absolutely manage that bit herself. It's her car, after all, whether it has a blue door or not.

After she's stood with one hand clasped in the other in front of the petrol pump for ten minutes, the back door opens and Vega crawls out of a tangle of arms, legs, football boots and dog heads, and comes to stand next to her, carefully positioning herself so that she blocks Sven's point of view.

'It's the one in the middle,' she says in a low voice to Britt-Marie without herself reaching for the petrol pump.

Britt-Marie looks at her in a panic.

'I didn't think about it until I got out of the car, you have to understand. That I don't know how you . . .'

Her voice cracks. Vega tries to make herself as broad-chested as she can so Sven can't see anything from the window. She reaches out and touches Britt-Marie's hand.

'It doesn't matter, Coach.'

Britt-Marie smiles faintly and tenderly removes a loose hair from the shoulder of Vega's jersey.

'Kent always filled up the car. He was always the one who . . . it's always been him.'

Vega points at the pump in the middle. Britt-Marie grabs hold of it as if worried that it might be live. Vega leans forward and unscrews the petrol cap.

'Who taught you all this?' asks Britt-Marie.

'My mother,' says Vega.

Then she grins so you can see more clearly than ever that she's Sami's sister.

'You don't have to support Liverpool from the day you're born, Coach. You can learn to do it when you're grown up.'

It's a day for the football cup, and for farewells, and it's the day Britt-Marie puts fuel in her own car. She would have been capable of climbing mountains or crossing oceans, if someone had asked her to.

30

Britt-Marie is not sure exactly at what point the sun broke through the eternal grey haze of the January sky, but it seems to be looking ahead into the new season. Borg somehow looks different today. They drive past Toad's house, the one with the greenhouse outside. A pregnant woman is moving about inside. They pass more gardens, with more people in them, which is deeply strange now Britt-Marie has got used to Borg's only road always being deserted. A few of them are young, a few have children, a few of them wave at the car. A man with a cap is standing there with a sign in his hand.

'Is he putting out a "For Sale" sign?' asks Britt-Marie.

Sven slows down and waves at the man.

'He's taking it down.'

'Why?'

'Things have changed. They're going to the football cup. They no longer want to go, they want to see what happens next. It's been a while since anyone in Borg wanted to know what happens next.'

The white car with the blue door travels through Borg, and only when they go past the sign announcing that they are now leaving Borg does Britt-Marie realise that they are being followed by other vehicles. History will remember this as the first time there's ever been a traffic jam in Borg.

Max lives in one of the big houses beyond the boundaries of the village, on its own secluded street and with windows so big that they could only have been put there by someone who thought it more important for people to be able to look in than out. Sven explains to Britt-Marie that the residents here have fought with the local council for years, with mounting hostility, to put them under the jurisdiction of the town rather than remaining a part of Borg. In the next moment he slams his brakes on as a BMW backs out without looking from a garage at the far end of the street. Fredrik is wearing sunglasses, spinning the wheel as if it's fighting his efforts to do so. Sven waves, but the BMW roars past; it might as well have driven straight through them.

'Bloody lemon arse,' mutters Vega and gets out of the back seat.

Britt-Marie follows on behind. Max opens the door before they have even pressed the doorbell, barges his way out and, looking stressed out, closes the door behind him. He's still wearing the tracksuit top with 'Hockey' printed across the chest, but he has a football under his arm.

'No need to bring a ball, Vega has already put one in the car,' Britt-Marie informs him.

Max blinks uncomprehendingly.

'Surely you don't need more than one ball?' Britt-Marie goes on.

Max looks at the ball. Looks at Britt-Marie.

'Need?'

As if that's a word that bears any relation to footballs.

'Well *I* need to use your loo,' moans Vega, moving impatiently towards the door. Max's hand catches her shoulder; she instantly slaps it away.

'You can't!' he says, looking worried. 'Sorry!'

Vega peers suspiciously at him.

'Are you worried I'll see how bloody over-the-top your house is? You think I care if you're millionaires?'

Max tries to push her away from the door, but she's too quick; she slips under his arm and goes in. He bundles in after her, then they stand there, both rooted to the spot. She with her mouth wide open, he with his eyes closed.

'I . . . what the hell . . . where's your furniture?'

'We had to sell it,' mumbles Max after a moment, closing the door without looking at the room.

Vega peers at him.

'Don't you have any money?'

'No one has any money in Borg,' says Max, opening the door and stepping out, heading towards the car.

'So why doesn't your dad just sell his bloody BMW, then?' Vega calls out after him.

'Because then everyone will know he's given up,' says Max with a sigh, and climbs into the back seat.

'But . . . what the . . .' Vega starts saying as she climbs in after him, until she's stopped by a hard shove from Omar.

'Drop it, sis, what are you? A cop or something? Leave him alone.'

'I only want to kn—' she protests, but Omar gives her another shove.

'Leave it! He talks like one of them but he plays football like one of us. You got it? Leave him alone.'

Max doesn't say a word on the way into town. When they stop outside the leisure centre, he gets out of the back seat with his football tucked under his arm, drops it on to the asphalt and drills a shot into the wall that is just about the hardest Britt-Marie has ever seen a ball being struck. Britt-Marie lets out the dog and Toad from the boot. Bank follows them inside. Dino, Omar and Vega come behind. Sven is at the back. Britt-Marie counts them several times and tries to work out who's missing, then hears Ben's voice, sounding rather pathetic, from somewhere around the far corner of the back seat.

'Sorry, Britt-Marie. I didn't mean to.'

When she can't immediately locate the voice he manages to say:

'I've never played in a cup before. I got so . . . nervous. I didn't want to say anything when we were at the petrol station.'

Britt-Marie still isn't quite sure she can hear what he's saying, so she sticks her head into the car. Sees the dark patch on his trousers and the seat where he's sitting.

'Sorry,' he says, squeezing his eyes shut.

'Oh . . . I . . . sorry. Don't worry about it! It'll come off with bicarbonate of soda!' Britt-Marie stutters, and goes to dig out some spare clothes from the boot.

Because that's the sort of person she's become in Borg, she realises. Someone who goes to football competitions with spare clothes in the boot.

She holds the bamboo screen over the window while Ben gets changed inside. Then she covers the seat with bicarbonate of soda. Brings his trousers into the sports hall and rinses them in a washbasin in a dressing room.

He stands beside her with an embarrassed pout around his mouth, but his eyes are sparkling, and when she's done he blurts out:

'Mum's coming here to watch today. She's taken the day off work!'

The way he says it, it's as if the building they're in is made of chocolate.

The other children are kicking two footballs around the corridor outside, and Britt-Marie has to exert considerable self-control not to rush out and give them a stern ticking-off about the unsuitability of kicking balls around indoors. She actually feels it's inappropriate even having sports arenas indoors, but she has no intention of being looked at as if *she's* the one with crazy opinions on the matter, so she keeps schtum about it.

The sports hall consists of a tall spectators' stand and a flight of stairs of equal height, leading down to a rectangular surface full of colourful lines running to and fro, which Britt-Marie assumes is where the football matches will be played. Indoors.

Bank gathers the children in a circle at the top of the stairs and tells them things that Britt-Marie does not understand, but she comes to the conclusion this is another one of those pep talks they're all so taken with.

After Bank has finished she waves her stick in the air towards where she's figured out Britt-Marie is standing, and then says:

'Do you have anything you want to say before the match, Britt-Marie?'

Britt-Marie has not prepared for this sort of eventuality, it's not on her list, so she grips her handbag firmly and thinks it over for a moment before saying:

'I think it's important that we try to make a good first impression.'

She doesn't know what exactly she's driving at with this, it's just something Britt-Marie finds a good general rule in life. The children watch her, with their eyebrows at varying heights. Vega keeps eating fruit from the bag and nodding sourly at the spectators in the stand.

'A good impression on who? That lot? They hate us, don't you get it?'

Britt-Marie has to admit that most of the people in the stand, many of them wearing jerseys and scarfs emblazoned with the name of their own team from their own town, are looking at them as you might look at a stranger on the underground who just sneezed in your face.

Halfway down the stairs stands the old codger from the council and the woman from the football association, the same ones that paid a visit to the training session in Borg a couple of days ago. The woman looks concerned, the old codger has his arms full of papers, and next to them stands a very serious man wearing a jersey on which it says 'Official', and another person with long hair and a tracksuit top with the name of the team from town printed on one side and the word 'Coach' on the other. He's pointing at Team Borg and bellowing something about how this is 'a serious competition, not a nursery!'

Britt-Marie doesn't know what that's supposed to mean, but when Toad hauls out a soft-drink can from his pocket she decides that this is certainly not a way of making a good first impression, so she cautions him not to open it. Toad immediately insists that his blood sugar is a bit on the low side, whereupon Vega gets involved and shoves his shoulder, while hissing:

'Are you deaf or what? Don't open that can!' Unfortunately

she catches Toad off balance and he falls backwards helplessly. He tumbles halfway down the stairs, shrieking with every step, until his body thumps into the legs of the woman from the football association, the old codger from the local council, the official and the coach person.

'DON'T OPEN THAT CAN!' roars Vega.

Upon which he decides to open the can.

It's not what you'd in any way describe as a top-notch first impression, it really isn't.

By the time Britt-Marie and Bank have reached the section of the stairs where Toad came to a stop, the coach person is yelling with even greater indignation, for reasons already described. The old codger and the woman and the papers are whirling about in a persistent rain of lemonade. The coach person has such an amount of lemonade in his hair, on his face and over his clothes that the amount of lemonade in the can must in some way have bypassed the natural laws of physics. The coach person points at Bank and Britt-Marie, so angry by this stage that the pointing action is executed by both hands, which, at this kind of distance, makes it difficult to determine whether he's actually pointing at all, or just demonstrating the approximate size of a badger.

'Are you the *coach* of this so-called *team*?'

He makes deranged quotation marks in the air when he says 'coach' and 'team'. Bank's stick pokes at the coach person by accident the first time, and possibly a little less by accident the following five times. The woman looks concerned. The old codger with the papers moves behind her and, chastened by experience, keeps his hand over his mouth.

'We're the coaches,' Bank confirms.

The coach person grins and looks angry at the same time.

'An old biddy and a blind person, *seeeriously*? Is this a *seeerious* competition? Huh?'

The official shakes his head gravely. The woman, more concerned than ever, peers at Bank.

'One of the players in your team, this Patrik Ivars . . .'

'What about me?' Toad bursts out anxiously from the floor.

'What about him?' growls Bank.

'Yeah, what about Patrik?' asks a third voice.

Toad's father is standing behind Britt-Marie now. He has combed his hair neatly, and dressed up. There's a red tulip tucked into the lapel of his jacket. Kent stands next to him in a wrinkled shirt. He smiles at Britt-Marie, and she immediately wants to take him by the hand.

'Patrik is two years younger than the others. He's too young to play in this competition without exemption being granted,' says the woman, coughing down at the floor.

'So organise the exemption then!' snorts Bank.

'Rules are rules!'

'Really? REALLY! COME HERE YOU LITTL . . .' yells Bank, striking furiously at the coach person with her stick, whereupon the coach person tries to grab her stick in order to avoid falling, and at the same time manages to pull her with him down the stairs, whereupon they both lose their footing and drop over the ledge, before a big hand in a single, forcible movement closes like a handcuff around the tracksuited arm and stops their fall.

The coach person hovers, leaning backwards over the stairs, with eyes wide open as he looks at Kent, who keeps his implacable grip on his arm and leans forward and declares in that clear and straightforward way of his, which he makes use of when explaining to people that he's actually going to do business with Germany:

'If you try to push a blind woman down a staircase I'll sue you in the courts until your family is buried in debt for the next ten generations.'

The coach person stares at him. Bank regains her balance by happening to put her stick in the coach person's stomach two or maybe three times. The concerned woman, trying a different tack, holds out a piece of paper.

'There has also been a protest from your opponents concerning this "Viga" in your team, we can see by her social security number that . . .'

'My name is VEGA!' snarls Vega from further up the stairs.

The woman scratches her earlobe self-consciously. Then smiles, as if after a local anaesthetic. And turns to Britt-Marie, who by now seems to be the only reasonable person in the assembled company.

'You have to have an exemption before girls and younger players can take part.'

'So you're going to ban Patrik and Vega, purely because this town team is too scared to play against a girl and a kid who's two years younger!!' says Kent.

'YOU'RE SCARED!' yells Bank and accidentally pokes her stick into the tracksuit top and a bit into the old codger with papers.

'We're not bloody sc . . .' mumbles the coach person.

And that is how Vega and Patrik get their exemptions so they can play. Patrik goes down the stairs to the pitch with his dad's arms around his shoulders, looking so happy you'd think he'd sprouted wings.

The other children run on to the pitch and start taking some warm-up shots at the goal, which admittedly looks as if they're taking general warm-up shots at everything except the goal.

Britt-Marie and Kent stay there on the stairs, just the two of them. She picks up a hair from the shoulder of his shirt, and adjusts a crease on his arm so softly that it's as if she never even touched him.

'How did you know to say that thing about them being scared?' she asks.

Kent laughs in a way that makes Britt-Marie also start laughing inside.

'I have an older brother. It always worked for me. You remember when I jumped off the balcony and broke my leg? All the dumbest things I ever did started with Alf telling me he didn't think I had the guts to do them!'

'It was nice of you. And you were sweet to leave the tulips,' whispers Britt-Marie, without asking if she was also one of those dumb things he did.

Kent laughs again.

'I bought them off that Toad boy's dad. He's growing them in a greenhouse in the garden. What a lunatic, eh? He nagged the heck out of me about how I had to get the red ones instead because they're "better", but I told him you like the purple ones.'

She brushes some invisible dust from his chest. Controls herself.

In a common-sense approach, she clasps one hand in the other and says:

'I have to go. They'll be on soon.'

'Good luck!' says Kent, leaning forward and kissing her on the cheek so warmly she has to grasp the metal banister to avoid falling down the stairs.

When he goes to sit in the last empty seat in the away section, she realises that this is the first time Kent is somewhere for her sake. The first time in their lives that he has to present himself as being in her company, rather than the other way around.

In the seat next to him sits Sven. With his eyes fixed on the floor.

Britt-Marie breathes in deeply with each step. Bank and the dog are waiting for her on a bench next to the pitch. Somebody as well, with a particularly satisfied expression on her face.

'How did you get here?' asks Britt-Marie.

'Drove, you know,' Somebody answers casually.

'What about the pizzeria and the grocery store and the post office, then? What about the opening hours?'

Somebody shrugs.

'Who will come to shop, Britt? Everyone in Borg – here!'

Britt-Marie adjusts invisible creases in her skirt at such a speed that it looks as if she's trying to start a fire. Somebody pats her calmingly.

'Nervous, huh? No problem, Britt, I said to that official, huh: I will sit on the sideline with Britt. Because I have one of those, what's-it-called? Calming effect on Britt, huh. The official just said "Forget it," so I said "Can't see one of those disability areas here, illegal, huh." I said: "Could sue you, you know." So now: I sit here. Best seat, isn't it?'

Britt-Marie excuses herself, leaves the sidelines, walks down a corridor and into a toilet, where she vomits. When she comes back to the bench, Somebody is still talking, her fingers nervously drumming against anything within reach. The dog sniffs in Britt-Marie's direction. Bank offers her a pack of chewing gum.

'It's normal. You often get food poisoning just before important games.'

Britt-Marie chews the gum with her hand covering her mouth, because people might come to the conclusion that she has tattoos (or similar). Then the spectators burst into applause, the referee walks on to the pitch and a team from Borg that does not even have its own pitch starts playing.

With vocal support from an entire community where just about everything has been closed down. But only just about.

The first thing that happens is that Dino gets tackled – or elbowed, to be more precise – by a large boy with a complicated haircut. The next time Dino gets the ball, exactly the same thing happens, only even harder. A few metres away from Britt-Marie the coach person bounces up and down in a soaking wet tracksuit jacket while yelling his encouragement:

'*Exaaactly* like that! Make them *respeeect* you!'

Britt-Marie is convinced she's about to have a heart attack, but when she explains this to Bank, Bank says 'That's how it's meant to be when you're watching football.' Who on earth would want to watch football, then, Britt-Marie thinks to herself. The third time Dino gets the ball the big boy accelerates from the other side of the pitch and runs at full speed with his elbow raised. The next moment he's lying on his back. Max stands over him with his chest out and his arms straightened. He's already walking back towards the bench before the referee has sent him off.

'Max! Huh! You're such a, what's-it-called?' Somebody says, overwhelmed with joy.

Bank taps her stick against Max's shoes.

'He talks like one of them. But he plays like one of us.'

Max smiles and says something, but Britt-Marie can't hear what.

The match resumes, and Britt-Marie finds, to her surprise, that she's standing up. Her mouth is hanging open and she doesn't even know how. On the pitch, three players have collided and the ball has bounced haphazardly towards the touchline, and suddenly it's just lying there at Ben's feet, and he has a clear shot at the goal. He stares at it. The entire crowd in the sports hall stares at him.

'Shoot,' whispers Britt-Marie.

'Shoot!' yells a voice from the stand.

It's Sami. Next to him stands a red-faced woman. It's the first time Britt-Marie has ever seen her wearing anything but a nurse's uniform.

'SHOOOOOOOOOOOOOOOOT!!!' cries Bank, waving her stick to and fro in the air.

So Ben shoots. Britt-Marie hides her face in the palms of her hands, Bank almost overturns Somebody's wheelchair while she yells:

'What's happening? Tell me what's happening!'

The stand is silent as if no one can quite believe how this has happened. At first, Ben looks as if he's going to burst into tears, then as if he's looking for a hiding place. And he doesn't have time to do much more than that before he finds himself at the bottom of a screaming pile of arms and legs and white shirts. Borg are in the lead by 1–0. Sami charges around in the stand with his arms held out, like an aircraft. Kent and Sven bounce up from their seats so abruptly that they accidentally start hugging one another.

A red-faced woman makes her way out of the chaos and runs down the stairs. A couple of officials try to get in her way when they see she's going to run on to the pitch, but they can't stop her. They couldn't have stopped her even if they were carrying guns. Ben dances with his mum as if no one can take this away from him.

Borg lose the match 14–1. It makes no difference. They play as if it makes all the difference in the universe.

It does make a difference.

31

At a certain age almost all the questions a person asks him or herself are really just about one thing: how should you live your life?

If a human being closes her eyes hard enough and for long enough, she can remember pretty well everything that has made her happy. The fragrance of her mother's skin at the age of five and how they fled giggling into a porch to get out of a sudden downpour. The cold tip of her father's nose against her cheek. The consolation of the rough paw of a soft toy she has refused to let them wash. The sound of waves stealing in over rocks during their last seaside holiday. Applause in a theatre. Her sister's hair, afterwards, carelessly waving in the breeze as they're walking down the street.

And apart from that? When has she been happy? A few moments. The jangling of keys in the door. The beating of Kent's heart against the palms of her hands while he lay sleeping. Children's laughter. The feel of the wind on her balcony. Fragrant tulips. True love.

The first kiss.

A few moments. A human being, any human being at all, has so perishingly few chances to stay right there, to let go of time and fall into the moment. And to love someone without measure. Explode with passion.

A few times when we are children, maybe, for those of us who are allowed to be. But after that, how many breaths are we allowed to take beyond the confines of ourselves? How many pure emotions make us cheer out loud, without a sense of shame? How many chances do we get to be blessed by amnesia?

All passion is childish. It's banal and naïve. It's nothing we learn, it's instinctive, and so it overwhelms us. Overturns us. It bears us away in a flood. All other emotions belong to the earth, but passion inhabits the universe.

That is the reason why passion is worth something, not for what it gives us but for what it demands that we risk. Our dignity. The puzzlement of others and their condescending, shaking heads.

Britt-Marie yells out loud when Ben scores that goal. The soles of her feet are catapulted off the floor of the sports hall. Most people are not blessed with that sort of thing in the month of January. The universe.

You have to love football for that.

It's late at night, the cup was over several hours ago, and Britt-Marie is at the hospital. She's rinsing the blood out of a white football jersey in the washbasin while Vega sits on the toilet next to her, her voice still euphorically effervescent. As if she can't sit still. As if she could have run vertically.

Britt-Marie's heart is still beating so wildly that she still can't understand how anyone could have the energy to live like this – that is, if it's true what the children are saying, that it's possible to have a football team that plays a match every week. Who would be willing to do this to themselves on a weekly basis?

'I absolutely can't understand how you could get it into your head to behave in this sort of way,' Britt-Marie manages to whisper, because her voice no longer carries, having been yelled to shreds.

'They would have scored otherwise!' explains Vega for the thousandth time.

'You threw yourself right in front of the ball,' hisses Britt-Marie with a reproachful gesture from the washbasin and the bloodstains on the jersey.

Vega blinks. It hurts when she does that, because half her

face is dark purple and swollen from her lacerated eyebrow, down across her bloodshot eye, her nose with coagulated blood in her nostrils, and her split lip at the bottom so big that it looks as if she's tried to eat a wasp.

'I covered the shot,' she asserts.

'With your face, yes. For goodness' sake, one doesn't cover shots with one's face,' but it's unclear if she's mainly angry because Vega got blood on her face or blood on her jersey.

'They would have scored,' shrugs Vega.

'I can't for the life of me understand why you love football so much you're prepared to risk your life in that way,' hisses Britt-Marie as she furiously rubs bicarbonate of soda on the jersey.

Vega looks thoughtful. Then hesitant.

'Have you never loved anything like that?'

'Ha. No. I . . . ha. I don't know. I actually don't know.'

'I don't feel pain any more when I'm playing football,' says Vega, her eyes fixed on the number on the back of the jersey soaking in the washbasin.

'What pain do you mean?'

'Any pain.'

Britt-Marie goes silent, ashamed of herself. Turns on the hot water. Closes her eyes. Vega leans her head back and peruses the ceiling of the bathroom.

'I dream about football when I'm sleeping,' she says, as if this is quite reasonable, and then she asks, with sincere curiosity, as if she cannot understand what else you could dream about:

'What do you dream about?'

It just slips out of Britt-Marie; she whispers instinctively:

'Sometimes I dream about Paris.'

Vega nods understandingly.

'In that case football for me is like Paris for you. Have you been there a lot?'

'Never.'

'Why not?'

'It's one of those things that just . . . never happened. Come here now and wash your face—'

'Why not?'

Britt-Marie adjusts the tap so the water is not too hot.

Her heart is still thumping so hard that she can count the beats. She looks at Vega, tries to smooth away a few hairs from her forehead and gently probes the swelling at the edge of her eye, as if it is hurting Britt-Marie more than Vega. Then she whispers:

'You have to understand that when I was small my family and I went to the seaside. My sister always found the highest rocks to jump off into the water, and when she dived and came up to the surface, I was always still there at the top of the rock, and she would call out to me, "Jump, Britt-Marie! Just jump!" You have to understand that when one is just standing there looking, then just for a second one is ready to jump. If one does it, one dares to do it. But if one waits it'll never happen.'

'Did you jump?'

'I'm not the sort who jumps.'

'But your sister was?'

'She was like you. Fearless.'

Then she folds a paper tissue and whispers:

'But not even she would have got it into her head to throw herself face first in front of a football like an utter madwoman!'

Vega stands up and lets Britt-Marie dab her cuts.

'So that's why you don't go to Paris now? Because you're the type that doesn't jump?' asks the girl.

'I'm too old for Paris.'

'How old is Paris?'

To which Britt-Marie has no decent answer. Even though it sounds like an absolutely excellent crossword clue. She glimpses herself in the mirror. It's all quite ludicrous, of course. She's a grown woman, she is, and here she stands in a hospital for the second time in just a few days. A child sits here on a toilet seat, her face covered in blood, while, in another room at the end of the corridor, another child lies with a broken leg.

Because they were covering shots. Who would want to live like that?

Vega meets her eyes in the mirror, then laughs so the blood runs from her lip across her teeth. Which makes her laugh even more, the lunatic.

'If you're not the type that jumps, Britt-Marie, how did you bloody well end up in Borg, then?'

Britt-Marie presses the paper tissue against her lip and hisses something at her about not using inappropriate language. Vega mumbles something angry through the tissue, so Britt-Marie presses it down even harder. Then she pulls the girl outside into the waiting room before she says anything else.

Which is obviously not a very well thought-through idea, because that's where Fredrik is. He's pacing back and forth outside the toilet door. Toad, Dino, Ben and Omar are sleeping on the benches in a corner. Fredrik immediately points at Britt-Marie in a hostile manner.

'If Max has broken his leg and misses elite training camp I'll make sure you never get anywhere near h . . .'

His voice fades as he closes his eyes and tries to calm himself down. Vega pushes in front of Britt-Marie and slaps at his finger.

'Shut up, will you! The leg will heal! Max was covering a shot!'

Fredrik clenches his fists and backs away from her, as if, in his despair, he's afraid of what might otherwise happen.

'I banned him from playing football before the elite training camp. I told him that if he injures himself now it could damage his whole career. I told hi—'

'What bloody career is that? He's at bloody secondary school!' Vega cuts in.

Fredrik points at Britt-Marie again. Sinks down on a bench as if someone just dropped him.

'Do you know what it means to go to elite training camp when you play ice hockey? Do you understand what we have sacrificed to give him this opportunity?'

'Did you ask Max if he wants to, or not?'

'Are you retarded or something? It's the elite camp! Of course he wants to!' bellows Fredrik.

'No one needs to shout at him for playing football!' Vega bellows back.

'Maybe you could do with someone shouting at you!'

'AND MAYBE YOU COULD DO WITH SOME FURNITURE!'

They stand with their foreheads locked together, breathing heavily, and both utterly exhausted. Both have tears in their eyes. Neither of them will ever forget the cup matches Borg played today. No one in Borg will.

Admittedly they lost their second game 5–0. The match had to be stopped for several minutes halfway through because Toad saved a penalty and everyone had to wait until he had stopped running around the pitch like an aircraft. The crowd sounded as if Borg had won the World Cup, which, after repeated explanations, Britt-Marie understood was another football competition, of particular importance if you were that way inclined.

In the third and last game the noise in the sports hall was so loud that all Britt-Marie could hear was a sort of sustained roar, and her heart thumped so hard that she lost her sense of touch, while her arms waved around her body as if they were no longer hers. Their opponents were in the lead by 2–0, but with another few minutes to go Vega thumped in a goal for Borg with her whole body. Immediately afterwards, Max dribbled his way through the entire opposing team and scored, watched every step of the way by his begrudging father. When his head popped out of the pile of arms and legs of his team-mates, Fredrik turned around in disappointment and walked out of the door. Max stood motionless by the sidelines, staring at him as the referee blew the whistle to restart the game. By the time the roaring spectators had woken the boy up, their opponents had hit the post once and the crossbar once, and the whole team except for Vega was lying scattered on the floor. Then one of the opposing players gathered himself to take a shot at the open goal, and that was when Vega threw herself in front of the ball and covered the shot. With her face. There was blood on the ball when it bounced back to the player.

He could have killed the match by tapping the ball in with the side of his foot, but despite this the player stretched his foot for a hard shot. Max ran straight into the pile of bodies and threw himself forward with his leg stretched out. He made contact with the ball but the opponent hit his leg. Max yelled so loud that Britt-Marie felt as if she was the one with the broken leg.

The match finished 2–2. It was the first time in a very, very long time that Borg had not lost a football match. Vega sat next to Max on their way to the hospital, singing extremely unsuitable songs all the way.

Ben's mother is standing in the doorway. She looks at Vega, then at Britt-Marie, then she nods as you do at the end of a long shift.

'Max wants to see you two. Just you two.'

Fredrik swears loudly but Ben's mother is implacable.

'Just these two.'

'I thought you were having the evening off,' says Vega.

'I was. But when Borg plays football the hospital has to call in extra staff,' she says severely, even though she's quite clearly trying not to laugh.

She throws a blanket over Ben on one of the benches, and kisses him on the cheek. Then she does the same with Dino, Toad and Omar, all still sleeping on the other benches.

Britt-Marie feels Fredrik's hateful stare at her back as she and Vega follow her down the corridor, so she slows and walks behind Vega, to stop his stares hitting the girl. Max lies in a bed with his leg hoisted up towards the ceiling. He grins when he sees Vega's swollen face as she comes walking in.

'Nice face! Totally an improvement on how you looked before!'

Vega snorts and nods at his leg.

'You think the doctors can screw on your leg straight this time, so you can learn to shoot properly, or what?'

He sniggers. So does she.

'Is my dad pissed off?' asks Max.

'Do bears shit in the woods?' Vega answers.

'Really, Vega! Is that the sort of language you use when you're in a hospital? Well, is it?'

Vega laughs. Max too. Britt-Marie inhales, deeply self-controlled, turns and leaves them and their language to it.

Fredrik is still standing in the waiting room where they left him. Britt-Marie stops, at a loss. Resists the impulse to pick one of Vega's hairs from his arm, where it landed while they were locking heads and yelling at one another.

'Ha,' whispers Britt-Marie.

He doesn't answer. Just glares down at the floor. So she summons what voice she has left in her throat and asks:

'Have you ever loved anything as much as these children do, Fredrik?'

He raises his head and drills his eyes into her.

'Do you have any children of your own, Britt-Marie?'

She swallows heavily and shakes her head. He looks down at the floor again.

'Don't ask me about what I love, then.'

They sit on their chairs without saying anything else, until Ben's mother re-emerges. Britt-Marie stands up, but Max's dad stays seated as if he can't summon any more energy. Ben's mother puts her hand consolingly on his shoulder and says:

'Max wanted me to tell you that he'll most likely be able to start playing ice hockey within six months. His leg will be completely back to normal. His career shouldn't be in any danger at all.'

Max's father doesn't move. Presses his chin hard against his throat. Ben's mother nods at Britt-Marie. Britt-Marie sucks in her cheeks. Ben's mother is heading for the door when Max's father finally lifts his hands to his eyes in two quick movements, tears dripping between his fingers, down into his beard. He doesn't have a towel. The tears stain the floor.

'Football, then? When can he start playing football again?'

At a certain age almost all the questions a person asks himself are about one thing: how should you live your life?

32

Britt-Marie sits alone on a bench on the pavement outside the accident and emergency wing. She has a bouquet of tulips in her arms, can feel the wind in her hair, and is thinking about Paris. It's strange, the power a place can have over you, even if you've never been there. If she closes her eyes she can nonetheless feel its cobblestones under her feet. Maybe more clearly now than ever. As if when she jumped into the air when Ben scored, she came back down to earth as a different person. The sort of person that jumps.

'Mind if I sit with you?' asks the voice.

She can hear the voice is smiling. She also smiles, even before she has opened her eyes.

'Please do,' she whispers.

'Your voice is hoarse,' says Sven with a smile.

She nods.

'It's the flu.'

He laughs out loud. She laughs inside. He sits down and holds out a ceramic vase for her.

'Well, yeah, I made it for you. I'm doing a course. You know, I thought you could put your tulips in it.'

She grips it and holds it tightly in her arms. The surface is slightly rough against her skin, like a soft toy you wouldn't let your parents wash.

'It was quite fantastic today. I have to admit it. Absolutely wonderful,' she manages to say.

'It's a wonderful sport,' says Sven.

As if life was so simple.

'It's been heavenly to feel enthusiastic again,' she whispers.

He smiles and turns to her, looking as if he's about to tell her something, so she stops him by gathering up all her common sense in a single, suffocating breath and saying:

'If it's not too much trouble I'd be very grateful if you had time to run the children home.'

She sees him sitting there growing smaller in the seconds that follow. Her heart twists inside her. Also inside him.

'I have to assume that this, that this means that, well . . . I have to assume that it'll be Kent who's driving you home then,' he manages to say.

'Yes,' she whispers.

He sits in silence with his hands gripping the edge of the bench. She does the same, because she likes holding it while he's also holding it. She peers at him and wants to say that it's not his fault. That she's just too old to fall in love. She wants to tell him that he can find himself someone better. That he deserves something perfect. But she doesn't say anything, because she's afraid he'll say she is perfect.

She's still clutching the vase as she sits in the car, the town and the road swishing by. Her chest is aching with held-back longings. Kent talks all the way, of course. Initially about the football and the children, but before long his focus switches to business and Germans and plans. He wants to go on holiday, he says, just the two of them. They can go to the theatre. Go to the sea. Very soon; a few plans just have to fall into place first. When they drive into Borg he makes a joke about how this place is so small that two people could stand on top of the welcome signs at either end, having a conversation without even having to raise their voices.

'If you lie down here you'll find your feet are already in the next village!' he guffaws, and when she doesn't immediately laugh he says it again.

'OK, pop in and get your stuff now, and then we'll be off!' he says as the BMW stops outside Bank's house.

'Right away?'

'Yes, I have a meeting tomorrow. Let's get going now so we're ahead of the traffic.' He drums his fingers against the dashboard impatiently.

'We actually can't just leave in the middle of the night,' protests Britt-Marie, her voice scarcely audible.

'Why not?'

'Well, only criminals drive around in the middle of the night.'

'Oh, good God, darling, you have to pull yourself together now,' he groans.

Her nails dig into the vase.

'I haven't even handed in notice to my employers yet. I can't just disappear without handing in my notice. The keys have to be returned, you have to understand.'

'Please darling, it's not exactly much of a "job", is it?'

Britt-Marie sucks her cheeks in.

'It's a job as far as I'm concerned.'

'Yes, yes, yes, that's not how I meant it, darling. Don't get irate now. Can't you just call them while we're on the road? It's not that important, is it? Come on, I have a meeting tomorrow!' He says this as if he's the one who's being flexible here. She doesn't answer.

'Do you even get a salary for this "job"?'

Britt-Marie's nails hurt as they bend against the ceramic vase in her lap.

'I'm not some criminal. I'm not travelling around in the car at night. I just won't do it, Kent,' she whispers.

'No, no, no, OK then,' sighs Kent, 'Tomorrow morning if it's so important. I can't believe how this village has got under your skin, my darling. You don't even like football!'

Britt-Marie's nails start slowly retracting from the ceramic vase. Her thumb dives over the rim and adjusts the tulips inside.

'I was given a crossword the other day, Kent. There was a question about Maslow's Hierarchy of Needs in it.'

Kent has started fidgeting with his mobile, so she raises her voice:

'It's popular in crosswords, it really is. The Hierarchy of Needs. So I read about it in a newspaper. The first stage is about people's most basic needs. Food and water.'

'Mmm,' says Kent, tapping away.

'Air as well, I have to assume,' adds Britt-Marie so quietly that she's almost not sure herself whether she says anything.

The second stage of the Hierarchy of Needs is 'safety', the third is 'love and belonging', the fourth is 'self-esteem'. She remembers it quite clearly, because this Maslow fellow is remarkably popular in crosswords. 'The highest step of the ladder is self-actualisation. That was how all this felt to me, Kent. It was a way of actualising myself.'

She bites her lip.

'You just think it's silly, I suppose.'

He looks up from his telephone. Looks at her, breathing deeply and loudly, like he does just before he falls asleep and starts snoring.

'Yes, yes! Of course I can understand the whole darned thing, darling. I get it. It's superb, really superb! Self-actualising. Bloody superb. So now you've got it out of your system. And tomorrow we can go home!'

She bites her lip and lets go of his hand. Takes a firm grip on the vase and clambers out of the car.

'Damn it, darling! Don't get annoyed again! I mean how long does this job last? How long will you be employed?'

'Three weeks,' she forces herself to say.

'And then? When those three weeks are over and you don't have a job any more? Will you be staying on in Borg as an unemployed person, then?'

When she doesn't answer he sighs and gets out of the car.

'You do understand this is not your home, don't you darling?'

She is walking away, but she knows he's right.

He breaks into a run and catches up with her. Takes the ceramic pot with the tulips from her, and carries them into the house. She walks slowly behind him.

'I'm sorry, my darling,' he says, with his hands cupped softly around her face, as they stand there in the hall.

She closes her eyes. He kisses her on the eyelids. He always used to do that, in the beginning, just after her mother had died. When she was at her loneliest in the world, until one day when he stood there on the landing in their apartment building, and then she was no longer at her loneliest. Because he needed her, and you are not alone when someone needs you. So she loves it when he kisses her eyelids.

'I'm just a bit stressed. Because of the meeting tomorrow. But everything is going to be all right. I promise.'

She wants to believe him. He grins and kisses her cheek and tells her not to worry. And that he will be picking her up tomorrow morning at six o'clock, so they don't end up in the morning rush hour traffic.

Then he scoffs: 'But you never know, if all three cars in Borg are out at the same time it could get a bit crowded!' She smiles, as if that's funny. Stands in the hall with the door closed until he drives away.

Then she goes up the stairs and makes the bed. Puts her bags in order. Folds all the towels. Goes down the stairs again, out of the door, and walks through Borg. It's dark and silent as if no one lives here, as if the football cup never even took place.

But the lights are on in the pizzeria; she can hear Bank and Somebody laughing in there.

There are other voices too. Clinking glasses. Songs about football, and other songs sung by Bank, the lyrics of which, certainly as far as Britt-Marie is concerned, do not bear repeating.

She unlocks the recreation centre and turns on the kitchen light. Sits on a stool and hopes the rat will turn up. It fails to do so. Then she sits with her mobile held in her cupped hands, as if it was liquid and might otherwise be spilled. She waits for a long time before she can bring herself to make the call.

The girl from the unemployment office answers on her third attempt.

'Britt-Marie?' she manages to say, sounding drowsy.

'I should like to hand in my notice,' Britt-Marie whispers.

It sounds as if the girl is stumbling about and knocking something over at the other end of the line. A lamp, perhaps.

'No, no, Mummy is just talking on the telephone, darling, go back to sleep, sweetie . . .'

'I beg your pardon?'

'Sorry. I was talking to my daughter. We fell asleep on the sofa.'

'I wasn't aware you had a daughter.'

'I have two,' the girl replies, and it sounds as if she walks into a kitchen and turns on a lamp and starts making coffee. 'What time is it?'

'Hardly a good time to be drinking coffee,' answers Britt-Marie.

'What can I do for you, Britt-Marie?'

'I should like to hand in my notice. I need to . . . come home,' whispers Britt-Marie.

'How did the football cup go?' the girl asks after a long silence.

Something about that question impacts on Britt-Marie. It may be the case that after Ben's goal she really did come back to earth as a different human being. She doesn't know. But she takes a deep breath and tells the girl everything.

About communities situated by main roads and rats and people who wear their caps indoors. About boys' first dates and jerseys hung up on pizzeria walls. It all pours out of her. About Faxin and bamboo screens, beer bottles presented in cellophane, and IKEA furniture. Pistols and crossword supplements. Policemen and entrepreneurs. Doing the Idiot in the beam of a truck's headlights. Blue doors and old football matches. Purple tulips and whisky and cigarettes and dead mothers. Flu. Soft-drink cans. 1–0 against the team from the town. A girl who covers a shot with her face. The universe.

'I suppose this must all sound very . . . silly,' she concludes.

The girl at the other end of the line can't quite keep her voice steady as she replies:

'Have I told you why I work here, Britt-Marie? I don't know if you know this, but you're at the receiving end of an unbelievable amount of crap when you work at the unemployment office. People can be incredibly mean. And when I say "crap", Britt-Marie, you should know that I really do mean that quite literally. One time, someone sent me some shit in an envelope. As if it's my fault that there's a financial crisis, sort of thing?'

Britt-Marie coughs.

'Might one ask how on earth they got it into the envelope?'

'The shit?'

'It must have been quite hard to . . . aim.'

The girl laughs loudly for several minutes. Britt-Marie is pleased about losing her voice, because it means the girl can't hear that she's also laughing. It may not be the universe, maybe not so, but the emotion levitates her slightly off the stool.

'Do you know why I work when there's all this crap, Britt-Marie?'

'Why?'

'My mother worked for the social services all her life. She always said that in the middle of all the crap, in the thick of it all, you always had a sunny story turning up. Which makes it all worthwhile.' The next words that come are smiling:

'You're my sunny story, Britt-Marie.'

Britt-Marie swallows.

'It's inappropriate to talk on the telephone in the middle of the night. I should like to contact you again tomorrow.'

'Sleep well, Britt-Marie,' says the girl softly.

'You too.'

Britt-Marie sits on the stool with the palms of her hands cupped around the telephone.

She catches herself wishing so fervently for the rat to turn up that when there's a knock on the door, she thinks it finally has. Then she comes to her senses and realises that rats can't knock on doors, because they don't have knuckles. At least she thinks they don't.

'Anyone home?' Sami calls out from the door.

Britt-Marie flies off her stool.

'Did something happen? Has there been an accident?'

He stands calmly leaning against the doorpost.

'No. Why?'

'It's the middle of the night, Sami. Surely one doesn't just show up unannounced at people's homes like some vacuum cleaner salesman unless something has happened!'

'Do you live here?' asks Sami, with a grin.

'You must surely understand what I mean—'

'Chill, Britt-Marie. I was driving past and I saw your lights were on. Wanted to see if you fancied a cigarette. Or a drink.'

He laughs at her expense. She doesn't appreciate that at all.

'Certainly not,' she hisses.

'OK, cool,' he laughs.

She adjusts her skirt.

'But if you'll make do with a Snickers instead you can come in.'

They each take a stool by the kitchen window. Look at the stars through the cleanest windows in Borg.

'It was nice today,' says Sami.

'Yes. It was . . . nice.' She smiles.

She wants to tell him she has to leave Borg first thing tomorrow and go home, but before she has time to open her mouth he says:

'Right, I have to go into town. I have to help a friend.'

'What sort of friend is that? It's the middle of the night.'

'Magnus. He's having problems with a few guys there. Owes them money, you know.'

Britt-Marie stares at him. He nods. Smiles ironically at himself.

'I know what you're thinking. But this is Borg. We forgive each other in Borg. We don't have a choice. If we didn't there wouldn't be any friends left to get pissed off at.'

She stands up. Gently takes his plate. Hesitates for a long time, then at long last tenderly lays her bandaged hand against his cheek.

'You don't always have to be the one that steps in, Sami.'

'Yes I do.'

She washes up. He stands next to her, drying the plates.

'If something happens to me can you promise you'll look out for Omar and Vega and make sure they're all right? Can you promise me you'll find good people to look after them?'

'Why would something happen to you?' she asks, the colour draining from her face.

'Ah, nothing is going to happen to me, I'm fucking Superman. But you know. If something does happen. Will you make sure they can live with some good people?'

She elaborately dries her hands on the towel, so he won't notice that they are shaking.

'Why are you asking me? Why don't you ask Sven or Bank or . . .'

'Because you're not the type to walk out, Britt-Marie.'

'Neither are you!'

He places himself on the threshold and lights a cigarette. She stands to one side behind him, breathing in the smoke.

The sun hasn't come up yet. She picks a hair off the arm of his jacket. Puts it in a handkerchief and folds it up.

'What football team did your mother support?' she asks quietly.

He grins, as if it's quite obvious, and answers the question as all sons with mothers do:

'Our team.'

He drives her to Bank's house. Kisses her hair. She sits on the balcony with her packed bags and watches him driving off towards town. He has made her promise that she won't sit up all night waiting for his car to come back.

But she does it anyway.

33

'I should like you to know that I've handed in my notice. I have to go home, you understand.'

Britt-Marie fiddles with the bandage around her ring finger.

'Admittedly I can perfectly understand that you don't understand. But I belong with Kent. A person has to have a home. Obviously I don't mean to say that you also have to have a home. I'm not sticking my nose into that. I'm quite sure you have a perfectly adequate home.'

The rat sits on the floor, looking at the plate in front of it as if the plate had stepped on its tail and called it a blithering idiot.

'I ran out of Snickers,' Britt-Marie says apologetically.

The rat looks at the jars on the plate.

'That one is peanut butter. And this is something known as "Nutella",' she says proudly. 'They'd run out of Snickers in the grocery, but I've been informed that in all important respects this is the same thing.'

It's still the middle of the night. Somebody was not at all pleased about being woken up, but Britt-Marie couldn't bring herself to sit on her own with her bags on Bank's balcony. Couldn't bear it. So she came back here, to say goodbye. To both the rat and the village.

Britt-Marie stands by the window. It'll soon be dawn. Somebody has turned out the lights in the pizzeria and gone to bed again, in the hope that Britt-Marie won't be banging on her door again because she needs peanut butter and chocolate. The party is long since over. The road lies deserted. Britt-Marie rubs her wedding ring with a potato smeared with bicarbonate of soda, because that is the best way to clean wedding rings. She often does that with Kent's wedding ring; he often leaves it on his bedside table. He's often so distracted, Kent is, whenever he's about to meet with the Germans.

Britt-Marie usually cleans the ring until it gleams, so he won't be able to avoid noticing it when he gets out of bed the next morning.

This is the first time she has cleaned her own ring. The first time she has not worn it on her finger. She whispers, without looking at the rat:

'Kent needs me. A person needs to be needed, you have to understand.'

She doesn't know if rats sit awake in their kitchens at night, thinking about how they are going about their lives. Or who they are going about their lives with.

'Sami told me I'm not the type to clear off, but you have to understand that that is most certainly exactly what I am. Whichever way I turn, I'm leaving someone behind. So the only thing that's right must be to blasted well stay where you belong. In your normal life.'

Britt-Marie tries to sound sure of herself. The rat licks its feet. Makes a little semi-loop on the napkin. Then dashes out of the door.

Britt-Marie doesn't know if it thinks she talks too much. Doesn't know why it keeps coming here. The supply of Snickers, obviously, but she hopes there's something more to it. She takes the plate and puts cling film over the remains of the peanut butter and Nutella, then puts everything in the fridge out of an old habit, because she's not one to throw away food. She wipes her wedding ring carefully and folds it in a piece of kitchen roll before tucking it into her jacket pocket. It'll be nice to take off the bandage and put the ring back on her finger. Like getting into her own bed after a long journey.

A normal life – she has never wanted anything but a normal life. She could have made other choices, she tells herself, but she chose Kent. A human being may not choose her circumstances, but she does choose her actions, she insists quietly to herself. Sami was right. She's not the kind that clears off. So she must go home, where she is needed.

She sits on the stool in the kitchen, staring at the wall and waiting for a black car. It does not come. She wonders if Sami thinks about how one should live one's life, if he has ever had that luxury. A human being can't choose his circumstances, admittedly, but in Sami's life there have been more circumstances than events. She asks herself if choices or circumstances make us the sort of people we become – or what it was that made Sami the sort of person who steps in. She wonders what takes the most out of a person: to be the kind that jumps, or the kind that doesn't?

She wonders how much space a person has left in her soul to change herself, once she gets older. What people does she still have to meet, what will they see in her, and what will they make her see in herself?

Sami went to town to protect someone who doesn't deserve it, and Britt-Marie is getting ready to go home for the same reason. Because if we don't forgive those we love, then what is left? What is love if it's not loving our lovers even when they don't deserve it?

The headlights from the road give off a sudden gleam, slowly reach out of the darkness like arms in the water, passing the 'Welcome to Borg' sign.

They slow down by the bus stop. Turn off into the gravelled parking area. Britt-Marie is already standing in the doorway.

Later, when people speak of it, it will be said that a few young men found Magnus in the early hours of morning, standing outside a bar. One of them was holding a knife. Another man stepped in between them. He was the kind that always steps in.

The car stops gently on the gravel. Makes a little warm sigh as the engine is turned off. The headlights are switched off at the same time as the pizzeria lights are turned on. In certain types of communities people always know what it means when cars stop outside their windows before dawn. People know it is never because something good has happened. Somebody comes rolling on to the porch; her wheelchair stops at once when she sees the police uniform.

Sven stands with his cap in both hands and his bottom lip full of teeth marks, caused by his attempt to hold it all in. Despair, which has run down his cheeks and caused red lines, speaks volumes about just how futile his attempt has been.

Britt-Marie yells out. Falls to the ground. And lies there under the weight of another human being, who no longer exists.

34

This is no slow grief. It does not emerge at the tail end of denial, anger, negotiation, depression or acceptance. It flares up at once, like an all-consuming fire within her, a fire that takes all the oxygen from the air until she's lying on the ground, lashing at the gravel and panting for air. Her body tries to twist into itself, as if there's no spine, as if it is desperately trying to quench the flames inside.

Death is the ultimate state of powerlessness. Powerlessness is the ultimate despair.

Britt-Marie doesn't know how she gets back on her feet. How Sven gets her into the car. He must have carried her. They find Vega halfway between the flat and the recreation centre, and she's lying in the gravel. Her hair is plastered to her skin, her words come out in stuttered gurgles, as if tears have filled her lungs. As if the girl is drowning from the inside.

'Omar. We have to find Omar. He'll kill them.'

Britt-Marie doesn't know if, sitting there in the back seat, she's holding Vega so tightly herself, or if, in fact, it's the other way around.

Around them, the dawn gently wakes Borg like someone breathing into the ear of someone they love. With sun and promises. Tickling light falls over warm duvets, like the smell of freshly-brewed coffee and toasted bread. It shouldn't be doing this. It's the wrong day to be beautiful, but the dawn doesn't care.

The police car hurtles along in these first few moments of

morning, the only thing moving on the road. Sven's fingers are curled so hard around the steering wheel it must surely be hurting him. As if he has to keep the pain in some place. He speeds up when he sees the other car. The only car that has any reason to leave Borg at this time of morning. The only brother left for Vega to save.

Every death is unjust. Everyone who mourns seeks someone to blame. Our fury is almost always met by the merciless insight that no one bears responsibility for death. But what if someone was responsible? And what if you knew who had snatched away the person you love? What would you do? Which car would you be sitting in, and what would you be holding in your hands?

The police car roars past and cuts off the other car. Sven's feet hit the asphalt before any of them have even come to a stop. For an eternity he stands there in the road, alone, his face streaked with red lines and his lip buckled with bite marks. Finally a car door opens and Omar steps out. A man's eyes in the body of a boy. Is this the end of a childhood?

It's the sort of night that can't be undone in a person.

'What, Sven? What are you going to tell me? That I have too much to lose? What the fuck do I have to lose?'

Sven holds out his palms. His eyes flicker towards what Omar is holding in his hands. His voice hardly makes itself heard.

'Tell me where it ends, Omar. When you've killed them, and they've killed you. Tell me where it ends after that.'

Omar just stands there dumbly, as if he also has to focus his pain somewhere. Two young men in the back of the car open the doors, but they don't get out, merely sit there waiting for Omar to make a choice. Britt-Marie recognises them. They play football with Sami and Magnus in the glare of headlights from Sami's black car . . . how long ago did they last play? Days? Weeks? A whole lifetime ago. They are almost boys.

Death is powerlessness. Powerlessness is desperation. Desperate people choose desperate measures. Britt-Marie's hair moves in the draught when the door of the police car opens and Vega steps out. She looks at her brother. He's on his knees now. She keeps his head pressed against her throat and whispers:

'Where would Sami have stood?'

When he doesn't immediately answer she repeats:

'Where. Would. Sami. Have stood?'

'Between us,' he pants.

The two young men give Sven one last look. At another time, perhaps, they could have been stopped. One day it may be possible to stop them again. But not tonight.

The car leaves Britt-Marie, Sven and two children in the road. Dawn rises over them.

The police car slowly drives back through Borg, exits on the other side, continues down a gravel track. Keeps driving for ever, until Britt-Marie no longer knows if she has fallen asleep or just gone numb. They stop by a lake.

Britt-Marie wraps the pistol in every handkerchief she's got in her bag, she doesn't know why, mainly perhaps because she doesn't want the girl to get dirty. Vega insists she's got to be the one that does it. She gets out and throws it as hard as she can into the lake.

Britt-Marie doesn't know how the hours turn into days, or how many of them pass by. By night, she sleeps between the children in Sami's bed. The beating of their hearts in her hands. She stays there for several nights. It is not something she plans, no decision has been made, she just stays there. One dawn after another seems to merge with dusk. Looking back, she has a vague memory of having spoken to Kent on the telephone, but she can't remember what was said. She thinks she may have asked him to arrange some practical things, possibly she asks him to make some telephone calls, he's good at those things. Everyone says Kent is good at those things.

One afternoon, she's unsure when it is, Sven comes to the apartment. He has brought a young woman with him from the social services. She is warm and pleasant. Sven's neck doesn't seem capable of holding up all his thoughts any longer. The woman sits with them all at the kitchen table, speaking slowly and softly, but no one is able to concentrate. Britt-Marie's eyes keep straying out of the window, one of the children is looking up at the ceiling, and the other is looking down at the floor.

The following night, Britt-Marie is woken by a sound of slamming in the flat. She gets up and fumbles for the light switch. The wind is blowing in through the balcony door. Vega moves maniacally back and forth in the kitchen. Tidying up. Cleaning everything she finds. Her hands scrub frenetically at the draining board and frying pans.

Again and again. As if they were magic lamps that could give her everything back. Britt-Marie's hands hesitate in the air behind her shaking shoulders.

Her fingers grip without touching.

'I'm so sorry, I know you must feel—'

'I don't have time to feel things. I have to take care of Omar,' the girl interrupts vacantly.

Britt-Marie wants to touch her, but the girl moves away, so Britt-Marie fetches her bag. Gets out some bicarbonate of soda. The girl meets her eyes, and her sorrow has nothing else to say. Words cannot achieve anything.

So they keep cleaning until morning comes again. Although not even bicarbonate of soda can help against this.

It's a Sunday in January. While Liverpool are playing Stoke one thousand kilometres away, Sami is buried next to his mother, sleeping softly under a carpet of red flowers. Mourned by two siblings, missed by a whole community. Omar leaves a scarf in the churchyard.

Britt-Marie serves coffee in the pizzeria and makes sure each of the mourners has a coaster. Everyone in Borg is there. The gravelled parking area has lit candles around its boundary. White jerseys have been neatly hung up on the wooden plank fence next to it. Some of them are new, and some so old and faded that they've turned grey. But they all remember.

Vega stands in the doorway, in a freshly ironed dress and with her hair combed. She receives people's condolences as if they have a greater right to mourn than herself. Mechanically shakes their hands. Her eyes are empty, as if someone has turned off a switch inside her. Something is making a thumping noise outside in the parking area but no one listens to it. Britt-Marie tries to get Vega to eat, but Vega doesn't even answer when spoken to. She allows herself to be led to the table and lowered into a chair, but her body reacts as if it's sleeping. It turns so that she faces the wall, as though she wants to avoid any possible physical contact. The thumping gets louder.

Britt-Marie's despair intensifies. People have different ways of experiencing powerlessness and grief, but for Britt-Marie it's never so strong as when she's unable to get someone to eat.

The mumbling voices from the crowded pizzeria grow into a hurricane in her ears, her resigned hand fumbles for Vega's shoulder as if it were reaching over the edge of a precipice. But the shoulder moves away. Glides towards the wall. And the eyes flee inwards. The plate remains untouched.

When the thumping from the parking area gets even louder, as if trying to prove something, Britt-Marie turns angrily towards the door with her hands clenched so tightly that the bandage comes loose from her fingers. She's just about to scream when she feels the girl's body pushing past her, through the throng of people.

Max is standing outside, leaning on his crutches. He suspends himself from his armpits, his whole weight swinging through the air, and then swings his uninjured leg at the football, firing it at a tight angle so it flies first against the wall of the recreation centre, then at the wooden fence where the white jerseys are hanging, then back at him. *Du-dunk-dunk*, it sounds like. *Du-dunk-dunk. Du-dunk-dunk.*

Du-dunk-dunk.

Like a heartbeat.

When Vega gets close enough he lets the ball roll past him without turning around. It rolls up to her, and stops against her feet. Her toes touch it through her shoes. She leans over it and runs her fingertips over the stitched leather.

Then she cries without measure.

One thousand kilometres away, Liverpool win 5–3.

35

Omar and Dino are the first to throw themselves into the game with Vega. At first they are guarded, as if every movement is made in sorrow, but before long they are playing as if it's just another evening. They play without memory, because they don't know any other way of doing it. More children turn up, first Toad and Ben but soon others too. Britt-Marie doesn't recognise every one of them, but they all have jeans that are ripped over their thighs. They play as if they live in Borg.

'Britt-Marie?' says Sven in a formal tone that she's not used to.

He's standing beside her with a very tall man. Really astonishingly tall. Britt-Marie doesn't even know how one could manage to have fully functional lighting at home with him around.

'Ha?' she says.

Sven presents Dino's uncle in an English marred by a heavy accent, but Britt-Marie doesn't criticise; she's not the sort of person that criticises.

'Hello,' says Britt-Marie, this being about the long and short of the conversation for her part.

It's not that Britt-Marie can't speak English. It's just that she doesn't know how to speak it without feeling like an utter prat. She wouldn't even know how to say 'utter prat' in English. As far as she's concerned this illustrates her point very well.

The very tall man, who really is quite unreasonably tall,

points at Dino and explains that they lived in three countries and seven cities before they came to Borg. Sven helpfully translates. Britt-Marie understands English perfectly well, but she lets him go on, fearing that she might otherwise be expected to say something. The tall man's mouth judders up and down in a melancholy way when he says that small children don't remember things, which is a blessing. But Dino was old enough to see and hear and remember. He remembers everything they had to flee from.

'He's saying he still hardly says anything. Only with them . . .' Sven explains, pointing out of the window.

Britt-Marie clasps one hand in the other. The tall man does the same.

'Sami,' he says with a sort of music in the way he pronounces the name, as if he's nursing every nuance of sound. Her eyelashes grow heavy.

'He says that Sami saw a boy walking on his own in the road. Vega and the others called out and asked him if he wanted to play, but he didn't understand. So Sami rolled a ball over to him, and then he kicked it,' says Sven.

Britt-Marie looks at the tall man and her common sense prevents her from saying that once when she and Kent were staying at a hotel and someone had left a foreign newspaper behind, she almost solved a crossword in English entirely on her own.

'Thank you,' says the tall man.

'He wants to thank you for coaching the team. It meant a lo—'

Britt-Marie interrupts him, because she understands:

'I'm the one who should say thank you.'

Sven starts translating to the tall man, but he stops him because he also understands. He presses Britt-Marie's hand.

She goes back into the pizzeria, with Sven following, and helps Somebody clear glasses and plates from the tables.

'It was a beautiful funeral,' says Sven, because that's what you say.

'Very beautiful,' says Britt-Marie, because you have to say that as well.

He gets something out of his pocket and hands it to her. The keys to her car. His eyes flicker. Through the window they see Kent's BMW pulling into the parking area.

'I assume you'll be going home now, you and Kent,' says Sven, his eyes remote.

'It's best that way,' says Britt-Marie, sucking in her cheeks, but then a few more words slip out of her in spite of it all: 'Unless I'm needed here with . . . Vega and Omar . . .'

Sven looks up and crumples in the brief instant between the first question and the realisation that what she's asking is whether the children need her. Not whether he does.

'I . . . I, of course, of course, I have contacted the social services. They have sent a girl to Borg,' he says with a grim expression, as if he's already forgotten that it was actually several nights earlier that he first brought the girl to the children.

'Of course,' she says.

'She's . . . you'll like her. I've worked with her many times before. She's a good person. She wants what's best for them, she's not like . . . like you imagine the social services could be.'

Britt-Marie mops the sweat from her brow with a handkerchief, so he doesn't notice that she's also mopping her eyes.

'I promised Sami they'd be all right. I promised . . . I want . . . they have to have an opportunity to . . . there must be a sunny story in their lives, Sven. At some point,' she manages to say at long last.

'We're going to do our best. We'll all do everything we possibly can.'

'Of course, of course,' she replies, directing her words at her shoes.

Sven fingers the police cap in his hands.

'The girl from the council, yes, she'll be staying with the children for a few days. Until they've sorted it all out. She's very considerate, you don't have to worry about that, I, well, I've been asked to drive the children home tonight.'

It takes a few seconds before the significance of what he has said sinks in for Britt-Marie. Before she's hit with the insight that she's no longer needed.

'Obviously, obviously. It's best that way, obviously,' she whispers.

Outside on the football pitch, Kent has got out of his BMW. He sees Britt-Marie and Sven through the window and puts his hands in his pockets, slightly nonplussed, looking as if he's standing on a street corner and not quite willing to admit that he's lost. He's never been good at talking about death, Britt-Marie knows that. He's the kind of person who can sort out all the practicalities, he can make calls, he'll kiss your eyelids. But he's never been good at feeling things.

His eyes seem to be considering walking into the pizzeria, but his feet steer off in the opposite direction. He makes a few movements with which he seems to be heading back into the BMW, but then the football comes rolling up and stops by his feet. Omar is standing a few metres away. Kent puts the sole of his shoe on the ball and looks at the boy. Kicks the ball to him. Omar stops it with the side of his foot, so it bounces back to Kent.

Thirty seconds later Kent is in the middle of the pile of children, his shirt creased and hanging down outside his belt, his hair untidy. Instantly he's happy. When the ball comes flying to him at knee-height, he gathers himself and kicks as hard as he can, misses the ball, and watches one of his shoes flying off and clearing the top of the fence along the side of the recreation centre.

'Mother of God,' mumbles Britt-Marie from the window. The children watch the shoe flying off. Turn to Kent. He looks back at them and starts laughing. They also laugh. He plays the rest of the match with one shoe, and when he scores he runs around the pitch with Omar perched on his back.

Omar hugs him a little too hard. A little too long. As teenagers get few chances to do outside of a football pitch. Kent hugs him back. Because football allows him to do it.

Sven has turned away from the window when he mumbles:

'Don't dislike me, Britt-Marie, for not calling the social services earlier. I just wanted to give Sami the chance to get things organised. I thought . . . I . . . I . . . I just wanted to give him the chance. Don't dislike me for it.'

Her fingers skim through the air between them as close as they can without actually touching him.

'Quite the opposite, Sven. Quite the opposite.'

He looks about to say something, so she quickly interjects:

'There are more kids here now than earlier. Where are they all from?'

Sven puts his police cap back on his head. It ends up slightly wonky.

'They've been coming here every evening since the cup. More and more of them every evening. If it carries on like this, soon Borg won't be a team, it'll be a club.'

Britt-Marie doesn't know what that means, but it sounds beautiful. She thinks Sami would have liked it.

'They look so happy. Even in the midst of all this they can look so happy when they're playing,' she says, almost enviously.

Sven rubs the back of his hand against his beard stubble. He looks tired. She has never seen him tired. But at long last the corners of his mouth twitch slightly, his eyes glitter at her and he says:

'Football forces life to move on. There's always a new match. A new season. There's always a dream that everything can get better. It's a game of wonders.'

Britt-Marie straightens out a crease in his shirt, her hand landing as lightly as a butterfly, without actually touching his body under the fabric.

'If it's not too inappropriate, I should like to ask you a very personal question, Sven.'

'Of course.'

'What football team do you support?'

Surprised, his face releases and changes.

'I've never supported a team. I think I love football too much. Sometimes your passion for a team can get in the way of your love for the game.'

It seems quite fitting for a man like Sven that he should believe more in love than in passion. He's a policeman who believes more in justice than in the law. It suits him, she thinks to herself. But she doesn't tell him as much.

'Poetic,' she says.

''Course.' He smiles back.

She wants to say so much more. Maybe he does too. But in the end all he can manage to utter is: 'I want you to know, Britt-Marie, that every time there's a knock on my front door, I hope it's you.'

Maybe he is also intending to say something bigger, but he holds off and he walks away. She wants to call out to him, but it's too late.

The door tinkles cheerfully behind him, because doors really don't seem to get when the moment is or isn't right.

Britt-Marie dabs her cheeks with her handkerchief so no one can see she's wiping her eyes. Then she walks purposefully through the pizzeria to Somebody. There are still people everywhere. Ben's mother and Dino's uncle and Toad's parents, but also a lot of other people whose faces Britt-Marie can only dimly recall from the football cup. They are cleaning up and putting the chairs in order, and she only just manages to resist the urge to straighten them again.

'It was, what's-it-called? Beautiful funeral, huh?' says Somebody, her voice a little gravelly.

'Yes,' agrees Britt-Marie, before getting out her wallet and immediately continuing: 'I should like to ask what I owe you for the car door.'

Somebody drums the edge of her wheelchair.

'Well. I been, you know, thinking about that car, huh, Britt-Marie. I don't have good car mechanic, huh? Maybe did it wrong, you know? So first you check the work, huh? Then you come back. Pay.'

'I don't understand.'

Somebody scratches her cheek so no one can see she's wiping her eyes as well.

'Britt-Marie very honest person, huh. Britt-Marie does not steal. So then I know Britt-Marie comes back to Borg, huh. To pay.'

'Of course', she replies, turning away. 'Of course.'

She wants to get busy cleaning up, but then has a merciless realisation that the people she does not know, inside the pizzeria, have already done it. Somebody has already told them all what to do. And now there is nothing left to finish.

Britt-Marie is not needed here any more.

She stands on her own in the doorway until the children stop playing. They go home, one after the other. At a distance, Sven waits patiently for Vega and Omar. He lets the children take the time they need. Vega goes directly to the back seat and closes the door behind her, but Omar wanders on his own along the plank and runs his fingers across the white jerseys. He leans over the candles on the ground, carefully picks one up that has gone out and relights it by holding it over the flame of another, then puts it back. When he straightens up he sees Britt-Marie in the doorway. His hand moves almost unnoticeably away from his hip, in a little wave. A wave from a young man is much more than a wave from a child. She waves back as much as she can without showing him that she is crying.

She goes down to the parking area just as the police car pulls into the road and heads off towards the children's house. Kent is waiting for her, sweaty, his shirt creased and hanging loose, his hair on end to one side of his large head – and he still only has one shoe. He looks quite, quite mad. It reminds her of how he used to look when they were children. Back then it never bothered him that other people would shake their heads at him; he was never afraid of making a fool of himself. He never needed anyone's affirmation except hers.

He takes her hand and she presses her eyelids against his lips. Says, almost panting:

'Vega is afraid even if she mainly seems angry. Omar is angry, even if he mostly seems afraid.'

'Everything is going to be all right,' says Kent into her hair.

'I promised Sami their lives would work out,' sobs Britt-Marie.

'They're going to be fine, you have to let the authorities take care of this,' he says calmly.

'I know. Of course I do know that.'

'They're not your children, darling.'

She doesn't answer. Because she knows. Obviously she knows that. Instead, she straightens her back and wipes her eyes with a tissue, adjusts a crease in her skirt and several in Kent's shirt. Collects herself and clasps her hands over her stomach and asks him:

'I should like to take care of a last errand. Tomorrow. In town. If it's not too much trouble.'

'I'll go with you.'

'You don't always have to stand next to me, Kent.'

'Yes I do.'

Then he smiles. And she tries to.

But when he starts walking back to the BMW she stays where she is with her heels dug into the gravel, as you do when enough is finally enough:

'No, Kent, certainly not! I am certainly not going into town with you if you don't first put on both your shoes!'

36

One remarkable thing about communities built along roads is that you can find just as many reasons for leaving them as excuses to stay. Some people never quite stop devoting themselves to one or the other.

In the end it's almost a whole week after the funeral before Britt-Marie gets into her white car with its blue door and drives off along the road that leaves Borg. Admittedly it's not entirely the fault of the council employees in the town hall. Possibly, they are only trying to do their jobs. It is not their fault that they are not wholly aware of Britt-Marie's precision when ticking off her lists.

So on the first day, a Monday, the young man who's working temporarily on reception at the town hall looks as if he thinks Britt-Marie is trying to be amusing. The reception opens at 8.00, so Britt-Marie and Kent have turned up at 8.02 because Britt-Marie doesn't want to come across as pig-headed.

'Borg?' says the temporary receptionist in the sort of tone you might use when pronouncing the names of beasts in fairy tales.

'My dear boy, surely you can't be working for the council without knowing that Borg is a part of the local council!' Britt-Marie says.

'I'm not from here. I'm a temp.'

'Ha. And I suppose that's meant to be an excuse for not having to know anything at all.'

But Kent nudges her encouragingly in the side, and whispers to her that she should try to be a little more diplomatic, so she grimly collects herself, smiles considerately at the young man and says:

'It was very brave of you, putting that tie on. Because it looks absolutely preposterous.'

Following this, there is a series of opinions exchanged that could not exactly be described as 'diplomatic'. But in the end Kent manages to calm down both combatants to the extent that the young man promises not to call the security guards, and Britt-Marie promises not to try to strike him with her handbag again.

One curious thing about communities built along roads is that you don't need to spend very long in them before you're deeply and personally offended when young men don't even know these places are there – that they even exist.

'I've come here to demand that a football pitch should be built in Borg, for your information,' Britt-Marie explains with her most goddess-like patience.

She points at her list. The young man looks through a file. He turns demonstratively to Kent and says something about a 'Committee', which is currently held up in a meeting.

'For how long?'

The young man continues going through the file.

'It's a breakfast meeting. So, more or less, until about ten o'clock.'

Whereupon both she and Kent have to leave the town hall, because a newly aggressive Britt-Marie has taken umbrage at the idea of a breakfast that lasts until ten o'clock, causing the young man to break his promise about not calling the security guards. They come back at ten o'clock, only to learn that the Committee is in a meeting until after lunch. They come back after lunch, when they find out that the Committee is in a meeting for the rest of the day. Britt-Marie clarifies her errand to the young man, because she does not believe it should have to take a whole day to get it done. The security guard who the

275

young man has called takes the view that her clarity is somewhat overstated. He tells Kent that if Britt-Marie does this one more time he'll have no option but to take her handbag away from her. Kent sniggers and says in that case the security guard is a braver man than Kent. Britt-Marie doesn't know whether to feel insulted or proud about it.

'We'll come back tomorrow, darling, don't worry about it,' Kent says soothingly as they are walking out.

'You have your meetings, Kent. We have to go home, I understand that, of course I do understand that. I just hope that we manage to . . .'

She takes a breath so deep that it seems to be extracted from the bottom of her handbag.

'When Vega plays football she doesn't feel any pain any more.'

'Pain about what?'

'Everything.'

Kent lowers his head for a moment in thought.

'It doesn't matter, darling. We'll come back tomorrow.'

Britt-Marie adjusts the bandage on her hand.

'I'm aware of the fact that the children don't need me. Obviously I am aware of that, Kent. I just wish I could give them something. At least if I could give them a football pitch.'

'We'll come back tomorrow,' Kent repeats, as he opens the car door for her.

'Yes, yes, you have your meetings, I understand that you have your meetings, we have to go home,' she says with a sigh.

Kent scratches his head distractedly. Coughs gently. Fixes his gaze on the rubber seal between the glass and the metal of the door, and answers:

'The fact is, darling, I only have one meeting. With the car dealer.'

'Ha. I didn't realise you were planning to buy a new car.'

'I'm not buying. I'm selling this one,' says Kent, with a nod at the BMW that she has just got into.

His face is dejected, as if it knows this is what is expected of it. But when he shrugs he does it as a young boy might, and his shoulders are light and relaxed as if they have just been liberated from a heavy burden.

'The company has gone bankrupt, darling. I tried to save it for as long as I could, but . . . well. It's the financial crisis.'

Britt-Marie gawps at him.

'But I thought . . . I thought you said the crisis was over?'

He considers this for a moment, then simply says, 'I was wrong, darling. Totally, totally wrong.'

'What are you going to do?'

He smiles, unconcerned and youthful.

'Start again. That's what you do, isn't it? Once upon a time I had nothing, remember?'

She does remember. Her fingers seek out his. They may be old, but he's laughing:

'I built a whole life. A whole life! I can do it again.'

He holds her hands in his and looks into her eyes when he promises:

'I can become that man again, my darling.'

They're halfway between town and Borg when Britt-Marie turns to him and asks how things have gone for Manchester United. He laughs out loud. It's heavenly.

'Ah, it's gone to pot. They've had their worst season in more than twenty years. The manager is going to get kicked out any moment.'

'How come?'

'They forgot what made them successful.'

'What do you do when that happens?'

'You start again.'

He rents a room from Toad's parents for the night. Britt-Marie doesn't ask if he'd prefer to stay in Bank's house, because Kent admits 'that blind old bat scares me a bit'.

The next day they go back to the town hall. And the next. Probably some of the people who work at the town hall believe that sooner or later Britt-Marie and Kent will give up, but these people are simply not aware of the profound implications of writing your lists in ink. On the fourth day they are allowed to see a man in a suit who's a member of a committee. By lunch-time he has called in a woman and a man, both wearing suits. Whether this is because of their expertise in the relevant area, or simply because the first suited man wants to improve his odds of not being hit in the event that Britt-Marie starts lashing out with her handbag, is never clarified.

'I've heard a lot of good things about Borg. It seems so charming there,' says the woman encouragingly, as if the village some twenty kilometres from her office is an exotic island only accessible through reliance on magic spells.

'I am here about a football pitch,' Britt-Marie begins.

'There's no budget for that,' the second suited man informs them.

'As I already said,' the first suited man points out.

'In that case I have to demand that you change the budget.'

'That's absolutely out of the question! How would that look? Then we'd have to start making changes in all the budgets!' says the second suited man, terrified.

The suited woman smiles and asks if Britt-Marie wants some coffee. Britt-Marie doesn't. The suited woman's smile intensifies.

'The way we understood it, Borg already has a football pitch.'

The second man in a suit makes a dissatisfied humming sound from between his teeth, and almost yells:

'No! The football pitch was sold off for the eventual building of apartments. It's in the budget!'

'Well, in that case I have to ask you to buy back the land.'

The humming from between the suited man's teeth is now also accompanied by a fountain of saliva. 'How would that look? If that happened EVERYONE would want to sell their land back! We actually can't just go around building football pitches everywhere! We'd be swimming in football pitches!'

'Well,' says the first man in a suit and looks at his watch with a very bored expression.

Kent has to grip Britt-Marie's handbag quite firmly at that point. The suited woman leans forward disarmingly and pours coffee for everyone, although no one actually wants any.

'We understand that you were employed at the recreation centre in Borg,' she says with a mild smile.

'Yes. Yes, that's right, but I have . . . I have handed in my notice,' says Britt-Marie, sucking in her cheeks.

The woman smiles even more mildly and pushes the coffee cup closer to Britt-Marie.

'There was never meant to be a position there, dear Britt-Marie. The intention was to close down the recreation centre before Christmas. The vacancy was a mistake.'

The second suited man is droning like an outboard engine.

'A position not in the budget. How would that look?'

The first suited man stands up.

'You'll have to excuse us. We actually have an important meeting.'

And on this note, Britt-Marie leaves the town hall. Having come to realise that her arrival in Borg was all a mistake. They are right. Obviously they are right.

'Tomorrow, darling. We'll come back here tomorrow,' Kent tries to tell her again as they sit in the BMW. Silent and dejected, she leans her head against the window and keeps a tissue under her chin. A sort of determination appears in Kent's eyes when he sees this, almost like something vengeful, but she doesn't notice it at that point.

The fifth day at the town hall is a Friday. It's raining again.

Kent has to force Britt-Marie to go. When she insists that it's all useless anyway, he has no choice in the end but to threaten to write a lot of mischievous, quite irrelevant things in ink on her list. At this point she snatches back the list as if it was a flower pot he had threatened to throw off a balcony, and then she reluctantly gets into the BMW, all the while muttering that Kent is a 'hooligan'.

A woman is waiting for them when they arrive at the town hall. Britt-Marie recognises her as the woman from the football association.

'Ha. I suppose you're here to stop us?' notes Britt-Marie.

The woman looks at Kent, surprised. Nervously starts wringing her hands.

'No. Kent here called me. I am here to help you.'

Kent pats Britt-Marie on the shoulder.

'I made a couple of calls. I took the liberty of doing what I'm good at.'

When Britt-Marie steps into the suited people's office, there are even more suits in there. Under existing circumstances, it seems, the football pitch in Borg has become a matter of interest for more committees than just the one.

'It has come to our attention that strong interests are backing the initiative for more football pitches within our council boundaries,' says a new suit, with a nod at the woman from the football association.

'It has also come to our attention that local business interests are ready to exert a certain amount of . . . pressure,' says another suit.

'Fairly unpleasant pressure, actually!' a third suit interjects, producing a plastic folder with various papers inside, and putting this on the table in front of Britt-Marie.

'We have also been reminded both by mail and various telephone calls that this is election year,' says the aforementioned suit.

'We have been reminded in a fairly abrasive and persistent way, in fact!' the latter suit adds.

Britt-Marie leans forward. The papers are headed as 'Working Group of Borg's Official Partnership of Independent Business Interests'. In these papers it can be clearly seen that the owners of Borg's pizzeria, Borg's cornershop, Borg's post office and Borg's car repairs workshop have sat down together over the course of the night and signed a collective demand for a football pitch. For safety's sake, the owners of the very recent start-ups, 'Law Firm Son & Son', 'Hairdressing and That' and 'Borg Good Wine Importers Ltd' have also signed this demand. As it happens, all in the same handwriting. The only document that stands out as different is one from a man named Karl, who according to the document has just opened a florist's.

Everything else is in Kent's handwriting. He stands behind Britt-Marie with his hands in his pockets, slouching slightly as if he does not wish to make too much of his presence. The woman with a suit serves coffee and nods excitedly:

'Actually, I had no idea there was such a flourishing business community in Borg! How charming!'

Britt-Marie's common sense has to work hard to stop her running around the room with her arms stretched out like an aircraft, because she's almost certain this would not be very appropriate.

The first man with a suit clears his throat and wishes to say another few words. He says:

'The thing is, we have now also been contacted by the unemployment office in your home town.'

'Twenty-one times. T-w-e-n-t-y-o-n-e times, we've been contacted,' another suit points out.

Britt-Marie turns and looks at Kent for guidance, but he's now standing with his mouth agape, looking just as shocked as she is. An apparently randomly picked suit points at another paper.

'It has come to our attention that you have been employed at the recreation centre in Borg.'

'Mistakenly so!' the woman in a suit says with a mild smile.

The random suit continues without missing a beat:

'The unemployment office in your town has made us aware of certain political responsibilities arising out of this. We have also been made aware of a certain amount of flexibility in the local council budget concerning further recruitment, which could be acted on now that . . . well . . . now that we are in an election year.'

'Twenty-one times. Twenty-one times we have been made aware of this!' another suit interjects angrily.

Words fail Britt-Marie. She stutters and clears her throat and then at long last manages to burst out:

'Might I just ask what on earth all this is supposed to mean?'

All of the suits in the room make restrained groans about how this must surely be quite plain and obvious. The suit sleeves slide back collectively to check if it isn't time to have lunch. It is. A great impatience arises. One of the suits finally takes it upon himself to clarify the whole thing, and then looks wearily at Britt-Marie:

'It means that the local council will either budget for a new football pitch, or budget for you to keep your job. We can't afford to do both.'

It's not a reasonable choice to give a human being.

One remarkable thing about communities built along roads is that you can find just as many reasons for leaving them as excuses to make you stay.

37

'I must ask you to try to understand that it isn't a reasonable choice to give a human being,' says Britt-Marie.

When she doesn't get an answer, she explains:

'It's just intractable, you have to understand. I want to ask you to try not to hold it against me.'

She still doesn't get an answer, so she sucks in her cheeks and adjusts her skirt.

'It's very neat and tidy here. Of course I don't know if this makes any difference to you now, but I hope it does. It's a very neat and tidy churchyard, this.'

Sami doesn't answer, but she hopes he's listening when she says:

'I want you to know, darling boy, I'll never regret coming to Borg.'

It's Saturday afternoon. The day after the local council gave her an unreasonable choice and the very same day that Liverpool are playing Aston Villa a thousand kilometres from Borg. Early this morning Britt-Marie went to the recreation centre.

On Monday there'll be bulldozers on the gravel outside, the council has promised. Kent forced them to promise, because he said otherwise he would not let them go to have their lunch. And so they promised and crossed their hearts that turf would be laid down and there would be proper goals with nets. Proper chalked sidelines. It was not a reasonable choice to give a human being, but Britt-Marie remembered what it was like losing a sibling, she remembered just how much one could lose oneself. With this in mind, she felt this was the best possible thing she could give someone who was every bit as lost. A football pitch.

She could hear voices through the open door of the pizzeria, but she didn't go in. It was best that way, she felt. The recreation centre was empty, but the door of the refrigerator was ajar. The rat teeth marks on the rubber seal of the door made it clear enough what had happened. The cellophane over the plate had been chewed away and every last crumb of peanut butter and Nutella on it had been licked clean. On its way out the rat had stumbled on Britt-Marie's tin of bicarbonate of soda, over-turning it on the draining board. There were tracks in the white dust. Two pairs, in fact. The rat had been there on a date, or a meeting, or whatever they called it these days.

Britt-Marie sat on one of the stools for a long time, with a towel in her lap. Then she mopped her face and cleaned the kitchen. Washed up and disinfected and made sure everything was spotless. Patted the coffee machine, which had once been damaged by flying stones, ran her hand over a picture with a red dot hanging at precisely the right height on the wall, telling her exactly where she was.

The knocking on the door didn't surprise her, oddly enough. The young woman from social services standing in the doorway gave her the impression of being exactly in the right place. As if she belonged here.

'Hello Britt-Marie,' said the girl, 'I hope I'm not disturbing you. I saw that the lights were on.'

'Certainly not. I only came to leave the keys,' Britt-Marie informed her in a low voice, feeling like a guest in someone else's house.

She held out the keys to the recreation centre, but the girl did not take them. Just smiled warmly as she looked at the premises.

'It's very nice here. I've understood that this place means so much to Vega and Omar, I wanted to have a look at it so I could understand them better.'

Britt-Marie fumbled with the keys. Stifled everything welling up inside her. Checked several times that she had put all of her things in her handbag, and that she had really turned off the lights in the bathroom and kitchen. Galvanised herself several times to say what she wanted to say, even though her common sense was fighting tooth and nail to stop her.

'Would it make any difference if someone offered to take care of the children?' she wanted to ask. Obviously she knew it was preposterous. Obviously she did. Yet she had time to open her mouth, and then to say:

'Would it, I should just like your leave to ask whether, obviously it's quite preposterous, certainly it is, but I should like to enquire about the whither and whether of whether it might happen to make any difference if someone . . .'

Before she got to the end of the sentence she noticed Toad's parents standing in the doorway. The mother had her hands on her pregnant stomach, and the father held his cap in his hands.

'Are you the one who's picking up the children?' Karl demanded to know.

The mother elbowed him softly in his side, and then turned in a very forthright manner to the girl from the social services.

'My name is Sonja. This is Karl. We're Patrik's parents; he plays in the same football team as Vega and Omar.'

Of course it is quite possible that the girl from the social services was intending to answer, but Karl did not give her the chance:

'We want to take care of the children. We want them to come and live with us. You can't take them away from Borg!'

Sonja looked at Britt-Marie. Saw her hands, perhaps, so she crossed the room and, without any sort of prior warning, gave her a hug. Britt-Marie mumbled something about having washing-up liquid on her fingers but despite that Sonja kept hugging her. Something was rattling in the doorway. The girl from the social services began to laugh a little, as if this was her natural impulse every time she opened her mouth.

'The fact is I've had the same suggestion from both Ben's mother and the uncle of . . . Dino . . . is that his name?'

The rattling sounds from the doorway intensified and were complemented by a person demonstratively clearing her throat.

'Those kids! Can live with me, huh? They're like, what's-it-called? Children for me, huh?' Somebody looked ready to fight about it with everyone in the room. She waved at the football pitch; there were still white jerseys hanging along the fence and the candles had been thoughtfully lit again earlier that morning.

'It takes, what's-it-called? Takes a village to bring up a child, huh? We have a village!'

Sonja reluctantly let go of Britt-Marie, like you do with a balloon that you know will fly off as soon as you loosen your grip.

Karl wrung his cap and pointed both exactingly and fearfully at the girl from the social services. 'You can't take the children away from Borg, they could end up living with anyone! They could end up with a Chelsea supporter!'

By that stage, Britt-Marie had already put the keys to the recreation centre on the draining board and sneaked out behind them. If they did notice, and maybe they did, they let her go without a word, because they liked her enough to do that.

Afternoon turns to evening in Borg, quick and merciless, as if dusk is pulling a plaster off the daylight. Britt-Marie kneels with her forehead against Sami's headstone.

'My darling boy, I'll never regret that I was here.'

On Monday the bulldozers are coming to Borg. Britt-Marie doesn't know if she is religious, but she imagines that it's good enough, the knowledge that God has plans for Borg.

She has grass stains on her tights when she walks on her own down the road through the village. The white jerseys are still there on the fence. New candles have been lit underneath. The recreation centre is lit up by the glow of a television and she can see the shadows of the children's heads inside. More children now than ever. A club more than a team. She wants to go in, but she understands this would not be appropriate. Understands that it's best this way.

In the gravelled parking area between the recreation centre and the pizzeria are two quite gigantic old trucks with their headlights turned on. A group of grown men with beards and caps are moving about in the beams of light, huffing and puffing, groaning and shoving each other. It takes a good while before Britt-Marie understands they are playing football.

They are playing.

She continues down the road. Stands for a few heartbeats outside a modest little house with a modest little garden. If you didn't know it was there you could easily walk past without paying any attention to it and, in this sense, the house has a great deal in common with its owner. The police car is not parked outside, the windows are not lit up. Once she's absolutely certain that Sven is not at home, Britt-Marie sneaks up to the door and knocks on it. Because she wanted to do that once in her life.

Then she quickly moves off, keeping herself to the shadows, and walks the remaining distance to Bank's house. The flower bed outside no longer stinks. The 'For Sale' sign on the lawn has been removed. There's a smell of fried eggs when Britt-Marie steps into the hall; the dog is sleeping on the floor, Bank is sitting in her armchair in the living room with her face pressed up so close to the TV that Britt-Marie actually wants to warn her that it might be harmful to her eyes, but on second thoughts realises it would be better not to.

'Might one ask who's playing?' she says instead.

'Aston Villa and Liverpool! Aston Villa are leading 2–0!' says Bank, very agitated.

'Ha. So should I presume, then, that you also support Liverpool, like all the children seem to?'

'Are you mad? I support Aston Villa!' hisses Bank.

'Might I ask why?' asks Britt-Marie, because when she thinks about it more closely, it occurs to her that this is the first time she has ever seen Bank pay any attention to a televised football match.

Bank looks as if this is a preposterous question. Thinks for a moment. Then answers, grumpily:

'Because no one else supports Aston Villa . . . And because they have nice jerseys.'

Britt-Marie finds the second argument a touch more rational than the first. Bank lifts her head, turns down the volume on the TV. Takes a pull at her beer and clears her throat.

'There's food in the kitchen. If you're hungry.'

Britt-Marie shakes her head, clutches her handbag hard.

'Kent is coming soon. We're going home. He's driving his car, and I am driving mine, but he'll drive in front of me of course. I don't like driving in the dark. It's best if he's at the front.'

Bank gets to her feet with a lot of laborious cursing at the armchair, as if it's the chair's fault that people get older.

'Not that I want to get involved, but I think you should learn to drive in the dark.'

'That's very sweet of you,' answers Britt-Marie into her handbag.

Bank and the dog give her a hand with the bags and the balcony box from upstairs. Britt-Marie washes up and cleans the kitchen. Sorts cutlery. Pats the dog behind its ears. A person on the TV starts yelling loudly. Bank disappears into the living room, and comes back looking irascible.

'Liverpool just scored. Now it's 2–1,' she mutters.

Britt-Marie walks around the house one last time. Straightens rugs and curtains.

When she comes down into the kitchen she says:

'I'm not the kind to stick my nose in, but I could hardly avoid noticing that the "For Sale" sign on the lawn has been taken down. I'd just like to congratulate you on getting your house sold.'

Bank laughs bitterly.

'Are you joking? Who would buy a house in Borg?'

Britt-Marie adjusts her skirt.

'It wasn't an unreasonable assumption to make given that you'd just removed the sign . . .'

'Ah, I thought I'd stay on in Borg for a while, that's all. I was thinking I'd go and have a word with my old man. I thought it might be easier now he's dead, because he can't interrupt me all the time.'

Britt-Marie wants to pat her on the shoulder, but she realises it's best to leave it. Not least because Bank has her stick within reach.

There's a knock. Bank goes into the hall but then continues on into the living room without opening the door, because she knows who it is.

Britt-Marie looks around the kitchen one last time. Runs her fingers close enough to the walls to feel them, but not close enough to touch them. They are very dirty, after all. She hasn't had time to sort them out. She would have needed more time in Borg for that.

Kent smiles with relief when she opens the door.

'Are you ready to go?' he says anxiously, as if he still fears she may change her mind.

She nods and grasps her bag. Then the commentator on the TV suddenly starts roaring like mad. It sounds as if someone has walloped him.

'What on earth is going on?' Britt-Marie exclaims.

'Let's go now! Or we could get stuck in the traffic!' Kent tries, but it's too late. Britt-Marie goes into the living room. Bank is swearing and hissing at a young man in a red shirt who's charging about yelling until his face turns purple.

'2–2, Liverpool have equalised, it's 2–2,' she mutters, kicking the armchair as if it's responsible for the situation.

Britt-Marie is already halfway out of the door.

Kent's BMW is parked in the street. He comes running and reaches out to her, but she pulls away. Of course, it's not appropriate at all, a grown woman running as if she was a criminal fleeing justice. She stops herself by the edge of the pavement, her breath hot in her throat, and she turns around and looks at Kent with tears streaming down her face.

'What are you doing, darling? We have to go now,' he says, but his voice breaks because he can probably recognise very clearly what she's doing.

Her skirt is creased, but she doesn't adjust it. Her hair is almost untidy, as untidy as it is possible for Britt-Marie's hair to be. Her common sense throws in the towel in the end, and allows her to raise her voice:

'Liverpool have equalised! I think they're going to win!'

Kent allows his chin to sink towards his chest. He shrinks.

'You can't be their mother, darling. And even if you can, what'll happen after that? When they don't need you any more? What happens then?'

She shakes her head. But defiantly, rebelliously, not with sadness and dejection. As if she's fully intending to jump off an edge, even if only the edge of the pavement.

'I don't know, Kent. I don't know what happens after that.'

He closes his eyes, looking once again like a young boy on a landing, and then says in a quiet voice:

'I can only wait till tomorrow morning, Britt-Marie. I'll stay with Toad's parents. If you don't come knocking on the door in the morning I'm going home on my own.'

He tries to say it in a confident way, even though he knows he has already lost her.

She is already halfway to the recreation centre.

Omar and Vega see her before she sees them. She has already run past them when she hears them calling out irritably to her.

'Goodness grac . . . Liverpool have . . . well I certainly don't know exactly what they've done, but I am under the impression that they're going to win against these . . . whatever their name was. Villa something!' pants Britt-Marie, so out of breath that she sees stars and has to steady herself, in the middle of the road, by resting her hands on her knees. The neighbours must surely be wondering whether she's started using narcotics.

'We know!' Omar joins in eagerly. 'We're going to win! You could see it in Gerrard's eyes when he scored that we're going to win!'

Britt-Marie looks up, breathing so heavily that she feels a migraine coming on.

'May I ask what on earth you are doing here in the middle of the road, then?'

Vega faces her with her hands in her pockets, shaking her head as if she has come to the conclusion that Britt-Marie is even slower than she'd thought.

'When we turn it around we want to see it with you.'

Liverpool never turn that match around. The final score is 2–2. It makes no difference and it makes all the difference in the world.

They have eggs and bacon in Bank's kitchen that night. Vega and Omar and Britt-Marie and Bank and the dog. When Omar puts his elbows on the table it's Vega who tells him to take them off.

Their eyes meet for a moment, and then he does as she says without protest.

Britt-Marie stands in the hall as they put on their jackets. She curls up her toes in her shoes and brushes their arms until they have to hold her hands to make her stop.

The young woman from the social services is standing on the lawn, waiting for them.

'She's OK, she doesn't like football but she's OK,' says Vega to Britt-Marie.

'We'll teach her,' Omar assures her.

Britt-Marie sucks in her cheeks and nods.

'I . . . the thing is that I . . . I just want to say that I . . . that you . . . that I never,' she begins.

'We know,' mumbles Vega deep into the fabric of Britt-Marie's jacket.

'It's cool,' Omar promises.

The children have reached the road when the boy turns around. Britt-Marie hasn't moved at all, as if she wants to preserve the image of them on her retinas until the very last. So he asks:

'What are you doing tomorrow?'

Britt-Marie clasps her hands together on her stomach. Inhales for as long as she can.

'Kent will be waiting for me to knock on his door.'

Vega shoves her hands in her pockets. Raises her eyebrows. 'And Sven?'

Britt-Marie inhales. Exhales. Lets Borg bounce around inside her lungs.

'He told me he hopes it's me every time there's a knock on his door.'

The children look so small, illuminated by the streetlights. But Vega stretches, straightens her back and says:

'Do me a favour, Britt-Marie.'

'Anything,' she whispers.

'Don't knock on any door tomorrow. Just get in the car and drive!'

Britt-Marie stands on her own in the dark long after they have gone. She never said anything, has not promised anything. She knows it would have been a promise she could not keep.

She stands on the balcony of Bank's house, feeling Borg blowing tenderly through her hair. Not so hard that it ruins her hairstyle, just enough to feel the breeze. The newspaper delivery drives past while it's still dark. The women with the Zimmer frames slowly make their way out of the house opposite, towards their postbox. One of them waves at Britt-Marie and she waves back. Not with her whole arm, obviously, but with a controlled movement, a discreet movement of one hand at the level of her hips. The way a person with common sense waves. She waits until the women have gone back into the house. Then she sneaks down the stairs and carries her bags out to the white car with the blue door.

Before dawn she's standing outside a door, and knocking.

38

If a human being closes her eyes hard and long enough, she can remember all the times she has made a choice in her life just for her own sake. And realise, perhaps, that it has never happened. If she drives a white car with a blue door slowly down a road through a village, while it's still dark, and if she winds down the window and takes deep breaths, then she can remember all the men she has fallen in love with.

Alf. Kent. Sven. One who deceived her and left her. Another who deceived her and was left by her. A third who is many things she has never had, but possibly none of the ones she has been longing for. And she can slowly, slowly, slowly unwrap the bandage from her hand and look at the white mark on her ring finger. While dreaming of first love and other chances, and weighing up forgiveness against love. Counting the beats of her heart.

If a human being closes her eyes she can remember all the choices in her life. And realise they have all been for the sake of someone else.

It's early morning in Borg, but the dawn seems to be holding off. As if it wants to give her time to raise her hand. Make up her mind.

And jump.

She knocks on the door. It opens. She wants to say everything she feels inside, everything she has been carrying, but she never gets the chance. She wants to explain exactly why she's here and nowhere else, but she is interrupted. It makes her disappointed to realise she was expected – and that she's so predictable.

She wants to say something about how it feels, to open her chest and let everything flow for the first time, but she is not given the opportunity. Instead she is led with a firm hand back to the road. The pavement is dotted with plastic petrol cans. As if they've fallen off the back of a lorry.

'Everyone in the team collected money. We've worked out the exact distance,' says the boy.

'Those of us who can count have worked it out, yes,' the girl interjects.

'I can count!' the boy cries angrily.

'Just about as much as you can kick a ball, so, yeah, like, you can count to three!' grins the girl.

Britt-Marie leans forward and feels the plastic jerrycans. They stink.

Something brushes against her arms and it takes a good while before she realises the children are holding both of her hands.

'It's petrol. We've worked it out. There's enough here to get all the way to Paris,' whispers Omar.

'And all the way back,' adds Vega.

They stand there waving while Britt-Marie gets into the driver's seat. They wave with their entire bodies, the way grown-ups never do. Morning comes to Borg with a sun that controls itself and waits respectfully on the horizon, as if wanting to give her enough time to make a last choice, and then to choose for herself for the first time. When daylight finally streams in over the rooftops, a white car with a blue door starts pulling away.

Maybe she stops. Maybe she knocks on just one more door.

Maybe she just drives.

God knows Britt-Marie certainly has enough fuel.

It's January in a place that is one of millions rather than one in a million. A place like all the others, and a place like no other.

In a few months, a thousand kilometres away, Liverpool will almost win the English Premier League. In one of the last matches they will be leading 3–0 against Crystal Palace, but in eight surreal minutes they will let in three goals and lose the League title. No one in Liverpool will ever know anything about Borg, they won't even know the place exists, but no one who drives down this road with their windows rolled down will be able to avoid hearing the whole thing as it happens.

Manchester United fire their manager and start again. Tottenham promise that next season will be better. Somewhere out there, people can still be found who support Aston Villa.

It's January now, but spring will come to Borg. A young man will rest beside his mother in a churchyard under a blanket of scarfs, two children will fall over themselves to deplore useless referees and pathetic sliding tackles. A ball will come rolling and a foot will kick it, because this is a community where no one knows how not to. A summer will come when Liverpool lose everything, and then autumn will arrive and along with it a new season, when they have another chance to win everything. Football is a mighty game in that way, because it forces life to go on.

Borg is exactly where it is. Where it has always been. Borg is a place by a road that exits in two directions. One direction home and one to Paris.

If you merely drive through Borg it's easy to notice only the places that have been closed down. You have to slow down to see what's still there. There are people in Borg. There are rats and Zimmer frames and greenhouses. Wooden fences and white jerseys and lit candles. Newly laid turf and sunny stories. There's a florist where you can only buy red flowers. There's a cornershop and a car mechanic and a postal service and a pizzeria where the TV is always on whenever there's a match, and where it's no shame to buy on credit. There isn't a recreation centre any more, but there are children who eat bacon and eggs with their new coach and her dog in a house with a balcony, in a living room where there are new photos on the wall. There are marginally fewer 'For Sale' signs along the road today than there were yesterday. There are grown men with beards and caps who play football in the beams of headlights from old trucks.

There's a football pitch. There's a football club.

And whatever happens.

Wherever she is.

Everyone will know Britt-Marie was here.

AUTHOR'S THANKS

Neda. The greatest blessing in life is to be able to share it with someone who's much smarter than oneself. I'm sorry you'll never get to experience that, it really is unbeatable. Asheghetam. Sightseeing.

Jonas Axelsson. My publisher and agent, who never loses sight of the fact that I am still a beginner, and that his foremost task is to help me get better at writing. **Niklas Natt och Dag**, who, in his texts and his respectful artistry, reminds me every day that this is a privilege. **Céline Hamilton** and **Agnes Cavallin** at Partners in Stories, where a large houseful of competence is slotted into the walls of a fairly small house – using equal parts of brain and heart they have kept this project on course. It wouldn't have worked without you. **Karin Wahlén** at Kult PR, who got it from day one. **Vanja Vinter**, grammatical elite soldier and uncompromising, outstanding proof-reader, editor, and critic, although her cutlery drawer is one prolonged disappointment. **Nils Olsson**, who patiently, sensitively, and with great love, has designed three fantastic book covers. **Andrea Fehlauer,** who stepped in as the editor of key sections of the book, bringing both his experience and his precision to the task, and without a doubt improving the book as a result.

The readers of my blog. Who were there from the very start. All this is actually mostly your fault.

Torsten Wahlund, Anna Maria Käll, and **Martin Wallström**, who recorded my stories as audio books and gave voices to my characters in ways I did not think possible. They are more yours than mine now. **Julie Lærke Løvgren**, who has overseen the publication of my books internationally. **Judith Toth**, who got me there. **Siri Lindgren** at Partners in Stories, who makes sure the boat does not capsize when Jonas refuses to sit still in it. **Johan Zillén**. First in, last out.

Everyone who was and still is involved in my books at Forum, Månpocket, Bonnier Audio and Bonnier Rights. Especially **John Häggblom**, without whose help I would not be here today. **Liselott Wennborg**, the editor of "Saker min son behöver veta om världen" [Things My Son Needs to Know about the World]. **Adam Dahlin**, who saw the potential. **Sara Lindegren** and **Stephanie Tärnqvist**, who have always been far more patient with me than I deserve.

Natur och Kultur, who have given us their support, especially **Hannah Nilsson** and **John Augustsson**.

Pocketförlaget and A Nice Noise, who believed in all this.

All who have reviewed, written about, blogged, tweeted, face-booked, instagrammed, and spoken about my books. Especially those of you who really did not like them, and took your time to rationally and instructively explain why. I can't promise that I became a better writer as a result, but at least you forced me to think. I don't think that can be a bad thing.

Lennart Nilsson in Gantofta. The best football trainer I ever had.

Most of all, thanks to all of you who read my books. Thanks for your time.

Questions For Discussion

1. What did you learn about Britt-Marie from her interactions with the people in Borg? Do they change her?

2. Think about the children on Borg's football team: to what extent are they responsible for Britt-Marie's growth, and how? Does one particular child have greater influence on Britt-Marie than the others? If so, who, and why?

3. 'She has difficulties remembering the last time she said anything at all, until one day she left him without a word. Because of this it always feels like the whole thing was her fault' (page 151). To what extent do you think Britt-Marie contributed to the unravelling of her and Kent's relationship with her silence, if at all?

4. How have Britt-Marie's experiences as a girl and a young woman made her into the woman she is at the start of the novel?

5. Did learning about her childhood change the way you felt about Britt-Marie as a character?

6. When we first meet her, Britt-Marie seems a fairly conservative person, yet in the course of the novel she is exposed to many new situations. What does she learn through these experiences and what do we learn about her?

7. Consider the role of football in this story. What does football represent to the citizens of Borg, particularly to the children?

8. 'What is love if it's not loving our lovers even when they don't deserve it' (page 283). Do you agree with this statement, or does love without limits tend to lead to a relationship like Britt-Marie and Kent's at the start of the novel?

9. Why do you think that Kent decides to fight for Britt-Marie's football pitch? Do you believe he's really a changed man?

10. Why do you think Britt-Marie ultimately makes the choice she does at the end of the story?

Turn the page for an extract of Fredrik Backman's
New York Times bestselling novel

A MAN
CALLED OVE

At first sight, Ove is almost certainly the grumpiest man you
will ever meet. He thinks himself surrounded by idiots –
neighbours who can't reverse a trailer properly, joggers, shop
assistants who talk in code, and the perpetrators of the
vicious coup d'etat that ousted him as Chairman of the
Residents' Association. He will persist in making his daily
inspection rounds of the local streets.

But isn't it rare, these days, to find such old-fashioned clarity
of belief and deed? Such unswerving conviction about what
the world should be, and a lifelong dedication to making it
just so?

In the end, you will see, there is something about Ove that is
quite irresistible . . .

'Warm, funny, and almost unbearably moving'
Daily Mail

SCEPTRE

A MAN CALLED OVE DOES NOT PAY
A THREE-CROWN SURCHARGE

Ove gives her the plants. Two of them. Of course there weren't supposed to be two of them. But somewhere along the line there has to be a limit. It was a question of principle, Ove explains to her. That's why he got two flowers in the end.

'Things don't work when you're not at home,' he mutters, and kicks a bit at the frozen ground.

His wife doesn't answer.

'There'll be snow tonight,' says Ove.

They said on the news there wouldn't be snow, but, as Ove often points out, whatever they predict is bound not to happen. He tells her this; she doesn't answer. He puts his hands in his pockets and gives her a brief nod.

'It's not natural rattling around the house on my own all day when you're not here. It's no way to live. That's all I have to say.'

She doesn't reply to that either.

He nods and kicks the ground again. He can't understand people who long to retire. How can anyone spend their whole life longing for the day when they become superfluous? Wandering about, a burden on society, what sort of man would ever wish for that? Staying at home, waiting to die. Or even worse: waiting for them to come and fetch you and put you in a home. Being dependent on other people to get to the toilet. Ove can't think of anything worse. His wife often teases him, says he's the only man she knows who'd rather be laid out in a coffin than travel in a mobility service van. And she may have a point there.

Ove had risen at quarter to six. Made coffee for his wife and himself, went round checking the radiators to make sure she hadn't sneakily turned them up. They were all unchanged from yesterday, but he turned them down a little more just to be on the safe side. Then he took his jacket from the hook in the hall, the only hook of all six that wasn't burgeoning with her clothes, and set off for his inspection. It had started getting cold, he noticed. Almost time to change his navy autumn jacket for his navy winter jacket.

He always knows when it's about to snow because his wife starts nagging about turning up the heat in the bedroom. Lunacy, Ove reaffirms every year. Why should the power company directors feather their nests because of a bit of seasonality? Turning up the heat five degrees costs thousands of crowns per year. He knows because he's calculated it himself. So every winter he drags down an old diesel generator from the attic that he swopped at a jumble sale for a gramophone. He's connected this to a fan heater he bought at a sale for thirty-nine crowns. Once the generator has charged up the fan heater, it runs for thirty minutes on the little battery Ove has hooked it up to, and his wife keeps it on her side of the bed. She can run it a couple of times before they go to bed, but only a couple – no need to be lavish about it ('Diesel isn't free, you know'). And Ove's wife does what she always does: nods and agrees that Ove is probably right. Then she goes round all winter sneakily turning up the radiators. Every year the same bloody thing.

Ove kicks the ground again. He's considering telling her about the cat. If you can even call that mangy, half-bald creature a cat. It was sitting there again when he came back from his inspection, practically right outside their front door. He pointed at it and shouted so loudly that his voice echoed between the houses. The cat just sat there, looking at Ove. Then it stood up elaborately, as if making a point of demonstrating that it wasn't leaving because of Ove, but rather because there were better things to do, and disappeared round the corner.

Ove decides not to mention the cat to her. He assumes she'll only be disgruntled with him for driving it away. If she was in charge the whole house would be full of tramps, whether of the furred variety or not.

He's wearing his navy suit and has done up the top button of the white shirt. She tells him to leave the top button undone if he's not wearing a tie; he protests that he's not some urchin who's renting out deckchairs, before defiantly buttoning it up. He's got his dented old wristwatch on, the one that his dad inherited from his father when he was nineteen, the one that was passed on to Ove after his sixteenth birthday, a few days after his father died.

Ove's wife likes that suit. She always says he looks so handsome in it. Like any sensible person, Ove is obviously of the opinion that only posers wear their best suits on weekdays. But this morning he decided to make an exception. He even put on his black going-out shoes and polished them with a responsible amount of boot shine.

As he took his autumn jacket from the hook in the hall before he went out, he threw a thoughtful eye on his wife's collection of coats. He wondered how such a small human being could have so many winter coats. 'You almost expect if you stepped through this lot you'd find yourself in Narnia,' a friend of Ove's wife had once joked. Ove didn't have a clue what she was talking about, but he did agree there were a hell of a lot of coats.

He walked out of the house before anyone in the street had even woken up. Strolled up to the parking area. Opened his garage with a key. He had a remote control for the door, but had never understood the point of it. An honest person could just as well open the door manually. He unlocked the Saab, also with a key: the system had always worked perfectly well, there was no reason to change it. He sat in the driver's seat and twisted the tuning dial half forward and then half back before adjusting each of the mirrors, as he did every time he got into the Saab. As if someone routinely broke into the Saab and mischievously changed Ove's mirrors and radio channels.

As he drove across the parking area he passed that pregnant

foreign woman from next door. She was holding her three-year-old by the hand. The big blond Lanky One was walking beside her. All three of them caught sight of Ove and waved cheerfully. Ove didn't wave back. At first he was going to stop and give her a dressing down about letting children run about in the parking area as if it was some municipal playground. But he decided he didn't have the time.

He drove along, passing row after row of houses identical to his own. When they first moved in here there were only six houses; now there were hundreds of them. There used to be a forest here but now there were only houses. Everything paid for with loans, of course. That was how you did it nowadays. Shopping on credit and driving electric cars and hiring tradesmen to change a light bulb. Laying click-on floors and fitting electric fireplaces and carrying on. A society that apparently could not see the difference between the correct plug for a concrete wall and a smack in the face. Clearly this was how it was meant to be.

It took him exactly fourteen minutes to drive to the florist's in the shopping centre. Ove kept exactly to every speed limit, even on that 50kph road where the recently arrived idiots in suits came tanking along at 90. Among their own houses they put up speed bumps and damnable numbers of signs about 'Children Playing', but when driving past other people's houses it was apparently less important. Ove had repeated this to his wife every time they drove past over the last ten years.

And it's getting worse and worse, he liked to add, just in case by some miracle she hadn't heard him the first time.

Today he hadn't even gone two kilometres before a black Mercedes positioned itself a forearm's length behind his Saab. Ove signalled with his brake lights three times. The Mercedes flashed its full beam at him in an agitated manner. Ove snorted at his back mirror. As if it was his duty to fling himself out of the way as soon as these morons decided speed restrictions didn't apply to them. Honestly. Ove didn't move. The Mercedes gave him a burst of its full beam again. Ove slowed down. The

Mercedes sounded its horn. Ove lowered his speed to 20. When they reached the top of a hill the Mercedes overtook him with a roar. The driver, a man in his forties in a tie and white cables trailing from his ears, held up his finger through the window at Ove. Ove responded to the gesture in the manner of all men of a certain age who've been properly raised: by slowly tapping the tip of his finger against the side of his head. The man in the Mercedes shouted until his saliva spattered against the inside of his windshield, then put his foot down and disappeared.

Two minutes later Ove came to a red light. The Mercedes was at the back of the queue. Ove flashed his lights at it. He saw the driver craning his neck round. The white earpieces dropped out and fell against the dashboard. Ove nodded with satisfaction.

The light turned green. The queue didn't move. Ove sounded his horn. Nothing happened. Ove shook his head. Must be a woman driver. Or roadworks. Or an Audi. When thirty seconds had passed without anything happening, Ove put the car into neutral, opened the door and stepped out of the Saab with the engine still running. Stood in the road and peered ahead with his hands on his hips, filled with a kind of Herculean irritation: the way Superman might have stood if he'd got stuck in a traffic jam.

The man in the Mercedes gave a blast on his horn. Idiot, thought Ove. In the same moment the traffic started moving. The cars in front of Ove moved off. The car behind him, a Volkswagen, beeped at him. The driver waved impatiently at Ove. Ove glared back. He got back into the Saab and leisurely closed the door. 'Amazing what a rush we're in,' he scoffed into the back mirror and drove on.

At the next red light he ended up behind the Mercedes again. Another queue. Ove checked his watch and took a left turn down a smaller, quiet road. This entailed a longer route to the shopping centre, but there were fewer traffic lights. Not that Ove was mean. But as anyone who knows anything knows, cars use less fuel if they keep moving rather than stopping all the time. And, as Ove's wife often says: 'If there's one thing you could write in Ove's obituary, it's "At least he was economical with petrol."'

As Ove approached the shopping centre from his little side road, he could just make out that there were only two parking spaces left. What all these people were doing at the shopping centre on a normal weekday was beyond his comprehension. Obviously people no longer had jobs to go to.

Ove's wife usually starts sighing as soon as they even get close to a car park like this. Ove wants to park close to the entrance. 'As if there's a competition about who can find the best parking spot,' she always says as he completes circuit after circuit and swears at all the imbeciles getting in his way in their foreign cars. Sometimes they end up doing six or seven loops before they find a good spot, and if Ove in the end has to concede defeat and content himself with a slot twenty metres further away, he's in a bad mood for the rest of the day. His wife has never understood it. There again, she never was very good at grasping questions of principle.

Ove figured he would go round slowly a couple of times just to check the lay of the land, but then suddenly caught sight of the Mercedes thundering along the main road towards the shopping centre. So this was where he'd been heading, that suit with the plastic leads in his ears. Ove didn't hesitate for a second. He put his foot down and barged his way out of the junction into the road. The Mercedes slammed on its brakes, firmly pressing down on the horn and following close behind. The race was on.

The signs at the car park entrance led the traffic to the right, but when they got there the Mercedes must also have seen the two empty slots, as he tried to slip past Ove on the left. Ove only just managed to manoeuvre himself in front of him to block his path. The two men started hunting each other across the tarmac.

In his back mirror, Ove saw a little Toyota turn off the road behind them, follow the road signs and enter the parking area in a wide loop from the right. Ove's eyes followed it while he hurtled forward in the opposite direction, with the Mercedes on his tail. Of course, he could have taken one of the free slots, the one closest to the entrance, and then have the kindness of letting the Mercedes take the other. But what sort of victory would that have been?

Instead Ove made an emergency stop in front of the first slot and stayed where he was. The Mercedes started wildly sounding its horn. Ove didn't flinch. The little Toyota approached from the far right. The Mercedes also caught sight of it and, too late, understood Ove's devilish plan. Its horn wailed furiously as it tried to push past the Saab, but it never stood a chance: Ove had already waved the Toyota into one of the free slots. Only once it was safely in did Ove nonchalantly swing into the other space.

The side window of the Mercedes was so covered in saliva when it drove past that Ove couldn't even see the driver. He stepped out of the Saab triumphantly, like a gladiator who had just slain his opponent. Then he looked at the Toyota.

'Oh damn,' he mumbled, irritated.

The car door was thrown open.

'Hi there!' the Lanky One sang merrily as he untangled himself from the driver's seat. 'Hello hello!' said his wife from the other side of the Toyota, lifting out their three-year-old.

Ove watched repentantly as the Mercedes disappeared in the distance.

'Thanks for the parking space! Bloody marvellous!' The Lanky One was beaming.

Ove didn't reply.

'Wass ya name?' the three-year-old burst out.

'Ove,' said Ove.

'My name's Nasanin!' she said with delight.

Ove nodded at her.

'And I'm Pat . . .' the Lanky One started saying.

But Ove had already turned round and left.

'Thanks for the space,' the Pregnant Foreign Woman called out after him.

Ove could hear laughter in her voice. He didn't like it. He just muttered a quick 'Fine, fine,' without turning round and marched through the revolving doors into the shopping centre. He turned left down the first turning and looked round several times, as if afraid that the family from next door would follow him. But they turned right and disappeared.

Ove stopped suspiciously outside the supermarket and eyed the poster advertising the week's special offers. Not that Ove was intending to buy any ham in this particular shop. But it was always worth keeping an eye on the prices. If there's one thing in this world that Ove dislikes, it's when someone tries to trick him. Ove's wife sometimes jokes that the three worst words Ove knows in this life are 'Batteries not included'. People usually laugh when she says that. But Ove does not usually laugh.

He moved on from the supermarket and stepped into the florist's. And there it didn't take long for a 'rumble' to start up, as Ove's wife would have described it. Or a 'discussion' as Ove always insisted on calling it. Ove put down a coupon on the counter on which it said: '2 plants for 50 crowns'. Given that Ove only wanted one plant, he explained to the shop assistant, with all rhyme and reason on his side, he should be able to buy it for 25 crowns. Because that was half of 50. However, the assistant, a brain-dead SMS-tapping nineteen-year-old, would not go along with it. She maintained that a single flower cost 39 crowns and '2 for 50' only applied if one bought two. The manager had to be summoned. It took Ove fifteen minutes to make him see sense and agree that Ove was right.

Or, to be honest about it, the manager mumbled something that sounded a little like 'bloody old sod' into his hand and hammered 25 crowns so hard into the till that anyone would have thought it was the machine's fault. It made no difference to Ove. He knew these retailers were always trying to screw you out of money, and no one screwed Ove and got away with it. Ove put his debit card on the counter. The manager allowed himself the slightest of smiles, then nodded dismissively and pointed at a sign that read: 'Card purchases of less than 50 crowns carry a surcharge of 3 crowns.'

Now Ove is standing in front of his wife with two plants. Because it was a question of principle.

'There was no *way* I was going to pay three crowns,' rails Ove, his eyes looking down into the gravel.

Ove's wife often quarrels with Ove because he's always arguing about everything.

But Ove isn't bloody arguing. He just thinks right is right. Is that such an unreasonable attitude to life?

He raises his eyes and looks at her.

'I suppose you're annoyed I didn't come yesterday like I promised,' he mumbles.

She doesn't say anything.

'The whole street is turning into a madhouse,' he says defensively. 'Complete chaos. You even have to go out and reverse their trailers for them nowadays. And you can't even put up a hook in peace,' he continues as if she's disagreeing.

He clears his throat.

'Obviously I couldn't put the hook up when it was dark outside. If you do that there's no telling when the lights go off. More likely they'll stay on and consume electricity. Out of the question.'

She doesn't answer. He kicks the frozen ground. Sort of looking for words. Clears his throat briefly once again.

'Nothing works when you're not at home.'

She doesn't answer. Ove fingers the plants.

'I'm tired of it, just rattling round the house all day while you're away.'

She doesn't answer that either. He nods. Holds up the plants so she can see them.

'They're pink. The ones you like. They said in the shop they're perennials but that's not what they're bloody called. Apparently they die in this kind of cold, they also said that in the shop but only so they could sell me a load of other shit.'

311

He looks as if he's waiting for her approval.

'The new neighbours put saffron in their rice and carry-on like that; they're foreigners,' he says in a low voice.

A new silence.

He stands there, slowly twisting the wedding ring on his finger. As if looking for something else to say. He still finds it painfully difficult being the one to take charge of a conversation. That was always something she took care of. He usually just answered. This is a new situation for them both. Finally Ove squats, digs up the plant he brought last week and carefully puts it in a plastic bag. He turns the frozen soil carefully before putting in the new plants.

'They've bumped up the electricity prices again,' he informs her as he gets to his feet.

He looks at her for a long time. Finally he puts his hand carefully on the big boulder and caresses it tenderly from side to side, as if touching her cheek.

'I miss you,' he whispers.

It's been six months since she died. But Ove still inspects the whole house twice a day to feel the radiators and check that she hasn't sneakily turned up the heating.

Also by Fredrik Backman

my grandmother sends her regards and apologises

Everyone remembers the smell of their grandmother's house.

Everyone remembers the stories their grandmother told them.

But does everyone remember their grandmother flirting with policemen? Driving illegally? Breaking into a zoo in the middle of the night? Firing a paintball gun from a balcony in her dressing gown?

Seven-year-old Elsa does.

Some might call Elsa's granny 'eccentric', or even 'crazy'. Elsa calls her a superhero. And granny's stories, of knights and princesses and dragons and castles, are her superpower. Because, as Elsa is starting to learn, heroes and villains don't always exist in imaginary kingdoms; they could live just down the hallway.

As Christmas draws near, even the best superhero grand-mothers may have one or two things they'd like to apologise for. And, in the process, Elsa can have some breath-taking adventures of her own . . .

'Firmly in league with the likes of Roald Dahl and Neil Gaiman. A touching, sometimes funny, often wise portrait of grief.' *Kirkus*

SCEPTRE

Join a literary community of
like-minded readers who seek out
the best in contemporary writing.

From the thousands of submissions Sceptre
receives each year, our editors select the books
we consider to be outstanding.

We look for distinctive voices, thought-provoking
themes, original ideas, absorbing narratives and
writing of prize-winning quality.

If you want to be the first to hear about our
new discoveries, and would like the chance to
receive advance reading copies of our books
before they are published, visit

www.sceptrebooks.co.uk

Follow @sceptrebooks

'Like' SceptreBooks

Watch SceptreBooks